MOTHER EARTH
and Other Stories

Vera T. Reck is presently doing research on Pilnyak and his era at the School of Slavonic and East European Studies at the University of London. A native of Russia, she was formerly a lecturer in Russian at the University of California at Irvine and received her degrees from Cornell University and the University of California at Berkeley.

Michael Green is at the Russian and East European Studies Center at the University of California at Los Angeles. He received his B.A. from the School of Slavonic and East European Studies at London University and did graduate work at Moscow University.

Boris Pilnyak

Boris Vogau

MOTHER EARTH

AND OTHER STORIES

TRANSLATED FROM THE RUSSIAN
AND EDITED BY

VERA T. RECK *and* MICHAEL GREEN

FREDERICK A. PRAEGER, *Publishers*
New York • Washington

BOOKS THAT MATTER

Published in the United States of America in 1968
by Frederick A. Praeger, Inc., Publishers
111 Fourth Avenue, New York, N.Y. 10003

© 1968 by Frederick A. Praeger, Inc.

Library of Congress Catalog Card Number: 68-26787

Printed in the United States of America

The translators dedicate their work
to the memory of
the author

ACKNOWLEDGMENT

The translators are indebted to Mr. Gary Henkel for his kindness in reading the manuscript and offering valuable suggestions.

EDITORS' NOTE

When we met at the University of California, where we were teaching in the embryonic Russian department on the new campus at Irvine, we were pleased to discover that we shared an admiration for Pilnyak, and decided to join forces in translating a selection of his stories.

Our method of work took shape at the very beginning of the project—the first pages of "A Chinese Story," a semijournalistic work that was eventually left out of the collection. Together we drafted the translation, unraveling Pilnyak's rugged paragraphs, sentence by sentence, and reshaping them into English. Meaning and style were discussed; suggestions how best to render Pilnyak's unexpected and sometimes difficult turns of speech were offered, weighed, accepted or rejected; and items to be looked up were noted.

Research into the special vocabulary of Pilnyak's day and into the events that surrounded him and are so much a part of his stories went on as translation progressed.

Then came revisions of drafts—as many as three or four.

We feel we have come close to achieving our goal: a volume of some of Pilnyak's best work, with a text as truly faithful to the author as our combined abilities and best efforts could make it.

CONTENTS

INTRODUCTION

Boris Pilnyak

> *How good it is sometimes when you are young*
> *to shout with the thunder, to outshout the storm!*
>
> MOTHER EARTH

For a tragically brief period following the 1917 Revolution, there was the promise of a new and brilliant age of Russian prose. New talents sprang up. Graduates from the tough school of revolution, they were not inclined to apply rouge and powder to the truth as they saw it; they liked the hard image, the abrupt transition, the ironic contrast. Among these writers, few were so gifted and unpredictable—or so widely imitated—as Boris Pilnyak. His work was "difficult"—allusive, elliptic, convoluted—and yet he was one of the most popular writers of the time, perhaps because, gazing into the chaos of the Revolution, he saw there the rebirth of the true, the immemorial Russia.

Like many of his most talented contemporaries, Pilnyak was condemned by the brilliance and independence of his early work to a lingering literary death in the thirties, and his eventual physical death in Stalin's purges was little more than the brutal confirmation of an already established fact. (He was arrested in 1937, apparently on charges of Trotskyism and spying for Japan, and little is known of his subsequent fate; Soviet official publications give 1941 as the year of his death.) His work has not since been republished in the Soviet Union, and he has yet to be brought back from the literary limbo he has shared with so many others. There are, however, signs that his "rehabilitation" will not be long delayed.

Pilnyak was born in 1894; his real name was Boris

Andreyevich Vogau. The man who identified himself so passionately with the Slavs and their destiny carried in him the blood of several peoples: "German with a touch of Jewish," as he puts it himself, on his father's side, "Slavic and Mongol" on his mother's. Both his parents came from the Volga; his father, a district veterinary, had married the daughter of an old Saratov merchant family. Like many of the provincial intelligentsia in the eighteen eighties and nineties, they took an active interest in the Populist movement, carrying on educational work among the peasants.

Pilnyak's boyhood passed in the towns of Moscow Province, towns which clustered about their ancient kremlins, paying the slow centuries little heed; their poetry entered deep into the boy, and he was later to make them the settings—indeed, almost the main characters—of some of his best stories. The Volga steppe, with its tumultuous springs and burning summers—the homeland of his German ancestors—was also part of his boyish world, and would be memorably evoked by the mature writer.

Pilnyak records that he began to write at the age of nine, and that his very first production described "night and the steppe, the cry of the eagle owl." His career as a writer began in 1915. Some of his early stories are a celebration of the primitive, sensual, unreasoned life—of birds, beasts, and the animal man. Primitivism was in the air at the time, an illustration, perhaps, of Wilde's dictum that "simplicity is the last refuge of the complex"; it was also a reaction against the endless abstractions and refinements of the Symbolists. Other stories of this period reveal his debt to Chekhov and Bunin: the "Tales of Seas and Mountains" are filled with the quiet desperation of provincial life and are autumnal in mood and landscape; in "The Forest Dacha" night is about to fall on the gentry after their long Chekhovian twilight.

Pilnyak welcomed the Revolution in his own way and for his own reasons. For him it had little to do with Marx and the urban proletariat: it was a "peasant revolt," it was Slavic Russia erupting and obliterating the alien European civilization so brutally imposed by Peter the Great. Pilnyak's revolution was symbolized by the blizzard and the wolf; it was elemental, anarchic, a creature of the forest. Naïve and romantic as these ideas may seem, they did enable Pilnyak to make sense of what seemed to many a descent into chaos, and even to sound a note of exhilaration in the midst of the cataclysm—to "shout with the storm."

This mood is very much in evidence in *The Naked Year,* which on its appearance in 1922 immediately established Pilnyak's reputation. Although Pilnyak calls it a novel, some of its sections had been published earlier as self-contained works. For Pilnyak there was nothing unusual in this practice: the boundaries of literary genre hardly existed for him, and he was always ready to quarry material from old works to build new ones; sometimes the connection between the assembled parts seems tenuous, almost as if they had been flung together haphazardly. It is as if the harsh wind of the Revolution had blown through this prose, fragmenting and reassembling it to the shape of the times. Pilnyak hears the moaning of this wind, mixed with the exultant cries of Russia's ancient gods and demons, in the frequently bizarre new words (usually compounded from the initial letters or syllables of the names of the new Soviet institutions) brought into being by the Revolution.

The Naked Year and other works of this period, such as "Ivan-and-Marya," "The Third Capital," and (in the present volume) "Ryazan Apples," are poems in prose in which people and events whirl about the invisible axis of the Revolution. The influence of Andrey Bely is strongly felt in these works, in their loose musical structure, incantatory digressions, repetitions of whole segments and key phrases as a unifying device, obsessive word play ("words to me are like coins to a numismatist"), and experiments with typographical layout; more distantly, there are echoes of the Russian folk epic. A device much used in these stories, and of which Pilnyak was never to tire, is the introduction of quotations from documents, works of obscure erudition, newspapers, public notices, popular songs—the pungent ephemera of the passing day—as if to validate the poetry of art with the prose of life.

In "Mother Earth" Pilnyak discards much of the extravagance of his earlier style; this magnificently detailed picture of peasant life, with its atmospheric evocation of forest and steppe, is tighter in structure and is built around a central character—the Bolshevik Nekulyev. Primitive Russia goes on, unchanged, unchanging, as Reds and Whites surge back and forth across the land; to the peasants, immersed in their own concerns, the struggle is meaningless. The narrative moves at different speeds, switching masterfully from the easy pace of the folk tale to the jagged, insistent rhythms suggesting Nekulyev's tightening nerves and a terror always just outside the door.

Like many writers of the time, both in Russia and elsewhere, Pilnyak turned his thoughts to the mechanistic society of the future; in *Machines and Wolves* he attempted to come to terms with the machine, but was ultimately unable to reconcile intellectual acceptance with a deeper instinctive fear. "The Bridegroom Cometh," on the surface a nature story, is really a horrified glance into a future where "the state is a machine, the state does not tolerate individuality, ownership, freedom of instinct." We are very close here to the world of Zamyatin's *We*, and indeed, not only in its central theme, but in the hypnotic rhythms of its prose, the story reads almost like a parody of Zamyatin.

The early twenties were years of comparative freedom for the "fellow travelers"—the name given to writers who, like Pilnyak, accepted the Revolution without total commitment. It was a time when Trotski could deplore Pilnyak's philosophy of history as retrograde and yet praise him for his splendid portrayal of the Revolution from the point of view of the peasant in the provinces. Pilnyak made his own position quite clear in a piece published in 1924:

". . . I do not acknowledge that one must write choking with enthusiasm when one is writing about the Russian Communist Party, as very many do—particularly the quasi-Communists, who thus give our revolution a disagreeable bragging, self-praising tone; I do not acknowledge that a writer ought to live with the 'will not to see,' or, to put it bluntly, to lie; and lying is what results when some kind of statistical proportion is not observed. For example, we have the European-equipped Kashira power station, but half of Russia still lives without kerosene—so it is more to the point to write that our Russia sits in darkness in the evenings than to write that we now have electrification. And another example: I remember reading in *Gudok* in 1920, 'Victory on the labor front: the workers of Lyubertsy loaded seventeen carloads of firewood.' It seems to me that if you remember British loading cranes it would be truer to say, 'Disaster on the labor front.' I am not a Communist, and so I do not acknowledge that I ought to be a Communist and write like a Communist; I do acknowledge that Communist power in Russia was not achieved by the will of the Communists, but was brought about by the historic destiny of Russia, and to the extent that I trace (as best I can, and as my conscience and intelligence dictate to me) this historic destiny of Russia, to that extent I am with the Communists (now, at this time, that means more than ever before, since I cannot be in the philistine camp); I acknowledge that the destiny of the Russian Communist Party interests me less than the destiny of Russia; that for me the Russian Communist Party is only a link in the history of Russia; I know that I must be absolutely objective, that I must not be grist to anybody's mill, not deceive anyone, and—I acknowledge that I may be completely mistaken, but I know very well that I am not able to write otherwise than I write now, I do not know how, I will not, even if I wanted to, violate myself; there is a law of literature which prohibits, makes impossible, the violation of a literary gift. . . ."

Pilnyak was to refute this "law of literature" within a decade; he was to become the center of two literary scandals; the second scandal would break his spirit and destroy him as an independent artist.

In October 1925 M. V. Frunze, the People's Commissar of the Army and Navy, died on the operating table, and

the rumor quickly spread that the surgeons had been ordered to kill a man whom Stalin regarded as a dangerous
rival. In May of the following year the literary magazine
Novy Mir printed a story by Pilnyak entitled "The Tale of
the Unextinguished Moon," in which, so it seemed to
many, the circumstances of Frunze's death were set forth
in only the thinnest of fictional disguises. It was probably
his artist's instinct rather than any deliberate attempt at
portraiture that led Pilnyak to draw in his "Number One"
—"the unbending man"—a cold and paranoid bureaucrat
with a dangerous resemblance to Stalin. The issue of *Novy
Mir* containing the story was hurriedly withdrawn, and the
editorial board admitted that it had made a "gross and
obvious error" in publishing the work. The critic Aleksandr
Voronski, to whom "The Tale of the Unextinguished
Moon" had been dedicated, rejected the honor with in-
dignation, calling the story "a malicious slander on our
Party." That Pilnyak could write such a work was a sign
either of considerable courage or of political naïveté—perhaps the latter, since he had prefaced the story with a
bland denial that there was any connection between it and
Frunze's death.

Chastened by this episode, Pilnyak hurried abroad as
soon as he was able to obtain a passport. He was all his
life an insatiable traveler; he had a reporter's feeling for
the arresting detail, and his journalistic writing retains its
freshness even today. "Chinese Story" and "The Roots of
the Japanese Sun," both published in 1927, are sharp-eyed
accounts of his travels in the Far East. Under very different circumstances, a visit to the United States in 1931 re-
sulted in his "American novel," *O.K.*—not a novel, in fact,
but a rambling travelogue in which spontaneous reportage
is judiciously interlayered with the disapproving comment
expected of a Soviet writer. The imaginative writer and
the reporter are strangely compounded in Pilnyak: as there
are journalistic elements in his fiction, so there are fictional
elements in his reportage.

"Mahogany" is the last work in which Pilnyak is himself.
There was nothing unusual in the fact that it was brought

out, in 1929, by the Berlin publishing house "Petropolis";
in the twenties, for reasons of copyright, it was quite common for Soviet writers to bring out their work abroad before it appeared in the Soviet Union. The names of many
established Soviet writers appeared regularly in the "Petropolis" list. "Mahogany" had already been accepted for
publication, albeit with some cuts, by *Krasnaya Nov*, a
leading literary magazine. Pilnyak was therefore quite un-
prepared for the savage campaign of vilification launched
against him; he was accused of writing an anti-Soviet
novel and passing it on to a counterrevolutionary organization abroad.

Pilnyak's attempts to defend himself were drowned in
shouts of abuse from every corner. It is difficult, perhaps,
for us to imagine the virulence and terrible unanimity of
such a campaign. The whole of Soviet society seemed bent
on destroying the transgressor; there were very few who
dared to raise their voices in protest, or even in a plea for
mercy.

The campaign, of course, had its purpose and was not
allowed to let up until that purpose had been achieved.
Pilnyak was at this time president of the Moscow branch
of the All-Russian Writers' Union; Zamyatin occupied a
similar position in Leningrad. These two independent-
minded men had to be removed from their posts before
the Writers' Union could be brought to heel. Zamyatin,
whose novel *We* had been published abroad without his
permission, came under no less vicious attack. A man of
the rarest integrity, Zamyatin stood his ground, and wrote
his famous letter to Stalin asking permission to leave the
country. Pilnyak, with his passionate need to feel himself
at one with Russia, lacked that ultimate certitude of iden-
tity which enables a man to stand alone.

Pilnyak abased himself and promised to make amends.
"Mahogany" was dismantled and worked into a full-length
novel, *The Volga Falls into the Caspian Sea;* centered
about a huge waterways project, the novel attempted to
capture the spirit of socialist construction. Unfortunately,
"Mahogany" did not lend itself to incorporation into an

optimistic framework; it is a dirge for the passing of the old Russia, for the ancient, crumbling towns and the exquisite art they had produced—the Russia in which, for good or ill, Pilnyak's talent was rooted.

The Volga Falls into the Caspian Sea, broken-backed as it is, still has many a Pilnyakian page and certainly stands out in the gray procession of socialist construction novels. Little needs to be said about Pilnyak's subsequent works; their political orthodoxy is irreproachable and they will be enjoyed by the politically orthodox.

MOTHER EARTH

and Other Stories

MOTHER EARTH

A peasant named Stepan Klimkov from the small village of
Kadom went into the forest at Willow Spring to steal
bark, climbed an oak, lost his footing, fell, and, caught by
the bindings of his bast shoes, was left hanging head down-
ward in the branches; both his eyes burst from the rush
of blood to his head. That night the forest watchman Kandin took the thief to forestry headquarters and reported
to Nekulyev that he had brought a "citizen forest thief."
The forester Nekulyev ordered Stepan Klimkov's release.
In the darkness Klimkov stood at attention, barefoot—his
shoe bindings had been cut by Kandin when he pulled him
down from the oak, and his shoes had fallen off on the
way. Klimkov said calmly:

"I could do with a guide, mister comrade; my eyes
have run out down to the last drop."

Nekulyev leaned close to the peasant and saw a thicket
of beard; what had been eyes were two dead slits, and
blood trickled from the ears and nose.

Klimkov stayed at forestry headquarters for the night;
they bedded down in Kuzya's hut. Kuzya, forest watchman
and teller of tales, had been telling them the story about
the three priests and the Masses, the wily peasant Ilya
Ivanych, his wife Annushka, and the drunkard Vanyusha.
It was a moonlit June night. At the foot of the hill the Volga
kept silence. Sometime during the night Ignat the wise
man arrived—Minka the shepherd had run to fetch him
from his cave. The wise man announced that there was no
getting back Stepan Klimkov's eyes—neither by prayer nor
spell—and that they should apply plantain leaves "so his
brains won't run out."

· · · ·

The hero of this tale of forests and peasants (apart from the forester Anton Ivanovich Nekulyev, apart from the tanner Arina—Irina Sergeyevna Arsenyeva—apart from summer, ravines, and whistles in the night), the hero is a wolf pup, the little wolf pup Nikita, as he was named by Irina Sergeyevna Arsenyeva—that woman who was to die so senselessly and to whom the wolf pup—to die for his pelt —stood for so much. The wolf pup was bought for a few kopeks that spring in Tetyushi, in the Province of Kazan, on the Volga. A peasant boy was trying to sell it on the wharf, but nobody was buying; it was lying in a basket. And Irina Sergeyevna bought it.

It was barely able to open its eyes; its pelt was the color of black leaf tobacco and there was a reek of dog about it. She put it inside her coat and warmed it at her breast. She herself likened the color of its fur to that of tobacco—smaller than a kitten, it clouded her mind like tobacco with its enchanting remoteness. The boy who was selling the pup told how it had been found in a forest clearing: some boys went into the forest after birds' eggs and stumbled upon a litter of wolf pups (they were still blind); five of the pup's little brothers died of hunger and it alone survived. The pup was unable to lap milk. Irina Sergeyevna let the steamer go on without her, and managed—by means of a special authorization—to obtain in Tetyushi a rubber nipple, the kind used to feed babies, and with this nipple she fed the pup. She whispered to the wolf pup as she fed it:

"Eat, my little silly; suck, Nikita, and you'll grow big and strong!"

She came to spend hours talking to the pup as a mother would to her child. The wolf pup was a wild creature; it never lost its fear of Irina Sergeyevna; it would creep into dark corners, curl its fluffy little tail under it, and from the darkness its black, watchful eyes would follow with a concentrated gleam every movement of Irina Sergeyevna's hands and eyes, and when their eyes met, the eyes of the wolf pup, unblinking, would become more hostile than ever, staring out of its triangular head like two intelligent, gleaming buttons; but the triangular head itself—the pointed muzzle, the black and likewise pointed ears—was silly, and not fierce at all. A terrible smell of dog came from the pup, and the rankness of it permeated everything.

· · · ·

There is a kind of dryness about the land along the quiet reaches of the Volga between Samara and Saratov. The Volga—the ancient waterway of Russia—flows among great plains, among solitudes and wildernesses. In July the grass of the hills is dried up, the smell of wormwood is everywhere, flint gleams in the moonlight; the traveler's feet become dusty and sore; the leaves of the oaks and maples are stiff, as if made of tin, and it takes more than a man's strength to split a pine; only the Tartar maple stands unperturbed; there are no flowers, and the bonfires on the hills—there is no mistaking them for lightning flares—are visible from the Volga for many versts[1] through the dust clouds rolling up from Astrakhan. And that is when you know that the dust is born of grasshoppers, of the grasshoppers' June chirping. To the right are wooded hills, and beyond the hills—the steppe; to the left are floodlands, and beyond the floodlands—the steppe. In the distance un-Russian church towers can be seen through the haze beyond the Volga: these are the German *kolonkas*.[2]

Many years ago, one of the tsars, most likely Paul, gave Prince Kadomski a title deed in which was written in the imperial hand:

> . . . *Your Excellency will come to the town of V. on the Volga; thirty versts thence lies the hill of Medyn. Your Excellency will mount this hill, and everything that the eye of Your Excellency will behold will be yours.* . . .

Along the Volga, where it enters the steppe, the Medynski forests sprang up on hills and islands, extending

[1] A measure of distance, about seven tenths of a mile (Editors).

[2] German "colonies"—settlements established in the Trans-Volga region in the latter half of the eighteenth century (Editors).

seventy versts along its bank; pines for building timber, oaks, maples, elms, thickets, virgin forest, fir stands, saplings—covering an area of twenty-seven thousand dessiatines.[3] In a hollow at the foot of Medynski Hill stood the Prince's house—stunned by the year 1917. In the forests there was nothing except watchmen's huts and guard posts: villages, big and small, moved away from the forests, making way for them and for the Prince. This is what the forester Nekulyev wrote to his friends on the Provincial Committee about his journey there: ". . . you have to get to the village of Vyazovy by steamer; in Vyazovy you have to find either the forest watchman Tsipin —and he will jolt you for sixteen versts in his cart through woods, over hills, across gullies—or the fisherman Vasili Ivanov Starkov (you have to ask for Vasyatka the fisherman)—and he will pull you twelve versts up the Volga by the strength of his own back. It's a lie that only in China are people used as beasts of burden: this is also the practice hereabout—Starkov harnesses himself to the towline, his son takes the rudder, you get into the boat, and towing —just as people did three hundred years ago—by their own strength, taking turns, they'll pull you to forestry headquarters. If you ask this Starkov, 'How many Communists have you in Vyazovy?' he will answer, 'We don't have many Communists, what we have around here is mostly common folk, there's only two families of Communists.' And if you press him further as to who exactly these common folk are, he will say, 'Common folk, like everyone knows, is common folk. Common folk is something like what you might call Bolsheviks.'"

The forests stood drooping, silent in the night. But if there had existed a giant ear able to catch every sound in the countryside thereabout, it would have heard among the murmurs and rustlings of the forest at night many a crash as trees were sawed through by forest thieves, ringing of saws, talk of moonshiners and deserters in hollows, on hills, in caves and lairs; it would have heard footsteps,

[3] A measure of surface equal to 2.7 acres (Editors).

shouted challenges, warning fire of watchmen and forest guards, whistled messages and exchanges, cries of owls and cries of men, groans of the beaten, the thud of horses' hooves. At night forest bonfires are visible from afar, and if these bonfires have been lighted in hollows, the smoke drifts far over the dewy ground; night bonfires are frightening, and frightening deeds are recounted at night around the bonfires of Russia. Wolves keep well clear of the bonfires. Days in the forest—in July—are always spacious; the smell of Tartar maple is everywhere. The men of the forest—foresters, watchmen, mounted guards, woodcutters— have the unshakable conviction that the whole of humanity is divided into two camps: themselves—foresters, watchmen, and woodcutters—and "citizen forest thieves."

. . . .

It was a brisk, sunny day when the forester Anton Nekulyev, a brisk and cheerful man, succeeded in finding Tsipin the watchman in the village of Vyazovy, told him he was the new forester and a Party member, there had been a hell of a crush on board the steamer, he had to get to the village soviet, he had to be in Medyn that night, and Lenin had a head on his shoulders, he'd be damned if he didn't! He made no mention of the sixteen trained men who were to follow him to protect the forests from plunder, or of the authority with which he had been invested to take strong measures—up to and including shooting. At the village soviet, in a drowsy, fly-buzzing silence, the chairman and secretary sat drinking *samogon*[4] and eating catfish; the chairman ordered the secretary to bring a third glass for Nekulyev. Tsipin was a man who listened and took careful note of things: that morning, as soon as Nekulyev arrived, he had sent an estafette to Medyn by way of the cordons, ordering Kuzya to come and fetch the new forester; the words "estafette" and "cordon"[5] were embedded in the vocabulary of the forest men, and dated

[4] Home-distilled liquor usually made from grain or potatoes (Editors).

[5] Estafette—relay message; cordon—guard post (Editors).

back to the time of the princes. Tsipin listened carefully
to Nekulyev, but, being a passionate hunter, responded
with tales of grouse, foxes, and double-barrels. He did,
however, tell how the peasants had killed the forester's
predecessor: they killed him in the house, slit him open,
pulled out his guts, with the guts they bound his hands
and feet, tried hard to stuff him into the grand piano, but
couldn't do it, so they threw both him and the piano down
the steep bank of the Volga—the piano hangs there to this
day, stuck in the bush willows; and the hunting in these
parts is fit for a king: if, say, a man should be greedy
enough to lay traps in January when the fox is starved, he
could pick up as many as a hundred skins in a single winter
—but of course that's not the thing for a hunter with a gun
to do: it would be a disgrace. Kuzya arrived in a carriage,
the front wheels of which had been replaced by cart
wheels, while those at the back still had rubber tires. He
pulled himself to attention, arms stiffly at his sides, and
began, army-style, "I have the honor to report . . ."
Nekulyev gave him his hand, clapped him on the shoulder.
Kuzya said:

"I have the honor to report . . . I mean, we'd better
spend the night here or else—you never know—they're like
to bash our head in, them forest thieves. I have the honor
. . . I mean, people are really swine these days; it's a disgrace, that's what."

Tsipin turned out to be of a different opinion about
the situation. He reasoned:

"What? Touch Comrade Anton Ivanovich Nekulyev?
Him, a Party member and a Bolshevik? The forests are
ours now. What, dare to touch him? I'll come with you as
far as Willow Spring; we'll take the steppe route, the
roundabout way. Anton Ivanovich has a revolver, you have
a rifle—I have a rifle—I'll tell my boy to go on ahead and
give him a double-barrel. We'll shoot the lot of them, and
no doubt about it! What, touch a Bolshevik? That's why
he's come here—because the forests are ours. You can take
as much as you like now without stealing, that's what the
law says."

The steppe in July is stifling; the chirping of grasshoppers oppresses, and the air is filled with the smell of wormwood. Heat lightning winked incessantly. They descended a hill, crossed a ravine, passed some windmills, and suddenly the steppe was all around them, ancient as the ages. They took the roundabout route. Tsipin soon dozed off, Kuzya hummed to himself. It was very dark and quiet, only the grasshoppers kept up their rasping. They went down into another ravine and soon heard marmots squealing and whistling close by; Kuzya got down from the carriage and took the horse by the bridle: he said marmots had dug their burrows all over the track—the horse could likely break a leg. They came to the top of a hill and saw the sky—far away in the steppe, above the hills, over the Volga—torn with silent lightning: the thunder's roll did not reach them. "There's going to be a storm," said Tsipin sleepily. And again the sky flew open—silently—but this time to the left, above the steppe itself. The horse set off at a trot, the dry, black earth resounded to the thud of hooves and the rattle of wheels; the grasshoppers seemed to have quieted down, and one enormous half of sky was silently rent from east to west, opening up its infinities. By the side of the track sunflowers bent their heavy heads, and then the enormous distant thunder cart rolled over the steppe; the atmosphere became suffocating. Now lightning flares came thick and fast; the sky was ripped to tatters, and became a bowling alley where the boisterous elements sent balls of thunder rolling. Tsipin woke up and said, "We'll have to go to the shepherds' dugout, Kuzya; we'll sit out the rain there; I don't fancy getting wet."

The storm, the open spaces, the thunder and lightning—all seemed a rare joy to Nekulyev, and all his days in the forests he remembered that night: how good it is sometimes when you are young to shout with the thunder, to outshout the storm! They did not reach the shepherds' dugout in time: the wind began tearing about the steppe; lightnings darted and thunder roared on all sides; a torrent of rain came down on them when they were about a hundred paces from the dugout, and instantly soaked them to the skin. The black earth of the path leading to the dug-out turned to mud in a moment, water poured into the dugout in a stream. Someone shouted in alarm, "Who the hell is that out there?" The horse stopped obediently by the wicket fence. In a brilliant flash of lightning Nekulyev saw his way to the dugout and—in the impenetrable rainy darkness—tumbled into a puddle. Through the thunder he heard people talking close by, "That you, Potap? It's me, Tsipin." "Our matches are soaked. Did the Devil bring you out hunting?" "No, I'm taking a *barin*[6] somewhere—Party member, the new forester." Again the sky was rent by lightning; a little boy ran past into the dugout and said, as both he and the dugout were swallowed up by the dark-ness, "Dad, the wolves are here again, a pack of them. There's a strange horse standing out there, not ours, right where the pack is!" Kuzya had stayed behind with the horse, taking shelter under the carriage. They went out to the horse, Tsipin and Nekulyev carrying guns, and the old shepherd a stick. They found the horse up the wicket fence, snorting, while Kuzya stood shaking off mud, snivel-ing and muttering curses. "I get under the carriage, and there's a big flash of lightning! And that gray nag takes a big jump up the fence! It's a wonder my neck wasn't broken." "It's wolves, you fool!" "N-o-o?" They pulled the horse down from the fence, replaced the broken bellyband with a rope. They decided to go on. They set off. The track had quickly turned to mud and running streams. They went down into a small ravine. Tsipin said, "Don't take the bridge way, Kuzya: the horse'll break a leg. It was there at the bridge," he explained to Nekulyev, "that the peasants killed the *barin*—the Prince." A stream whirled through the ravine. It had stopped raining; the storm was passing, lightning and thunder were less frequent. They began to climb out of the ravine; the horse slid about in the mud and went sprawling; the travelers climbed out. They began to push the carriage, got halfway up the hill and started to slide down again, all together—horse, carriage, and men;

[6] A member of the gentry; also a form of address and refer-ence roughly equivalent to "Master" (Editors).

the horse fell down and had to be unharnessed. Lightning blazed, and suddenly they saw a pack of wolves sitting side by side, above, on the edge of the ravine, not more than ten paces away. Tsipin said, "We'll have to pull the cart out, we can't spend the night here: the wolves won't leave us alone." They led the horse out first, then dragged out the carriage. Nekulyev was in high spirits all the time.

The rain had passed. They moved into the forest—into darkness, rustlings, fragrances, and water splashing down from leaves. Tsipin got down, dropped behind, and went to the hut of a watchman friend. Nekulyev wondered how Kuzya could find his way and not get lost in this damp and odorous darkness, where a man might just as well have been blind. Kuzya was silent for a while.

"When the peasants took it into their heads to kill the *barin*—the Prince—this Tsipin goes to Prince Kadomski and says, 'Seeing as how things are, you'd better leave; they're going to loot the house—the peasants are after your blood.' The Prince says to his lackey, 'Have the troika ready!' And Tsipin says to him, 'There won't be any horses for you, Your Excellency, we won't allow that.' The Prince started rushing about, dressing himself up something like a tradesman—he took his coachman's boots, his cap too, and his red neckcloth. His wife put on a shawl. They left at night, as quiet as could be, and there by the bridge Tsipin comes up to them, 'Seeing as how things are, Your Excellency, how about a little tip from Your Grace for the warning?' The Prince gave him a coin—a silver ruble—but who killed the Prince nobody knows."

Kuzya fell silent. Nekulyev too was silent. They rode slowly in the pitch darkness. Here and there on the ground glowworms were burning.

"And, speaking of that, here's another thing. In a village there lived a peasant—a very cunning, thrifty man—his name was, let's say, Ilya Ivanych," Kuzya began in a leisurely singsong. "And he had a young wife—a beauty, and faithful, too—Annushka by name. The village was a big one—it had three churches, mark you, all consecrated to different saints. . . . And so one day Annushka goes to Mass. And let me tell you that Mass began at a different time in each church. So Annushka is walking along, and she meets a priest; he says to her, 'Good day to you, Annushka!' and then, under his breath, 'Annushka, how about us meeting some evening at sundown?' 'What are you saying, Father?' says Annushka, and runs straight to the second church as fast as her legs can carry her. And she meets a second priest, and he says, 'Good day to you, Annushka!' and, under his breath, like the other one, 'Annushka, how do you like the idea of spending a night with me?' "

"What on earth are you talking about?" Nekulyev asked in bewilderment.

"I'm telling a story, that's what; people like the way I tell stories."

. . . .

And once again it was a brisk, sunny day—a day which emerged in benevolent sunshine from the wet darkness of a stormy night in the steppe, a day filled with the intoxicating smells of forest's and earth's abundance. The lungs swelled like a sponge in water—how good it smells when maples are baking in the sun! The stunned white house with its lizards and broken glass basked in the sun, and, at the slightest touch, ripe raindrops fell from the grapevine on the veranda. Below the steep bank the Volga was melting the sun, you couldn't look at it. All that had to be done was to put in windows, screw on doorknobs, fix vents and doors in the stoves, replace the stolen parquetry with new flooring—and the house would be in just as good shape as before—it wouldn't take much! And from the inner rooms to the one which bore the sign "Office" on its outside door, strode—the ceiling dully echoing his firm steps—a brisk man, handsome, curly-haired, youthful, wearing a dark-blue high-collared blouse and hunting boots. The pince-nez on his nose sat neatly—in contrast with the rioting hair above. In the office, dull as all the bookkeeping in the world, plans and maps lay on one drawing table; the green baize of the other one was stained with the ink

and candlewax of many nights and many scribblers;
through the windows the sun brought in the vitality of
the whole world. Holding his arms stiffly at his sides,
Kuzya stepped forward to meet Nekulyev; he was barefoot
and wearing the dark-blue woolen trousers of a gendarme's
uniform and a shirt faded with age; he wore no belt and
his collar was unbuttoned; Kuzya had enormous—terrifying
—brown whiskers which, far from making his good-natured,
round face fearsome, merely gave it a rather foolish look.
Kuzya said:

"I have the honor to report there are guards and peasants outside: the guards have brought in some forest
thieves. And there's a woman asking to see you too. Do I
let them in?"

"Let them all come in!"

"I have the honor to report, the old forester used to
talk to everyone through this window—he ordered a hole
to be made in the wall just for that."

"Let them all come in."

For a few minutes the office was the scene of an open
meeting; the peasants came trooping in; there was no telling which of them had been caught stealing wood and
which had come as petitioners. The guards lined up army-
style, rifles at their sides. The peasants all began talking
at once; they were peacefully disposed, but still on their
guard: "The forests are ours now, we own them!" "Seeing
as how you're a Communist, comrade—we want to cut
wood in Wet Gulley, seeing as how it belongs to Kadom!"
"Those Germans across the river—if they set foot in the
forests on our side, we'll break their legs for them!" "The
same for Tartars and Mordvinians." "Look at it this way,
comrade *barin*, we did the cutting and we want to sell
the wood at a good price in Saratov!" Nekulyev said
gaily: "It's no use acting dumb, comrades, no use playing
the fool. It's true I'm a Communist, but I'm not letting
anyone plunder the forests. You know yourselves it's no
good; as for shouting, I can do that too—I've got a strong
throat." A peasant, barefoot, wearing a coarse woolen
coat and holding a fur cap in his hands, came up and

stood by Nekulyev, who said, "Don't stand there cap in
hand—aren't you ashamed?—put it on!" The peasant was
abashed, he shot a glance at Nekulyev, hastily put the cap
on, yanked it off again, and replied angrily, "This is a
house, ain't it? There's icons here!" Two by two, unhurriedly, quietly, six men came into the room—Germans, all
wearing vests, but ragged like the Russians. *"Können Sie
Deutsch sprechen?"* asked one of them. The peasants broke
into shouting about the Germans, "Get out, the forests
are ours!" Nekulyev sat down on a table, stretched out his
legs, rocked back and forth a few times, and began in a
businesslike way: "Comrades, why don't you sit down—
oh, on the window sills—and let's talk sense. Some of the
men here are under arrest; I'll let them go and give them
back their saws and axes—but that's not the issue. You
can't cut down trees just any old way; judge for yourselves," and he began to speak about things which to him
were as clear as day. Peasants and Germans went away in
silence; many of them, though, had put on their caps toward the end of his talk. To those who left last Nekulyev
said in a friendly manner, "I shall take what action is
necessary, comrades—I shall do what has to be done, and
you may do as you please!" Nekulyev was a no-nonsense
sort of man.

Kuzya pulled himself to attention and said:

"I have the honor to report . . . would you like a few
eggs or some milk, perhaps? We haven't got any ourselves,
but Maryasha can take a boat to the Germans across the
river."

"I want to have a talk with your wife anyway—about
her getting my meals. Let's eat together. Buy some
eggs. . . ."

And so it was a sunny morning, and Nekulyev was
cheerful and handsome in his youth and vigor, and Kuzya
with his foolish face was standing barefoot at attention,
when Arina Arsenyeva, the tanner, came into the room.
The green office baize was spotted with many waxes and
many inks.

"I have to get a permit from you for bark. We'll strip

it ourselves. Here's the order—I need the bark for the Shikhany tanneries." And in the top right-hand corner of the order were the words "Workers of the World Unite!" and on her documents, on her Party card were words beautiful to both of them: Communist Party of Russia. "They killed the man who was here before you? They killed the Prince?" "The peasants hereabout are fighting a war of their own against the forests." Their conversation was long, strange, and intense, with the intensity of the sun itself. For him—long ago and far away—a forestry institute in Germany, factories and factory settlements in Russia; being a revolutionary is a profession; dim lights are burning in the corridors of mill barracks, and sleep seems so sweet at the hour when the man on night duty begins to bang on the doors of the cubicles ("Get up! Get up! It's your shift, the whistle's blown!"); and the world is beautiful, the world is full of sunlight because one's will is strong and one's faith in the goodness of the world is strong—and there's no nonsense about it: the will and the faith drawn from his childhood in the Urals (a mountain rises above valleys, and beyond the mountain is a wilderness where it seems that no man has ever set foot—bears, and a hermit in a mud hut), from books in cardboard covers: the will and the faith which had sustained him through the forestry institute and the trenches of the Naroch front. All this was Nekulyev's, and all this had the precision of a game of chess—both out here in the Medyn forests and back there: in Moscow, Halle, Paris, London, and the mills of the Urals. And for her: the Volga, the Volga steppe and the land beyond, the fence at the edge of the village: on the other side of the fence—the outlaw steppe and rough trails; and on her side—vats with soaking skins and the corpselike smell of skins and tanbark; and everything had this smell, even the house, even the Sunday pies—light as a feather—and the feather beds—light as Sunday pies; and her mother's incense (her mother died when she was thirteen, and she had to take her place in the house and learn the tanning business as well); and her father—himself like a tanned bull hide from

the vat; and the cuckoo clock; and the house-goblin behind the stove, and the devils; and at the age of thirteen
she was in her third year at the *Gymnasium*—her breasts
already formed beneath the brown school uniform—and by
the age of seventeen the young Volga beauty had grown
to abundant womanhood; St. Petersburg and her studies
there unfolded in misty regularity, but the mists were low
like the ceilings at home—and she had to rid her cubbyhole
on Shestnadtsataya Liniya of bedbugs—yet later, when her
father died, the ceilings at home seemed even lower—
oppressive, smoke-blackened; the house-goblin was no
longer behind the stove, but the smell of skins brought
back the mysteries of her childhood; she entered the
house as the moon enters the night; the head clerk
grumpily brought in greasy account books, and the police
came, scuttling like rats, rummaging and rustling; there
could never be any reconciliation with the house, the account keeping, and the rats; beauty gave the right to shout
in protest, and the straight lines of prison corridors merged
with the regularity of Petersburg, where there is no way
of putting out the moon. All this was Arina Arsenyeva's
—and all this, too, had the precision of a game of chess—
and tanneries (the smell of them filled her childhood)
are needed by the Red Army and must be put back into
operation. With the years moonlight replaces sunlight in
a woman's life: the abundance of seventeen is a heavy
wine by the age of thirty when there has never been any
time for wine. "I know the country round here through
and through—the forests, the land along the Volga."

In the sunshine the green of the vine leaves makes the
light greenish, and the air becomes liquid. Nekulyev noticed that in the green light the blood vessels in the whites
of Arina's eyes turned blue, while the pupils deepened to
an abyss—and suddenly it seemed to him that from her
eyes came the smell of tanned hide. Three people came
into the office: a peasant family—a man, a woman, and a
boy. The man said uncertainly:

"I have the honor to report—I'm second watchman after

Kuzya from the eleventh cordon. Yegor Nefedov. And this is my wife Katya. And this is my son Vasyatka."

The watchman was interrupted by his wife, who began in an injured tone: "You told Kuzya, *barin*, that you want to eat with Maryasha. Do as you please—you're the master—but you could eat with us, too, and most likely no worse than at Maryasha's. We're building a new house, my husband's not strong, he got a rupture; we're from Kadom. Do as you please—you're the master. But Maryasha's got three kids, one smaller than the next, and there's only three of us." Katya pursed her lips, stuck her hands on her hips and waited belligerently for an answer. Nekulyev said, "Go, God be with you—I'll decide later." And in the sunlight Arina Arsenyeva noticed: the bluish shaven skin of his cheekbones was firm and tough. Arina said softly, with a touch of bitterness:

"Do you know, to this day when they have the 'crawling in'—that's what they call moving into a new house—the peasants around here first let in a rooster and a cat, and only then do people go in—according to popular belief this has to be done by the light of a full moon. It's at night too that they drive the cattle over to the new place. And the same night, before dawn, the woman runs around the house three times—naked. All this is done to please the house-goblin. . . ."

Chapter One: Nights and Days

Ask Maryasha, Katyasha, Kuzya, or Yegor about the forest—they will tell you:

In the depths of the forest and among the pines lives the wood-devil—the Lyad. The forests stand dark, reaching from earth to sky, and there is no end to the things that Maryasha knows about them. The bluish woods rear an impenetrable wall. Man can hardly force a way through the close-growing pines; in the heart of the forest everything is slowly dying and turning to wilderness. Here by

the side of new growth stand withered oaks and firs, eventually to crash to earth—smothering everything beneath
them—and to be covered with a rich funereal brocade of
mosses. Even in a July noon it is gloomy and damp here,
and seldom does a bird cry out; if a wind blows in from
the steppe the ancient oaks rub against one another, groaning, shedding decaying limbs and showers of powdery
rotten wood. Here Kuzya, Maryasha, Katyasha, and Yegor
are overcome by feelings of terror, nothingness, loneliness,
and impotence; their flesh creeps. The devil who is known
as the Lyad has made his home in the pine woods from
time immemorial, and Kuzya would even tell what he
looks like: a wide belt of red cloth, kaftan buttoned up
from left to right instead of right to left; bast shoes on the
wrong feet, eyes glowing like coals, and himself all
made up of mosses and fir cones. If you want to see the
Lyad, you have to look over the right ear of a horse.

.   .   .   .

By day the white house in the hollow near Medynski
Hill stood quietly amidst greenery, cool as a pond. At
night the house went mad: for Nekulyev's straining eyes
—searching the darkness—there was broken furniture,
bindings of torn books, all sorts of junk. In a rubbish heap
on the veranda Nekulyev found an hourglass; it took five
minutes for the sand to run from one glass sphere to the
other; on moonlit nights the glass of the spheres had a
faint greenish gleam; during the day Nekulyev never gave
the hourglass a thought, but at night he spent many a five
minutes with it. He was a no-nonsense sort of man; he
was not aware that—independent of consciousness and will
—every rustle in the house, every stupid mouse-skitter
across the floor, raised goose pimples on his back, and he
fell into the habit of staying awake at night; he never lost
his nerve, but all the time somebody else seemed to be
there—some elusive, remote presence—and every night was
the same. The moon was up, and hundreds of moons were
shattered in the water at the foot of the hill; the house
was numb; the trees surrounding it were of silver; a silence

settled, broken only by owls. Moonlight furrowed the parquet floor in the ballroom. Nekulyev had carefully closed the windows, but there was no glass in them. He had barricaded the room's three doors with broken furniture, and wedged them with staves. A sofa stood by one of the doors, and on it lay Nekulyev. A revolver in an unbuttoned holster hung on a chair close by; a rifle was propped against the foot of the sofa. On the sofa lay a large, healthy, handsome body—the very same body which absurdly came out in goose pimples at every rustle. Nekulyev was calm in the knowledge that two trained men, Kandin and Konkov, were guarding the forest at Willow Spring—they were tough and wouldn't bungle the job. You couldn't cross the hills on foot, let alone in a cart, but if anyone got through to the house, then he'd go down to the cellar through a secret door which he had stumbled on by chance, and which dated back to the time of the Prince who used to own the estate; and from the cellar—through an underground passage—into the ravine; once there—just try and find him! . . . To distract attention, a small, battered lamp had been left burning in the right wing of the house, where the windows were carefully covered up. The moon peered through the windows into the wrecked interior of the house. Nekulyev got up from the sofa, picked up his revolver, removed the stake from the door, and made his way through the dark rooms— hesitantly, because he was still unused to the house; he took a drink of water from a bucket in the kitchen, and went back; in the doorway he stood and listened to the sounds of the house—unaware of the goose pimples which rose all over his body; he wedged the stake against the door—and took it away again quickly: when he had picked up the bucket he had laid his revolver on the window sill and forgotten it; hurriedly he started back. In the dusty moonlight the hourglass lay on the window sill in the ballroom; Nekulyev began running the sand from one sphere to the other, bending his curly head over the dull glass.

· · · ·

And then, all of a sudden, someone began knocking on the window in the room where the lamp was burning, and a voice called uncertainly, "Hey, whoever's there, come out. The militiaman wants you!" Lithe as a cat, Nekulyev picked up his rifle and looked out of the broken window without making a sound: there in the moonlight by the house stood a boy with a boat hook, looking warily around in the silence. Nekulyev said calmly, "And who may you be?" The boy replied, relieved, "Come on, the militiaman wants you!" "What are you doing with that boat hook?" "It's to keep off dogs. Any dogs here? The militiaman's down below, in the boat!"

The boy, Kuzya, and Nekulyev (the last two carrying rifles) went down the steep bank to the Volga. Three flat-bottomed boats were moored by the bank. A militiaman, holding a revolver in one hand and a saber in the other, a rifle slung over one shoulder, was pacing the bank. The militiaman shouted:

"What the hell are you doing sleeping when timber's being stolen? I was out after moonshiners, got two boats —been out three days, haven't slept. I was just going past Wet Hill, and what do I see: logs flying down from the top of the hill—timber thieves are at work and you're sleeping! I'd have taken the thieves myself, but all I've got is two witnesses: the rest are moonshiners caught red-handed. If I leave them, they'll run for it. Forty buckets of *samogon* I'm carrying—haven't slept in three days! . . . They come hurtling down right from the top, and two empty boats waiting on the river! . . ."

The militiaman climbed into the boat, gave an order to the moonshiners, and the peasants harnessed themselves to the towline and started pulling the string of boats in silence. The militiaman barked orders and moved his revolver threateningly. The moon shone down silently, and hundreds of moons were splintered in the water. River and hills were numb. The boats disappeared beyond a spit of land. Kuzya brought up two horses, one of them saddled, the other with a sack of hay on its back. Without a word Kuzya and Nekulyev started at a gallop along forest paths and over hills in the direction of Wet Hill, rifles at the ready; they left the horses in Wet Ravine and came out to the Volga. River, hills, silence—a screech owl called, gravel loosened underfoot, the smell of wormwood drifted in from somewhere—silence—and on top of the hill a tree came crashing down, fell, rolling over the steep bank and dragging rocks after it. Kuzya and Nekulyev started to walk along the river below the sheer drop of the bank —two boats had been wedged among bush willows, one already piled high with logs; another log hurtled down from the hilltop, and close by—no more than ten paces away—a man whistled softly; another whistled on the hill, and a third . . . and then the world played dead. Suddenly a solitary rifleshot burst on the hill. Kuzya crouched behind a rock; Nekulyev gave him a prod forward with his knee, flicked the bolt of his rifle and strode resolutely toward the boats, pushed the empty boat out, and threw himself on the loaded one to get it moving. From above came a rifleshot; a bullet splashed in the water. "Kuzya, come and push!" Above the drop came a red flash, a pop; a bullet splashed. Immediately Nekulyev fired in the direction of the flash, and somebody shouted from the hill, "Oi, what are you doing, you devil? Let the boats be!"

Nekulyev said:

"Kuzya, push off, push with the oar, take over the rudder, get it away from the shore or they'll hit us!"

．　．　．　．

The moon splashed from the oar. Shouts came from the bank, "Forgive us, *barin*, for the love of Christ give us back our boats!"

Nekulyev said:

"Damn it, what if they steal the horses?"

Kuzya replied:

"How can they? We've got them now. Nothing to be afraid of. The peasants have come to their senses—they've got the fear of God in them."

．　．　．　．

The boat touched shore at Wet Ravine; three men— peasants—one of them with a rifle—all from Vyazovy—came up tearfully and began to beg for their boats. Nekulyev said nothing, looked away. Kuzya, also without a word, went into the ravine, brought back the horses and harnessed them to the towline; then he made a stern pronouncement: "Stealing wood, you swine! Get in the boat, you're under arrest! They'll get to the bottom of this, they'll show you how to steal wood!"

The peasants fell on their knees. Nekulyev whispered crossly:

"Why arrest them? What are we going to do with them?"

"That's all right—no harm in giving them a scare!"

Slowly the horses made their way along the shore over the rough stones. Hills and river were still, but the moon had already disappeared; in the vast spaces beyond the Volga the sky was ripening to red as day drew near; the dawn brought a chill, dew soaked their shirts.

"How about me telling you a story?" asked Kuzya.

They took the loaded boats around the spit of land below Medynski Hill, and moored them securely. (The boats disappeared in the night two days later—somebody stole them.)

. . . .

And again there came a hammering at the windows in the night. "Anton Ivanovich! Comrade forester! Nekulyev! Get up quick!" And the house was filled with the clumping of boots, with whispers, and rustlings; candle and lighter flames rocked the ceilings. "Seeing as how you're a Communist, the peasants from Kadom—the whole lot of them, and the priest, too—have gone to cut firewood near Red Ravine; estafettes have gone out to all cordons; the peasants have tied up Ilyukhin the watchman and dragged him off to the lockup!" Near the stable yard, opposite the servants' hut stood lathery horses, and there was a strong smell of horse sweat (a smell sweet to Nekulyev from childhood); a bright star was caught on the hilltop (what star was that?) and a glowworm burned under a tree nearby. Kuzya led out the horses, but they were one horse short, and he had to run.

"Yegor, you carry the rifle a bit—save me dragging it."

Into the saddle and off at a gallop to the hills, to the forest. "Damn it! The trails are choked. One of these branches could take your eye out!"

The forest stood black, silent; on the hilltops the air was parched and dusty; there was a smell of dry grass. The hollows were damp and chill; fog crept along the ground, unknown birds cried out ("Oh, how beautiful the Volga nights!"). There was a strong smell of horse sweat; the horses knew the way.

"What swine these lousy peasants are! It isn't what they take—it's what they knock down and trample! These peasants have no sense of responsibility at all! They've tied up Ilyukhin like a bandit and taken him to the village— they've locked up his wife and kids in the watchman's hut and left someone to guard them; their boy Vanyatka crawled into the cellar, where the dog had dug a hole, got out through the hole into the yard, and ran to Konkov. Otherwise we wouldn't know anything about it. And it's every night you have to be on the lookout!"

Running at a trot, Kuzya caught up with the horsemen and said to Yegor:

"Yegorushka, you run awhile and I'll ride and rest a bit."

Yegor dismounted and started running after the horsemen. Kuzya punched the bag which served as a saddle to make it more comfortable, settled down, got his breath back, and said cheerfully:

"Wouldn't it be fine to strike up a song, like the robbers in the old days!" And his long-drawn-out robber's whistle pierced the blackness of the forest; nearby a large bird flapped its wings.

. . . Spread out among the trees at the edge of Red Ravine, a thin line of watchmen had been lying in wait since evening. A road led through the green wall of the forest among trails which cut the forest into squares, and disappeared into the hills. Nothing much was happening. The sun had sunk beyond the steppe; the moment had passed when—for a moment—trees and grass and earth and sky and birds fall silent; bars of deep blue fell across the earth; an owl flew out of the forest and winged by silently; no sooner had it passed than an unknown night bird cried out among the trees. And then, far away in the steppe, a string of peasant carts came into view as they moved through a pass in the hills. But they were swallowed up by night, and it was only an hour later that the crude rattlings and creakings of native Russian wooden carts reached the edge of the wood. Then the dust cloud rolled up to the forest; creaking of wheels, rattling of wheel rims, snorts of horses, whispers of people, crying of a baby —converged, crowding against the forest. Two ancient oaks standing at the intersection of the road and a forest trail had been sawed almost through at the roots—the slightest push and they would topple and block the road.

And then out of the darkness—the stern voice of a mounted guard:

"Hey there! You Kadom people! You men! It's no good, turn back!"

And then from the line of carts all at once—shouting and laughter from a hundred throats; there is no making out the words or whether people are shouting or men and horses are trying to outneigh each other; and the carts creep forward. Then two bold trained men, Kandin and Konkov—agility, daring, a final effort—send the trunks of the two oaks crashing down across the road; two shots explode convulsively into the sky. From the peasant camp —in the direction of the forest—comes a random hail of shots from revolvers, rifles, and shotguns. Half the carts jerk to a halt, horses rear onto the tailboards of carts in front. "Get off the trail!" "Go back!" "Shoot!" "Look out, you've run over a woman!" "The priest, hold the priest!" The forest is dark, incomprehensible; you can't get a horse off the trail; horses shy away from trees, from shots; shafts run into tree trunks, wheels crack against stumps. "The horse, leave the horse alone! You'll tear the collar, you swine!" Nobody knows who is shooting and why.

Nekulyev galloped up at dawn. A bonfire was burning near the edge of the forest. Watchmen were sitting around the fire, two of them singing a monotonous song. Rifles had been thrown in a heap by the fire. Horses stood dejectedly among carts in a little clearing. Peasants—men, women, and children—stood under guard to one side, together with the priest. Dawn was catching fire above the forest. The crude encampment was a sorry sight. Kandin, who had come with Nekulyev to protect the forests, went to meet him, took him aside, and began in a distraught whisper:

"Things are a mess. We blocked the road, you see, knocked down two oaks, thinking we'd take, oh, maybe five carts; we cut them off. I fired a warning. We didn't use another bullet. It was the peasants themselves who did the shooting; they killed a boy and a horse, and another horse got trampled. When things got out of hand, I thought we'd make ourselves scarce while we could and let the peasants get out of the mess themselves, so we'd be out of it, but by that time there was no holding back our boys; they started chasing people, arresting, taking weapons away. . . ."

Nekulyev was holding a revolver; he said helplessly:

"Oh hell, what a mess!"

A crowd of peasants rushed up to Nekulyev, fell on their knees, and began to plead with him:

"Beloved *barin* and protector! For the love of Christ, let us go. We won't do it again, we've learned our lesson!"

Nekulyev roared—in bitter anger, no doubt:

"Get up this very minute! To hell with you, comrades! You've been told in plain language: I won't let you rob the forests, not for anything!" And in bewilderment, no doubt: "And look what you've done—you've killed a boy. A fine thing! Where is he? Every cart in the village is wrecked. A fine thing!"

"For the love of Christ, let us go! We'll never do it again!"

"Do me a favor—get out of my sight! That won't bring the boy back. Get it into your heads, for Christ's sake, that I'm on your side!" And threateningly: "And if any one of you calls me 'barin' once more, or pulls his hat off to me— I'll have him shot! Go wherever you like—please!"

Konkov, a Party member who had come with Nekulyev to protect the forests, turned on him angrily:

"What about the priest?"

"What about him?"

"We can't just let the priest go. That swindler ought to be sent to Cheka headquarters!"

Nekulyev said indifferently:

"All right then, send him!"

"I hope they shoot the swine!"

The sun rose above the trees—it was a glorious morning; the crude encampment was a sorry sight.

. . . .

And once again it was night. The house was silent. Nekulyev went to the window, stood gazing out into the darkness. And then in the bushes nearby—Nekulyev saw it—there was a sudden flash of rifle fire, a shot echoed, and a bullet hit the ceiling with a sharp click; plaster showered down. They were shooting at Nekulyev.

. . . .

And then came a brisk, sunny morning; it was Sunday, Nekulyev was in the office. Two moonshiners were brought in; Yegor was bent under the weight of a distilling vat. Tsipin arrived from Vyazovy with a message from the village soviet: "In view of the raising of the question concerning relegation of the forest, Comrade Nekulyev is to report immediately in person." Tsipin had been elected chairman of the village soviet. Nekulyev decided to go; they rode through the steppe, listening to the ground squirrels; Tsipin told hunting tales and was calm, deliberate, matter-of-fact. Later, when Nekulyev recalled that day, he knew it had been the most terrifying day of his life, and that only a stupid accident—human stupidity—had saved him from a most gruesome death—from being lynched, torn to pieces—arms, legs, and head torn from his body. In the steppe the squeaking of the ground squirrels seemed one with the suffocating heat. In the village young men and girls were milling in front of the church and the soviet building, and a young fellow, barefoot but

wearing spurs, was furiously dancing the squat dance;
Nekulyev was struck by those spurs and got down from
the cart to have a closer look: yes, that's what it was—
spurs on bare heels, but the boy's face was not stupid. In
the village soviet the peasants were waiting for Nekulyev.
They were drunk. The room was unbearably stuffy. When
Nekulyev entered, silence descended upon the gathering
—he could not hear so much as a fly's buzzing. Nekulyev
and Tsipin went through to the table together, and
Nekulyev suddenly noticed that Tsipin's expression, which
throughout their ride had been relaxed and amiable, had
become cunning and malicious. Tsipin began:

"All right, men! The meeting is open! Here he is—he's
arrived! A Party member, too! Let him say what he has
to say."

Nekulyev fingered the revolver in his pocket; the spurs
came to his mind; the spurs confused his thoughts. He
began:

"What's the matter, comrades? You demanded that I
come here to make a report. . . ."

"The forests are ours now, we want to split them up,
like the law says—to each man his share!"

Someone interrupted:

"To each household its share!"

There were shouts from all sides:

"No, to each man!"

"No, to each household!"

"No, I say, to each man!"

"What's the use of talking to him, men! Get the forester,
let's get him!"

Nekulyev shouted:

"Comrades! You demanded that I come here to make
a report. . . . Our land is mostly steppe, there isn't much
forest. There's a civil war going on, comrades. Maybe you
want the landowners back? If all the forests are cut down,
you won't be able to make good the damage in forty years.
Trees should be cut sensibly, according to a plan. There's
a civil war going on, we're cut off from coal. These forests

supply the whole of southeast Russia. You want the landowners back? I won't let anyone rob the forests. . . ."

"Listen, men! Everything is ours now! Let him answer
—how come the Kadom people can steal and we can't?
Who is he to plague us?"

"We want to choose our own forester!"

"Get him, men—let's get our hands on him!"

All his life Nekulyev remembered those savage, drunken
eyes closing in on him, full of hatred. He understood then
that a mob smells of blood, even though no blood has
been shed. Nekulyev shouted with something like gaiety:

"Damn it, comrades, I won't let anyone touch me. You
see this revolver? I'll stretch six of you out, and then I'll
turn it on myself!" Nekulyev pulled the table toward him
and got into the corner behind it, gun in hand. The crowd
pushed toward the table.

Tsipin bellowed:

"Minka, run get the rifle—we'll see who shoots who!"

"Shoot him, Tsipin; let's get him!"

Nekulyev shouted:

"Comrades, let me speak, damn you!"

The crowd assented:

"Let him speak!"

"Are you your own enemies, or what? Listen to me.
Let's talk sense: suppose you kill me—what sense is there
in that? You sit down, and I'll sit down, and we'll
talk. . . ." That day Nekulyev talked about everything:
forests, reforestation, what the Communists were doing,
what was going on in Moscow and Brussels, the locomotives that were being built, Lenin. He talked about everything because while he was speaking the peasants quieted
down, but the moment he stopped they began shouting,
"What's the use of talking—let's get him!" And Nekulyev
would begin to feel dizzy from the smell of blood. Tsipin
had been standing in the doorway with a rifle for some
time. Day gave way to that time of dusk when swallows
cut the air. Peasants came and went; the crowd got more
and more drunk. Nekulyev knew that there was no escape, that they would kill him, and many times when his

throat got dry it was only by a tremendous effort of will
that he was able to conquer his pride—not to shout, not
to send them all to hell, not to throw himself into the mob,
but to keep on talking—talking about whatever came into
his head.

Nekulyev was saved by chance. A group of young men,
members of the Union of Front-Line Fighters, blind drunk,
one of them with an accordion, staggered into the building; their leader—no doubt their chairman—climbed on the
table in front of Nekulyev; he was barefoot, and wore
spurs; he surveyed the crowd contemptuously, and began
with an air of authority:

"Listen, you graybeards! It's not up to you to judge
Comrade Nekulyev, the forester! It's up to us, the front-
line fighters. Look at Rybin there—shouting louder than
anyone, but has he sat in the forester's cooler? No, he
hasn't. Only them that's been caught stealing wood can
judge him, and them that hasn't—get the hell out of here.
And they think they can take the forest over—just like
that! We're the ones that were caught and put in the
cooler—so we've got first claim, and we're the ones to judge
him—and Tsipin along with him, seeing how he's his
right-hand man—the old devil!"

The swallow dusk had already given way to a night
filled with the chirping of grasshoppers. The young fellow
was drunk, and around him stood his friends, also drunk.
There was uproar: "Liar!" "That's right!" "Kill 'em!" "Get
Tsipin, the old devil!" Then a shouting, gasping, knock-
down fight broke out; beards, cheekbones, bruises went
flying on all sides. Nekulyev was forgotten. Very slowly,
barely moving his feet, apparently motionless, he reached
the window, and like a streaking cat threw himself out.
Never before had he run with such headlong speed—so
blindly; he regained memory and consciousness only at
dawn, in the steppe, among the squeaking of ground squirrels—as oppressive as the heat itself.

(In the village soviet no one noticed Nekulyev's disap-
pearance in the heat of the fighting, and that same evening Mother Grunya, the wife of Starkov the fisherman,

said—and by morning many women were saying it—that with her own eyes—may the earth open up and swallow her if she was lying—she saw Nekulyev's skin darken; saw him strain every muscle, saw his eyes fill with blood, foam drip from his mouth, fangs sprout from his jaws, saw him turn as black as black earth—strain every muscle—and plunge into the earth, sorcerer that he was.)

· · · ·

And something else happened to Nekulyev. Again, as on a dozen previous occasions, a mounted guard galloped up and reported that the Germans from the other side of the Volga were on their way to Green Island in their flat-bottomed boats—to cut firewood. Nekulyev and his stalwarts set off in his flatbottom to the rescue of the forests. Green Island was a sizable stretch of land; the forest men moored and went ashore unnoticed. It was a brisk day. They approached the Germans meaning to reason with them, but the Germans met them with an attack organized on the best military lines. Nekulyev gave the order to fire; from the German side came the rat-tat-tat of a machine gun, and the Germans began to advance in a perfectly controlled line, attacking in accordance with all the rules of war. Nekulyev and his band soon ran out of ammunition and were faced with a dilemma: either to surrender or to try to escape in the boat; but the boat was a very good target for the machine gun, and the watchmen assured him that if a German gets really angry he will spare nothing. The Germans took them prisoner, but later released all of them, except Nekulyev, whom they took back with them to the other side of the Volga, together with the wood and Nekulyev's boat. Nekulyev spent five days as a German prisoner. He was bailed out—for reasons incomprehensible to him—by the Vyazovy village soviet, headed by Tsipin (and it was Tsipin who crossed the Volga as negotiator). The passenger steamer which served the entire area stopped only at Vyazovy, and the Vyazovy peasants let the Germans know that if Nekulyev was not released, they would not let them cross to their side, and that any German caught would be killed; the Germans had to deliver butter, meat, and eggs to the ship; they let Nekulyev go.

Chapter Two: Nights, Letters, and Resolutions

In the evening Kandin came, bringing with him a forest thief; the thief had climbed a tree, was stripping bark, lost his footing, was caught in the branches by the bindings of his bast shoes; he was left hanging, his eyes ran out. Nekulyev ordered the thief's release. The peasant stood barefoot at attention in the darkness, and said calmly, "I could do with a guide, mister comrade—my eyes have run out." Nekulyev leaned close to the peasant, saw a thicket of beard; the empty sockets had already drawn together; the peasant stood cap in hand—and Nekulyev felt sick; he turned, went into the house. The house was alien, hostile; in this house they had killed the Prince; in this house they had killed his—Nekulyev's—predecessor: the house was hostile to these forests and this steppe— and Nekulyev had to live here. Again it was a moonlit night, and hundreds of moons splintered in the water at the foot of the hill. Nekulyev stood by the window, turning the hourglass over and over; abruptly he flung it away; it broke, spilling sand. . . . Sometimes when he was free Nekulyev would climb alone to the bald rock at the top of Medynski Hill; there he would light a fire and sit by it, thinking; below was the broad sweep of the Volga and the land beyond; and there was a bitter smell of wormwood in the air. Nekulyev left the house and walked through the grounds; on the threshold of the servants' quarters sat Maryasha and Katyasha; Yegor and Kuzya sat below; a broad-shouldered giant of a peasant, dressed unseasonably in a kaftan and bast shoes with white leggings, sat in a chair. Nekulyev did not come down from the hills until late.

Everything was peaceful near the servants' quarters. The moon glinted on the manure piled in front. Behind

the hut, a hill overgrown with hazel and maple reached
up toward the forests. Maryasha kept listening for the
sound of a bell among the hazels, lest the cow should
stray too far. The door of the hut was open, and the
groans of the blinded peasant came from within. Kuzya
got up from the log he was sitting on, stretched himself
out on the manure pile in front of the hut, and took up
his tale.

"... and so Annushka runs to the third church as fast
as her legs can carry her, and she meets a third priest,
who says, 'Good day to you, Annushka!' and then, under
his breath, 'How would you like to spend some time with
me, te-ta-te?' And so Annushka didn't get to Mass at
all; she came home and cried for shame, let me tell you.
She told her husband everything without fail, mark you.
And her husband, Ilya Ivanych—a cunning one—says, 'Go
to church, wait until the priest comes from Mass, and then
tell him to come at half past nine. And tell the second
priest to come about ten, and the third priest—and so on.
And keep your mouth shut.' Annushka sets off and sees
one of the priests coming from church. 'Well, Annushka,
how about sundown?' 'Come about half past nine, Father;
my husband will be visiting his cousin and he'll get dead
drunk, for sure.' And she meets the second priest. 'Well,
Annushka, how about spending the night?' Well, she said
what her husband had told her to say, and so it went
on. ... Evening came, and let me tell you, it was the
middle of winter, the time of the Epiphany frosts. The
priest arrives, smooths his beard, crosses himself in front
of the icon in the corner, and takes out from under his
coat, mark you, a bottle of vodka, the very best. 'Well,'
he says, 'hurry up with the samovar and the herring, and
then—to bed.' And she says to him, 'What's the hurry,
Father? The night is long, we can sleep all we want—
enjoy your tea.' Well, let me tell you, the way things are,
two's company and three's a crowd. No sooner has the
priest warmed up, sat close to her, slipped his hand inside
her blouse, when—'knock-knock' on the window. Well,
Annushka is thrown into a dither. 'Oh-oh! My husband!'

The priest tries to hide under a bench, can't squeeze himself in, starts groaning—he's real scared. And Annushka says, like her husband ordered, 'I just don't know where to hide you! Maybe in the storeroom; my husband's making a new bin—get in there.' The first priest hides himself, and the second one takes his place; he's brought vodka too—the very best. And no sooner has he slipped his hand inside her blouse, when—'knock-knock' on the window. And so the second priest finds himself in the bin, lying on top of the first, and there they are, whispering, pinching, and cursing each other. And as soon as the third priest begins to snuggle up, there's a knock at the gate and the husband shouts, playing drunk, 'Open up, woman!' And so the three priests find themselves piled one on top of the other. The husband, Ilya Ivanych—mark you—walks in and asks his wife in a whisper, 'In the bin?' Annushka replies, 'In the bin!' And now the husband, Ilya Ivanych, starts to throw his weight around like a drunk. 'Woman,' he says, 'I wish to put the new bin out in the cold, in the barn, and fill it with oats!' He starts climbing up to the storeroom. What Ilya Ivanych had in mind to do, mark you, was to put the priests out in the cold, lock them up in the barn, and let them freeze there for a day or so; in the end the cold would get them, they wouldn't be able to stand it, they'd break out of the barn, run like crazy, and be the laughingstock of the whole village. But things turned out quite different, and there was nothing to laugh at: he started to drag the bin down from the storeroom, the priests were fat—each of them weighed nine poods[7]— too heavy for Ilya Ivanych, and the bin went flying down the stairs. And the way it landed, the priests all cracked their heads open and gave up the ghost on the spot . . . ! Yes. . . ." Kuzya took out his tobacco pouch, squatted down, and began to roll himself a dog-leg[8]—carefully sealing the piece of newspaper with his tongue—about to go on with his story.

[7] A measure of weight, about 36 pounds (Editors).
[8] A paper funnel filled with tobacco and bent in the middle (Editors).

The moon got caught on top of the hill. The cowbell tinkled peacefully close by; the cow was chewing the cud. Nekulyev went by, walking uphill toward the steep bank. They fell silent, followed him with their eyes until he was lost in the darkness. Yegorushka said in a whisper:

"Look, there goes Anton! He's off again, he's on his way. To burn fires. . . . Grunya from Vyazovy—she's a sharp one—says he's a sorcerer for sure. I went up there and had a look: he breaks up dry branches, builds a fire, lies down beside it, props his head up with his hands—and looks and looks into the fire; his eyes are terrible to see, and those glasses on his nose glow like coals—and all the time he's chewing a blade of grass. . . . It's real frightening! Sometimes he stands with his back to the fire, right at the edge of the rock, hands behind his back—and there he stands and stands looking across the Volga; it's a wonder he don't fall off. Well, I got scared, and kept crawling and crawling until I got to the trail—and home at a run. Then I see him walking home just like nothing's happened."

"And he goes to see his woman," said Kuzya. "He gets there, and right away they go walking in the steppe, holding hands. And they start making a fire there too, mark you. . . . One time they went into a wood; I hid myself, and they sat down—oh, no more than two paces from me, no farther than that; I couldn't move, and the gnats were eating me up. They began talking about communes, and kissed once—genteel-like—they put up with the gnats, but I couldn't—and I couldn't move neither, and so I said, 'Excuse me, Anton Ivanych—the gnats are eating me alive!' She jumped up, and turned on him, 'What does this mean?'—angry-like. He didn't say anything to me, like nothing'd happened. . . ."

"I've got to read the Hours; I'll be off—good-bye to you," said the old peasant in the kaftan.

"Go, and may God be with you; time for bed," responded Maryasha, and yawned.

Kuzya struck a spark, kindled a piece of tinder, and lit a rolled cigarette; his cat whiskers could be seen in the glow. "And so, the way things are, there's no help for the man's eyes?" he asked sternly. "Neither by prayer nor spell?"

"There's no help for him at all—the wood-devil's gouged out his eyes. You have to lay on plantain leaves so his brains won't run out," said the old man. "I take my leave of you!" He got up and started to walk unhurriedly down toward the Volga, cudgel in hand; his white leggings and bast shoes showed pale below his kaftan.

Katyasha called after him, "Father Ignat, come by sometime, don't forget—see if you can heal my walleyed bull calf!"

Kuzya began in a singsong voice, "Yes. . . . And so that's how it turned out, let me tell you—Ilya Ivanych wanted to play a joke on the priests, but things turned out quite different. . . ."

"I brought you some eggs, Maryash," said Katyasha, interrupting him. "For the *barin*. What do you get for them?"

"Forty-five."

"I gave the Germans twenty. We'll settle later."

"How are you off for flour, Yegorushka?" asked Kuzya.

"We don't have any—we've spent everything on the house. The peasants don't buy wood anymore—they steal it themselves. As for flour—things couldn't be worse. Now, my brother had a lucky break in town, you might say he really struck it lucky. A brother-in-law of his comes to him from the depot and says, 'Here's forty poods of flour, sell it for me in the market and I'll make it worth your while—I just don't have time to do the selling.' So my brother agreed, sold all the flour, hid the money in a barrel and buried it—there were only three poods of flour left. And then the militia got him, my brother—it turns out the flour's been stolen from the depot. So they take him off to the cooler. 'Where's the rest of the flour?' 'I don't know.' 'Where did you get the flour?' 'At the market from somebody—don't remember who.' He stuck to it like a bull in a gate, didn't give his brother-in-law away; three weeks they kept him in jail—questioned him all the time—then, of course, they had to let him go. The brother-

in-law lost no time in coming around, but my brother
jumped on him: 'You no-good bum, selling stolen goods!
You should thank me on your knees for not giving you
away!' 'What about the money?' 'They took everything,
brother; thank God I got off with a whole skin. . . .' And
so the brother-in-law went away empty-handed; he even
thanked my brother and stood him a drink of *samogon*. . . . The money started my brother off, he opened
up a shop, he wears galoshes now—there's luck for you
straight out of the blue." Yegor was silent for a while.
"The eggs are in my cap—eight of them. Take them,
Maryash."

"The forester, let me tell you, ever since he arrived he's
lived on butter and eggs; he puts bread away and thinks
nothing of it—brought flour with him. And he notices
everything, doesn't miss a thing, mark you, he's got real
sharp eyes," said Kuzya.

"He eats and eats, nothing but sour cream, and butter,
and eggs—he's living like the gentry!" began Maryasha
animatedly. "He brought some buckwheat—in all my born
days I've never seen it, we don't sow it around here; I
cooked it and took some for myself—the kids ate it licking
their lips like it was sugar. And his underwear he tells me
to wash with soap; he wears it a week and takes it off—it's
as clean as can be, and still with soap! . . . I was washing
dishes and he says, 'Wash them with soap!' and I say to
him, 'In these parts we hold soap to be unclean! . . .'"

Suddenly inside the hut a bucket fell with a clatter, a
crushed chick squeaked, a hen started clucking, and a
peasant appeared in the doorway—the one who had been
blinded; his white shirt was bloodsoaked, his arms were
stretched out in front of him, his bearded head was thrown
back, the dead sockets could not be seen; his hands groped
the air. Suddenly he shrieked in unbearable pain and rage:

"Give me back my eyes, my eyes, my sharp eyes! . . ."
He stumbled on the threshold and fell forward into the
manure.

"That'll learn you to steal bark," Kuzya said comfort-

ingly. "You saw we called Father Ignat, and he said nothing can be done."

Kuzya and the women began dragging the man back
into the hut. Yegorushka walked a few paces away from
the hut toward the barn and the riverbank to relieve himself; he returned and said thoughtfully, "The fire's out,
that means he's coming back. Time for bed." He yawned
and made the sign of the cross over his mouth. "So give
him the eggs, we'll settle later." Yegor and Katyasha went
home to the watchman's hut at the other end of the
grounds. In the servants' quarters Kuzya lit a homemade
candle and took off his cap—cockroaches skittered over
the table. The peasant lay groaning on a bunk. The children were sleeping on the stove ledge. A cradle hung in
the middle of the room. From the oven Kuzya took an
iron pot. The potatoes were cold; he poured a little mound
of salt on the table (a cockroach came running up, took a
sniff, and went away slowly); he began eating a potato,
skin and all. Then he lay down, as he was, on the floor in
front of the stove. Maryasha also ate some potatoes, took
off her dress, but kept on a shift made of sacking; she let
down her hair, gave the cradle a gentle push, threw
Kuzya's sheepskin coat on the floor beside him, blew out
the candle, and, scratching herself and sighing, lay down
by Kuzya's side. Before long the baby in the cradle began
crying; taking up an incredible posture, one leg in the air,
Maryasha began to rock the cradle with her foot, and,
rocking—slept. In the passage a cock crowed peacefully.

· · · ·

In the morning both Kuzya and Yegorushka had things
to do. Maryasha got up at dawn, milked the cow; her
swollen-bellied children, who had not been washed for a
year, ran about the yard after her; the eldest, six-year-old
Zhenka—the only one who could talk—tugged at the hem
of her mother's skirt, crying: "A-rya-rya-rya, tyap-tya,
tyap-tya,"—asking for milk. The cow was drying up and
gave little milk; what there was Maryasha took down to
the cellar, and the children got none. Later, Maryasha sat

out on the veranda of the manor house, waiting—bored—
for the forester to wake up, chasing the children away lest
their noise should disturb Nekulyev. The forester, in a
cheerful mood, came out into the sun, and went down to
the Volga to bathe. He greeted Maryasha—she snickered,
dropped her head, stuck her hand inside her blouse, and,
murder in her face—"Get away, you little devils!"—ran
straight into the hut, dragged the samovar out onto the
veranda, then brought the milk pot up from the cellar and
the eight eggs—caught up in her skirt. Katyasha passed
by carrying water buckets and said with venom and envy
in her voice, "Trying hard? He'll take you to bed with him
soon!" Maryasha snapped back, "What of it—it'll be me
and not you!" Maryasha was no more than twenty-three,
but she looked like a woman of forty—tall and skinny as a
rake. Katyasha, on the other hand, was short, big-boned,
and covered with wrinkles like a dried-up puffball, as be-
fitted her thirty-five years.

That morning Kuzya went into the forest; he hung the
rifle from his shoulder by a string, barrel down, and stuck
his hands in his pockets; he walked unhurriedly, looking
solemnly from side to side—not along the track, but taking
hidden paths known to him alone. He went down into a
ravine, climbed a hill, and came to a wild and overgrown
part where oaks and maples grew thickly together, with
hazel pushing up from below. He began to descend a
steep bank, grabbing hold of bushes, sending stones down
in a cloud of dust. Among some dry leaves he found a
slough—a castoff snakeskin—picked it up, smoothed it out,
put it inside the lining of his cap, and stuck the cap on
his head at a rakish angle. He walked another quarter
verst along the slope and came to a cave. Kuzya called
out, "Anybody there? Andrey? Vasyatka?" A young man
came out, said, "Father's gone down to the Volga, he'll be
back right away." Kuzya sat down on the ground near the
cave, lit a cigarette; the young man went back inside and
said, "Want a glass of the new stuff?" "No," said Kuzya.
They fell silent; the stifling smell of raw *samogon* came
from the cave. Ten minutes or so later a peasant with a

beard an *arshin*[9] long came up the hill. Kuzya said: "Stilling as usual? I'm out of flour and grain. Get me, let's say, two poods. And Yegor'll be having his crawling-in feast, so he'll need *samogon*, the best you've got. Bring everything over. In the afternoon the forester'll go to the bark-stripping, and later he'll stop by at his woman's place. That's the time to aim for—leave everything with Maryasha." They talked about their affairs, how high prices were, the quality of *samogon*, then said good-bye. The young man came out of the cave, said, "Kuzya, let me have a bang!" Kuzya handed him the rifle, replied, "Shoot!" The young man fired; his father shook his head dejectedly, said, "You know, Vasili's a Red Army deserter. . . ."

On his way back Kuzya stopped at Ignat's bee garden in Linden Valley; they sat and smoked together. Ignat, nicknamed the Renter, sat on a stump and discoursed on the vagaries of life. "For example, once I was sitting on this very stump, and a siskin says to me from a tree, 'You'll be drinking vodka today!' And I say to him, 'What's this foolishness you're talking, where should I get vodka?' But it turned out as he said: a cousin of mine came in the evening and brought some *samogon!* . . . Birds are the wisdom of God. Or take your new *barin*, for example: I stopped at his place, we got talking; I ask what does he think—during the marriage rite should you walk around the lectern with the sun or against the sun? And he says, 'If you have to take the sun into account in such a matter, you'll have to stand still and have them carry the lectern around you, because the sun stands still in the sky and it's the earth that goes around.' Yes, he shot right back at me! And I say to him, 'If that's so, then Joshua stopped the earth and not the sun?' And it was Koopernik who started it all. They burned this Koopernik at the stake; too good for him—I'd have cut him up with my own hands, piece by piece, bone by bone. . . . As for tobacco,

[9] A measure of length, approximately twenty-eight inches (Editors).

it's true that it's the Devil's own weed. I planted some
here for smoking and had to throw away two hives of
honey. . . ."

When he was quite close to home, near the grounds of
the estate, Kuzya came across a clearing overgrown with
sorrel. He lay down on the ground, crawled all over the
clearing on his belly, eating sorrel. At home Maryasha
gave him a dish of *kvas*[10] with bread and onions in it. He
ate and went out to groom the horse; he curried it, washed
it down, and started harnessing it to the droshky. Nekulyev
came out of the house, and they set off for the forest.

. . . .

Katyasha and Yegorushka had been building a new
house in the village. The house was finished, and it only
remained to have it blessed and to celebrate moving-in.
Some time before Yegorushka had made an icon-case
from one of the Prince's mahogany cabinets, and since
early morning, after milking the cow, Katyasha had been
busy with its adornment. Somehow she had managed to
get hold of some brewery labels—"Volga Hawk Beer"—
with a golden hawk in the middle; she was pasting them
all over the mahogany of the icon-case, some upside down,
as she could not read. For Yegorushka and Katyasha, the
moving-in was a holiday; Nekulyev had given Yegor a
week's leave. That same morning Yegorushka and Katyasha visited Father Ignat in his bee garden to have their
fortunes told. Ignat did his best to fill them with terror.
He was sitting on a coffer in his hut and did not even
glance at Yegorushka and Katyasha, but simply waved
his hand for them to sit down. Between his feet Ignat had
placed an earthenware cook pot; he began peering into
it and saying—heaven knows what. He spat to the right,
to the left, and on Katyasha, who wiped herself submissively; then a spasm began to twist his face. Presently he
got up, came from behind the table, went into the storeroom, beckoned silently to Yegor and Katyasha to follow

[10] A thin, sour beer made by pouring warm water on rye or
barley and letting the mixture ferment (Editors).

him; inside it was dark and stuffy, and there was a stifling smell of honey and dry grass. Ignat picked up two church candles from a shelf; he took Yegor's hands and turned him around three times with the sun, ending up with Yegor behind him; he bent forward and began to twist the candles together in an intricate fashion; he gave one candle to Yegor and the other to Katyasha, mumbling something rapidly to himself; then he took the candles back, pressed them together, and, holding them at both ends, sank his teeth in at mid-point, his face contorted in a snarl, while Yegorushka and Katyasha stood in awe-stricken silence. Ignat began hissing, roaring, and gritting his teeth; his eyes filled with blood, so it seemed to Yegorushka and Katyasha in the darkness. He shouted: "May he be racked with convulsions, head over heels, feet in the air! May he be broken into seven hundred and seventy-seven pieces, may the sinew of his gut be stretched thirty-three *sazhens!*"[11] When this was all over, Ignat explained with perfect calm that they would live well in their new house, eat their fill, and reach a ripe old age; they would have a black-haired daughter-in-law, and only one misfortune would befall them: "after a dark number of days, nights, and months have passed"—the bull calf would go blind and would have to be slaughtered. Katyasha and Yegorushka walked home happy, in re-newed harmony, a little subdued by all these wonders; Ignat had given them the candles with instructions as to what was to be done with them: in the new house they were to go to the gatepost, light their candles, and singe the post; then they were to go into the house with the lighted candles and stick them to the doorjamb—this to be repeated three nights running; they were to see to it that on the last night the candles burned right down and went out together, but the first two nights they were to put out the candles with the thumb and fourth finger of the left hand, without fail, and not to get it wrong, or else their fingers would drop off. Nekulyev had already left when

[11] A measure of length equal to seven feet (Editors).

Katyasha and Yegor got back; a *vedro*[12] of *samogon* had
been delivered. Yegor began harnessing the horse; Katyasha lingered, caught up in preparations, sticking labels
on the icon-case: "Volga Hawk Beer," "Volga Hawk
Beer." To while away the time, Yegorushka went into the
manor house, wandered into the room which Nekulyev occupied, felt the bed, lay down, trying it out for size; on the
table were some leftover sour cream and some granulated
sugar in a box which had once contained hard candies—
several times he wet a finger and stuck it first in the sour
cream, then in the sugar, then licked the finger; on
the window sill lay some toothpowder, a toothbrush, and
a razor; Yegorushka lingered here for some time—he tasted
the powder, chewed it, and spat it out, shaking his head
in bewilderment; he picked up a mirror and brushed his
beard and whiskers with the toothbrush; near the mirror
lay a safety razor, and several blades were scattered
about. Yegorushka examined them all, counted them,
picked out one of the rustier ones and stuck it in his
pocket. In the office he sat down at Nekulyev's writing
table, put on a stern face, rested his hands on the arms
of the chair, spreading out his legs and elbows, and said,
"All right, them as are forest thieves! Come forward!" In
the domestic life of Yegorushka and Katyasha, it was
Katyasha who had the upper hand. Soon a loaded cart
was standing in front of the house; in the cart were the
icon-case covered with "Volga Hawks," a broken-down
armchair with a gilt back, two baskets—one with a black
rooster (obtained from Maryasha and paid for in kind)
and the other with a black tomcat (kept specially since
spring; both rooster and tomcat were needed for the
moving-in)—and a trunk containing the possessions which
Katyasha had brought with her as a bride. On the very
top of the load sat Katyasha herself; she had already been
at the *samogon;* she was waving a red kerchief, bouncing
up and down, and singing "Saratov" and *"Sharaban,* my
sharaban"[13] at the top of her voice. Maryasha with the

[12] A liquid measure equal to 2.7 gallons (Editors).
[13] *Char-à-banc* (Editors).

children stood near the cart, looking on entranced and envious; Katyasha said, "Let's go! God be with us!" She called out to Maryasha, "Look after the animals; when Ignat comes, show him! . . ." They started; Yegor went on foot, holding the reins; again Katyasha began shrieking, "My *sharaban*, my two-wheeled carriage, and me, I'm just a no-good baggage! . . ."

. . . .

It was during Nekulyev's time as forester that the only meeting of the Workers' Committee took place. It was called by those good fellows Kandin and Konkov, trained workers and Party members. Many of those attending arrived the day before the meeting was scheduled—some had to travel as many as forty versts. In the evening they built a bonfire on the croquet court in the park and cooked potatoes and fish. The shrewdest among them, and the Party members, gathered at Nekulyev's in order to get things settled before the committee got down to business. Konkov was sullen and determined; Kandin did his best to be patient; they talked about the Revolution, about the forests, and about thieving—the absolutely unheard-of amount of thieving that was going on in the forests; they talked quietly, sitting in the ballroom in a close circle by the light of a single candle; Nekulyev lay on the sofa. Konkov said unhappily, "Shoot them—that's what we'll have to do, comrades—and our own men first of all to show we mean business. The way things are, what have we got? We fight the peasants, and the more cunning among them go to a forest watchman they know, talk him round, slip him a pood of grain, and the watchman lets them take whatever they want. What we've got, comrades, is nothing but hypocrisy and plain disgrace. Forgive me, comrades, but I'll confess: a peasant from Shikhany kept after me to let him have some wood for a house— two whole days he won't leave me alone—and there I am starving, and he keeps pushing *samogon* and white flour at me; I couldn't stand it any longer, and gave him such a beating they had to take him to the hospital!" Kandin replied, "I'll tell you straight, I've given more than one beating, not that it does much good. On the other hand, you have to take this into account: a forest watchman receives a wage of one and a half rubles to buy bread; he can't live on that, and so he's forced to steal; just look how they live—the gentry's pigs used to live more decently. You can't manage forests without statistics: we have to set a limit on what they can steal, and pretend not to notice, because they're stealing from need. And if they steal over the limit, that means they're stealing out of devilry, and in that case shooting might be a good idea. We're none of us saints—but we have our job to do!" They talked about the Workers' Committee. The Committee had to be formed to bind everyone together in collective responsibility. Nekulyev was silent, listening; the candle cast its light no further than the sofa. Neither Konkov nor Kandin knew how they were to conduct the meeting of the Workers' Committee in the morning in such a way as not to set the rest of the forest men against them. In the park a song rose and faded; Nekulyev went out to join the others. People sat by the bonfire, a ragged crowd, no two of them dressed alike, all with rifles. Kuzya lay by the fire, resting his head on the palms of his hands; he was staring into the fire and telling a story. Alarmed by the blaze, crows were screaming in the trees. Nekulyev sat down by the fire and listened.

Kuzya was saying:

". . . And so, like I was saying, Ilya Ivanych wanted to play a joke on the priests, but it turned out different. Ilya Ivanych opens the bin, and there are the three priests lying one on top of the other, all dead and stiffening in the cold already. Ilya Ivanych gets scared, carries the priests into the barn, and lays them out side by side; he goes back to the house, sits down at the table, puts on his thinking cap, and, mark you, he's in a cold sweat. . . . But Ilya Ivanych was a clever one; he sat there for an hour or so racking his brains—and all of a sudden he slapped himself on the forehead! He went into the barn— the priests were stiff by now—took hold of one of them, stood him up by the shed, and poured water over him—icicles were soon hanging from him. Then Ilya Ivanych went to the tavern, and, mark you, took a bottle along with him—the one the priest hadn't finished. At the tavern an accordion is playing, people are sitting around, and it so happens that Vanyusha the drunkard is sitting by the counter waiting for someone to treat him to a drink. Ilya Ivanych goes straight up to Vanyusha: 'Have a drink!'—gives him the bottle. Vanyusha tosses it back and gets drunk straight away. And Ilya Ivanych says to him: 'I'd give you some more, but there's no time. I've got to go—a drowned man has come into my yard; I'll have to carry him to the river and drop him through a hole in the ice.' Well, Vanyusha grabs at the chance: 'I'll carry him, if you'll treat me!' And this is just what Ilya Ivanych is waiting for; he says, unwilling-like, 'Well, all right—if it's for friendship's sake—you take him away, come back to the house, and I'll treat you!' Vanyusha can't get there fast enough. 'Where's the drowned man?' 'Over there!' Vanyusha grabs hold of the priest, throws him over his shoulder, and makes straight for the gate. And Ilya Ivanych says to him, 'Wait a bit, you'd better put him in a sack, or you'll scare people.' So they put him in a sack, mark you; Vanyusha sets off with his load, and in the meantime Ilya Ivanych brings the second priest out of the barn, stands him up, pours water over him, and waits. Vanyusha comes running, straight to the house: 'Where's the drink?' But Ilya Ivanych says to him, 'Just a minute, brother; you did a poor job of carrying him away; you didn't say the right word—he's come back again.' 'Who has?' 'The drowned man.' 'Where is he?' They go out into the yard. The priest is standing by the shed. Vanyusha's eyes pop out of his head, and he gets angry: 'Oh, you so-and-so, you want to make trouble!' He grabs hold of the second priest and runs toward the hole in the ice. And Ilya Ivanych shouts after him, 'When you're shoving him in, say "May his soul rest in peace," and then he'll go in easy!' This was so that the priest had some kind of prayer said for him. No sooner is Vanyusha gone than Ilya Ivanych brings out the third priest and stands him up by the shed. Vanyusha comes running, and Ilya Ivanych tells him off: 'You're a fine one, Vanyusha! Can't even carry away a drowned man—look, he's come back again. Seems like I'll have to go with you myself to make sure things are done good and proper. You carry him, and I'll walk behind and see how you handle things.' So they carried off the third priest; Ilya Ivanych watched and saw that Vanyusha had been launching the priests like he ought to, so he stopped worrying, and said, 'Well, all right, Vanyusha, you've worked hard enough, come on—I'll treat you!' And he got Vanyusha so drunk that he couldn't remember a thing and forgot how he hauled away the drowned men. And they never found out about the priests—what the Devil had done with them. And so ends my story, and mine be the glory," said Kuzya.

Nekulyev walked away from the bonfire into the darkness, skirting the grounds; he went up the hill toward the riverbank, to be alone with his thoughts for a while. The tale seemed to him a bad omen.

In the morning, on the same croquet court where many had bedded down for the night by the fire, about seventy men—woodcutters and forest watchmen—gathered. A table was set up under a linden tree, benches were brought —but many of the men lay on the grass around the court. The fire was kept going. Rifles were stacked army-style. A presidium was elected.

The following minutes of this meeting survive:

REPORTS	RESOLUTIONS
1. Comrade Konkov made a report on the international situation.[1]	1. Duly noted.
2. Comrade Kandin made a report on the plan of activities of the Workers' Committee.	2. In view of the wide dispersion of forest workers throughout the forests, no cultural commission to be elected; a collective subscription to a news-
a. Cultural-educational work.	

b. Income and expenditure of the Workers' Committee.

paper for each watchman's hut to be made;[2] expenses:

a. Office supplies.

b. Transportation to town.

c. Daily allowances.

3. Comrade Konkov proposed that a contribution should be deducted from wages toward the fund for the building of a monument to the Revolution in Moscow.

3. One day's pay to be deducted.

4. Chairman of the Kadom village soviet Nefedov charged that there were fictitious names on the payroll of the twenty-seventh cordon, for which mounted guard Sarychev collected. Sarychev produced the above-mentioned payroll and pointed out that its correctness was certified by the stamp and signature of Chairman Nefedov, who had made the above-mentioned charge.

4. In view of the absurdity of making a charge against oneself, an inquiry should be initiated by sending a copy of the charge to the Department of Criminal Investigation.

5. The case of the pedigreed bull eaten by mounted guards and woodcutters of the seventh cordon: the bull was hired from the breeding farm on a collective guarantee—it was killed and eaten and a report sent to the breeding farm to the effect that the bull had died of anthrax.

5. In view of the illegal act concerning the bull, three days' pay to be withheld monthly from woodcutters Stulov, Sinitsin, and Shavelkin and from mounted guard Usachev, and sent to the cashier's office of the breeding farm.

6. Comrade Soshkin expressed a wish that no general meetings should be held on Sundays.[3]	6. Carried.
7. Mounted guard Sarychev proposed that all present immediately join the Russian Communist Party.	7. No action to be taken at present.[4]

[1] In his report Konkov made a mistake in indicating that Europe and Russia are geographically situated in different continents.

[2] It was discovered that half of the forestry workers were illiterate; as he voted, Kuzya whispered to Yegorushka, "It's all right, we'll use them for smokes!"

[3] A barefoot young fellow in a coat of coarse cloth got up from the grass and said in some agitation: "This is what I think, comrades; it seems like we shouldn't have meetings of the Workers' Committee on Sunday, as citizen forest thieves are all out in the fields on weekdays—you can't catch them there—but on Sunday they sit at home, and that's the place to go after them with the militia."

[4] Comrade Kandin said at this point that the question of joining the Russian Communist Party should be left to each man's conscience. Sarychev took offense at Kandin's remarks, and said: ". . . and if you think that Vaska Nefedov from Kadom, chairman and informer, was telling the truth about me, let me tell you he's the biggest crook himself; as for the names that were signed, those people were from other parts; by now they'll have gone home to Vetluga."

Here is part of the first letter which Nekulyev wrote from the Hills of Medyn—he never finished it:

". . . in the middle of nowhere—there is no post office for sixteen versts, and no railway for a hundred—in an accursed house on the Volga, a house which has passed the curse of the landowners on to me; the heat and the goings-on here are truly devilish! I live like Robinson Crusoe, I sleep without sheets, eat raw eggs and milk—nothing cooked—and go about half-naked. All around me there is savagery, shame, abomination. The nearest village is sixteen versts from us, but the 'Great Waterway' flows at the foot of the steep bank, and I often talk with the men who haul boats on the Volga; there are a great many—a good

score of flatbottoms pass by every day, and the men often
stop for a rest and cook their fish stew near our place.
About five days ago a peasant was pulling his wife tied
up in a boat; he informed me that she was possessed by
three devils, one under the heart, another in the backbone,
and a third in the armpit, and that there was a remarkable
soothsayer some hundred versts from us who could cast
out devils—and so he was taking his wife to him; yesterday
he was on his way back, and this time it was his wife who
was in harness, while he took it easy in the boat; he told
me that the devils had been cast out. The people I am
living with are two watchmen and their wives and children. One of them has built himself a house out of stolen
wood—the wood which it is his duty to guard—and filled
it with broken pieces of furniture from the estate; but
that's not the main thing; the main thing is that before
moving into the house he let in a black cat and a rooster,
put a hunk of bread and salt under the stove for the
house-goblin, and his wife ran around the house naked
'to ward off the evil eye.' His bull calf got sick—its eyes
started running; there's a veterinary not far away—in
Vyazovy—but he called in a local soothsayer (this soothsayer, a peasant who rents an apiary, came around once
or twice to talk to me; I had no idea he was a sorcerer—
he seemed just like any other peasant, only a bit sharper;
he can read, and talks some nonsense about Copernicus),
and so this soothsayer examined the bull calf, whispered
something over it, removed (!) some kind of film (!) from
its eyes, sprinkled salt in them—and the calf went blind!
Then Katyasha, Yegor's wife, got hold of a snake slough,
dried it, ground it to powder—and this snake slough is
what she uses to treat the calf, sprinkling the powder in
its already blind eyes. The other watchman's wife is called
Maryasha. At first I called her Masha, but she said to me,
'What's that you're calling me? Everybody calls me
Maryasha!' She has three children and is about twenty-
three years old; my 'way of life' makes her drool: 'Eee,
and everything with butter, and milk to your heart's content!' She gives no milk to her children—she sells it to me;

this disgusts me, but I know—if I don't buy from her I'll
die of hunger, as I'm not used to constant starvation the
way they are, and she would only use it to make butter
and cottage cheese and sell it all the same. Maryasha has
never been to town—her own District town, thirty versts
away; she has three children living, who run about naked,
and had two that died; she is twenty-three and already
has some kind of female ailment which her husband Kuzya
readily talks about to all and sundry; none of her children
was delivered . . . not even by the local wise woman:
she gave birth alone, cut the umbilical cord herself, and
herself cleaned up the blood afterward, sending her husband out into the forest for the occasion. What savagery,
what horror, God damn it all! This is their attitude toward
me: yesterday a German from across the Volga came and
offered to sell me butter. I asked, 'How much?' 'The same
price you paid before—twenty-five.' And Maryasha, Kuzya,
and Katyasha had been charging me sixty. My patience
gave way, and I called Maryasha and Katyasha and told
them they ought to be ashamed of themselves, and that
I knew very well they were cheating and robbing me right
and left—after all, hadn't I treated them as friends and
been fair with them? From now on I should be forced to
consider them thieves and no longer respect them—such a
lyrical homily I read them! They didn't bat an eye: 'We
did it special, on purpose like! . . .'

"And that very day at dinner time they suddenly bring
me a sterlet:[14] 'This is a present to you from us!' I told
them to go to hell with their sterlets. For them I'm just the
barin and nothing else: I don't plow, I wash my clothes
with soap, do things incomprehensible to them; I read,
live in the manor house, and so—I'm the master; if I were
to order them to crawl on all fours—they'd do it; if I ordered them to lick the floor clean—they'd do it; and they'd
do it 50 per cent out of servile fear and 50 per cent because—who knows?—maybe the *barin* really needs it done,
because much of what I am doing—what we are doing—

[14] A small sturgeon (Editors).

seems as absurd to them as licking floors; they will do anything you like, still I have got into the habit of making sure there is no one behind me, as I never know if Katyasha or Kuzya may not find it unavoidable at a given moment to stick a knife in my back: perhaps this is a superfluous precaution, because they look upon me as their milch cow, and I have heard Katyasha say enviously that I was 'a godsend' to Maryasha, because Maryasha, in getting the samovar for me and cleaning my room and office, has every right and every opportunity to rob me systematically—with Katyasha's approval! Yes, that's how it is—and I am an honest Party member. I don't understand our peasants' conception of honor—after all, they must have honor. They live understanding nothing, nothing at all—and here is Yegor building a new house according to all the soothsayers' rules at a time when the world revolution is taking place! All the people I see every day are like that, and in addition to them there are the unseen ones—the hundreds, perhaps even thousands, who all around me are carrying off the forests, and with whom I am engaged in a fight to the death. I have a feeling that all those who surround me are thieves, one worse than the next, and I don't understand how it is they don't steal each other—but I was forgetting that I was stolen myself by the Germans and kept prisoner in a dark storeroom! . . . Maryasha's children run about naked because they have nothing to put on, and they're covered with terrible itching sores; at first I used to eat at Kuzya's table, but I was nauseated by the filth and felt ashamed to eat in front of the children because they were hungry; they don't even get enough bread and potatoes—as for meat or butter, say, or eggs—they never see them. . . . And then take Mishka the shepherd—who talks to cows in cow language that hardly resembles human speech, and is almost unable to talk like a human being—he found a tumbledown hut in a ravine in a remote part of the forest; the hut had sunk into the hill, and inside was a crumbling Psalter—no doubt some pious man had sought salvation there; it would be interesting to know if he considered

soap holy or unholy. . . . And a siskin foretells when the
soothsayer—the one they call the Renter—is going to drink
samogon. As for Minka the shepherd himself—he is famous
because last year, before I came, a cow in his herd gave
birth to a calf with a human head; the women killed the
calf, and rumor decided that Minka was the father. Of
course that couldn't have happened, but if Minka, who
talks to cows more easily than to human beings, had lusted
after cows—let that be on his own conscience. . . ."

Nekulyev did not finish the letter. He sat down to write
it in the evening, after coming back from the hill, where
he had lit a fire, and remained at the table late into the
night. He was writing in the office; two candles burned on
the table, dripping wax which spilled onto the green baize,
adding to the marks of other candlewax nights passed in
the house, this house bitter as honey gathered from tobacco flowers. And suddenly Nekulyev felt his flesh creep
—for the first time he became aware of the goose pimples
which had so often made his skin tingle—quickly he felt
for his revolver, jumped up from behind the table,
grabbed the revolver, ready to shoot—at that moment Konkov walked into the office, revolver in hand, covered with
dust, his face the color of earth. Konkov said:

"Comrade Anton! Ilya Kandin has been killed—by peasants he caught stealing wood. Reconnaissance detachments have arrived in Kadom, Vyazovy, and Belokon
—we can't find out if they're Whites or Reds. The peasants
are rioting!"

*Chapter Three: About Mother Earth and
the Beauty of Love*

If you ask a peasant about Mother Earth, and if you are
weary as you listen, there will rise before you terrors,
devils, and that mighty force concealed in the earth with
which the legendary hero Mikula, had he found it, would
have turned the world around. Peasants—old men and
women—will tell you that ravines were dug out and hills

piled up with their horns by huge devils, such as no longer exist, at the very time when the archangels were driving them out of Paradise. Mother Earth, like love and sex, is a mystery: for her own secret purposes she divided mankind into male and female; she lures men irresistibly; the peasants kiss the earth like sons, carry her with them as an amulet, talk softly to her, cast spells in her name to charm love and hatred, sun and day. The peasants swear by Mother Earth as they do by love and death. Spells are woven over her, and in the night a naked widow who has known all things is harnessed to a plow, and the plow is guided by two naked virgins who have the earth and the world before them. It is for a woman to take the part of Mother Earth. But Mother Earth herself is fields, forests, swamps, coppices, hills, distances, years, nights, days, blizzards, storms, calm. . . . You can either curse Mother Earth or love her. . . .

. . . .

Nekulyev's task was a difficult one. The Don and Ural Armies were cutting off the southeast; the Czechs were marching from Penza toward Kazan. The Volga was caught, pressed from all sides. The Volga was saved by places like Medyn. At various Wet Ravines, Hamlets, Islands, Old Fields—at dozens of places—barges were being loaded with firewood, timber, eight-inchers, twelve-inchers, boards. By day and by night steamers arrived, at their last gasp; in the darkness they sent up showers of sparks, and took on firewood—their life's sustenance—in order to slap the daybreak waters with their wheel paddles, frightening the empty distances. From Saratov, from Samara, from provincial districts, from steppe towns, came bands of people with saws, people with the will to achieve victory and not to die—factory workers, professors, students, women teachers, mothers, doctors—old and young, men and women; they went to the forest, they sawed wood, bruising hands and knees, raising blood blisters, fighting for life with blunt saws. At night they burned bonfires, sang hungry songs, slept on the forest grass, wept and cursed the night and the world—and still the steamers came, coughing up wood smoke; professors worked as stokers, their jackets became oil-stained like work shirts. Nekulyev was here, there—dashing from one place to another astride the Prince's bay, while Kuzya limped behind on a lame gelding; everything they did had to be done—at all costs—and Kuzya had occasion to wave his revolver about often enough.

. . . .

It was night. Nekulyev had not finished his letter; the candles were recording a new wax chronicle on the green office baize. It was then that Konkov walked into the room, revolver in hand, covered with dust, his face the color of earth, and said in a whisper, like a conspirator: "Comrade Anton! Ilya Kandin has been killed—by peasants he caught stealing wood. Reconnaissance detachments have arrived in Kadom, Vyazovy, and Belokon—we can't find out whether they're Whites or Reds. The peasants are rioting!" Nekulyev met Konkov in goose-flesh fear, both hands grasping a revolver; he lowered it and sat down helplessly on the table to mark his friend's death by a moment of silence. Suddenly both of them tightened their grips on the handles of their revolvers as they drew closer together: from outside the window came the rustle of a dozen stealthy footsteps, rifle locks flicked, and the next moment the black holes of rifle barrels appeared in doorways and windows; a sailor walked into the room, calm and businesslike, his revolver still in its holster. "Don't move, comrades. Hands up, comrades. Your papers!" "Are you a Communist, comrade?" "You're under arrest. You will come with us to the ship." The earth was moving into autumn, the night was black, and the broad reaches of the Volga breathed a damp hostility. Near the boat the women were wailing in the darkness, and Yegorushka and Kuzya were taking leave of them like recruits leaving home. Steamers were snorting, but none of them had lights on board. They got into the boat and cast off. Kuzya eased down next to Nekulyev: "What's happening—are they taking us to be shot?" He was silent for a moment. "I figure at least I'm barefoot—I'll jump in and swim for it." A sailor shouted, "No whispering!" "All right then, where are you taking us?" Kuzya snapped back. "You'll find out when you get there." The boat nudged the side of a steamer. "Grab the line." "Make fast!" The steamer was humming with voices. Nekulyev was the first to climb on deck. "Take me to the deckhouse!" The deckhouse was crowded with armed men; some had belts hung with hand grenades the way Indians' belts are hung with feathers; others wore machine-gun cartridge belts slung around their hips; the smell of makhorka[15] was enough to knock you over.

And this is what had happened:

The Seventh Revolutionary Peasant Regiment had lost its chief of staff, and he had been the only one on board who could read German—a map torn from a German atlas served as a field map; it was spread out on the table in the deckhouse, upside down. The Seventh Peasant Regiment was on its way to fight the Cossacks and break through to Astrakhan, but the further they went following the map, the more confused they became. Nekulyev turned the map around; they argued, not trusting him. In the end Nekulyev sat all night with the staff officers—sailors—teaching them how to read Russian words in Roman script; the sailors were quick to understand, and hung on the wall a sheet of paper with the Russian equivalents of the Roman letters. Dawn came through the fading glass of portholes. Nekulyev was released; Konkov said he would remain on board; Yegorushka and Kuzya were asleep by the funnel; Nekulyev shook them awake.

And when they had already pushed away from the steamer a cannon shot exploded beyond the hill, and with a roar the water near the boat leaped wildly skyward. It was the Cossacks firing, those who were advancing to meet the Seventh (also the First and Twentieth) Revolutionary Peasant Regiment, named in honor of the sailor Chaplygin.

· · · ·

[15] A coarse tobacco, grown especially in the Ukraine (Editors).

Men like Nekulyev are shy in love: they are chaste and truthful in all things. Sometimes, for political reasons and for the sake of life, they tell lies—but this is not lying and hypocrisy, but rather a blithe cunning; within themselves they are chaste and innocent, straightforward and exacting. That first day in Medyn the sun burst into the office, and everything was full of life; and then a few days later in the moonlit and dewy darkness, Nekulyev said, "I love you, I love you," swearing by the sun itself and by all that is finest in man, so that this love would be all sun and humanity. There was an intoxicating smell of linden, the moon was red, and they were coming into the fields from the wood where Arina and her workmen stripped bark— living bark from living trees—to tan dead hide. Arina Arsenyeva's childhood had been filled with the smell of rich pies, but she had wanted to reshape it to the regularity of Petersburg; she grew abundantly, like Mother Earth, like the steppe, tulip-covered for a brief two weeks in the spring—Arina Arsenyeva the leather tanner, a woman. The house was as it had always been, but her days were different—very spacious; there were neither clerks, nor bookkeepers, nor father, nor mother. Work had to be done at all costs. Everything had to be cut to a new pattern. The house was the same, but the pies had vanished, and where the dining room (a place to eat those pies) had been stood workmen's bunks, and Arina was left with an attic, a suitcase, a basket of books, a bed, a table, a rifle, samples of leather; and in the corner lived the wolf pup. But beyond the house and the fences—the house stood at the edge of the village—was the steppe, as always dried up, lonely, with its long, low hills and ravines, the moonlit steppe so well remembered from her childhood. And every woman is a mother. She had to rush to the forest in her tarantass to supervise bark-stripping; she had to rush to the Council of National Economy in town and have things out with them; she had to throw herself into all sorts of battles at village meetings and at town conferences; she had to know about rawhide, flesh side, derma, liming, tanning, scraping, drying, about *shaksha* (meaning bird droppings); and sometimes she had to curse workmen out—necessity is a stern master—using language that made even the leather dressers respect her; inside the fence were low barracks, vats for washing and liming stood in rows; at the back a small slaughter yard had been added; the barracks were being built to house the soap and glue works; there was a shed where horse bones were ground up: everything had to be rebuilt, done over again in an entirely new way. She had to wear a man's jacket, to carry a revolver on a strap, but boots—for those small feet—had to be made to order. And in the evenings she shouldn't—she really shouldn't—have bent over the wolf pup, looking into its eyes, saying tender words to it, breathing in its bitter forest smell. And one brisk, sunny day the urgings of Mother Earth rose within her, choking her, and she fell in love—in love! And in that same moonlit week, in the moonlit and dewy dark when Nekulyev said, "I love you, I love you," there were only the moon and Mother Earth; she gave herself to him—a woman of thirty and a virgin—yielding up everything she had garnered in those thirty springs. He would come to see her in the evenings and go up to the attic; sometimes she was not at home, and then, as he waited, he would rummage through books, strange to him, about the tanning industry, and try to play with the wolf pup; but the pup was hostile: it would cower in its corner, and two eyes—alien, unblinking, utterly watchful—would stare out, following every movement, not missing a thing; and the wolf pup would bare its little teeth in a helpless snarl; there was a vile smell of dog about it, something rancid, repellent to man. . . . Arina would come in, and every time it seemed to Nekulyev that the sun was coming into the room, and he was blinded with happiness. Nekulyev accepted unthinkingly the good things she always gave him to eat: ham, pork, and very often there were either pies as light as a feather or rich puffs which—somehow she found the time!—Arina baked herself. He gave no thought to the strange, indefinable smell which permeated everything in the house, even the pies—could it be leather? Later Nekulyev and Arina would go out into the steppe together and descend into the ravine—at the top sunflowers bowed their suns, and at the bottom marmots whistled to each other and froze like sentries; then they would climb up the other bank and find themselves in places where man had never set foot, where not even the Tartar hordes had passed. Arina gave herself to Nekulyev with all the abandon of Mother Earth; it seemed to Nekulyev that he held the sun in his arms. They had no need of a moving-in with black rooster and black cat (although the moon was full)—because they were happy and in love.

And this happiness was smashed to pieces as earthenware is smashed to pieces at peasant weddings in the villages. Nekulyev suddenly understood the smell that surrounded Arina and could not overcome his revulsion.

One day he arrived in the afternoon. The attic was deserted, except for the wolf pup. At the gate of the tannery sat a watchman, an old man, who said, "The army sent us some mangy nags, no good and half dead—Arina Sergeyevna went over." Nekulyev started to walk through the tannery, passed huge, stinking vats; he was too squeamish to enter the barracks, and went through the gate into the other yard—and there he saw . . . In the yard stood forty or so horses, complete wrecks—hairless, blind, "legless" (when horses become "legless" their legs are bent like bows); the horses looked like hideous old beggar women; crazy with fear, they bunched together, heads to the center; they had no tails, only gray, scaly stumps which trembled convulsively. And it was here, behind a low fence, that the horses were slaughtered one after another, each one dragged away forcibly from the herd. The small gate leading to the slaughter yard opened, and four men began to shove a struggling horse through, one of them twisting its tail stump, forcing the horse on to the slaughter—Arina came out through the gate and struck the horse on the neck with a club; it staggered and lurched forward. Arina was wearing a blood-soaked apron and leather pants. Nekulyev started running toward the gate. When he ran into the slaughter yard the horse was already lying on the ground; the legs jerked convulsively; the dead lips sagged away from teeth which clenched a tongue covered with yellow saliva, and a pair of workmen were busy with the horse, cutting open the still-living skin; the broken tail stump stuck up in the air. Nekulyev shouted, "Arina, what are you doing?" Arina began to speak in a matter-of-fact way, but hurriedly—so it seemed to Nekulyev. "The skin is used for leather, the fats are used in soapmaking, we feed the proteins to the pigs. The bones and sinews go to the glue works. Then the bones are ground to make fertilizer. We waste nothing here." Arina's hands were covered with blood; the ground was running with blood; workmen were skinning the horse; other carcasses lay about already skinned; using a pulley, they hung the horse by its legs from a gallows. And then Nekulyev understood: the smell here was the same as Arina's smell, and he suddenly felt his throat contract in a spasm of nausea. He pressed his hand to his mouth, as if to hold back his vomit, turned around, and without a word walked out of the yard into the steppe. Nekulyev was chaste in love. He had always been a cheerful and no-nonsense kind of man—and now he was walking through the steppe like a fool; he was without his cap—he had left it in the wolf pup's attic. Nekulyev never saw Arina again.

. . . .

The forests lay in wait, silently—the wood-devil (according to Kuzya) lived in the depths of the forest, and among the pines; at night bonfires burned, ill-omened fires. If there had existed a giant ear, it would have heard watchmen shouting to each other, trees falling—millions of logs (to fuel the Volga and the Revolution)—it would have heard whistles which conveyed all kinds of messages, warning shouts, yells. Beneath the forests lay Mother Earth. It was dawn when shells came flying over the forest —shells that were to establish truth. Nekulyev went into the house, calling to Kuzma and Yegor to follow him; standing behind a table, he said:

"Comrades. We have to decide what to do. There's

fighting on all sides. Are we going to stay, or are we going to leave? . . ."

Kuzya did not answer at once; he asked Yegor, "What do you think, Yegorushka?" Yegor replied, "I can't go—I've built a new house, I can't go noways, they'll carry off every last thing; I'd better hide in the village." Standing at attention, Kuzya answered for both of them:

"I have the honor to report we're staying with the forests!"

Nekulyev sat down at the table, and said: "Go now; I'm staying too. We'll shoot it out. If I get killed, divide up whatever things there are between you. Kuzma, come in an hour's time, and I'll give you some letters; you can deliver them." Kuzma and Yegor went out. A shell burst over the house.

Nekulyev began to write, slowly:

"To Irina Sergeyevna Arsenyeva. Arina, forgive me. I have been honest, both with you and with myself. Goodbye, good-bye forever; you have taught me to be a revolutionary. . . ."

. . . .

But he never finished the letter, because suddenly goose pimples rose all over his body, the smell of rotting skins and tobacco honey came flooding in; his hands began to tremble, the hair on his head stirred; there came fear, horror. Night was giving way to gray murk, far away the east was lilac, far away shells burst; around him all was quiet. Nekulyev crouched down behind the table, straining his ears; his eyes were the eyes of a madman; he ran on tiptoe to the door: it was quiet outside; he put out the candle on the table, held his breath, shouted, "Go away!" Then he sprang to the window, flung it open, vaulted out; he ran headlong like one possessed toward the hills. Goose pimples covered his skin ever more thickly; his curly hair must have been turning gray as it stirred on his head. . . .

. . . .

The next morning Kuzya found the letter on the table—just the three lines—and set off to deliver it.

About the Wolf Pup

It was a moonless night. A fine rain was falling. Irina was returning from the steppe; she passed through the village, listened to the dogs howling; the village seemed dead in the silence and darkness. She entered the yard, passed by the vats, meeting no one, and went up to her attic. She listened intently to the silence—the wolf pup was breathing somewhere close by in the room. She lit a candle, bent over the pup, whispered, "My darling, my little animal, don't be shy, come to me! . . ." The wolf pup crouched in the corner, its fluffy tail curled under it, its black eyes following every movement of Irina's hands and eyes. And when their eyes met, the pup's unblinking gaze became more than ever remote and eternally hostile. When Irina found the pup it was still blind; she fed it with a rubber nipple, she nursed it as if it were a baby, she sat with it for hours at a time, whispering to it again and again all the tender words she had learned from her mother; the wolf pup thrived in her care, learned to lap from a saucer and to eat unaided, but it sensed that it was and always would be Irina's enemy. There was no taming it; the bigger the wolf pup grew, the more hostile and remote it became; it ran from Irina's hands, and stopped eating in her presence; for hours they sat facing each other, its dish between them; she knew it was hungry, she coaxed it with the tenderest words, "Eat, eat, my darling, don't be silly, eat—because I won't leave until you do!" The wolf pup followed her eyes and hands with its little, glinting eyes, not moving, refusing to look at the dish—until she left, and then it gulped the food down; it would growl and bare its teeth when she stretched her hand out to it; it was and always would be her enemy; there was no taming it. Irina had often noticed that when it was alone the pup led a very contented life, absorbed in its own concerns: it ran about the room, examining and sniffing things, basked in the sun, chased flies, lay about at its ease, rolled on its back—but the moment she walked in it would retreat into its corner, and two black and utterly vigilant eyes would stare out. . . . Irina put the candle on the floor, squatted down in front of the wolf and began talking: "My darling, my little animal, my little Nikita, don't be shy, come to me; you haven't got a mamma—I'll take you in my arms and stroke you!" The candle was smoking, winking; the world—the world of Irina and the wolf pup—was confined by the back of the bedstead, a wall, a stove; even the ceiling was out of sight, because the candle was smoking and because both pairs of eyes were looking into each other. Irina stretched out a hand to stroke the pup—and it threw itself on the hand with boundless hatred, in a fight to the death; it sank its teeth into the fingers and fell over in its rage, jaws still clenched; Irina snatched her hand back, but the wolf pup hung on by its teeth; then it dropped, tearing the flesh from her fingers, hitting against the bed—and immediately retreated to its usual place in the corner: a pair of unblinking, utterly vigilant eyes looked out as if nothing had happened. And Irina wept bitterly: it was not the pain, not the blood flowing from her hand; she wept from loneliness, hurt, and helplessness; love a wolf pup as you may, it still looks to the forest; Irina was powerless before instinct—before the little, stinking, fluffy bundle of forest and animal instincts now entrenched behind the bed, powerless before those instincts which were alive within her and ruled her, and which had driven her out into the rain, into the steppe, to weep on the hill where she had given herself to Nekulyev; and in her helplessness, hurt, and loneliness (the more she loved the wolf pup, the more savage it was toward her) she hit the pup hard about the head and eyes, and fell in tears on the bed in her loneliness and misery. The candle remained on the floor near the wolf pup's corner. . . .

At that moment a stone hit the window, glass scattered, and someone outside called in a stifled voice:

"Comrade Arsenyeva! Run for it! What are you waiting

for?—everyone's gone. The Cossacks are in the village!
Quick! To the woods!"

And from outside came the rapid beat of a horse's
hooves . . . away from the village, toward the steppe,
toward the forests. . . .

* * * *

In fall the steppe fades all at once, enveloped suddenly
in a vast, gray sadness. Morning came in rain and sleet,
unwashed, dreary. A detachment of Cossacks rode past
the shattered gate of the tannery, singing lustily. Three
Cossacks rode out of the gate and mingled with the rest;
no one heard them talking about the beautiful woman
Communist they had been lucky enough to have for the
night. . . . And when the singing died away the shattered
gate of the tannery again stood in silence. Vats reeking of
dead skins and tanbark stood in the tannery yard; a stake
had been driven into the central vat, and Irina—Arina
Sergeyevna Arsenyeva—was impaled on the stake. She
was naked. The stake was driven between her legs; her
feet were tied to the stake. Her face—the face of a beautiful woman—was hideous with horror, the eyes popping out
of their sockets. She was alive. She died toward evening.
The whole of that day no one went into the tannery yard.

* * * *

Kuzya was late in delivering Nekulyev's letter to Arina.
He came at night. House and yard were unlocked; there
was no one about. He made his way to the attic, lit a
match; everything was in wild disorder. In the corner
behind the bed a holder with a candle stub was standing
on the floor; two wolf eyes stared out from behind it.
Kuzya lit the candle, examined the room carefully, picking
at the bloodstains on the floor with his fingernail, and said
to himself aloud, "Killed her, have they? Or just wounded
her maybe—and they've smashed up things here too, the
devils!" Then he fixed his attention on the wolf pup,
looked at it closely, chuckled, and said, "And they said
it was a wolf pup—they're not all there! It's a fox!" Kuzya
heaped together all the movables in the room, wrapped

them in a blanket, and tied a rope around; he took the sheet from the bed, calmly picked up the fox cub by the scruff, wrapped it up, threw the bundles over his shoulder, put out the candle, stuck the candle holder in his pocket, and went out of the room.

Soon Kuzya was walking through the forest. The forest was silent, black, still. Nekulyev would have wondered how Kuzya could move in the dark without having his eyes poked out by branches. He took the shortest route, following narrow paths over hills; he gave no thought to the wood-devil, but he did not whistle either. The bundles were heavy.

The affair of the wolf pup must have made a great impression on Kuzya, because Yegor, Maryasha, and Katyasha each heard the story many times over: "And they said it was a wolf pup—they're not all there!—It was a fox all the time! A wolf's tail is like a cudgel, but this one has a black tuft on the end, and the ears are black, mark you. Of course, how should the gentry know about that?—Not every hunter can tell the difference—but I know!"

By the time the snows came that fall there was no longer any doubt that the wolf pup had turned out to be a fox. Kuzya killed the fox, skinned it, and from the pelt made himself a cap with earflaps.

November 20, 1924

MAHOGANY

Chapter One

Paupers, soothsayers, beggars, mendicant chanters, lazars, wanderers from holy place to holy place, male and
female, cripples, bogus saints, blind psalm singers, prophets, idiots of both sexes, fools in Christ—these names, so
close in meaning, of the double-ring sugar cakes of the
everyday life of Holy Russia, paupers on the face of Holy
Russia, wandering psalm singers, Christ's cripples, fools
in Christ of Holy Russia—these sugar cakes have adorned
everyday life from Russia's very beginnings, from the time
of the first Tsar Ivans, the everyday life of Russia's thousand years. All Russian historians, ethnographers, and
writers have dipped their quills to write about these holy
fools. These madmen or frauds—beggars, bogus saints,
prophets—were held to be the Church's brightest jewel,
Christ's own, intercessors for the world, as they have been
called in classical Russian history and literature.

A noted Muscovite fool in Christ—Ivan Yakovlevich,[1] a
onetime seminarian—who lived in Moscow in the middle of
the nineteenth century died in the Preobrazhenskaya Hospital. His funeral was described by reporters, poets, and
historians. A poet wrote in the *Gazette:*[2]

> *What feast is in the Yellow House[3] afoot,*
> *And wherefore are the multitudes there thronging,*
> *In landaus and in cabs, nay e'en on foot,*

[1] Koreisha, Ivan Yakovlevich (about 1780–1861): for many
years an inmate of a Moscow asylum for the insane; his fol-
lowers regarded him as a saint and a seer (Editors).

[2] *Moskovskiye Vedomosti*, a conservative Moscow daily
(Editors).

[3] Synonym for insane asylum (Editors).

And ev'ry heart is seized with fearful longing?
And in their midst is heard a voice of woe
In direst pain and grief ofttimes bewailing:
"Alas, Ivan Yakovlevich is laid low,
The mighty prophet's lamp too soon is failing."

Skavronski, a chronicler of the times, relates in his *Moscow Sketches* that during the five days that the body lay unburied, more than two hundred Masses for the repose of the dead were sung over it. Many people spent the night outside the church. An eyewitness of the funeral, N. Barkov, the author of a monograph entitled *Twenty-six Muscovite Sham Prophets, Sham Fools in Christ, Idiots, Male and Female*, relates that Ivan Yakovlevich was to have been buried on Sunday "as had been announced in the *Police Gazette*, and that day at dawn his admirers began flocking in, but the funeral did not take place because of the quarrels which broke out over where exactly he was to be buried. It did not quite come to a free-for-all, but words were exchanged, and strong ones they were. Some wanted to take him to Smolensk, his birthplace, others worked busily to have him buried in the Pokrovski Monastery, where a grave had even been made for him in the church; others begged tearfully that his remains be given to the Alekseyevski Nunnery; still others, hanging on to the coffin, tried to carry it off to the village of Cherkizovo. . . . It was feared that the body of Ivan Yakovlevich might be stolen." The historian writes: "All this time it was raining and the mud was terrible, but nevertheless, as the body was carried from the lodgings to the chapel, from the chapel to the church, from the church to the cemetery, women, girls, ladies in crinolines prostrated themselves and crawled under the coffin." Ivan Yakovlevich—when he was alive—was in the habit of relieving himself on the spot: "He made puddles [writes the historian] and his attendants had orders to sprinkle the floor with sand. And this sand, watered by Ivan Yakovlevich, his admirers would gather and carry home, and it was discovered that the sand had healing properties.

A baby gets a tummy-ache, his mother gives him half a spoonful of the sand in his gruel, and the baby gets well. The cotton with which the deceased's nose and ears had been plugged was divided into tiny pieces after the funeral service for distribution among the faithful. Many came with vials and collected in them the moisture which seeped from the coffin, the deceased having died of dropsy. The shirt in which Ivan Yakovlevich had died was torn to shreds. When the time came for the coffin to be carried out of the church, freaks, fools in Christ, pious hypocrites, wanderers from holy place to holy place, male and female, were gathered outside. They had not gone into the church, which was packed, but stood in the streets. And right there in broad daylight, among the assembled, sermons were preached to the people, visions called up and seen, prophesies and denunciations uttered, money collected, and ominous roarings given forth." During the last years of his life Ivan Yakovlevich used to order his admirers to drink the water in which he had washed: they drank it. Ivan Yakovlevich made not only spoken but also written prophesies which have been preserved for historical research. People wrote to him; they would ask, "Will so-and-so get married?" He would reply, "No work —no supper. . . ."

Kitai-Town[4] in Moscow was the cheese in which the fools in Christ—its maggots—lived. Some wrote verse, others crowed like roosters, screamed like peacocks, or whistled like bullfinches, others heaped foulness on all and sundry in the name of the Lord, still others knew only a simple phrase which was held to be prophetic and gave the prophet his name; for example, "Man's life's a dream, the coffin—coach and team, the ride—as smooth as cream!" Also to be found were devotees of dog-barking who with their barking prophesied God's will. To this estate belonged paupers, beggars, soothsayers, mendicant chanters, lazars, bogus saints—the cripples of all of Holy Russia; to it belonged peasants, and townfolk, and gentry, and mer-

[4] Formerly a commercial district of Moscow near Red Square (Editors).

chants—children, old men, great, hulking louts, brood-
mares of women. They were all drunk. They were all
sheltered by the onion-domed, sky-blue calm of the Asi-
atic Russian tsardom; they were bitter as cheese and
onions, for the onion domes atop the churches are, of
course, the symbol of oniony Russian life.

. . . .

. . . And there are in Moscow, Petersburg, and other
large Russian towns other kinds of queer fish. Their family
tree is rooted in the Russia of the emperors rather than
the Russia of the tsars. The art of Russian furniture, established by Peter, came into its own under Elizabeth.
This serf art has no recorded history and the names of its
practitioners have been obliterated by time. It was an art
of solitary men, of cellars in towns, of cramped back rooms
in servants' huts on country estates. It was an art that had
its being in bitter vodka and cruelty. Jacob and Boulle
were the teachers. Serf boys were sent to Moscow and
St. Petersburg, to Paris, to Vienna—there they were taught
their craft. Then they returned—from Paris to the cellars
of St. Petersburg, from St. Petersburg to servants' cramped
back rooms—and created. For decades a craftsman would
work on a great sofa or dressing table, or on a small bureau
or a book cabinet—would work, drink, and die, leaving his
art to a nephew, for a craftsman was not supposed to
have children, and the nephew would either copy his
uncle's art, or develop it further. A craftsman would die,
but the things he had made would live on a century or
more on the landowners' estates and in their town houses;
people made love in their presence and died on the great
sofas, hid secret correspondence in the concealed drawers
of secrétaires; brides looked closely at their youth in the
little mirrors of the dressing tables, and old women—at
their old age. Elizabeth—Catherine—rococo, baroque—
bronze, scrolls, palisander, rosewood, ebony, curly birch,
Persian walnut. Paul is severe, Paul is a Knight of Malta;
Paul has soldierly lines, Paul has a severe repose, dark-
polished mahogany, green leather, black lions, and grif-

fins. Alexander—Empire, classic lines, Hellas. Nicholas—
Paul again, crushed by the majesty of his brother Alexander. Thus have epochs given their shape to mahogany.
In 1861 serfdom collapsed. The serf craftsmen were replaced by furniture factories—Levinson, Thonet, Viennese
furniture. But the craftsmen's nephews survived, thanks
to vodka. These craftsmen no longer make anything, they
restore the past, but they have kept all the skills and
traditions of their uncles. They are solitary men, and silent.
They take pride in their work, like philosophers, and they
love it, like poets. They live in cellars as before. You can't
put such a craftsman in a furniture factory, you can't make
him restore a piece later than Nicholas I. He is an anti-
quarian, he is a restorer. In the attic of some Moscow
house or in a barn on some country estate which has escaped burning, he will find a table, a three-leaved mirror,
a sofa—dating back to Catherine, Paul, Alexander—and for
months on end he will worry away at it in his cellar,
smoking, thinking, measuring with his eyes to bring back
life to dead things. He will love these things. And—who
knows?—he may find a yellowed bundle of letters in the
secret drawer of a small bureau. He is a restorer, he looks
back to the prime of these things. He is sure to be a queer
fish, and in his queer-fish way he will sell the restored
piece to a collector, as queer a fish as himself, with whom,
to seal the bargain, he will drink brandy—poured from a
bottle into a square glass measure of Catherine's time—out
of a wineglass which had once been part of the imperial
diamond set.

Chapter Two

The year is 1928.
The town is a Russian Bruges and a Muscovite Kamakura. Three hundred years ago the last tsarevitch of the
House of Ryurik was murdered in this town; on the day
of the murder the children of the boyar Tuchkov played
with the tsarevitch—and to this day Tuchkovs survive in

the town, as do the monasteries and many other families of less illustrious ancestry. . . . Relics of ancient Russia, the Russian provinces, the broad upper reaches of the Volga, forests, swamps, villages, monasteries, country estates, a chain of towns—Tver, Uglich, Yaroslavl, Rostov Veliki. The town is a monastic Bruges of feudal Russia, a town of narrow streets overgrown with camomile, of stone witnesses to murders and centuries. Two hundred versts from Moscow, and the railroad is fifty versts away.

Here ruins of country estates and mahogany have been left high and dry. The head of the local historical museum walks around in a top hat, a cape, check trousers, and has let his side whiskers grow, like Pushkin's; in the pockets of his cape are kept the keys to the museum and the monasteries; he drinks tea in the tavern, and vodka in solitude—in his storeroom; his house is piled with Bibles, icons, archimandrital cowls and miters, surplices, stoles, cuffs, cassocks, chasubles, chalice cloths, palls, altar vestments—of the thirteenth, fifteenth, seventeenth centuries; the furniture in his study is mahogany and once belonged to the Karazins; on the writing desk is an ashtray in the form of a nobleman's cap with a red band and a white crown.

Barin Karazin—Vyacheslav Pavlovich—served at one time in the Horse Guards and resigned some five and twenty years before the Revolution, because he was an honest man; one of his colleagues had been caught stealing, he was sent to investigate, reported the truth to his superiors, his superiors covered up for the thief—this was more than *Barin* Karazin could stand and he submitted a second report—his resignation—and settled down on his estate, going into his District town once a week to make purchases; he rode in a huge, old-fashioned carriage, accompanied by two footmen; with a white glove he would sign to the shop clerk to wrap up for him half a pound of the best caviar, three quarters of a pound of *balyk*,[5] and a small sturgeon; one footman would pay the

[5] Dried and salted sturgeon (Editors).

bill, the other would receive the purchases; on one occasion the shopkeeper made as if to shake hands with the *Barin*, but the latter withheld his hand, explaining this refusal with a curt, "No need for that!" *Barin* Karazin wore a nobleman's cap and a greatcoat in the style of Nicholas I; the Revolution had forced him from his estate and into town, but had left him his greatcoat and cap; *Barin* Karazin stood in queues wearing his nobleman's cap, preceded by his wife instead of footmen.

Barin Karazin existed by selling off old family possessions; it was to this end that he used to call on the museum curator; at the curator's he would see things that had been taken from his estate by the will of the Revolution, and look at them disdainfully; but one day he noticed on the curator's desk the ashtray in the form of a nobleman's cap.

"Take it away," he said curtly.

"Why?" asked the curator.

"The cap of a Russian nobleman cannot serve as a spittoon," replied *Barin* Karazin.

The two connoisseurs of antiquities quarreled. *Barin* Karazin went away in anger. Never again did he cross the curator's threshold. In the town lived a saddler who remembered with gratitude how *Barin* Karazin—when the saddler was a youngster and an errand boy in the *Barin's* service—how the *Barin* with one blow of his left hand had knocked out seven of his teeth for not jumping to it.

In the town impenetrable silence was congealing, howling with boredom twice a day in steamers' whistles, and ringing the ancient denizens of church belfries—until 1928, that is, for in 1928 the bells were taken down from many churches for the State Ore and Metal Trust. High up in towers, with the aid of pulleys, beams, and hemp ropes, bells were dragged from their belfries; they hung over the earth, then they were cast down. As the bells crept along the ropes they sang an ancient lament—and this lament hung over the town's close-packed, ancient stones. The bells fell with a roar and a great sigh, and sank a good two *arshins* into the ground.

In the days of the events described in this story the

town was groaning with the groans of these ancient bells.

The most useful thing in town was a trade-union card; in the shops there were two queues—those with cards and those without; to take a boat out on the Volga cost card-holders ten kopecks, and the rest forty kopecks, an hour; cinema tickets—to the rest twenty-five, forty, and sixty kopecks, to cardholders five, ten, and fifteen. A trade-union card, if there was one in the house, occupied the place of honor next to the bread card; as for bread cards —and that meant bread, too: four hundred grams per person per day—they were issued only to those who had the vote; to those who had no vote and to their children no bread was given. The cinema was in the trade-union park, in a heated barn; it had not been thought necessary to provide the cinema with a signal bell, but a signal was sounded from the power station to the whole town at once: first signal—time to finish your tea, second signal—put on your coat and be on your way. The power station operated until one, but when there were name days, *oktyabriny*,[6] and other unofficial festivities in the house of the Execu-tive Committee chairman, or the Industrial Combine chair-man, or of other higher-ups—electric lights were a long time going out, sometimes all night, and the rest of the popula-tion contrived to have their own festivities on these nights. And it was in the cinema one day that a representative of the People's Commissariat for Domestic Trade by the name of Satz, or maybe Katz, while in a state of perfect sobriety, bumped accidentally, simply through clumsiness, against the wife of the Executive Committee chairman; she, overflowing with disdain, uttered the words, "I am Kuvarzina"; representative Satz, being uninformed of the power of this name, apologized with raised eyebrows— and for those raised eyebrows was subsequently forced to leave the District. The higher-ups in the town lived in a tight little group, keeping a watchful eye, out of inborn suspiciousness, on the rest of the population; they sub-

[6] Secular ceremony of naming a child, taking the place of baptism. Its name derives from "October," the month of the Bolshevik Revolution (Editors).

stituted squabbles for constructive activity, and every year reelected themselves to one important District post after another, depending on the alignment of squabblers, on the principle of robbing Peter to pay Paul. The economy was juggled on the same principle. The Combine ran everything (the Combine came into existence the same year that Ivan Ozhogov—the hero of this story—became an *okhlomon*[7]). The board of the Combine consisted of Executive Committee Chairman Kuvarzin (his wife's husband) and Workers' and Peasants' Inspection Representative Presnukhin; Nedosugov acted as chairman. Their way of running things was by the slow dissipation of prerevolutionary resources, and stupid bungling, to which they brought loving care. The oil mill operated at a loss; the sawmill—also at a loss; the tannery—not at a loss, but not at a profit either, and without a depreciation fund. The previous winter a new boiler had been hauled over the snow to the tannery by forty-five horses and half the population of the District; they got it there and left it— because it was the wrong kind—entering its cost in the profit-and-loss account; they bought a bark crusher and abandoned it, too, as useless, entering it in the profit-and-loss account; then, for the purpose of crushing bark, they bought a chaffcutter—but abandoned it, since bark is not straw; that too was entered. They set out to improve the living conditions of the workers by a housing project: they bought a two-story wooden house, moved it to the tannery —and sawed it up for firewood—five cubic *sazhens* they got out of it—because the house turned out to be rotten: there were only thirteen sound beams in it; to these thirteen beams they added nine thousand rubles—and built a house just in time for the tannery to shut down because, al-

---

[7] *"Okhlomon"* is as strange a word in Russian as it is in English. It is probably derived from the Greek *ochlos*, mob, and *monos*, alone, and could be rendered as "apart from the mob," therefore "outcast." An early translator of Pilnyak who must have consulted the writer about the meaning of the word says: "The author affirms that it means just what its use in the novel implies" (Editors).

though unlike the other enterprises it made no losses, it made no profits either; the new house remained empty. The Combine covered its losses by selling off equipment from enterprises idle since before the Revolution, and also by such deals as the following: Chairman of the Executive Committee Kuvarzin sold lumber to Member of the Board Kuvarzin at the fixed prices with a 50 per cent discount—for twenty-five thousand rubles; Member of the Board Kuvarzin sold the same lumber to the population at large, and to Chairman of the Executive Committee Kuvarzin in particular, at the fixed prices without discount—for something over fifty thousand rubles. In 1927 the board expressed a desire to rest on its laurels; Kuvarzin was presented with a briefcase; the money for the briefcase was taken out of public funds, and then a subscription list was rushed around among the natives in order to return the money to the cashbox. In view of the narrowness of their interests and their lives, passed in secret from the rest of the population, the higher-ups are of no interest whatsoever to this story. Alcohol in town was sold in two forms only—vodka and sacramental wine, nothing else; vodka was consumed in quantity, and sacramental wine, too, although somewhat less in demand—for Christ's blood and *teplota*.[8] Cigarettes on sale in town were "Cannon," eleven kopecks a pack, and "Boxing," fourteen kopecks a pack; there were no others. There were two queues for both vodka and cigarettes—trade-union and non-trade-union. Steamers called twice a day, and in the ship's restaurant one could buy "Sappho" cigarettes, port, and rowanberry brandy—and "Sappho" smokers were obviously embezzlers, since there was no private business in town, and official budgets made no provisions for "Sappho." The townsfolk, looking forward to the day when the town would no longer be an administrative center, lived on their vegetable patches, supplying one another's needs.

Near Skudrin Bridge stood the Skudrin house, and in the house lived the peasants' agent Yakov Karpovich

[8] In the Russian Orthodox Church, wine diluted with warm water, given to communicants after Communion (Editors).

Skudrin, a man of eighty-five; besides Yakov Karpovich Skudrin there lived in the town—but not under the same roof as Yakov Karpovich—his two much younger sisters, Kapitolina and Rimma, and his brother, the *okhlomon* Ivan, who had changed his name to Ozhogov; more about them later.

For the last forty years Yakov Karpovich had suffered from a hernia, and when walking he supported this hernia of his with his right hand through the fly of his trousers; his hands were puffy and greenish; he salted his bread thickly with salt from the common salt dish, crunching it between his fingers, frugally sprinkling what was left back into the salt dish. Over the last thirty years Yakov Karpovich had lost the habit of sleeping normally; he would wake at night and keep vigil over the Bible until daybreak, and then sleep until noon; at noon he always went out to the public reading room to read the papers: there were no papers on sale in town and no money to take out subscriptions—papers were read in reading rooms. Yakov Karpovich was fat, white-haired, and bald; his eyes watered and as he got ready to speak he would go into protracted wheezings and snufflings. The Skudrin house had once belonged to the landowner Vereiski, who went bankrupt as an elected justice of the peace after the abolition of serfdom; Yakov Karpovich, having served his time in the prereform army, worked for Vereiski as a clerk, became adept in courtroom chicanery, and, when Vereiski went bankrupt, bought him out of house and position. The house had stood untouched since Catherine's time; in the century and a half of its existence it had darkened like the mahogany inside it, and its windowpanes had taken on a greenish tinge. Yakov Karpovich remembered the days of serfdom. The old man remembered everything, as far back as the *barin* of his serf village, as far back as the recruiting for Sevastopol; he remembered all the names, patronymics, and surnames of all the Russian ministers of state and people's commissars, all the ambassadors to the Russian Imperial Court and to the Soviet Central Executive Committee, all the foreign ministers of the great pow-

ers, all the prime ministers, kings, emperors, and popes.
The old man had lost count of years and used to say:

"I've outlived Nikolai Pavlovich, Aleksandr Nikolayevich, Aleksandr Aleksandrovich, Nikolai Aleksandrovich,
Vladimir Ilyich—and I'll outlive Aleksey Ivanovich too!"[9]

The old man had a nasty little smile, at once obsequious
and malicious; his whitish eyes watered when he smiled.
The old man was hard, and his sons took after him. The
eldest, Aleksandr—this happened long before 1905—having been sent to the landing stage with an urgent letter
and having missed the steamer, received from his father
a slap in the face accompanied by the words, "Get out,
you good-for-nothing!" That slap was the last drop of
honey; the boy was fourteen; the boy turned, walked out
of the house—and returned home only six years later, a
student of the Academy of Fine Arts. Sometime during
those years the father had sent his son a letter in which
he ordered his son to return and swore to withdraw
his parental blessing, laying on him an eternal curse; on
this very letter—just below his father's signature—the son
had written, "To hell with your blessing," and sent it back.
When, six years after his departure, Aleksandr walked
into the parlor one sunny spring day, the father went toward him with a gleeful smile and hand raised to strike
his son; with a cheerful grin, the son took hold of his
father's wrists, smiled again—a smile which sparkled with
strength; his father's hands were held in a vise; the son
forced his father to sit down in an armchair near the table
by applying the slightest of pressure to his wrists, and the
son said:

"Good day to you, Daddikins—don't put yourself out,
Daddikins—take a seat, Daddikins!"

The father began wheezing, tittering, snuffling; malevo-
lent kindliness passed over his face; the old man called
out to his wife:

"Maryushka, yes, hee-hee, a drop of vodka, my dear,

[9] Nicholas I, Alexander II, Alexander III, Nicholas II, Lenin,
Rykov (Chairman of the Council of People's Commissars, 1924–
30; executed in Stalin's purges in 1938) (Editors).

bring us a drop of vodka, cold from the cellar, and a bit of something cold to go with it—he's grown up, our boy, grown up—he's come back, our boy, to blight our old age, the s-son of a bitch!"

His sons went their ways: painter, priest, ballet dancer, doctor, engineer. Two of the younger brothers took after the eldest—the painter—and after the father; the two youngest left the house, like the eldest, and the younger of the two, the engineer Akim Yakovlevich, became a Communist; he never returned to his father's house, and on his visits to the town of his birth stayed with his aunts Kapitolina and Rimma. By 1928 Yakov Karpovich's eldest grandsons were married, but his youngest child, a daughter, was only twenty. She was his only daughter, and, amidst the thunders of the Revolution, she was given no education of any kind.

In the house lived the old man, his wife Mariya Klimovna, and their daughter Katerina. Half the house and the attic floor were not heated in winter. The house lived as people lived long before Catherine, even before Peter, although it was mahogany of Catherine's time that inhabited its silence. The old people lived off their vegetable garden. Industry supplied the house with matches, kerosene, and salt—nothing else; matches, kerosene, and salt were doled out by the father. From spring to fall Mariya Klimovna, Katerina, and the old man toiled over cabbages, beets, turnips, cucumbers, carrots, and licorice, which took the place of sugar. On summer dawns the old man could be met in his nightclothes, barefoot, his right hand thrust through his fly, a long switch in his left hand —grazing cows outside the town in dew and fog. In winter the old man would allow the lamp to be lit only when he was up—at other times mother and daughter sat in darkness. Every day at noon the old man went to the reading room to read the papers, soaking up names and news of the Communist Revolution. At those times Katerina would sit at the harpsichord practicing Kastalski's[10] spiri-

[10] Kastalski, Aleksandr Dmitriyevich (1856–1926): historian of Russian choral music, composer, choirmaster (Editors).

tual songs; she sang in the church choir. The old man came home at dusk, ate, and went to bed. The house sank into women's whisperings, into darkness. Then Katerina would go to the cathedral for choir practice. Her father would awake at midnight, light the lamp, eat, and bury himself in the Bible, reading it aloud from memory. About six o'clock he would fall asleep again. The old man had lost all sense of time, having ceased to fear death, having forgotten how to fear life. Mother and daughter kept silent in the old man's presence. The mother cooked porridge and cabbage soup, baked pies, baked[11] and curded milk, prepared pigs'-feet jelly (saving the knucklebones for her grandsons)—in other words she lived as the people of Russia lived in the fifteenth and in the seventeenth centuries; the food she prepared was also of the fifteenth and the seventeenth centuries. Mariya Klimovna was a dried-up old woman; she was a wonderful woman, the kind still preserved in Russia in the villages, together with ancient icons of the Virgin. The cruel will of her husband, who, fifty years earlier, the day after their wedding, when she put on a raspberry-colored velvet bodice, asked her, "What's that for?"—she did not understand the question —"What's that for?" asked her husband again—"Take it off! I know you as you are without the finery, and there's no cause for others to stare!"—and with this, licking his thumb, the husband painfully showed his wife how she should pull her hair back from the temples—the cruel will of her husband, which forced the wife to put away her velvet bodice in a chest forever, which banished her to the kitchen—was the wife's will broken by it, or was it tempered by subjugation? The wife became forever submissive, dignified, silent, sad—and was never false, not even in her heart. Her world did not reach beyond the gate—and there was only one path which led outside the gate: to the church, which was like a grave. With her daughter she sang Kastalski's psalms; she was sixty-nine years old. Pre-Petrine Russia was stiffening in the house. At night the old

[11] A method of preparing milk by slow cooking in an oven (Editors).

man read the Bible from memory, having ceased to fear life. Very rarely, once every few months, in the silent hours of the night, the old man would go to his wife's bed; he would whisper then:

"Maryushka, yes—k'he, hmm! . . . yes, k'he, Maryushka, this is life, Maryushka!"

He would be holding a candle, his eyes would be watering and laughing, his hands trembling.

"Maryushka, k'he, here I am, yes—this is life, Maryushka, k'he!"

Mariya Klimovna would cross herself.

"Shame on you, Yakov Karpovich! . . ."

Yakov Karpovich would put out the light.

Their daughter Katerina had little yellow eyes, which seemed unable to move from endless sleep. Around her swollen lids freckles bred all year round. Her arms and legs were like beams, her breasts were enormous, like the udders of Swiss cows.

. . . The town is a Russian Bruges and a Russian Kamakura.

Chapter Three

. . . Moscow rumbled with truckloads of actions, beginnings, achievements. Automobiles and buildings hurtled into distances and into space. Posters shouted Gorki's State Publishing House, cinemas, and congresses. Noises of streetcars, buses, and taxis affirmed the capital from one end to the other.

The train was leaving Moscow to enter a night black as soot. The feverish glows and thunders of Moscow were abating, and very quickly passed. Fields stretched out in black silence and silence settled down in the car. In a double compartment of a first-class car sat two men—the brothers Bezdetov, Pavel Fyodorovich and Stepan Fyodorovich, mahogany men, restorers. There was something puzzling about their appearance: they were dressed as merchants dressed in Ostrovski's time, in frock coats and

Russian-style overcoats, and their faces, although shaven, had the true Slavic cast of Yaroslavl folk; the eyes of both were empty and intelligent. The train was dragging time off into the black expanses of fields. The car smelled of tanned hide and hemp. Pavel Fyodorovich took out a large bottle of brandy and a small silver tumbler from a suitcase—poured, drank—poured and silently handed the tumbler to his brother. His brother drank and returned the tumbler. Pavel Fyodorovich put the bottle and the tumbler back into the suitcase.

"Are we taking beadwork?" asked Stepan.

"Certainly," replied Pavel.

Half an hour passed in silence. The train was dragging time along, bringing it to a halt with stations. Pavel took out the bottle and tumbler, drank, poured his brother a drink, put things away.

"Do we treat the girls? Are we taking porcelain?" asked Stepan Fyodorovich.

"Certainly," replied Pavel Fyodorovich.

And after another half hour of silence the brothers each drank another tumbler.

"Are we taking so-called Russian Gobelins?" asked Stepan.

"Certainly," answered Pavel.

At midnight the train reached the Volga, at a village famed throughout Russia for its handicraft boot industry. The smell of hide grew stronger and stronger. Pavel poured a final tumbler for each of them.

"We're not taking anything after Alexander?" asked Stepan.

"Out of the question," replied Pavel Fyodorovich.

At the station were heaped mountains of Muscovite boots —not a philosophical observation, but a concrete confirmation of the nature of Russian roads. The goods smelled of pitch. The darkness was as thick as the pitch it smelled of. Bootmakers ran about the station. Beyond the station everything was sinking into mud. Wasting no words, Pavel Fyodorovich hired a cart to the landing stage for forty kopecks. In the darkness coachmen were swearing like

bootmakers.[12] The damp rolled in from the vast dark of
the Volga. The far bank glowed with the electric lights
of bootmaking. In the ship's restaurant a party of Jewish
buyers was getting drunk; a young woman wearing a
monkey-fur wrap kept things lively, poured the vodka;
the party left after the third whistle. The steamer dimmed
lights. The wind began to grope the Volga's vastnesses,
dampness crept into the cabins. The waitress, an enormous
woman, while serving the Bezdetovs was making up beds
on the tables in the restaurant and talking about her lover,
who had stolen a hundred and twenty-two rubles from
her. The steamer was carrying off inside it the smells of
boot leather. Deck passengers were singing bandit songs
to keep out the cold. In the gray dregs of morning land-
scapes loomed—not from the fourteenth, but from some
prehistoric century—banks untouched by man, pines, firs,
birches, boulders, clay, water; the fourteenth century according to European chronology loomed in rafts, ferries,
villages. By noon the steamer had entered the seventeenth-
eighteenth century of the Russian Bruges: the town came
down to the Volga with its churches, its kremlin, and the
ruins left by the fire of 1920. (In that year a good half of
the town—the central part—burned down. The fire broke
out in the District Food Committee headquarters—the
townsfolk should have been fighting the fire, but instead
they began hunting *burzhuis*[13] and putting them in jail
as hostages; they hunted the *burzhuis* for three days—
exactly as long as the town burned—and stopped hunting
them when the fire had burned itself out without any in-
terference from firemen's hoses or population.) At the hour
that the antique dealers disembarked, crazed flocks of
jackdaws were flying over the town, and the town was
moaning the strange moan of bells dragged down from
church towers. Rain was getting ready to drip awhile over
the town.

[12] "To swear like a bootmaker," "to swear like a coachman":
both proverbial expressions in Russian (Editors).
[13] From *bourgeois*, often in the sense of "profiteer," "ex-
ploiter" (Editors).

Pavel Fyodorovich—without wasting words—hired a tarantass to Skudrin Bridge, to the house of Yakov Karpovich
Skudrin. The cab rattled off over ancient cobblestones
overgrown with camomile; the driver told them the town's
bell news, explaining that many people in the town had
developed nervous disorders from the strain of waiting for
the bells to fall and for the thunder of their fall, like inex-
perienced riflemen who screw up their eyes in anticipation
of the report. The Bezdetovs met Yakov Karpovich in the
yard; the old man was chopping kindling for the stove.
Mariya Klimovna was pitchforking manure out of the cowshed. Yakov Karpovich did not immediately recognize the
Bezdetovs, but when he did, he was pleased to see them,
he broke into smiles, began groaning and snuffling; he said:

"Aah, the buyers! . . . I've thought up a theory of the
proletariat for you!"

Mariya Klimovna bowed to the guests from the waist,
tucking her hands under her apron, and sang out hos-
pitably:

"Dear guests, long-awaited guests—welcome!"

Katerina, dirt-smeared, her skirt hitched up to her
thighs, dashed into the house—to change. Above the roof-
tops a falling bell roared, sending flocks of crows reeling;
Mariya Klimovna crossed herself; the bell boomed louder
than a cannon, the glass in the windows facing the yard
rang; it certainly was bad for the nerves.

They all entered the house. Mariya Klimovna went
through to her pots and pans, the samovar began to hum
at her feet. Katerina came out to the guests a young lady,
curtsied. The old man took off his felt boots, and circled
his guests barefoot, cooing like a pigeon. The antique
dealers washed off the grime of their travels, and sat down
at the table, side by side, in silence. The eyes of the guests
were empty, like those of dead men. Mariya Klimovna
inquired after their health and set out on the table a
variety of seventeenth-century food. The guests stood a
bottle of brandy on the table. During the meal only
Yakov Karpovich spoke; he tittered, hmm-ed, talked about

places to look for antiques which he had noted for the
benefit of the brothers Bezdetov.

Pavel Fyodorovich asked:

"So you mean to hold out?"

The old man fidgeted and tittered, answered in a whine:
"That's right, that's right. I can't, no, I can't. What's
mine is mine, I can still use it myself—time will tell, yes,
k'he. . . . Better let me tell you my theory. . . . I'll outlive you all yet!"

After dinner the guests went to take a nap—they pulled
the squeaking doors to, lay down on the feather beds, and
silently drank brandy out of antique silver. By evening the
guests were thoroughly drunk. All afternoon Katerina sang
psalms. Yakov Karpovich hung about the doors to the
guests' room, waiting for them to come out or to speak,
so that he would have an excuse to go in and talk with
them. The day was carried off by the crows; all through
sunset the crows were agitated, stealing the day piecemeal.
Dusk was carried from door to door in water-carriers'
barrels. The eyes of the guests, when they came out to tea,
were utterly dead, dazedly unblinking. The guests sat down
at the table, silently and side by side. Yakov Karpovich
squeezed himself in behind them to make sure of having
their ear. The guests drank tea from saucers, lacing brandy
with tea, unbuttoning their frock coats. A torchère of
Catherine's time was smoking near the table. The dinner
table was round, of mahogany.

Yakov Karpovich was choking on his words as he hastened to have his say:

"I've got an idea ready for you, k'he, an idea. . . . Marx's
theory of the proletariat will soon have to be set aside,
because the proletariat itself will have to disappear—that's
my idea! . . . And that means the Revolution was all for
nothing, a mistake, k'he, of history. By virtue of the fact
that, yes, two or three more generations and the proletariat
will disappear: first of all in the United States, in England, in Germany. Marx wrote his theory in an epoch
when muscular labor was supreme. Nowadays machines
are replacing muscles. That's my idea. Soon there'll be only

engineers tending the machines, and the proletariat will disappear, the proletariat will all turn into engineers. That, k'he, is my idea. And an engineer is not a proletarian, because the more cultured a man is, the less need he has to show off, and he's more content to have the same standard of living as everyone else, to spread material well-being evenly, so as to liberate thought, yes—take the English, both rich and poor sleep in the same way, in jackets, and live in the same kind of houses, the three-story kind; but the way it used to be with us—compare a merchant and a peasant: the merchant decked himself out like a priest, and lived in a palace. But I can go around barefoot and be none the worse for it. You'll say, k'he, yes, there'll still be exploitation. But how can there be? The peasant, who can be exploited because he's like a beast— you won't let him near a machine: he'd wreck it, and it costs millions. A machine is too costly to try to save a few kopecks on the man who operates it; the man must know the machine, the machine needs a man with knowl-edge—and there'll be one man where there were a hundred before. Such a man will be pampered. That'll be the end of the proletariat! . . ."

The guests drank their tea and listened with unblinking eyes. Yakov Karpovich grunted, hawked, and hurried on— but he did not have time to develop his idea to the full: Ivan Karpovich, his brother, arrived—the *okhlomon*, who had changed his name from Skudrin to Ozhogov. Neatly dressed in hopeless tatters, his hair neatly cut, galoshes on his bare feet, he bowed respectfully to all and sat down apart from the rest, in silence. Nobody responded to his bow. His face was the face of a madman. Yakov Karpovich fidgeted and showed signs of unease.

Mariya Klimovna said sorrowfully:

"Why did you have to come, brother dear?"

The *okhlomon* replied:

"To have a look at the different forms of the Counter-revolution, sister dear."

"What Counterrevolution could there be here, brother dear?"

"As far as you're concerned, sister dear, you are the everyday Counterrevolution," *okhlomon* Ozhogov began in a soft, mad voice. "But I have made you weep—that means that you have the seeds of Communism in you. But Brother Yakov hasn't wept once, and I very much regret that I didn't put him up against the wall and shoot him when things were going my way."

Mariya Klimovna sighed, shook her head, said:

"And how's your boy?"

"My boy," answered the *okhlomon* proudly, "my son is finishing university, and he doesn't forget me, he visits my domain on vacations, warms himself by the kiln; I make up revolutionary verses for him."

"And your wife?"

"I don't see her. She manages the Women's Division. Do you know how many managers we have for every two production workers?"

"No."

"Seven. Too many cooks spoil the broth. As for your guests, they are the historical Counterrevolution."

The guests drank their tea, pewter-eyed. Yakov Karpovich was flooding with violet rage; he began to look like a beetroot. He advanced on his brother, tittered with politeness, began to grope about with his hands, rubbed them together energetically as if he were out in a frost.

"You know what, brother dear," began Yakov Karpovich in a hoarse whisper, very politely, "get to the Devil's mother out of here. I ask you in all earnestness! . . ."

"Beg pardon, Brother Yakov, I didn't come to see you, I came to take a look at the historical Counterrevolution, and to have a few words with it," Ivan replied.

"And I'm asking you—go to the Devil's mother!"

"I'm not going to the Devil's mother!"

Pavel Fyodorovich slowly turned the pewter of his left eye to his brother, and said:

"We can't be talking to fools; if you don't leave I'll have Stepan throw you out on your neck."

Stepan returned his brother's glance, and shifted in his chair. Mariya Klimovna pressed her palms to her cheeks

and sighed. The *okhlomon* sat in silence. Stepan Fyodorovich got up slowly from the table and moved toward the
okhlomon. The *okhlomon* timorously half rose and started
backing toward the door. Mariya Klimovna sighed again.
Yakov Karpovich tittered. Stepan stopped in the middle of
the room—the *okhlomon* stopped by the door, grimacing.
Stepan took a step toward the *okhlomon*—the *okhlomon*
disappeared behind the door. From behind the door he
entreated:

"In that case, give me a ruble twenty-five kopecks for
vodka."

Stepan glanced at Pavel; Pavel said:

"Let him have enough for half a bottle."

The *okhlomon* went away. Mariya Klimovna saw him out
of the gate, pushed a piece of pie into his hand. The night
beyond the gate was black and motionless. *Okhlomon*
Ozhogov was walking toward the Volga through dark alleys,
past monasteries, across vacant lots, following paths known
to him alone. The night was very black. Ivan was talking
to himself, mumbling unintelligibly. He went down to the
Combine brickyard, where he squeezed through a hole in
the fence, and started across the clay pits. A kiln was
burning among the pits. Ivan crawled down into the kiln
pit—there it was very warm and very stuffy; through the
cracks of the kiln door came a red glow. Here on the ground
several derelicts lay about, overgrown with matted hair—
Ivan Ozhogov's Communists, men who had a tacit agreement with the Combine: they kept the brickyard kiln going
for nothing—the kiln whose fire baked the bricks—and they
lived by the kiln for nothing, these people who had brought
time to a standstill in the era of War Communism, when
they elected Ivan Ozhogov their chairman. On some straw
by a board which served as a table lay three derelicts,
taking a rest. Ozhogov squatted down by them, shivered
for a while warming up, as people shiver in fever, put
down the money and the piece of pie on the table.

"They didn't weep?" asked one of the derelicts.

"No, they didn't weep," replied Ozhogov.

For a while no one spoke.

"It's your turn to go, Comrade Ognyov,"[14] said Ozhogov.

Two more men in beggars' rags, with matted beards and whiskers, crawled into the clay of the underground cave, lay down beside the others, put money and bread on the board. A man of about forty, an old man already, who had been lying in the darkest warmth—Ognyov—crawled over to the board, counted the money, and started to climb out of the cave. The rest remained sitting or lying in silence —except that one of the newcomers announced that in the morning they would have to start loading a barge with firewood. Ognyov soon came back with bottles of vodka. Then the *okhlomons* moved closer to the board, brought out their mugs, and sat down in a circle. Comrade Ognyov poured a round of vodka; they clinked mugs, emptied them in silence.

"Now I shall speak," said Ozhogov. "Once there were some brothers, called Wright; they made up their minds to fly up into the sky, and they perished when they crashed to earth, having fallen out of the sky. They perished, but people have not abandoned their work; they haven't let go of the sky—and people are flying, comrades, they are flying over the earth like birds, like eagles! Comrade Lenin perished like the brothers Wright—I was the first chairman of the Executive Committee in our town. In nineteen twenty-one everything came to an end. We are the only real Communists in the whole town—and look what things have come to: the only place left for us is this cave. I was the first Communist here, and I'll remain a Communist as long as I live. Our ideas will not perish. And what ideas they were! Now nobody remembers that except us, comrades. We are like the brothers Wright! . . ."

Comrade Ognyov poured a second round of vodka. And Ognyov interrupted Ozhogov:

"Now I'll have my say, Comrade Chairman! What deeds were done! How people fought! I was in command of a partisan detachment. We were pushing through the forest:

[14] The names taken by the outcast Communists all derive from words related to fire (Editors).

a day, a night, and then another day, and another night.
And suddenly at daybreak we hear—machine guns. . . ."

Ognyov was interrupted by Pozharov; he asked Ognyov:

"And how do you slash? How do you hold your thumb
when you're slashing, bent or straight? Show us!"

"On the blade. Straight," answered Ognyov.

"Everybody holds it on the blade. You show us. Here's
a knife, show us!"

Ognyov took the cobbler's knife which the *okhlomons*
used to cut bread, and demonstrated how he placed his
thumb on the blade.

"You do it all wrong!" shouted Pozharov. "That's not
the way I hold the saber when I'm slashing—I slice with it
like a razor. Give it here, I'll show you! You do it all wrong!"

"Comrades!" Ozhogov said quietly, and his face was
contorted by raging pain, "Today we must talk about ideas,
great ideas, not about slashing!"

Ozhogov was interrupted by a fourth man, who shouted:

"Comrade Ognyov, you were in the Third Division, and
I was in the Second; do you remember how your outfit let
them get across near the village of Shinki? . . ."

"We let them get across? No, it was you let them get
across, not us! . . ."

"Comrades!" again Ozhogov spoke in a soft, mad voice,
"It's ideas we must talk about! . . ."

At midnight the men in the cave were asleep by the
kiln—these derelicts who had stumbled upon the right to
live in the kiln pit of a brickyard. They slept in a heap,
one resting his head on another's knees, their rags pulled
over them. The last to go to sleep was their chairman
Ivan Ozhogov: for a long time he lay near the mouth of
the kiln, a sheet of paper before him. He lay on his belly
with the paper spread on the ground. He wet his pencil
with his tongue; he wanted to write a poem. "We have
raised a worldwide . . . ," he wrote and crossed out. "We
have set ablaze a worldwide . . . ," he wrote and crossed
out. "You who warm your thieving hands . . . ," he wrote
and crossed out. "You who are lackeys, or idiots per-
chance . . . ," he wrote and crossed out. Words would not

come to him. He fell asleep with his head on the scratched
sheet of paper. Here slept Communists who had been
called to duty by War Communism and discharged by the
year nineteen hundred and twenty-one, men of arrested
ideas, madmen and drunkards, men who, living together
in a cave and working together unloading barges, sawing
firewood, had created a strict fraternity, a strict Communism, having nothing of their own, neither money, nor
possessions, nor wives; anyway, their wives had left them,
their dreams, their madness, their alcohol. In the cave it
was very close, very warm, very bare.

Midnight was passing over the town, inert and black as
the history of these parts.

At midnight Stepan Fyodorovich, the younger of the
restorers, stopped Katerina on the stairs to the attic floor,
touched her shoulders, solid as a horse's, felt them with a
drunken hand, and said quietly:

"Pass the word on to your . . . sisters. . . . We'll do it
again. Find a place, tell them. . . ."

Katerina stood submissively and submissively whispered:
"All right, I'll tell them."

Below at that very moment Yakov Karpovich was ex-
pounding his theories of civilization for the benefit of Pavel
Fyodorovich. On a round table in the parlor stood a frigate
of bronze and glass intended to hold alcohol, which, poured
from the little tap into wineglasses, and from wineglasses
down men's throats, would enable them to sail in this
frigate from fancy to fancy. The frigate was an eighteenth-
century piece. The frigate was filled with brandy. Pavel
Fyodorovich sat in silence. Yakov Karpovich fussed around
Pavel Fyodorovich, hopping up and down like a lovesick
pigeon, supporting his hernia through his fly.

"Yes, k'he," he said. "What do you think, then, keeps
the world moving, what moves civilization, science, steam-
ships? Well, what?"

"Well, what?" Pavel Fyodorovich repeated the question.

"What do you think it is? Labor? Knowledge? Hunger?
Love? No! Civilization is moved—by memory! Just picture
to yourself—tomorrow morning everybody loses his memory

—instinct, reason remain, but memory is gone. I wake up in bed—and I fall out of bed, because it's through memory that I know about space, and once memory's gone, I don't know about it. My pants are lying on the chair, I'm cold, but I don't know what to do with the pants. I don't know how to walk—on my hands or on all fours, I don't remember the day before, and so that means I'm not afraid of death, for I know nothing about it. The engineer forgets all his higher mathematics, all streetcars and locomotives have come to a standstill. Priests can't find their way to church, and what's more, they don't remember anything about Jesus Christ. Yes, k'he! . . . I still have my instincts—though you might say they're a kind of memory too; but let's suppose I have them: I don't know what I should eat, the chair or the bread left on it from the night before, and when I see a woman, I might take my daughter for my wife."

The northeaster which filled the sails of the alcohol frigate on the table affirmed Yakov Karpovich's thoughts: in company with the frigate the eighteenth century had left behind among the parlor's mahogany a Russian Voltaire. Beyond the windows of the eighteenth century moved a Soviet provincial night.

Another hour and the Skudrin house was asleep. And then in the sour silence of the bedroom Yakov Karpovich's slippers flip-flapped toward Mariya Klimovna's bed. Mariya Klimovna, an ancient woman, was sleeping. The candle trembled in Yakov Karpovich's hand. Yakov Karpovich tittered. Yakov Karpovich touched Mariya Klimovna's parchment shoulder, his eyes watered with pleasure. He whispered:

"Maryushka, Maryushka, this is life, this is life, Maryushka."

The eighteenth century sank into Voltairian darkness.

In the morning bells were dying over the city, howling as they shattered. The brothers Bezdetov woke up early, but Mariya Klimovna had got up even earlier, and with morning tea there were hot mushroom and onion piroshki. Yakov Karpovich slept. Katerina was half-asleep. Tea was drunk in silence. Day came gray and slow. After tea the brothers Bezdetov went about their business. On a piece of paper Pavel Fyodorovich had drawn up a list of houses and families they were to visit. The streets lay in the silence of provincial cobblestones, stone walls, tall weeds under the walls, elders among ruins left by the fire, churches, church towers—and sank even deeper into silence when the bells began to whine; their silence became a scream when the bells bellowed in their fall.

The Bezdetovs would enter a house silently, side by side, and look around them with vacant eyes.

1. On Staraya Rostovskaya Street stood a lopsided house. In this house the widow Myshkina was ending her days; the widow was an old woman of seventy. The house stood with one corner to the street, because it had been built before the street came into existence; the house had been built not of sawed, but of hewn wood, because it was put up before Russian carpenters used saws and when the axe was their only tool—before Peter's time, that is. In those days the house might have been a boyar's. The house preserved a tiled stove and stove ledge dating back to that time; the tiles were decorated with sheep and boyars, and were ochered and glazed.

The Bezdetovs walked in through the gate without knocking. The old woman Myshkina was sitting on the *zavalinka*[15] in front of a pig trough; a pig was eating scalded nettles. The Bezdetovs bowed to the old woman, and sat down beside her without a word. The old woman responded to the greeting, flustered, pleased, frightened. She was wearing torn felt boots, a cotton skirt, and a bright Persian shawl.

"Well, are you selling?" asked Pavel Bezdetov.

The old woman hid her hands under the shawl, lowered her eyes to the pig. Pavel Fyodorovich and Stepan Fyodorovich exchanged a look, and Stepan winked—she'll sell.

[15] An earthen ledge—part of the foundations—surrounding small Russian houses. In village life it has the function of the "front stoop" (Editors).

With her bony hand, lilac-nailed, the old woman wiped the corners of her mouth, and her hand trembled.

"I just don't know what's to be done," said the old woman, and glanced guiltily at the brothers. "Our grandfathers lived here and left it to us, and their fathers before them, and further back than anyone can remember. . . . And when my lodger died—God rest his soul—things just got too much for me; he did pay me three rubles a month for the room and buy kerosene—I didn't lack for anything. . . . And you know, my father and mother both died on that stove ledge. . . . What's to be done? . . . God rest his soul, the lodger was a quiet one, he paid three rubles, and died in my arms. . . . I've thought and thought, how many nights I haven't slept—you've upset my peace of mind."

Pavel Fyodorovich spoke.

"There are a hundred and twenty tiles on the stove and on the stove ledge. Twenty-five kopecks a tile, as we said before. And that makes thirty rubles for you all at once. That'll last you the rest of your life. We'll send the stove-setter, he'll take them out and put bricks in their place, and give them a coat of whitewash. And all at our expense."

"I'm not saying anything about the price," said the old woman. "It's a rich price you're giving. Nobody around here would give such a price. . . . And who needs them but me anyway? If only it wasn't for my parents. . . . I'm all alone. . . ."

The old woman was lost in her thoughts. She thought for a long time—or was she thinking at all? Her eyes became unseeing, sank deep into their sockets. The pig had finished its nettles, and was poking its snout at one of the old woman's felt boots. The brothers Bezdetov were looking at the old woman, businesslike and stern. Again the old woman wiped the corners of her lips with a trembling hand. Then she smiled guiltily, glanced guiltily around her—at the leaning fences of the yard and the vegetable garden—lowered her eyes guiltily before the Bezdetovs.

"So be it then, and God's blessing on you!" said the old

woman, and held out her hand to Pavel Fyodorovich—awkwardly and shyly, but as time-honored trading custom required—passing the tiles from hand to hand.

2. In the cathedral square in the semibasement of what had been their own house lived a family of landed gentry —the Tuchkovs. Their former estate had been turned into a dairy. In this basement lived two adults and six children; there were two women—old Tuchkova and her daughter-in-law, whose husband, a former officer, had shot himself in 1925, as death from tuberculosis drew near. The old colonel had been killed in 1915 in the Carpathians. Four of the children were Olga Pavlovna's, as the daughter-in-law was called; the other two were the children of the younger Tuchkov, who had been shot for counterrevolutionary activities. Olga Pavlovna was the breadwinner; in the evenings she played the piano in the cinema. At thirty she looked like an old woman.

The basement was unlocked, as are all poverty-stricken dwellings, when the brothers Bezdetov arrived. They were met by Olga Pavlovna. She nodded several times, inviting them to come in; she ran ahead of them into what was known as the dining room, to cover the bed so that the strangers would not see that there was no bed linen under the blanket. Olga Pavlovna glanced at herself in the triple mirror on a mahogany dressing table in the Empire style of Alexander's time. The brothers were businesslike and brisk. Stepan turned chairs upside down, pushed the sofa away from the wall, lifted the mattress from the bed, pulled out the drawers of the commode—examining mahogany. Pavel went through the miniatures, beadwork, and porcelain. The young old woman, Olga Pavlovna, still had a girl's lightness of movement and the ability to be embarrassed. The restorers wreaked silent havoc on the rooms, dragging dirt and poverty out of every corner. The six children clung to the mother's skirts, curious about these strange goings on; the two eldest were ready to help with the work of devastation. The mother was embarrassed for the children; the younger ones were sniveling as they held on to her skirt, distracting their mother from embarrassment.

Stepan set aside three chairs and an armchair, and he said:

"These are odd pieces, not a set."

"What did you say?" Olga Pavlovna asked, and turning to the children, cried helplessly, "Children, please leave the room! This is no place for you, I beg of you. . . ."

"These are odd pieces, not a set," said Stepan Fyodorovich. "There are three chairs, but only one armchair. The pieces are good, I don't deny it, but they'll need a lot of repairing. You see yourself—you live in a damp place. You'll have to get a complete set together."

The children quieted down as soon as the restorer began to speak.

"Yes," said Olga Pavlovna, and blushed, "we did have it all—but I doubt if it could be got together now. Some of it remained on the estate when we left, some was carried off by peasants, some was broken by the children, and, then again, there's the damp—I carried to the barn . . ."

"I suppose they gave you twenty-four hours to get out?" asked Stepan Fyodorovich.

"Yes, we left at night, without waiting for an order. We foresaw . . ."

Pavel Fyodorovich joined in the conversation; he asked Olga Pavlovna:

"You understand French and English?"

"Oh, yes," answered Olga Pavlovna, "I speak . . ."

"These miniatures wouldn't be—Boucher and Cosway?"

"Oh, yes! Those miniatures . . ."

Pavel Fyodorovich said, glancing at his brother:

"We can give you twenty-five each."

Stepan Fyodorovich interrupted his brother sternly:

"If you get together even half a set, I'll buy everything. If, as you say, the peasants have some of it, you could go to them."

"Oh, yes!" replied Olga Pavlovna. "If half a set . . . It's thirteen versts to our village—not much more than an easy walk. . . . Half a set can be got together. I'll go to the village today, and give you an answer tomorrow. But some of the pieces are broken. . . ."

"That doesn't matter, we'll reduce the price. And don't

bother with an answer, bring the things direct, so that we can receive everything from you tomorrow and have it packed. Sofas—fifteen rubles; armchairs—seven and a half; chairs—five each. We'll take care of the packing."

"Oh, yes, I'll go today; it's only thirteen versts to our village—not much more than an easy walk. . . . I'll go right away."

The eldest boy said:

"Then you'll buy me shoes, *Maman?*"

Beyond the windows was a gray day, beyond the town lay the country roads of Russia.

3. *Barin* Vyacheslav Pavlovich Karazin was lying on the sofa in the dining room, with a squirrelskin jacket, worn almost bald, thrown over him. His dining room, like the study-bedroom which he shared with his wife, had the appearance of a museum squeezed into the lodgings of a mail-coach driver. The brothers Bezdetov halted at the threshold and bowed. *Barin* Karazin subjected them to a lengthy scrutiny, barked:

"Out, s-swindlers! Out of here!"

The brothers did not move.

Blood rushed to *Barin* Karazin's face, and he barked again:

"Out of my sight, you scoundrels!"

The shouts brought his wife into the room. The brothers Bezdetov bowed to Karazina and retreated behind the door.

"Nadine, I can't stand the sight of those blackguards," said *Barin* Karazin to his wife.

"Very well, Vyacheslav, you go to the study, I'll talk to them. Oh, Vyacheslav, you know how things are!" replied *Barynya* Karazina.

"They have disturbed my rest. Very well, I'll go to the study. Only please, no familiarities with those serfs."

Barin Karazin left the room, trailing his jacket behind him; the brothers Bezdetov entered the room in his wake, and again bowed respectfully.

"Show us your Russian Gobelins, and also tell us the price of the small bureau," said Pavel Fyodorovich.

"Won't you sit down, gentlemen," said *Barynya* Karazina.

The door of the study flew open, the *Barin's* head thrust itself out. *Barin* Karazin shouted, looking to one side, at the windows, lest his eyes should accidentally fall on the brothers Bezdetov:

"Nadine, don't allow them to sit down! What can they understand of the beauties of art! Don't allow them to choose! Sell them those things which we find necessary to sell. Sell them the porcelain, the porcelain clock, and the bronze! . . ."

"We can go, if you want," said Pavel Fyodorovich.

"Oh, just a moment, gentlemen; let Vyacheslav Pavlovich calm down, he's very sick," said *Barynya* Karazina, and sat down helplessly at the table. "We do have to sell a few things. Oh, gentlemen! . . . Vyacheslav Pavlovich, I beg of you, shut the door, don't listen to us—go for a walk. . . ."

4–5–7–

Toward evening, after the jackdaws had torn the day to pieces and the bells had ceased howling, the brothers Bezdetov returned home and had their dinner. After dinner Yakov Karpovich Skudrin got ready to sally forth. In his pockets were money and a list provided by the Bezdetovs. The old man put on a wide-brimmed felt hat and a short sheepskin coat; on his feet were the remains of a pair of boots. He was on his way to the carpenter's, to the drayman's for ropes and matting—to make arrangements to have the purchases packed and taken to the wharf for shipment to Moscow. The old man was in his element; as he left he said:

"What we should do is leave the carrying and packing to the *okhlomons;* they're as honest as you'll find, even if they are idiots. But it can't be done. Dear Brother Ivan, their number-one revolutionary, wouldn't allow it—he wouldn't let them work for the Counterrevolution, hee-hee! . . ."

The brothers Bezdetov settled down in the parlor to rest. And the earth settled down for the night. All evening people kept knocking stealthily at Mariya Klimovna's windows; Katerina went out to them, and people, fawning like beggars, offered—"They say you have guests staying with you who buy all sorts of old things"—ancient rubles and kopecks, broken lamps, old samovars, books, candlesticks; these people did not understand the art of the old days—they were poverty-stricken in every respect. Katerina did not let them into the guests' presence with their copper lamps, suggesting that they leave the things until the morning when the guests, having rested, would take a look. The evening was dark. At sunset a wind rose, bringing clouds; a fine rain, immutably autumnal, began to fall; through the forest, through the mud of country roads (the same mud in which Akim Skudrin was soon to get stuck), walked Olga Pavlovna, a woman with an old woman's face and movements as light as a young girl's. The forest moaned in the wind, in the forest it was terrifying. This woman, with a young girl's terror of the forest, was walking to her village to buy from the peasants armchairs for which peasants could have no use.

About eight o'clock in the evening Katerina got her mother's leave to go, first to choir practice and then to a friend's; she put on her best clothes and left. Half an hour later Stepan and Pavel, the two Fyodoroviches, went out into the rain. Katerina was waiting for them on the other side of the bridge. Stepan Fyodorovich took Katerina's arm. In pitch darkness they set off along a path which followed the edge of a ravine, toward the outskirts of the town. That was where the old Skudrin aunts lived. Katerina and the Bezdetovs sneaked like thieves into the yard, and from there, like thieves, into the garden. At the far end of the garden stood a dark bathhouse.

Katerina knocked, and the door half opened. There was a light inside the bathhouse; three girls were waiting for the guests. The girls had blanketed the windows and moved a table to the steps leading to the steam shelf. The girls were wearing their Sunday best; they greeted the guests solemnly.

The brothers Bezdetov took out from their pockets bot-

tles of brandy and port, which they had brought from
Moscow.

The girls set out on the table—on paper—boiled sausage,
sprats, candy, tomatoes, and apples. The oldest of the girls
—Klavdia—brought out a bottle of vodka from behind the
stove. They all talked in whispers. The brothers Bezdetov
sat down side by side on the steps to the steam shelf. On
the shelf a tin lamp burned.

In an hour the girls were drunk—but still they talked in
whispers. The faces of drunken people, and women in
particular—when they are very drunk—become set in expressions which are the creation of alcohol. Klavdia was
sitting at the table, propping her head with a fist, like a
man, her teeth bared, her lips frozen in an expression of
contempt; from time to time her head would slip off her
fist, and then she would pull at her cropped hair, without
feeling any pain; she was smoking one cigarette after another and drinking brandy; her face glowed pink and she
was hideously beautiful. She was saying with disgust:

"Drunk, am I? Yes, I am. So what? Tomorrow I'll go to
school again and teach—and what do I know? What is it I
teach? And at six I'll go to a parents' meeting I called.
Here's my notebook, everything's written down here. . . .
I'm drinking—oh, what the hell!—and here I am drunk.
And what are you? What have you to do with me? You buy
mahogany? Antiques? You want to buy us, too, with your
wine? You think I don't know what life is? You're wrong,
I do—I'm going to have a baby soon, but who the father is
I don't know. . . . So what—so what?"

Klavdia's teeth were bared and her eyes staring. Pavel
kept teasing Zina, the youngest, a short-legged, giggly girl
with a head of blond curls; she was sitting on a block of
wood, a little apart from the rest, legs spread wide, hands
on hips. Pavel Fyodorovich was saying:

"I bet you won't take your blouse off, Zina, I bet you
won't undo your brassière, you wouldn't dare!"

Zina clapped her hand over her mouth so as not to burst
out laughing, burst out laughing, and said:

"Oh, yes, I will!"

"No, you won't! You wouldn't dare!"

Klavdia said contemptuously:

"She will. Zinka, show them your breasts! Let them look. Want to see mine? You think I'm a drunk? No, the last time I was drunk was when you were here before. And I came today to get blind drunk—blind drunk, you understand? Blind drunk! . . . What the hell! . . . Zinka, show them your breasts! Don't you show your Kolya? . . . Want to see mine?"

Klavdia yanked at the collar of her blouse. The girls rushed up to her. Katerina said sensibly:

"You mustn't tear your clothes, Klava, or they'll know at home."

Zina was barely able to stand; she embraced Klavdia, grasping her hands. Klavdia kissed Zina.

"I mustn't?" she asked. "Well, all right, I won't. . . . But you show them. . . . Let them look; we're not ashamed, we don't hold to old-fashioned ideas! . . . You buy mahogany?"

"All right, I'll show them," Zina said meekly, and set about unbuttoning her blouse.

The fourth girl went outside; she felt sick. Of course the Bezdetovs felt themselves to be buyers; buying was all they knew.

Outside the bathhouse it was raining, the trees rustled in the wind. At that hour Olga Pavlovna had already reached her village, and, happy and grateful to Grandpa Nazar for selling her some chairs and an armchair, was falling asleep on a bed of straw on the floor of Nazar's hut. At that hour *Barin* Karazin was writhing in a fit of senile hysteria. At that hour the *okhlomons* in their kiln pit were affirming with the eyes and voices of madmen the year nineteen hundred and nineteen, when everything was shared equally —both bread and labor—when nothing lay behind them, and ideas lay before them, and there was no money, because it was not needed. And in another hour the bathhouse was empty. The drunken women and the brothers Bezdetov had all gone home; the drunken girls were creeping to their beds. A notebook had been left lying on the floor in the bathhouse. In the notebook was written, "Call parents' meeting at six o'clock on the seventh. At meeting of Local Committee suggest everyone subscribe to government industrialization loan to amount of month's salary. Suggest Aleksandr Alekseyevich reread *ABC of Communism.*"

In the morning the bells were whining again, and in the morning cartloads of mahogany—Catherines, Pauls, Alexanders—were being dragged toward the wharf under Yakov Karpovich's supervision. The brothers Bezdetov slept until noon. By that hour a crowd waiting to know the fate of their old rubles, lamps, and candlesticks had collected in the kitchen.

The town is a Russian Bruges.

Chapter Four

. . . And it was about this time, two days after the brothers Bezdetov, that the engineer Akim Skudrin, the youngest son of Yakov Karpovich, arrived in the town. The son did not go to his father's house, staying with his aunts Kapitolina and Rimma. The engineer Akim was not in town on business, he had a week free.

. . . Kapitolina Karpovna goes to the window. The provinces. A crumbling red brick wall abuts on one corner an ochered house with a belvedere, on the other a church; beyond—the square, the town scales, another church. It is raining. A pig is sniffing at a puddle. A watercart comes around the corner. Klavdia goes out the gate; she is wearing greased boots, a black coat reaching to the tops of the boots, a blue kerchief on her head; she lowers her head, crosses the street, walks along the crumbling wall, turns the corner into the square. Kapitolina Karpovna's eyes are bright, she watches Klavdia for a long time. On the other side of the partition Rimma Karpovna is feeding her grandchild, the daughter of her elder girl Varvara. The room is very bare, very clean, very neat—nothing has changed for decades—as the room of an old maid, an elderly virgin, should be: a narrow bed, a small worktable, a sewing machine, a dressmaker's dummy, curtains. Kapitolina Karpovna goes to the dining room.

"Let me feed the baby, Rimmochka. I saw Klavdia leave. Did Varya leave too?"

These two old women, the two Karpovnas, Kapitolina and Rimma, were seamstresses and dressmakers, hereditary members of the lower middle classes and of an honored, well-established family. Their lives were as simple as the lifelines on the palms of their left hands. The sisters were born within a year of each other; Kapitolina was the elder. And Kapitolina's life was filled with the dignity of middle-class morality. Her whole life had been laid open before the town's eye and lived in full compliance with the town's rules. She was a respected member of the middle class. And not only the whole town, but she herself, knew that all her Saturday evenings were spent in church, that all her days were bent over the hemstitching and openwork of blouses and shifts—thousands of shifts—that not once had any man outside the family kissed her; and only she knew the thoughts, the pain of life's soured wine, that wither the heart; and yet her life had had its budding, its bloom, its Indian summer; and not once in her life had she been loved, had she known secret sins. She remained a model of obedience to the town's code, a virgin, an old woman who had soured her life with chastity, God, tradition. But the life of Rimma Karpovna, also a seamstress, had taken a different course. It had happened twenty-eight years before, it had gone on for three years—three years of shame, shame which was to remain with her throughout her life. It had happened at a time when Rimma's years were sinking beyond thirty—years which had taken away her youth and sown hopelessness. In the town lived a Treasury official, an amateur actor, handsome, and a swine. He was married, he had children, he was a drunkard. Rimma fell in love with him, and Rimma could not resist her love. Everything about it was shameful. In this love there was everything that shames a woman in the eyes of small-town morality, and everything went wrong. All around were woods where the secret could have been kept—she gave herself to this man one night in one of the town's little parks; she was ashamed to take home her torn, blood-stained (sacred blood, in truth) drawers—she stuck them in the bushes, and the next morning they were pulled out by some boys for all to see; and not once in all the three years of her shame did she meet her lover under a roof, meeting him in the woods and in the streets, in the ruins of houses, in deserted barges, even in fall and winter. Her brother, Yakov Karpovich, disowned her and drove her out of the house—even Kapitolina turned against her sister. In the streets people pointed fingers at her and cut her. The Treasury actor's lawful wife went to give Rimma a beating, and egged on the local roughs to beat her as well; and the town and its code were on the side of the lawful wife. Rimma gave birth to a daughter, Varvara, a witness to her shame and an embodiment of it. Rimma gave birth to a second girl, Klavdia, and Klavdia was a second witness to her shame. The Treasury amateur left town. Rimma remained alone with two children, in desperate poverty and shame, a woman then well past thirty. And since that time almost thirty more years have passed. Varvara, the elder daughter, is married, happily married, and already has two children. Rimma Karpovna has two grandchildren. Varvara's husband is in government service. So is Varvara. Rimma Karpovna runs a large household; she is the founder of a family. And Rimma Karpovna—a kindly old woman—is happy in her life. Old age has made her shorter, happiness has made her plump. How kind and how full of life are the eyes of this plump little old woman. And only one thing concerns Kapitolina Karpovna now: the lives of Rimma, Varvara, Klavdia, the grandchildren; her chastity, her town-wide reputation for uprightness, have turned out to be for nothing. Kapitolina Karpovna has no life of her own.

Kapitolina Karpovna is saying:

"Let me feed the baby, Rimmochka. I saw Klava leave. Did Varya leave too?"

Outside—the provinces, fall, rain. And then in the hall
the door pulley squeaks, a man's boots stamp the floor to
shake off wet and mud—and into the room walks a man,
looking around helplessly in the way that all nearsighted
people do when they take off their glasses. It is Akim
Yakovlevich Skudrin, the engineer, the image of his father
fifty years before. He has come—no one knows why.

"My respects to you, dear aunts!" says Akim, and kisses
Aunt Rimma first.

The provinces, rain, fall, the traditional samovar.

Engineer Akim was not in town on business. His aunts
welcomed him with the samovar, hurriedly prepared
lepyoshkas[16] and that warm hospitality found in the Russian provinces. Akim did not go to see his father or his
superiors. Dying bells whined over the town, the streets
were sound under their covering of camomile. Akim stayed
a day and a night, and left, having established that he
had no use for his birthplace; the town did not accept
him. The day passed with his aunts, in the roamings of
memory through time, in the futility of memory, in the
desperate poverty of his aunts, of their concerns, their
thoughts, their longings. Things in the house were as they
had been twenty, twenty-five years before, and the dressmaker's dummy, which had been terrifying in his childhood, no longer frightened. At dusk Klavdia came home
from school. They sat down together on the sofa, cousins,
ten years between them.

"How's life?" asked Akim.

They talked about this and that, and then Klavdia spoke
of what was most important to her; she spoke very simply.
She was very beautiful and very calm. Dusk lingered and
deepened.

"I want to ask your advice," said Klavdia. "I'm going to
have a baby. I don't know what I ought to do; I don't
know who the father is."

"What do you mean, you don't know who the father is?"

"I'm twenty-four," said Klavdia. "Last spring I decided
it was time I became a woman, and I became one."

[16] A round, flat cake, fried or baked (Editors).

"But you have someone you love?"

"No, I don't. There were several. I was curious. I did it out of curiosity, and after all—it was time, I'm twenty-four."

Akim was at a loss what else to ask.

"I was concerned not with love for someone else, but with myself and my own emotions. I chose men, different kinds of men, so as to experience everything. I didn't want to get pregnant; sex is joy, and I didn't think about a baby. But I did get pregnant, and I've decided not to have an abortion."

"And you don't know who the man is?"

"I can't say for sure. But it's of no importance to me. I'm the mother. I'll manage, and the state will help me; as for morality . . . I don't know what morality is, I've been taught not to know. Or perhaps I have my own morality. I answer only for myself and of myself. Why is it immoral to give myself to a man? I do what I want to do, and I'm under no obligation to anyone. The man? I don't want to tie him in any way; men are fine, but only when I need them and when they're not burdened with responsibility. I don't need a man in bedroom slippers, and I don't need a man to give birth. People will help me—I believe in people. People like you, if you have pride and aren't a burden to them. And the state will help. I slept with men I liked, because I wanted to. I'll have a son or a daughter. I'm not sleeping with anyone now, I don't need it. Yesterday I got drunk, for the last time. I'm telling you this as it comes into my head. I'm disgusted with myself for getting drunk yesterday. But perhaps the child will need a father. You left your father, and I was born without a father and never heard anything except filth about him; when I was a child this hurt me and I used to get angry with my mother. Still, I've decided not to have an abortion, the child fills my being. It's an even greater joy than . . . I'm young and strong."

Akim was unable to collect his thoughts. On the floor in front of him lay rag runners, the pathways of poverty

and meanness of spirit. Klavdia was calm, beautiful, strong
—very healthy and very beautiful. It was drizzling outside the windows. The Communist Akim wanted to hear
that a new way of life was coming; the old way of life
was rooted in the ages. But Klavdia's morality was both
new and strange to him; but could it be right, if Klavdia
saw it that way?

Akim said:

"Have the child."

Klavdia cuddled up to him, laid her head on his shoulder, tucked her feet up under her, became soft and helpless.

"I'm very physical," she said. "I like to eat, I like to
wash, I like to do exercises, I like it when Sharik, our dog,
licks my hands and feet. I enjoy scratching my knees
until the blood comes. . . . But life—it's big, it's all around
me, I can't make any sense of it, I can't make any sense of
the Revolution—but I believe in them, in life, in the sun,
in the Revolution, and I'm at peace with myself. I understand only what touches me. As for the rest, I'm not even
interested."

A tomcat walked along the runner to the sofa and made
his customary leap onto Klavdia's lap. Outside the windows it had grown dark. On the other side of the partition
a lamp was lit and the sewing machine began to stitch.
Peace had entered the darkness.

In the evening Akim went to see his Uncle Ivan, who
had changed his name from Skudrin to Ozhogov. *Okhlomon* Ozhogov came out of the kiln to greet his nephew.
The earth around brickyards is dug up and the roofs of
brick sheds are long and low—and because of this brickyards always look like places of ruin and mystery. The
okhlomon was drunk. It was impossible to talk with him,
but he was very pleased, very happy, that his nephew had
come to see him. The *okhlomon* could hardly stand up, and
trembled like a dog.

The *okhlomon* led his nephew into the brick shed.

"You've come, you've come," he whispered, pressing his
trembling hands to his trembling chest.

He turned a wheelbarrow upside down and made his nephew sit on it.

"Have they thrown you out?" he asked eagerly.

"Out of where?" asked Akim.

"Out of the Party," said Ivan Karpovich.

"No."

"No? They haven't thrown you out?" Ivan asked again, and sadness came into his voice—but he finished cheerfully, "Well, if they don't throw you out now, they will later; they'll throw out all the Leninists and Trotskyites!"

Here Ivan Karpovich fell into delirium; in his delirium he talked about his commune, how he had been the first chairman of the Executive Committee—what years they had been and how they were lost, those stormy years; how he had been driven out of the Revolution, and now went among the people to make them weep, and remember, and love—and again he talked about his commune, about the equality and brotherhood there; he insisted that Communism was, above all, love, the intense concern of man for man, friendship, brotherhood, shared labor; Communism was the renunciation of material things, and what mattered most in true Communism was love, respect for human beings, and—people. The neat little old man trembled in the wind, running his bony fingers, which were also trembling, over the lapels of his jacket. The brickyard spoke of ruin. Akim Skudrin, the engineer, was flesh of Ivan Ozhogov's flesh. . . . Paupers, beggars, soothsayers, mendicant chanters, lazars, wanderers from holy place to holy place, cripples, blind psalm singers, prophets, fools in Christ—all these are the double-ring sugar cakes of the everyday life of Holy Russia, now sunk into eternity— paupers on the face of Holy Russia, fools of Holy Russia for Christ's sake. These sugar cakes were the adornment of everyday life, Christ's own, intercessors for the world. Before the engineer Akim stood a pauper and beggar, a lazar and fool in Christ—a fool of Soviet Russia for Justice's sake, an intercessor for the world and for Communism. Uncle Ivan must have been a schizophrenic; he had his own par-

ticular obsession: he walked the town, he went to the
houses of acquaintances and strangers, and he implored
them to weep; he delivered fiery and insane speeches
about Communism, and in the street markets his speeches
made many people cry; he made the rounds of government offices, and it was rumored in town that at such
times certain important personages rubbed their eyes with
onion in order to gain, through the *okhlomons,* some much-
needed popularity. Ivan was afraid of churches, and he
cursed the priests, not afraid of them. Ivan's slogans were
the most leftist in the town. In the town Ivan was revered
as the people of Russia have learned over the centuries to
revere fools in Christ, through the mouths of whom Truth
makes itself known to men, and who for Truth's sake are
willing to go to their deaths. Ivan drank, destroying himself with alcohol. He gathered around him men like himself, cast out by the Revolution which had created them.
They found a place for themselves in the underground
cave; they lived in true Communism, brotherhood, equality, friendship—and each one of them had his own madness: the obsession of one was to correspond with the
proletarians on Mars; a second proposed that all fully
grown fish in the Volga be caught and that iron bridges
be built over the Volga, paid for by the sale of the fish;
a third dreamed of laying streetcar lines in the town.

"Weep!" said Ivan.

Akim, tearing himself from his thoughts, did not understand Ivan at first.

"What did you say?" he asked.

"Weep, Akim, weep, this very minute, for Communism
lost!" shouted Ivan, and pressed his hands to his chest,
bowing his head as people do in prayer.

"Yes, yes, I am weeping, Uncle Ivan," Akim replied.

Akim was strong, tall, massive. He stood up next to
Ivan. Akim kissed his uncle.

The rain beat down. The darkness of the brickyard
spoke of ruin.

.   .   .   .

Akim was making his way back through town from tne *okhlomons* by way of the market place. In a solitary window a light was burning. This was the house of the town eccentric, the museum curator. Akim went up to the window—in times past he and the curator had together rummaged around in the kremlin cellars. He was about to knock, but he saw something strange, and did not knock. The room was piled with surplices, stoles, chasubles, cassocks. In the middle of the room sat two men: the curator poured a glass of vodka from a huge bottle and lifted it to the lips of a naked man; the man did not move a muscle. On the head of the naked man was a crown. And then Akim realized that the curator was drinking vodka in solitude with a wooden statue of a seated Christ. The Christ was carved of wood and was life-size. Akim remembered —as a boy he had seen this Christ in the Divny Monastery; the Christ was seventeenth-century work. The curator was drinking vodka with Christ, lifting glass after glass to the lips of the wooden Christ. The curator had unbuttoned his Pushkin-style frock coat, his side whiskers were tousled. The naked Christ with his crown of thorns seemed alive to Akim.

Late that night Akim's mother, Mariya Klimovna, came to see him. The aunts left the room. His mother had come in a plain house dress; she had thrown a shawl over her shoulders and come running. She wore a pair of spectacles—held together with thread—to have a better look at her son. And the mother was solemn, as at Communion. The mother embraced her son, pressing her withered breast to her son's breast; the mother ran her bony fingers through her son's hair, the mother pressed her head to her son's neck. The mother did not even weep. She was very grave. Not trusting her eyes, she felt her son with her fingers. And she blessed him.

"You won't come, you won't come to see us, son?" the mother asked.

Her son did not reply.

"And me—what have I lived my life for then?"

The son knew that his father would give his mother a

beating if he found out that she had been to see her son. The son knew that his mother sat long hours in the dark, while his father slept, and thought of him, her son. The son knew that his mother would keep nothing from him and would tell him nothing new—nothing—and the old was accursed, but she was his mother—his mother!—all that is most rare, most wonderful, most beautiful, his mother, a saint, a martyr, a part of him by everything she had lived through. And the son did not reply to his mother, said nothing to his mother.

. . . .

Next morning the engineer Akim left. The steamer did not leave until evening; he decided to go fifty versts by carriage to catch the night train. A tarantass and a pair of bays were brought up. The day was changeable—rain one minute, sun and blue sky the next. They took the Moscow road. Mud came up to the wheelboxes and the horses' hocks. They rode through thick forests; the forests stood gloomy, wet, silent. The driver, old and taciturn, was perched on the box. The horses went at a walk. Halfway, when Akim was already beginning to worry that he might miss the train, they stopped to feed the horses. In the cooperative tearoom they were told that vodka was not sold there, but they managed to get some from the stiller across the street, the secretary of the village soviet. The driver had a bit too much to drink and began to talk. Tediously he told the story of his life—how he had worked for thirty years, as he put it, in meat, but gave it up when the Revolution came, being no longer needed. When the driver was thoroughly drunk he began to wonder at the ways of authority. "Well, there you are, that's how things go, God help us—I was in meat for thirty years and this commissar came and did it all in three weeks, and three weeks later he got rid of my brother, who was in flour, and my brother had been in the business thirty years, like me!" And there was no telling whether the driver spoke in bewilderment or in derision. They fed the horses, set off, again were silent.

The engineer Akim was a Trotskyite; his faction had been crushed. His birthplace, his town—it was clear to him now—was no longer of any use to him; he had set aside this week for thought. He should have been thinking about the fate of the Revolution and of his Party, of his own fate as a revolutionary—but these thoughts would not come. He looked at the forests—and thought of forests, wilderness, marshes. He looked at the sky—and thought of sky, clouds, space. The horses' ribs had long been covered with foam; the horses' bellies heaved in labored breathing. The road was deep in mud; lakes had formed in the road—for the simple reason that a road was there. Dusk was already falling. The forest was mute. Thoughts of forests, of country roads, stretching for thousands of versts, led Akim to thoughts of his aunts Kapitolina and Rimma—and for the thousandth time Akim justified the Revolution. Aunt Kapitolina had led what was known as an upright life— not a single sin in the eyes of the town, not a single transgression against town morality; and her life had turned out to be empty and of no use to anyone. In Aunt Rimma's passport there would always be written, as would have been written in the passport of the Virgin Mary had she lived in Russia before the Revolution, "Spinster—has two children"; Rimma's children had been her shame and her grief. But her grief had become her happiness, her dignity; her life was full, fulfilled; she, Aunt Rimma, was happy, and Aunt Kapitolina lived on her sister's happiness, having no life of her own. One must be afraid of nothing, one must be doing; every deed, even a bitter one, can be a happiness, but nothing—remains nothing. And Klavdia— wasn't she happier than her mother? She didn't know who the father of her child was; her mother knew she had loved a scoundrel. Akim's father came to his mind: it would have been better never to have known him! And Akim suddenly became aware that his thoughts about his father, Klavdia, his aunts, were really thoughts not about them, but about the Revolution. And for him the Revolution was the beginning of life, and life itself—and the end of life.

The forests and roads darkened. They came out into open country. The west had long been dying, the red sunset its mortal wound. They drove through fields—fields the same as they had been five hundred years before—entered a village, dragged through the mud of its seventeenth century. Beyond the village the road dipped into a ravine; they crossed a bridge; on the other side of the bridge was a pool that proved to be impassable. They drove into the pool. The horses lurched and came to a halt. The driver struck the horses with his whip—the horses pulled, but did not budge. All around was deep mud, the tarantass was sinking deeper and deeper in the middle of the pool—up to the linchpin of the left front wheel. The driver braced himself on the box and booted the shaft horse in the rump—the horse jerked and fell on top of the shaft, then sank up to its collar into the mire. The driver lashed the horses until he realized that the shaft horse could not get up; then he waded into the mud to unharness the horse. He took a step and sank knee-deep into the mud; he took another—and he was stuck; he could not pull his feet up, his feet came out of his boots, his boots were left in the mud. The old man lost his balance, and sat down in the pool. And the old man burst into tears —bitter, hysterical, helpless tears of rage and despair—this man, this specialist in the slaughter of cows and bulls.

The Trotskyite Akim missed the train, as he had missed the train of time.

Chapter Five

The art of mahogany was an anonymous art, an art of the useful. Master craftsmen drank themselves to death, but the things they had made were left behind, and lived; in their presence people loved and died, to them they entrusted secrets of griefs, loves, business affairs, joys. Elizabeth, Catherine—rococo, baroque. Paul is a Knight of Malta, Paul is severe—severe repose, dark-polished mahogany, green leather, black lions, griffins. Alexander—Empire, classic lines, Hellas. People die, but things live on; ancient things give forth "effluences" of bygone days, of epochs dead and gone. In 1928—in Moscow, in Leningrad, in provincial capitals—antique shops appeared, where bygone days were bought and sold by pawnbrokers, by the State Export and Import Office, by the State Museum Fund,[17] by museums; in 1928 there were many people who collected "effluences." People who bought ancient things after the thunders of the Revolution, indulging their passion for bygone days in the privacy of their own houses, breathed in the living essence of dead things. And Paul, the Knight of Malta—straight and severe, without bronze and scrolls—was held in high esteem.

The brothers Bezdetov lived in Moscow on Vladimiro-Dolgorukovskaya Street, on the Zhivodyorka,[18] as Vladimiro-Dolgorukovskaya Street used to be called in the old days. They were antiquarians, restorers—and of course they were queer fish. Such people are always solitaries, and they are silent. They take pride in their work, like philosophers. The brothers Bezdetov lived in a cellar; they were queer fish. They restored Pauls, Catherines, Alexanders, Nicholases—and they were visited by queer-fish collectors, who came to look at bygone days, at workmanship, to talk about bygone days and craftsmanship, to breathe in bygone days, to set their heart on something, and to buy it. If the queer-fish collectors bought anything, then the purchase would be christened with brandy poured into a square glass measure of Catherine's time and drunk out of glasses which had once been part of the imperial diamond set.

• • • •

. . . And back at Skudrin Bridge—nothing is happening.

The town is a Russian Bruges and a Muscovite Kamakura.

Yakov Karpovich would awake about midnight, light a

[17] Not a "fund," but an organization established in 1918 for the purpose of confiscating and disposing of privately owned objets d'art (Editors).

[18] Literally, "Flayers' Street" (Editors).

lamp, eat, and read the Bible aloud, from memory, as always, as he had done for forty years. Every morning the old man would be visited by his friends and by petitioners—peasants—for Yakov Karpovich was a peasants' agent. In those years the peasants were bewildered by the following—incomprehensible to them—problematical dilemma, as Yakov Karpovich put it. The problem's incomprehensibility lay in the fact that the peasants were divided about fifty-fifty. Fifty per cent of them got up at three o'clock in the morning and went to bed at eleven, and in their families everyone, young and old, worked day in and day out; if they were buying a heifer, they went over everything ten times before buying; they carried home any brushwood they found on the road; their huts were kept in good repair, as were their carts; their cattle were well fed and well cared for, as they themselves were well fed and up to their ears in work; taxes in kind and other state dues they paid promptly; they feared the authorities; and they were considered enemies of the Revolution, no more, and no less. The other 50 per cent of the peasants each had a hut open to the winds, a scraggy cow and a mangy sheep—and that was all they had; in spring they went to town to collect a state seed loan; half the seed loan they ate, for they had no grain of their own left; the other half they scattered—shouting distance from seed to seed—and so there was no harvest in the fall; they explained the poor crop to the authorities by the lack of manure from the scraggy cows and the mangy sheep; the state relieved them of tax in kind and repayment of the seed loan; and they were considered friends of the Revolution. Peasants among the "enemies" maintained that as far as the "friends" were concerned, 35 per cent of them were drunkards (and here, of course, it is hard to determine whether poverty came from drunkenness, or drunkenness came from poverty), 5 per cent or so had bad luck (chance isn't always on your side!), and 60 per cent were idlers, gabbers, philosophers, loafers, bunglers. In all the villages the "enemies" were har-

assed with the aim of turning them into "friends" and thus
ensuring that they would have no means of paying their
taxes in kind, while their huts became the property of the
winds. Yakov Karpovich wrote affecting and fruitless petitions. Among Yakov Karpovich's visitors was one Vasili
Vasilyevich, an enemy of the Fatherland, a man who had
gone out of his mind. Before the Revolution Vasili Vasilyevich had been a clerk of the Council—the District Council;
he became interested in agriculture and read every book
about it he could lay his hands on. In 1920 he went to
the land; he was given one dessiatine; he came to his
dessiatine, a man of forty, with nothing but bare hands
and boundless enthusiasm. In 1923 at the All-Russian
Agricultural Exhibition, he was awarded a gold medal on
paper and certificates of merit by the People's Commissariat of Agriculture for his cow and milk, and for his work
as chairman of the dairy collective; in the spring of '24
he was offered forty dessiatines to build a model farm—he
accepted twenty, and by '26 he had seventeen cows; he
hired a farmhand and—that was the end of him: he had
become a kulak; by '27 he had five dessiatines and three
cows left—the rest had gone in taxes, dues, and government bonds; in the fall of '28 he gave up everything, having decided to return to town and to clerking, in spite of
the fact that in the fall of '28—on rafts crossing the Volga,
on country roads, in pothouses, and in market places—
the peasants were talking figures: they gave you a ruble
and eighty kopecks for a pood of rye at the cooperative,
but if you bought a pood of rye at the same cooperative—
on a coupon—it was three rubles and sixty kopecks, and if
you sold a pood in the market—you got six rubles. Vasili
Vasilyevich returned to town and—went out of his mind,
not having the strength to break away from the kulak way
of life. In these parts you don't come across too many
villages and hamlets—mainly forests and swamps.

Yakov Karpovich had lost his sense of time and had
lost his fear of life. Besides petitions of no use to anyone,
he wrote proclamations and philosophical tracts. Vile—

heartachingly, nauseatingly vile—was Yakov Karpovich Skudrin.

The town is a Russian Bruges and a Muskovite Kamakura. In this town in the sixteenth century Tsarevitch Dimitri was murdered. It was then that Boris Godunov ordered the great bell of the Church of Our Saviour in the kremlin to be taken down—the very bell that the priest Oguryets had struck to cry the murder; Boris Godunov punished the bell, tore out its ear and tongue, scourged it in the town square together with other tongueless and earless citizens, and exiled it to Tobolsk in Siberia. Today the bells are dying over the town.

Yakov Karpovich Skudrin is alive—his life is uneventful.

.   .   .   .

In 1744 the leader of an expedition to China, Gerasim Kirillovich Lobradovski, upon arriving at the outpost of Kyakhta, took into his party one Andrey Kursin, a silversmith and a native of the town of Yaransk. Kursin, on orders from Lobradovski, journeyed to Peking in order there to obtain from the Chinese the secret of making china, *portselen,* as china was called in those days. In Peking, through the agency of Russian "apprentices of the rank of ensign," Kursin suborned a master craftsman from the Imperial China Works with a bribe of a thousand *lan,* two thousand rubles of the time. This Chinaman demonstrated to Kursin how to make *portselen* in abandoned Buddhist shrines thirty-five *li* from Peking. When Gerasim Kirillovich Lobradovski returned to St. Petersburg he brought Kursin with him and wrote a report to the Empress about the secret of *portselen*-making which he had carried with him out of China. There followed an imperial ukase, conveyed to Baron Cherkassov by Count Razumovski, that the new arrivals from China be sent to Tsarskoye Selo. Kursin was showered with honors, but his thievery did him no good, for, as it turned out, the Chinaman had deceived Andrey Kursin, had "acted perfidiously," as was reported at the time in a secret court circular. Kursin returned to his native Yaransk, fearing a flogging. In the same year, on the first of February, 1744, in Kristiania,[19] Baron Korf concluded a secret agreement with Christoph Konrad Hunger, a master chinamaker, who had learned his craft, he claimed, at the Meissen Works in Saxony. Hunger, striking a bargain with Baron Korf, came secretly to Russia, to St. Petersburg, on a Russian frigate. Hunger began building a china works which subsequently became the Imperial China Works—and began to conduct experiments, which he combined with drunken brawls and cudgel fights in company with his Russian assistant Vinogradov; he was thus fruitlessly engaged until 1748, when he was expelled from Russia for charlatanry and incompetence. Hunger's place was taken by the Russian mining engineer Dimitri Ivanovich Vinogradov—one of Peter's protégés, a hopeless drunkard and a man of great natural gifts—and it was he who founded the craft of Russian *portselen* in such a way that it owes nothing to anybody, being the invention of Vinogradov; nevertheless, Andrey Kursin, the man from Yaransk, who was roundly duped by the Chinese, and Christoph Hunger, the German, who duped everyone around, dangling Europe before their eyes, must be considered the fathers of Russian *portselen*. And Russian china had its golden age. Master craftsmen— of the Imperial Works, of old Gardner, of the *"vieux"*: Popov, Batenin, Mikhlashevski, Yussupov, Kornilov, Safronov, Sabanin—flourished under serfdom in a golden age. And continuing the tradition of Dimitri Vinogradov, those who gathered around chinamaking were connoisseurs and queer fish, drunkards and skinflints; the factories were run by the princely Yussupovs, the Vsevolozhskis of ancient lineage, by the queer-fish Bogorodsk merchant Nikita Khrapunov, flogged on the order of Alexander I for a statuette of a monk bent under the weight of a wheat sheaf wherein was hidden a peasant maid; all the masters stole secrets from each other, Yussupov from the Imperial Works, Kisselyov from Popov; Safronov would spy on a

[19] The name of Oslo until 1925 (Editors).

secret process through a hole in an attic late at night, like a thief. These master craftsmen and queer fish created beautiful things. Russian china is the most marvelous art adorning the earthly globe.

January 15, 1929

RYAZAN APPLES

Shasha[1]

> *Peasants, out of ignorance, call the automobile*
> fooroofooz.

The road is old, they call it the Astrakhan road. On Astrakhanskaya Street in Ryazan, on Astrakhanskaya Street in Kolomna, they boarded up the windows of the Gavrilov and Gromov hotels forty years ago, when the old Astrakhan road was eaten up by the Kazan Railroad. In Kolomna it is two and a half versts—one Kolomna verst, the way coachmen drove in those days—from the city gate with the eagles to the city gate with the stars. The road isn't even lined with willows, and isn't, strictly speaking, the Astrakhan road—it flung itself along the Volga, and came to rest there. Between Ryazan and Kolomna—going toward Moscow—the road came to rest along the Oka.

The summer of nineteen hundred and twenty-one was a fearful summer. Between Ryazan and Kolomna the road came to rest in the Black River Forest and the Zaraisk Marshes—and the road was overhung with smoke from grasses, cowberry, and charred forests. Turn left off the road, and you'll come to a village of the Zaraisk District—Zaraisk means "in heaven," "in Christ's bosom"—and that would be the village of Kobylino; but there is no village of Kobylino: the turf under the village burned away, the village went plunging to hell, like the town of Kitezh in the Province of Nizhni Novgorod[2]—to hell, if you please. The smoke is black over the Black Forest.

---

[1] A peasant version of the word *shossé* (French *chaussée*) (Editors).

[2] In Russian folklore, a town which sank into the earth at the

The road isn't even lined with willows, and it isn't the Astrakhan road: in July along the wires, from telegraph pole to telegraph pole, thundered the Third International, the Comintern. The road isn't even lined with willows, and the only noteworthy thing about it are the bridges for breaking automobile springs. And it isn't the Astrakhan road: it was to Moscow—to people's commissariats and board meetings—that the Ryazan Executive Committee slit the road in their automobiles, avoiding the cholera-packed trains.

> *Tra-trak-trak-tra!—the footfall of the automobile.*
>
> *Turn right off the road, and you'll come to the lands of Zaraisk—"in Christ's bosom"—the hills along the Oka, and meadows like steppe: Belo-omutskiye Meadows, Dedinovskiye Meadows—turn off to the right: that'll be Sapronov's village—Sapronov Hills. The car rattles along the road, two chauffeurs, Pugin, let's say, and Merinov—chase the versts, the car meets a stray sheep: the stupid sheep runs straight ahead, won't get off the road! The car chases the sheep, knocks it down, the sheep is thrown in the back—and in Ryazan the fruit of the crime is divided up fairly and squarely, and eaten with relish. On his next day off, Merinov, a thrifty peasant, goes home. His wife takes him to the shed straightaway.*
>
> *"Well, how's things?"*
>
> *"The other day some scoundrels stole the sheep."*
>
> *". . . ?"*
>
> *(A story could be written telling how Comrade Merinov demanded that Comrade Pugin give back the other half of the sheep—Merinov's sheep.)*
>
> *Tra-trak-trak-tra!—the automobile's footfall.*

Wires along the road trumpet the Third International to Ryazan. You won't scare the boys in the Executive Com-

---

time of the Tartar invasion; a lake formed where Kitezh had been, and on rare occasions certain favored individuals may hear the church bells of the lost town (Editors).

mittees with the Third International. The year was nineteen hundred and twenty-one.

A cart on two wheels is called "woe."

People walk along our tracks and trails—singing songs as quiet as those tracks and trails of ours; to some those songs are misery; we live and have lived in them, by them, through them. The highway from the Volga region —the *shasha:* sky, forest, coppices, fields, parching heat, and dust; the dust is like the sound "sh," the heat is like the sound "zh." In the wheatlands of the Samara and Saratov Provinces winter crops were plowed under, spring crops burned up, and taters were baked in the ground. Goosefoot in rye—no woe say I, rye nor goosefoot none— woe is begun, bitter dock lacks—woe on our backs. July laid bare our ancient Slavic fate—laid it bare in peasant caravans: by July that year bitter dock cost fifty thousand rubles a pood, and tree bark—forty thousand, and the Volga was so low that it could be forded near Saratov at Green Island. Peasant caravans strung along the highways —this is ours, our fate: July laid bare our ancient fate. That year the sun rose in smoke, and in smoke it set; there was parching heat, like the sound "zh"; the peasants shook icons in frenzy at the Lord God, abased themselves in prayer. And caravans set out along the highways: "woe" on two wheels in the dust, on the "woe" a little tent, at the back a goose in a wicket cage, between the shafts a pair of broken-down nags, in the tent—belongings and children. Russian gypsies—going wherever the road might lead, away from famine, for back there along the Volga, in Samara, Saratov, Astrakhan Provinces, there was famine. People walk along our tracks and trails—singing songs which are like those tracks and trails of ours. Along the Black River the forests were burning, villages went plunging to hell like so many Kitezh towns. To go wherever the road might lead. By July caravans of "woes" had rolled as far as the lands of Zaraisk—"in Christ's bosom"—following the Astrakhan highway, the *shasha.* For in Astrakhan cholera was sending two thousand human souls to the

Lord for every journey of the sun from east to west. The
dust of the *shasha* is like "sh."

> *Tra-trak-trak-tra!—the footfall of the* fooroofooz.
> *Wires along the route trumpet the Third In-*
> *ternational to Ryazan. The lands of Ryazan. The*
> *Zaraisk lands ate their fill, gorged the winter*
> *away on taters.*

The old truck—the *fooroofooz*—chased the road like a
pig the size of a hippopotamus, in a fit of hysterics from
having been smeared under the tail with turpentine, sending the Russian gypsies flying as it passed on its way to
commissariats, to board meetings. The peasants were glad
whenever an automobile got stuck on a bridge: the Provincial Committee would write a note to the Provincial
Executive Committee and the bridge would be resurrected within twenty-four hours—otherwise it would have
rotted for years. And the Provincial Committee, resting on
the grass by the side of the road in its velvet jacket, had
its first good look at the Russian gypsies and the cholera-
stricken lying on their belongings in the cart called "woe."
As for the chauffeurs, they sold kerosene.

"So where are you from then?"

"From Samara Province. People are starving there,
food's scarce. You can get a horse, say, for two poods of
grain—there's no grass."

"S-o-o, where you making for?"

"We don't know ourselves. Wherever God sends us, you
might say."

As for the chauffeurs—they sold kerosene. America built
the "White" to run on gasoline. Ryazan got the "White"
to run on kerosene, and when Ryazan got hold of some
gasoline, the chauffeurs announced that the "White" had
got out of the habit of running on gasoline—

> *because you couldn't get taters for gasoline.*

Famine.

It is not for our highways to be told of famine, poverty,
and parching heat. There in the wheat country, in places
with names like Kurdyum, Nurlat, or, say, Chicken Tits,

everything had burned to the ground—there was no food for man or beast, and taters were baked in the ground, May was like July, two poods of grain for a horse, and one pood for half a village of houses. It was for our peasant, the savage—the Slav—to ponder, to steel himself, to resolve: it wouldn't be the first time he walked the land, living the life of a nomad, fleeing from place to place! To ponder a day, to ponder another day—it was for the man who had spent his life breaking his back to wander about idly, to touch the earth with his hand, with the toe of his bast shoe (the earth was too hot to go barefoot), to stare at the sky, to stare at the steppe, to sit for hours on the coffer bench in his hut before a bowl of cow dung (they ate that, too), to go look in the grain bin, shiny as a bald patch—just in case—and to steel himself, to resolve.

"We have to . . . go . . . , wife,"—to say "wife" to his wife for the first time, and not "Dunka," not "bitch," without hitting her in the face.

To drag all his belongings to the "woe"—two blankets, the feather bed, the icon, the ax, the goose, the children; in one day to slaughter, sell, barter the cow, the calf, the sheep—to work all day breaking his back, as he has done all his life. And toward evening (they had to leave by evening without fail!), when the "woe" is already piled high and standing in the street, and the horses bow their heads before the long journey, and the gates are wide open —to go back into the hut for the last time, to glance, as he has done for so many years, at the icon corner, empty now, for even the tsars, generals, and deserters are rolled up in the "woe"—not even to cross himself, the corner being empty, but to stand there in his heavy coat and cap, his mittens stuck in his belt, to slap his knee broodingly with the whip handle (the whip takes the place of oats!), to poke at a cockroach with the whip handle, to sigh thoughtfully, and to stamp out of the hut, leaving the door gaping wide.

"Well . . . , let's be off then . . . , wife," and himself to go alongside on foot—thousands of versts to his grave.

And first, night byways, and then, highways, wherever

the road might lead, for peasants are not coachmen versed in geography. . . . It is not for our highways to be told of famine, poverty, parching heat—it is for them to do the telling. The *shasha*. . . . Thousands of versts: it wouldn't be the first time for thousands of us to be swallowed up by thousands of versts, by famine, cholera, and dark deeds, for—who will shelter us, and how? The *shasha!* . . .

> *The road trumpets the Third International along the wires!* . . .

The lands of Ryazan, of Zaraisk—were in Christ's bosom: they gorged the winter away on taters. But that year—the summer of nineteen hundred and twenty-one— was fearful even in the lands of Zaraisk. The flowering of the grasses and the scattering of the seed of their flower- ing—came all at once and was over in a few brief, blessed days. And then came parching heat, horror came; not even dew fell, and there was no rest even in the nights; the flowers of August finished blooming in May. The earth became stone, overhung with smoke, gutted by forest fires; the sun rose and set like a fiery serpent and the dry, sickly shoots were dark and dusty, like the windowpanes of the Ryazan Transit Prison. All over Russia that summer people ate bitter dock—horse sorrel—which horses will not eat. People lay down to rest and awoke with a prayer for rain, powerless before the elemental forces of fires and parching heat which baked everything hard, the earth and the toil of man's hands. In that year in a village some- where in the Ryazan lands somebody said to someone that the Revolution was over.

And the Astrakhan highway lay—as all Russian highways lie. Sky, and dust, and weariness. And hamlets, and vil- lages. And bridges. And hills, and copses, and burial mounds. If you turn off to the left—there's no village of Kobylino; if you turn off to the right—there are the Sap- ronov Hills, behind you—Ryazan, in front—Moscow, the lands of Zaraisk.

We, the swagbellied men of Ryazan, will eat our fill: of ta-ters. And the automobiles rattle as they do because kerosene has made them old before their time. Great is Mother Russia, Devil take her. *Shasha.*

Ryazan-Baba[3]

> *They planned it all on paper neatly,*
> *Forgot about ravines completely—*
> *And it's through them you have to go. . . .*
> LEO TOLSTOY[4]

Girls sing about the Sapronov Hills:

> *Strange goings on for sure*
> *Among Sapronov's hills and ditches. . . .*
> *All the gentry's called Yegor,*
> *And down to their last breeches.*

The Devil himself could break a leg on the topography and history of Sapronov Hills: there is an estate on every hill—six estates in all, and there are three peasant settlements—seven huts in each ravine. The surveyor Nil Nilovich Tyshko, who has been living these many months past in one of the boarded-up manor houses, couldn't make out for the life of him where and how the Devil broke his leg. The peasants lived and thought as they had at the time of Aleksey Mikhailovich,[5] and could not agree how to reapportion their land. Of the landed gentry the only ones who remained—remained in spite of everything—were the Yerliksovs and the Skurlatovs, side by side on two estates separated by a ravine, and a beekeeper, a former District official, Komynin, in a mud hut in his own sapling grove. Beyond Biryuchi Gulley—a wild spot—was the Commune

---

[3] *Baba*—a peasant word for woman, used by townsfolk in a derogatory sense. Here it means a coarse, wanton female (Editors).

[4] From a satirical piece in the form of a soldiers' song, attributed to Tolstoy. The song was current at the time of the Crimean War, and describes the battle of Chernaya Rechka. The piece is one of Tolstoy's few attempts at verse (Editors).

[5] Tsar of Russia, 1645–76 (Editors).

"Labor"; even Communists talked about the Commune in undertones.

The gentry were all Georgis and Yuris:[6] Yuri Georgiyevich—the old general, Yuri Yuryevich—a junior captain in the Great War, who had lost a leg, Marya Yuryevna—a Party member, and only Komynin was simply Yagor Yagorovich Komynin. The girls sing one version of a *chastushka;*[7] when the young men sing to the girls, they sing a different version:

> *Strange goings on for sure*
> *Among Sapronov's hills and ditches!*
> *All the gentry's called Yegor,*
> *And it's for . . . they itches!*

But then, there are a great many *chastushkas:* a woman's art, since, "Your sweetheart went to join the Reds, mine to Balakhovich fled—yours was hanged and mine was shot, and we must moan our widows' lot." A chronicler of everyday life can't afford to ignore them. "Oho, how now, how now! The *barin* walks behind the plow; his tears are flowing in a flood—now that he can't drink our blood." "A time there was, and that of late, they wouldn't let us in the gate—but now the front door's open wide: 'Buy skirts and blouses—come inside!' " "There's a rumor about, if you please, that they're taking a census of fleas: to count them each one as they breed—they're teaching the women to read." "The Communists, they keep their word; 'Land for all'—that's what they said: three *arshins* for a grave they give, and allocate it by the head."

Truly: "I'll call down trouble, I'll call down woe—I'll go to the john with no pass for to show; a pass I would get me if only I could, but a bribe takes money, and so it's no good." *Chastushkas* are a girls' art, an art born of merrymaking. A chronicler of everyday life has to take a song as he finds it. Young men are in very short supply.

. . . And back there, beyond Sapronov Hills—the Oka,

[6] Georgi, Yuri, Yegor—are all Russian variants of the name "George"; on occasion they are used interchangeably (Editors).

[7] Usually a four-line folk verse, humorous and topical, sung in a lively manner (Editors).

Dedinovskiye, Lyubytskiye, Lovetskiye, Belo-omutskiye
meadows: before, thousands of people made their living
from tens of thousands of dessiatines, supplying the whole
of Russia with millions of poods; now the grasses have
vanished from the meadows—wheatgrass, clover, fescue,
vetch, lucerne—smothered by nettle and sow thistle. And
still, every spring apple trees blossom in the old gardens
on Sapronov Hills and will blossom as long as earth remains. In the moonlight the gardens of white apple blossom
seem carved of bone, are motionless. All night frogs fill the
ravines with their croaking, and it is hard to sleep between
the purple of the west and the purple of the east, among
the brimming songs of nightingales, for is not the nightingale's song a goblet filled to the brim with honeydew
which the nightingale raises to the earth? The gardens are
old, dying, sparse. And in autumn the rains will come,
the Feast of the Intercession and the Feast of the Holy
Virgin of Kazan will come and go, white snows will fall,
the peasants will lay things away after the summer, will
shut themselves up in their huts for the winter—and the
gardens will again turn to bone with the first frosts, and
white snows will fall as long as earth remains.

The girls sing:

> *My daddy's fifth I am,*
> *My sweetheart's ninth, I make it—*
> *There's nothing ruins us poor girls*
> *Like love, the Devil take it.*

The young men reply:

> *Dilly come dance, it's off with your pants,*
> *Take a girl that's willing to bed.*
> *Soviet girls are the ones for me—*
> *You can sleep with them and never get wed.*

Ryazan is a town on hills above a river.

The word "Ryazan" is feminine in gender, and truly the
town of Ryazan is—a *baba* of forty. Women breed not
only children; they breed fleas, too. Ryazan is a fat *baba*;
fleas she has aplenty, she is fat, and lust still burns in the
fat; she is covered with gulleys and hills—her wrinkles;
she is obese—and she has laid herself down above the Oka,

legs spread wide. The merchants built houses specially
for rats and bedbugs, houses on fivefold foundations, with
windows too small for fat *baba* Ryazan to crawl out of,
and the merchants painted *baba* Ryazan with ochers. The
merchants gave up combing her hair forty years ago when
the Kazan Railroad pushed its way through town, having
eaten up the Astrakhan road; and *baba* Ryazan lies above
the Oka, legs spread wide—bareheaded, dirty, sweaty, vile.
On a fence near the station in Ryazan is a sign:

Undertaker's Warehouse

And people live on *baba* Ryazan. And *baba* Ryazan
herself has lived a thousand years: *baba* Ryazan's belly
is the kremlin; beneath the kremlin flows the river Trubezh. On *baba* Ryazan's belly, on the monasteries, cathedrals, and on the princes' palace, stone has inscribed upon
stone how Prince Yaroslav of Ryazan divided up the land,
how the princes of Moscow took the princes of Ryazan
prisoner, and how Ryazan set out with hue and cry in
pursuit of the Crimean Khan Girey. The name "Trubezh"
is an ancient one; the Trubezh—trumpeting through the
centuries of Khan Girey, of the princes of Ryazan, of
Prince Yaroslav of Ryazan—washes *baba* Ryazan's belly.
From the belly, from the kremlin hill, the water meadows
can be seen for scores of versts; there in the distance is
Belo-omut—the poetry of Ogaryov.[8] The Trubezh has
trumpeted through the centuries—but the Revolution is
over: down below at the foot of the cliff stands a post,
and to the post is affixed a notice of the Ryazan Health
Department:

Bathing in the Trubezh is strictly forbidden,
for reason of the river being infected with syphilis.

Undertaker's Warehouse

And people live on Ryazan—the *baba*. In Ryazan there
are: a health department, food committees, executive

[8] Ogaryov, Nikolai Platonovich (1813–77): poet, philosopher,
publicist, a famous exile from imperial Russia; at one time he
owned a large estate in the area (Editors).

committees, both Provincial and District, offices of the Workers' and Peasants' Inspection, the Cheka, the Seventeenth Division, telephones. Telephones and people. And centuries—trumpets which the Trubezh has sounded as the palace guards of the Ryazan princes used to sound their horns. Ryazan is a market town.

Telephones and people. Two men, both Jews. On some Seminarskaya Street or other stands a church—some Holy Virgin of Kazan or other—like a Kazan orphan[9]—and in the Kremlin Monastery, say, stands Our Saviour in the Churchyard: the churches were built to the glory of God—the Mystery of the Church is like the towns of Rostislavl[10] and Kitezh—their bell towers gaze up to the sky, raise their voices to the sky. Other centuries came (before the Kazan Railroad); the merchants burned candles each weighing a pood in the churches, but said: "Begging your pardon, God is One and Indivisible to be sure, but economic necessity leaves us no choice"—and put up *baba*-like houses all over the place, befouled the churches, squeezing them into alleyways with their fat bellies—incomparable churches, monuments of Mystery, of the past, and of civilization. Two men—both Jews—in a three-room mezzanine, in a house like a *baba*.

One—the first—the man, the Jew, the Zionist, slept on chairs, placing them side by side and laying a feather bed on top. During the day he went to the dental clinic where he worked, ran from one eating house to another; in the evening he molded teeth, and at night, before pushing his chairs together, he studied an Arabic grammar and an Arabic dictionary, for he dreamed of going to Palestine, his own country, and practicing there among the Arabs. He was fifty-two and as dried up as a mummy in the sands of Africa; he had seen nothing outside Ryazan and Odessa.

[9] Proverbially, one who tries to arouse sympathy by tales of nonexistent misfortunes (Editors).

[10] In the story Pilnyak uses several common variants of this name: Roschislavl, Raschislav, and others. This town on the Oka River was founded in the twelfth century by Prince Rostislav of Ryazan, or in his honor; it has since vanished, and in Pilnyak's time a small parish stood on its site (Editors).

Pal-es-tine and Arabs with bad teeth, whose teeth needed pulling, and with whom one would have to speak Arabic. Not even in Palestine had it been resurrected, the ancient Hebrew language, but he knew it; he slept two hours a night.

For twenty-five years a telephone had hung in his mezzanine—and then came the second—the man, the Jew, the Communist. After the Revolution only official personages were allowed telephones; the second was an official personage; he took down the telephone in the hall and moved it two and a quarter paces to his own room, and when there was a call for the first Jew, who had owned the telephone twenty-five years, the second replied:

"There's definitely no dentist here. This is the military commissar's residence."

The second had also seen nothing outside Odessa. Every morning, early, he left for his office, returned at five, and spent the whole evening talking on the telephone; near the telephone in his room stood an armchair, and when he talked to his subordinates, he sprawled in the armchair, legs spread wide; when he talked to his equals he sat like an ordinary human being; when he talked to those in authority he jumped to attention and jingled his spurs: these were three distinct voices; but there was a fourth which he used—on the telephone—when he talked to women. He never had any visitors at all; he went to sleep on his sofa between nine and ten, "decree time."[11]

The first and the second, the two Jews, were distantly related, both having come from Odessa, somewhat in the way that the two churches—the Holy Virgin of Kazan, let's say, and Our Saviour in the Churchyard—were related, both being in Ryazan, both befouled by the merchants who had put up *babas* all over the place for rats and bedbugs, having offered their apologies:

"Begging your pardon, God is One and Indivisible to be sure, but economic necessity leaves us no choice . . . , but touching on the question of the *babas'* hemming in, you might say . . ."

And the third—the man, the Russian, the prince. The

[11] Daylight saving time (Editors).

train crawled into Ryazan station, spilled people like typhus lice—people who had long been called not "hares,"[12] but "rabbits," for a startled hare makes a dash for it, but a rabbit chased by the railroad police just runs back and forth. Neither a louse nor a rabbit, the man in the cap and the English overcoat with collar pulled up to the ears, carrying a lean suitcase, got off the train, alone and unhurried. The man's face was like November. Unlike the rest, the man stood for a long time in the third-class waiting room, leaning against a wall, his November eyes lowered. Then the man walked briskly toward the center of town, to the state hostel on Astrakhanskaya Street. There he showed his papers and was assigned a bunk in a dormitory where forty men were already sleeping; the man examined the bed linen, sprinkled it thickly with flea powder from the lean suitcase, took a long time undoing his worn-out shoes and unwinding the wrappings from his worn-out feet, put the shoes in the suitcase, put the suitcase under his pillow, and, without taking off his coat, pulling his cap down firmly, having neither eaten nor drunk, lay down to sleep. Early next morning, without asking directions, he went out of town to the camp where Russian officers from the armies of Denikin and Vrangel captured in Russia were imprisoned. He did not stay there long, delivered several letters, talking and smiling for the first time, and then went on a round of Soviet government agencies, to the Provincial Executive Committee and the Provincial Land Department.

The prince must also have had his corresponding church, parish. Roschislavl, say.

There Is None But—The Lord of Hosts Alone

(OLD-BELIEVERS' HYMN)

Nightingales sang all night long. Nil Nilovich Tyshko spent the whole night walking with Yelena Yuryevna

12 A person using public transportation without a ticket (Editors).

Skurlatova in the monastery pine grove. There was mist in the bottom of Filimonov Ravine, its steep sides were covered with pines, and even at night before dewfall there was the same smell of melted resin as in the afternoon. The slopes of Filimonov Ravine were strewn with horse skulls; night wrapped the earth in moonlight. Below in the ravine the nightingales were spilling their overflowing goblets, and cuckoos were cuckooing as if there were wine in the air. Graceful Yelena spoke with a mocking smile about the wood-devil Yegor Yegorovich Komynin, about love; she stood—graceful, barefoot, in a white dress —on a horse skull and declaimed Pushkin:

Wise Oleg girds himself for war . . .

She sat down on the skull and undid her braids: her hair came down like black seaweed. Yelena kept giving little derisive laughs. Two of the skulls—at Yelena's command— Nil Nilovich dragged behind him on a strap, and they hung them up outside the Skurlatovs' house.

"Oh, silly, silly crocodile Nil. Just think, he doesn't even know that Yegor Yegorovich is a wood-devil, and all the women in the Commune are . . . witches," said Yelena, gave a little nervous laugh, and disappeared into the doorway between the horse skulls in her white dress, sheaves of meadowsweet in her hands.

Nilych replied:

"Hmm," and all the way home hmm's kept issuing from his clean-shaven mug.

Waking at twelve, Nil Nilovich spent a good hour on the veranda washing his bald head, cleaning his teeth, nails, boots; he tried on two pairs of trousers and finally put on a pair of dark-blue riding breeches with a leather behind, a military jacket, and Swedish jack boots—drank a jug of milk and, having pinned to the door with four thumbtacks a yellowed notice on vellum,

Back by six o'clock old time.
                    N. Tyshko

rode off on his bicycle to have dinner at the house of a married friend of his, a surveyor, fifteen versts away.

The same morning, the morning after the night when the lilacs first opened up, a commission left the town by car. In the sky above the fields clouds passed, melted, and came into being again, alive as the morning. Larks whistled, the fields smelled sharply of hill mustard, from coppices came a faint sweet drift of lily of the valley, and the breeze caressed as gently as a lily of the valley. The automobile rattled along the road as far as the turnoff to Sapronov Hills; here it shed cyclists who were to ride through the fields. The cyclists pedaled as if they were in a race, passing each other, tiring themselves needlessly, showing off, enjoying themselves. Halfway to Sapronovo they dropped in to see a friend, the chairman of the *volost*[13] soviet; they trooped into the hut, sweaty, high-spirited; they made a lot of noise, joked, spilled makhorka, drank milk, inquired about the land, asked—would there be cheating on taxes in kind? With a solemn face the chairman began to propose that they should sing the "International"—they told him to go to hell, scrambled onto their bicycles, set off, again as if in a race, sending the village dogs flying.

In Sapronovo, at the edge of the village, a boy ventured a question, "Where you going, then?"—but was told, "To the Politburo,"[14] and again they set about sending dogs flying. Alyoshka was about to stick his head out of the window—froze, and raced around the back yards to Filimonov Ravine, where other deserters soon gathered. Somewhere in the village a hand mill grunted and fell silent.

A cock flew up onto a perch in the stable and crowed: "Koo-koo-rk-koo-o!"

The commission tore down Nil Nilovich Tyshko's yellowed notice, and pinned up a new one:

The commission expects the crocodile.

—SIGNATURES

Among the members of the commission was the second —the man, the Jew, the Communist. He had ridden behind

[13] Formerly the smallest rural administrative unit (Editors).
[14] Political Bureau of the Central Committee of the Communist Party (Editors).

the rest, no doubt because he was hot in his leather jacket;[15] but there were others besides Communists in the commission.

In the Commune the commission was awaited by the *volost* cell of the Russian Communist Party; not all members of the commission belonged to the Russian Communist Party, but they all went to the meeting. The meeting opened and closed with the "International"; the meeting was held in the servants' quarters, flies whirled about, chicks peeped on tables, and on the conference table stood a large jug of *kvas*. They sang the "International" from beginning to end both times, with boredom, in the heat. "Saturday labor"[16] had been called off, although it wasn't even Saturday. For some reason all the members of the cell had whitish eyes—almost white, vacant; and everyone's eyes were set differently: people peered out of these eyes at different angles—wolfishly, foxily, owlishly. The brothers Merinov, Lipat, Login, and Sidor, sat at the table side by side in ascending order of age—chairman, secretary, chief of supplies—sticking up above the table like gnarled stumps, for like stumps they were. The Merinovs' faces were set in such a way that they all looked up at the sky; the faces were like gnarled stumps from the bottom of a pond—they had even turned green from the slime of their white eyes; the backs of their heads had degenerated into necks; there were no necks; they might have been beasts, or they might have been fish; and yet the faces were all different: Lipat's face was foxy, sharp, one enormous freckle; his ears stuck out, his eyes snuggled up to each other, his gaze moved quickly, secretly, missing nothing; Sidor's eyes had settled over his ears and were cut longways, rather than crossways; the eyes were like buttons on underpants and each weighed a pood; the face was at its broadest at the cheekbones, the nose stuck out like a duck bill, the mouth was a little, hairless hole. Lipat

[15] In Pilnyak "leather jacket" is often synonymous with "Communist"—Bolshevik (Editors).

[16] "Saturday labor," *subbotnik*—voluntary work for the State on days off (Editors).

Merinov said all the proper things, with a bob at every word.

"I hereby announce the agenda. I move that we begin by singing the international anthem of the workers. Does anyone wish to change the order?"

"When you can witness a person's insides with your own eyes, citizen, then you'll know what I wish to say."

In the discussion of current business the question somehow came up: should they or should they not confiscate the *burzhui*-teacher's cow? On one hand, the teacher ought to be punished for counterrevolutionary activities, but on the other hand—without the cow he'd die of hunger. Not everyone signed the minutes—not everyone could write; Marya Yuryevna Skurlatova, a member of the *volost* cell of the Russian Communist Party, announced hysterically:

"Comrades. I have been elected correspondent of our paper. Would you please pass on to me any interesting and useful material."

Not a single peasant came to hear the report on taxes in kind. Nil Nilovich Tyshko sent a note that he had tea ready. They inspected the Commune. That spring the Commune was infested with beetles—the Spanish fly; the entire Commune reeked of dog; beetles crawled down people's necks, got into their sleeves. The estate lay awkwardly in the woods: outbuildings, cattle yard, tool shed were flung about the hill, the smithy stood at the foot of the hill near the dam, the manor house was boarded up. Yegor Yegorovich Komynin came out of his mud hut to join in the inspection of the Commune; he walked around, smirking, with lame Marya Yuryevna Skurlatova. The members of the commission, most likely, were not endowed with sharp eyes, and, most likely, there was no point in their looking too closely. All the same a report was drawn up. In the Commune the only Communists were the brothers Merinov—the brothers Merinov walked around with the commission, not leaving them even for a minute.

In the report of the commission's inspection of the Com-

mune—a report to be swallowed up by eternity—was
written:

"No reading room, plenty of books, but not everyone
knows about them. In the Commune there are people (the
locksmith and the shepherd boy) who don't know: are
they members or not? No one remembers there ever having been a general meeting. Peasants who join the Commune bring in their own land, put up their huts in the
village for rent."

A peasant woman:

"Well, that's how it is, dear, we burned out, burned to
the ground, and so we came to the Camoon. You have to
eat, you know."

"I'm a beggar, dear. Christ's blessing on their heads for
giving a crust of bread to an old woman. I wash floors
and milk cows for it, for my bread."

There are only four families in the Commune: those of
the three brothers Merinov and their cousin. The rest are
alone in the world. They live in two houses and the bathhouse. In the bathhouse lives Sidor Merinov and his large
family. One house is a dacha, twelve by twelve,[17] four
rooms and a kitchen, eight people living in it: two brothers
Merinov and their wives, the relative and his wife, and
two girls. The other house, the servants' quarters, is eleven
by fourteen, twenty-three persons in it, one broken window stuffed with matting. In the house where the Merinovs live there are a great many beds, everything is neat
and clean, there is a cloth on the table, on the walls are
marks of squashed bedbugs; the women are young, clean,
healthy, wear shoes, and sit around the table, crocheting.
In the servants' quarters (which also serve as a kitchen)
it is dirty, cramped, flies whirl around, nothing but old
men and women in bast shoes—they sleep on the floor.
The books turned out to be in the manor house, in boxes,
interlayered with leaf tobacco to keep mice from eating
them. The books are very valuable—classics, many English
books. In the village the Merinovs had owned one hut,

[17] The unit of measurement is a *sazhen,* seven feet (Editors).

had not divided the property, had counted as a single household; the youngest and middle brothers had worked in town as yardmen.

	The Commune	The village
Dessiatines of arable land	200	70 20
Under winter crops	24 des.	(no space for more)
Horses	14	11
Cows	13	15
Pigs	8	—
Winnowers, seeders, threshers, plows	—	wooden plows, harrows
Houses	3	18
People	31	78
Meat eaten with		sorrel

Modern agriculture is unknown in both Commune and village. The village delivered its due of grain, meat, butter, eggs, potatoes, wool. The Commune delivered nothing.

This report was written by the second man—the Jew, the Communist. The commission were enjoying themselves; they learned nothing more, since everyone met the commission with silence. Nil Nilovich Tyshko came to the Commune to hurry them along, but the commission was held up a few minutes by some peasants—they came from the village, surrounded the commission, pulled off their caps, began shouting all at once.

"The Revolution's over now, just you wait, we'll ask their honors the commissars, the comrades. Right now you might say the Revolution's over, in a manner of speaking."

"He lived in the town, he did, in twenty, and we were hacking away at virgin soil. And he says—by the head! . . . And then there's this Camoon. . . ."

"Liar! It's idle, your land is! You pig, you want to eat for eight people. . . ."

"Wait a bit, citizeners. We'll tell it all to their honors, the commissars, right from the beginning, like before God. Take this for a fact, they rode about town in cabs for twenty years, and there was us hacking away at the land.

And seeing as how things are short in town, they say—by the head! . . . And what's more they haven't got no cattle, nor tools, all they've got is a hut patched up in a thunderstorm! . . . And that's the truth. . . ."

"Liar! It's idle, yours is!"

"Pig, everyone knows you're a pig!"

"Take him off half-time work!"

"So you want to spec'late? The taters you buried gone rotten?"

"Liar! I've got a girl and I married her off, and she got seeded, and like she was brought to bed—don't that make things come out right, by the head?"

And suddenly there was a shower of rapes which the peasants vowed to commit on each other's livers, spleens, eyes, mouths, souls, backbones. Nil Nilovich Tyshko said:

"Men. I'll take a piece of paper this very minute and I'll write a report. And anyone who says one more foul word I'll send to the *volost* lockup to cool off, and he'll get double cartage duty into the bargain."

The peasants fell silent—stood awhile in silence—and left.

. . . .

Hmm-ing, Nil Nilovich placed five buckets of water in a row on his veranda, and the commission washed, taking turns to pour water from the buckets over each other's heads. With their boot tops they fanned to flame the pine cones in the samovar, which they had got going in the meadow near the garden house (in the meadow children's shouts). Nil Nilovich's bald spot and leather behind gleamed. Bread, honey, and milk had been sent from the Commune. Sidor Merinov put in an appearance, stood there bowing, but declined tea. Marya Yuryevna limped around, carrying plates. Komynin lay down on the grass and stayed there, his heels blinking at the sky from the slippers sewn for him by Yelena. They drank tea from soup plates. In the evening swallows streaked the sky; the ashes of evening fell to earth to make the night deep blue. The last orioles shrilled like flutes, and there was a sweet smell of apple blossom. While they were still at tea they began singing student songs for some reason, although, except for Tyshko, there were no students among them. But then, Yegor Yegorovich Komynin also called all the commission students, lying as before—heels to the sky—in front of his plate, screwing up his eyes and conversing with a member of the commission—the second man, the Jew, the Communist.

"And allow me to ask you, then, mister stewdent, where does the word 'comrade' came from?"

"I don't know," answered the second.

"Well, I'll tell you, mister stewdent. When the Volga pirates raided barges at Zhiguli they used to shout, 'Scum to the bows,[18] come, raid. . . .' And that's where it came from, mister stewdent. . . . And what are women's rights, mister stewdent?"

"I don't know," said the member of the commission.

"Well, I'll tell you, mister stewdent—an insult."

"Why?"

"When a woman makes demands—that means a man's a fool, impotent. It's an insult to the male sex, mister stewdent. And do you know what a young leddy is, mister . . ."

But Yegor Yegorovich didn't finish because the whole company went to Marya Yuryevna Skurlatova's place. Marya Yuryevna, the Communist, lived with her sister in a converted brick greenhouse. Horse skulls hung by the door. It was frightening to go inside the house because dirt, flies, cockroaches, spiders, dust did not lie quiet, but whirled around frantically—and the dust was not gray, but like *terra di Siena;* walls, and ceilings, and windowpanes, and the books on the floor in the corner—Gleb Uspenski and Herzen[19]—were the color of *terra di Siena.*

[18] River pirates' command to barge haulers to get out of the way (Editors).

[19] Uspenski, Gleb Ivanovich (1843–1902): writer known for his somber, semijournalistic sketches of provincial and peasant life.

Herzen, Aleksandr Ivanovich (1812–70): writer best remembered for his memoirs; a famous exile, creator of the free Russian press abroad (Editors).

Junk was strewn around generously, as in attics, and although people lived here, it was like an attic nevertheless. Marya Yuryevna sat down on the sofa—from which springs shot out with plaintive squeaks—and shouted hysterically:

"Sit down, comrades. I'm a real peasant, I live like a peasant, damn it all. . . . I haven't got a thing to eat in the house . . . ," and she spoke the truth, because she was always half starved and managed to get something to eat only when the Commune fed her, for she was—in some obscure way—a member of the Commune. "Damn it all— I'm a true Communist, I've got nothing of my own," she burst out laughing, making a bid for some encouragement, and again she spoke the truth, for she had started digging a vegetable patch in maybe three places near the house —but had given up each time, having changed her mind or lost interest.

"And allow me to ask you, gentlemen stewdents," said Yegor Yegorovich apropos of nothing, "what is the emancipation of women?"

He paused, screwed up his eyes, and answered:

"It's that all women and young leddies can be divided into leddies and no-leddies.[20] That's what it is, gentlemen stewdents."

From the other room, from which she had not emerged, Yelena shouted:

"Throw Yegorka out!"

"And why have you hidden yourself, young leddy?" Yegor Yegorovich responded, brightening up.

"I'm not dressed, I'm hot. I'm going bathing."

"May I be allowed to see for myself?"

Sidor Merinov, who was standing respectfully in the doorway and, thanks to the peculiar set of the Merinov skull, looking up at the ceiling, wagged his head respectfully. Yegor Yegorovich gave the door a push—the door was locked. Then he said:

"And allow me to ask you gentlemen stewdents—what is a young leddy?"

[20] Play on words; the other meaning is, "I will give and I won't give" (Editors).

But he had no chance to give an answer, as the peasants came trooping into the house, and a hubbub broke out again.

"We want to do things in God's way, no cussing, and if we use language, it's 'cause we're iggorant folk."

"Liar, it's idle, your land is!"

"Wait a bit, men. I want to do things in God's way before the gentlemen comrades: . . . When . . . she painted her cheeks, she was . . . , and like when she washed, the paint came off her—and now nobody wants her!"

"We bled for the Soviets in the war, and now the Revolution's over—there's no land for us. They think they can take us in. . . ."

And again came a shower. . . .

The members of the commission went to the Commune to spend the night; they were put up in the barn. Beyond the open doors bats streaked a sky reduced to a square studded with white, vacant stars, and the frogs in the pond behind the barn croaked so ferociously and loudly that each might have been as big as a dog. In the barn, in addition to the smell of the Spanish pest, there was the smell of rats, and the whining of mosquitoes was as thin as their stings. The members of the commission lay side by side on quilts made up of triangular patches. On the scales stood a large jug of *kvas*. An owl flew into the barn, swerved suddenly after a bat, gave a hoarse cry and flew off into the night. From somewhere at the far end of the Commune, near the boarded-up manor house, came what sounded like hymn singing, which immediately died away. And then Sidor Merinov appeared in the doorway, leaned his shoulder against one of the doors.

"Sleeping?" he said. "We were wanting to ask you . . . Someone come over here and I'll tell 'em."

One of the members of the commission went over. Sidor Merinov whispered loudly, so that everyone heard.

"Would you be wanting a bit of skirt? We got some nice bits of skirt, and they'd like to do you a favor."

All the members of the commission but one accepted.

The one was the second—the man, the Jew, the Communist: he dreamed of a Jewish maiden and he was ascetically pure. This second man turned over on his belly, stretched—then got up and walked off into the night, away from the Russians.

Sidor Merinov insinuated himself into the barn, squatted down, and whispered:

"Only you can't go out of here on no account. They'll smell a rat. Why don't all of you take a corner—spread out a bit. Or they'll smell a rat. You can't go out of here on no account, I'm telling you. I'll go call 'em. I'll open the doors again."

Sidor Merinov went away, pushing the doors to behind him. The members of the commission dragged their quilts into the corners; for some reason they all made haste to take a swig of *kvas*, and suddenly the barn became very quiet; there was only the whining of the mosquitoes.

A door squeaked, a slit widened, in a deep-blue triangle of sky appeared two women and the head of Sidor Merinov; in the opening between the doors the women seemed huge; the one in front covered her face with her arm, the second walked sideways; one of the members of the commission thought that they were the same women he had seen sitting around the table in the Merinovs' house —most likely the Merinovs' wives. The door squeaked again, and pitch darkness filled the barn; for a quarter of a minute there was a strained silence. Then the women spoke, both at once:

"Oooh, what are you up to! . . ."—this, half-playful, half-whining, from one.

"Where do I go?"—this, calmly businesslike, from the other.

From behind the door came Sidor's whisper—his last gasp:

"In the corners, they're in the corners like . . ."

At that very moment, at the other end of the Commune, in the stable, in the passage between the stalls stood Login and Lipat Merinov. In the servants' quarters a small boy, their nephew, was trying to wake the locksmith:

"Hurry, hurry—get a move on! Lipat Ivanych, Login Ivanych want you right away!"

The ragged little peasant got to his feet, scratched himself, smoothed his beard—he slept in the same clothes he worked in during the day—hitched up his pants, and hurried out; the boy ran on ahead. Lipat Merinov, who usually looked up at the sky, bent double to peer with his whitish eyes into the God-foolish eyes of the locksmith. Login bent over him from the other side.

"So . . . so, you're not a member?" hissed Lipat.

"S-o-o, you're not a member?" echoed Login.

Lipat straightened up and with his left hand struck the locksmith a blow on the ear. Login also straightened up, gave a hop, and with a grunt struck the locksmith a blow on the neck.

The locksmith hiccuped, grunted, his head snapped forward, and he fell to his knees.

"Mercy! . . ."

"S-o-o, you're not a member? . . . Go blabbing to the bosses you're not a member? . . ."

And the same night just before dawn strange rustlings awoke Nil Nilovich Tyshko in the garden house. Mosquitoes whirled about, cracks in the door and shutters glimmered green. There was a bitter smell of birch, Nilych's sheets and nightshirt were damp with dew. The first thing Nilych heard was a cuckoo—then lowered voices.

"Sh-sh."

"It's all right, he's asleep. . . ."

"That old fool, what a scare he gave me. . . ."

It was women whispering.

"You know, in the old days they used to carry patches about with them in their snuffboxes, and they used to cut them out of black taffeta. And then they used to stick them on their faces, with a meaning: a patch near the right eye meant—'Tyrant'; on the cheek—'Parting'; on the chin—'I love, but cannot find you.' I read it in granny's diary."

"He's in love with you."

"Yes, but he's a fool. He just hmm-s, and doesn't understand that I want to be . . ."—there came a sound of an open palm slapping bare flesh. "Ugh, how they bite; they'd suck your blood to the last drop, may the! . . . And there were different kinds of faints too: Dido's faint, Medea's caprices, Omphale's vapors, faints at the right moment. . . ."

"How sick I am of this Commune. You know what I mean; they—I don't know—they're provided for, have plenty to eat, and that's why truth is not theirs, and they're seeking it, these Merinovs. . . . I don't know how to put it. . . . That's what Yegor Yegorovich also . . ."

"Listen, and Yegorka—what is he? . . ."

"He'll have his way with you, Yelena. Only he won't give you a family and home, he won't give you anything. . . . How dreary, Yelena. . . . But Tyshko—he's young and strong. . . . I'm hungry."

"Yes, Marya—young and strong. . . . But Yegorka—he's a bottomless pit. . . ."

Nearby, twigs snapped, a watchman's clapper clacked, there came a sound of heavy wheezing. The women ran off. The door of the garden house flew open with a bang; in the doorway stood Sidor Merinov in a sheepskin and a fur cap, clapper in hand.

"They here?"

"Who?"

"Them. You seen them?"

"Who?"

"Them. Stark naked."

"What exactly are you talking about—who do you mean?"

"I was going to the smithy over the dam, and spied them. You should have seen them dash past me, stark naked, hair flying in the wind, over the dam into the pool —Marya Yuryevna, crooked-leg, and Yelena Yuryevna for another. . . . They screamed like somebody grabbed them by the belly button, and went under, and not a peep out of them—just bubbles. So I start yelling—a-lya-lya-lya-lya . . . ! They jump out screaming and make for the ravine. Oho, I think to myself—they're either going to your place or to Yagor Yagorych's. I think to myself, if they're going to your place—they'll tickle you to death."[21]

"I suppose they were going bathing. Why should they want to tickle me?" asked Nil Nilovich.

Sidor lowered his head like a donkey to fix his whitish eyes on Nilych, and whispered with a touch of fear:

"They're witches."

"Wha-a-t?"

"Witches they are, both of them. And Yagor Yagorovich is a sorcerer too."

"You're talking nonsense, Sidor," said Nil Nilovich.

"Nonsense! Yagor Yagorovich is stirring up trouble among the women, and some of the men get caught in it too. He takes Marya to bed with him, and now he's trying to get round Alyona. One night last fall she comes after me in the barn—I was keeping an eye on the hay—Marya, that is, the fat one, with nothing on but a shift, hair hanging down over her breasts; she's all over me; 'Darling,' she says, 'I want a baby,' and she's crying like. And what's more, I saw through a crack the things Yagor Yagorovich did with her right in this here garden house—and in broad daylight . . . in broad daylight! . . . And then she starts crying again, crook-leg, 'Your blood's tainted,' she says, 'you haven't got no seed neither,' and then she goes on about a baby again. And what does she want a baby for? To drink baby blood maybe? And you say—n-o-o-nsense! . . ."

That morning Nil Nilovich burned pine cones in a chamber pot to drive away mosquitoes, and slowly traced on vellum the words:

> *Back by six o'clock Central European Time.*
> *N. Tyshko*

. . . .

And the apple trees—the apple trees bloom every year.

Every spring the apple trees bloom, apple blossom falls in the night, piling white drifts; no one knows, no one

---

[21] In Russian folklore water nymphs, *rusalkas,* sometimes kill mortals by tickling them (Editors).

cares who has come. The house might have belonged to
Gogol's old-world landowners—the same squeaking doors
and low ceilings, and little stairways, and all around the
lilac has run wild, covered with bloom. Preserved by
God or the Devil, some of the gentry still remained on
their estates. No one knows, no one cares who has come
—it is I who have come, the author. I am met by a stream
of Hungarian profanity coming from the run-down cattle
yard: this is the one thing the villagers learned from prisoners of war. There comes the sound of a wooden leg
scraping along the corridor; the man who appears is not
the elegant officer he once was: his face is covered with
stubble, his uniform tunic is beltless (because the crutch
would pull the tunic out from under the belt), the trouser
leg hangs dead on the dead limb.

One ought to ask, "Are you still alive?" but the question
that comes out is:

"You weren't asleep? Well, how are things?"

"Bad enough, thank God," Yuri Yuryevich Yerliksov
gives the by now habitual answer. "Come in," and somewhere into the darkness, "Is Ivan home? Has Lantush come
back? Come in, my dear fellow. We're very pleased to see
you."

The visitor tries not to make any noise.

"Don't worry, nobody's asleep," says Yuri Yuryevich
loudly, and adds softly, "When the raids were going on—
we used to wait for them. They always used to start fires
at dawn. We got into the habit of not sleeping nights."

In the corridor it is dark; in the dining room a candle
burns. The father, the old general Yuri Georgiyevich, is
sitting alone at solitaire in his hareskin jacket; the gaze of
his spectacles is stern, his forehead, merging into bald, red
patches at the temples, is also stern: an old general, a
veteran of two wars. He rises, wheezing, to greet the
visitor.

"You're not a Bolshevik?" says the old general in a stern
bass. "Let's have a look at you. So damn dark—can't see
how you look now. Bring any bread? We haven't any;
they've taken the cows, they req-ui-si-tioned the horses,

ha! Haven't got any money, either. Here, lift the candle up to your face—let's have a look. Dark. No kerosene."

"Don't, papa, don't get excited," says his son.

The old man flares up like gunpowder, turns red in the face, stamps his feet.

"You're not a Bolshevik? If you're a Bolshevik—out! Go to Mashka, that lame she-devil! . . . She's got her own sort to keep her company—Tishki-Trishki, Nily-Nionily! . . ."

His son Yuri puts a hand on his father's shoulder, says sternly:

"That's enough; calm yourself, father, calm yourself."

The old man shuffles the cards angrily and lays out his endless solitaire; the gaze of his spectacles is stern, the candle burns dimly. Nina Yuryevna, a student who has been away from her studies in Moscow for many years, enters, greets the visitor listlessly; she has a plaid shawl about her shoulders; she sits down on the stairs.

"How are you, Nina Yuryevna?"

"Bad enough, thank God." She smiles, looks very serious.

"How is she?" Her father leans back in his chair, gives a forced laugh, throws up his hands. "She isn't! Understand? She *is not!* The girl ought to be studying—the years go by—no money! Disgraceful. The girl ought to be having a good time—dresses, chocolates and all that, flowers, troika rides, a visit to a neighbor once in a while. No horses. Wolves they are, not human beings."

"There you go again, papa! Don't."

"All right, all right. I'll go. I'll keep quiet. I'll soon be dead and buried. The truth hurts. It's all because of those Bolsheviks! . . ."

Late that night the visitor and Yuri Yuryevich are standing on the veranda. The green moonlight furrows the rotting boards, the moon is caught in the lindens, a nightingale jugs three paces away in the lilac.

The visitor and Yuri Yuryevich are silent for a long time. With an effort Yuri Yuryevich pulls himself up onto the railing.

"Well then, shall it be literature, music, politics, or war

—what shall we talk about?" says Yuri Yuryevich, and lets his shoulders droop in an unofficerlike way.

The visitor is silent.

"Ah yes. . . ." Yuri Yuryevich is silent for a long time. "Life was just taking shape, and then . . . it did take shape, in a manner of speaking. . . . Father's going out of his mind, or perhaps he is out of his mind. He sleeps in a different place every time, cries out in his sleep—dreaming they've come. And once he crawled—you understand?— crawled over to me and begged me to save him: he wants to live. I understand—it's an elemental thing, human lava, there's nothing you can do about it; father doesn't understand, never will. He never did anything underhanded, was always an honorable man, and—he's a general. He'll never understand. And here I am, as you can see—with a stump. I got through the war without a scratch, and got a leg shot off at Tarnopol."

The nightingale jugs away as if possessed, pouring out goblet after goblet.

"Stupid. Very stupid—old ties, the blood of the gentry. The thing to do would be to drop everything, go away. Pride won't allow it—and cowardice. When they were raiding everyone around here—they didn't touch us: slaves. They got scared—we wouldn't have surrendered alive, we'd have shot the lot of them."

"And would you have been shooting?" the visitor asks.

"I would. With the greatest pleasure!" Yuri sounds like his father. "With the great-est pleas-ure! . . . To hell with them! Slaves! They've worn us out. They didn't come then. But later the authorities came. They took our horses, took our cows, they plow our land, there's the Commune—we're keeping it from father. Nina, my sister—is a shoemaker: she makes the peasant women cord slippers for milk. Marya Skurlatova has lost all semblance of herself; she lives like vermin, she's joined the Communists: I can't understand it—how did she get in? . . . I can't bear it. . . . It's stifling! Do you understand?—stifling!"

And at dawn in the meadow bordering the garden there

was Nina wearing a white kerchief on her head, carrying a spade.

"Oh, it's you?" She smiled, embarrassed. "I'm planting potatoes and beans. They've taken our land, you know. . . ." She must have blushed—in the moonlight her eyes looked out guiltily from behind her pince-nez.

"Only please don't tell papa that I'm digging—he'll be cross," she said softly.

And in the dawn light: on her breast, pinned to the worn cotton dress, a spray of apple blossom, pink-white petals. Lord, youth is sweet! . . .

Every spring apple trees blossom, and will blossom as long as earth remains. Morning came clear with joyful sunlight, with the coolness of dew and green shade. In the morning on the veranda where the grapevine cut green rivers on the white tablecloth, Nina was pouring tea. Chessmen lay about on the table.

Yuri Yuryevich walked up and down the veranda with a worried air, his wooden leg scraping the floor.

"What's the matter?"

"It seems that some commission or other arrived at the Commune yesterday. Is Lantush home?"

Chessmen lay about on the table.

The old man came out, saying briskly:

"Been playing chess? I'll bet you don't know how. All right, I'll teach you. All right, set them up."

"Yes, yes, father—that's right, give him a good lesson!"

And in the corridor Nina whispered, raising her eyes and opening them wide:

"Only please let papa win. He's a very sick man, you know."

> Every spring apple trees blossom, and will blossom as long as earth remains, shedding the white flowers of their flower gardens.

Undertaker's Warehouse

(SIGNBOARD)

When they moved in, the Commune "Labor" checked all movables against an inventory, and Sidor Merinov, wetting an indelible pencil with his tongue, wrote on every table, "table," on every chair, "chair," to make everything quite clear, and only then did he affix his signature to the inventory to acknowledge receipt of the tables and chairs. There was really no need to do this: there was plenty of junk which had not been listed lying about in the house and in the attic. The estate had belonged to the princes Rostislavski; in his time old Rostislavski, an engineer, had covered half of Russia and traveled the length of Siberia, prospecting: in the manor house, in the room next to his study, was a pile of theodolites and astrolabes; without noting it in the inventory, the Merinovs unscrewed the spherical lenses, and in spring, when the sun got warmer, they used them to light their tobacco in order to save matches; they even put a big lens for everyone on a window sill in the servants' quarters. There was little snow that winter, and a windy spring came early. The Merinovs passed the winter dully, in idleness; the calluses went from the hands of Lipat, the chairman; they sat the winter through in a warm house, stuffing themselves and sleeping, often going out to the road behind the cattle yard and standing there for hours gazing across the empty, snow-covered fields. In the village the Merinovs had counted as a single household, had lived in a single hut, Lipat and Login had gone to live in the town while still boys, working as yardmen. Lipat even then was making his mark in the world: he wormed his way into the bed of a Ryazan merchant's wife, and it was at that time too that his back and buttocks began to shrivel up; he always went about in felt boots, made visits to the doctor and to wise women—seeking a cure for the pox and telling everybody that he had a rupture; and from then on, from the time they moved to town, these Merinovs got out of the habit of doing peasant work. The Merinovs, however, were not all of a kind. Sidor Merinov—the eldest—all his life accustomed to breaking his back and to being busy from dawn to dusk for his bread, at first wallowed in satiety, then his idleness began to weigh on him: knocked out of his rut, he didn't know what to do with himself; it was he who unscrewed all the spherical lenses, who put makhorka leaves between books to keep mice away, and who wrote on tables, "table," and on chairs, "chair." The peasants looked askance at the Commune, resentful, sus- picious, and gave the communards a wide berth. In vil- lages all around grain was getting scarce and the peasants were tightening their pants' strings and steaming chaff, as they always did anyway in spring; the Commune ate its fill; once in a while—in exchange for taters—alcohol was brought in from town; then, toward nightfall, they would lock themselves in the house to drink and bawl out songs. Sometime during Lent an order came from headquarters: the Commune was to be cleared of all icons; they took the icons to the attic in the manor house; at that time they were not concerned with God one way or the other. Sidor Merinov, though, removed the silver casings from the icons and buried them. Winds blew that spring; spring winds must stir Russian souls as they do birds; spring winds lure—to roam, to take wing. The Merinovs did not sit at home—the house was steamy and sour-smelling from the good life—they walked about the estate, came out to the road, sat for hours on the coffer bench in the kitchen in the servants' quarters, having poked out the rags from broken windowpanes to let in the sun; they were so busy doing nothing that they did not have time to get ready for spring work in the fields. And in the fifth week of Lent, when snow began to cave in and long days of rivulets and rooks' screaming came, the men were suddenly roused: two of the Merinov brothers, their nephew, and their cousin drove out their wives and families; the Merinovs sent their wives begging, while the cousin and the nephew moved theirs into the hut in the village; and all four turned to matchmakers for new wives. No brides were to be found thereabouts: no one from the neighboring villages would marry without the blessing of the Church, and the Merinovs could not marry in church. Brides were found

with the help of Katsepov, an old man who had kept a
tavern by the road on the outskirts of the village for some
thirty years, and who was said to be a Khlyst, or perhaps
a Molokan, or a Skopets[22]—even though he had offspring
as eyebrowless and beardless as himself. For several days
the Merinovs made secret visits to Katsepov, and Katsepov
to the Merinovs; and after each visit Katsepov would
harness his bay colt, put on his woolen coat, and—always
at night—drive off, in that remote spring season, in search
of brides. Katsepov was a long time finding women, and
those he did find were all plump, big-breasted, shameless;
he went to many places—sometimes as far as sixty versts
away—before he found them; two he found among the
vegetable growers of Kashira, two among people like himself—either Skoptsy or Molokans—somewhere on the outskirts of Guslitsy, where horse thieves had always lived.
The women took the Merinovs without the blessing of
the Church, for money, settled themselves in the well-kept
house, littered the front steps with sunflower-seed husks;
and in the Merinov house a month passed in lechery,
shame, and revelry. In that month came and went the
blessed spring days of the earth's blooming when grasses
hastened to flower, when sow thistle was smothering fescue
and wheatgrass in Belo-omutskiye and Dedinovskiye meadows; in that month the Commune was invaded by the
Spanish fly—the pest; it oppressed with its smell of dog,

[22] Dissenters from the Russian Orthodox Church. The Khlysts
taught that Christ becomes incarnate in man through suffering;
they followed ecstatic practices, including flagellation. "Khlysts,"
the name bestowed upon them by the Church, is a corruption
of "Christs," which is what they called themselves; it also
happens to mean "whips." The Molokans, or "Spiritual Chris-
tians," were a rationalistic sect that stressed the authority of
the Bible as opposed to that of the Church, rejected ritual, and
observed certain dietary laws, which allowed drinking milk during Lent; hence the name "Molokans," from *moloko*, milk. The
Skoptsy (singular—Skopets) believed salvation was possible only
through mortification of the flesh, in particular sexual abstinence
and castration. "Skoptsy" means "eunuchs" (Editors).

crawled down collars, hummed like parching heat. And then days of parching heat came; as before, not even dew fell, and there was no rest in the night; horror came. The sun rose like a serpent and like a serpent it set. The Black River Forests burned and smoked; the sun turned orange, there was no air to breathe, even the marshes dried up, and the village of Kobylino plunged into the earth like the town of Kitezh. The peasants got up and lay down to rest in anguish and terror, praying for rain. The Commune lived within itself, and nothing was said about it.

And in that same month old Anfusa, the mother of one of the new Merinov wives, came to the Commune, all in black, with a jackdaw face. Anfusa began to bustle about, mistress of the estate, fussing and muttering; she picked out a room for herself in the manor house—the very one where theodolites had lain before—and prayed fervently; she did not move the icons to her room, but demanded the casings from Sidor; dressed the icons again, and hung them in the attic in the shadow under the roof, clearing a space in front of them and barricading, hiding them behind the attic junk. The very first evening she went to Katsepov's, and that night the three of them were seen together—she, Katsepov, and Yegor Yegorovich Komynin. People said that the same evening Yegor Yegorovich raped Anfusa, but this was not true, since Anfusa had known Yegor Yegorovich when he was still District chairman. The Khlyst and Yegor Yegorovich became quite at home in the Commune; the Khlyst and Anfusa fussed and bustled about in the manor house, while Yegor Yegorovich took his ease in the sun. And then the old woman—and after her the four wives—demanded imperiously that Yegor Yegorovich Komynin hear their confessions and marry them properly to the Merinovs. Komynin heard their confessions one by one in his mud hut, married them in the attic of the manor house, secretly, in the presence of Anfusa, Katsepov, and Sidor Merinov; and at the very first ceremony Katsepov, enraptured and ecstatic, spoke of the *new god Yegorushka*.

It was about this time that Sidor Merinov, the old man,

drove out his wife, and the new wife, for some reason, went through a wedding ceremony first with Yegor Yegorovich, and only then with Sidor; it was the Skopets Katsepov who now played the priest. And it was the Skopets who brought songs from somewhere on worn pieces of cloth, and the Merinovs repeated these songs over and over again so that they could sing them at night in the attic. They decided to give Yelena Skurlatova to Yegor Yegorovich as his Virgin Mary.

Stop!

Stop!

Stop! All this, of course, is written by me, the author. Nothing like this ever happened—nothing like this would ever have happened if I had not existed: all this about the Commune "Labor" degenerating into a sectarian commune (can you call it a commune?) because the Merinovs had betrayed some unwritten peasant law. Devil only knows—did the town of Rostislavl exist or not?

But then, there is a *Produce Gazette* which comes out in Russia, and in it appeared on the very day I am writing these lines:

> *There remains absolutely no hope for the grain harvest. The rye dried up before the grain filled out. In some places the spring sowing did not come up at all, while in certain* volosts *shoots are breaking through the dried-up and hardened crust, and where they have come up—they have turned yellow from lack of rain. Even potatoes, the last hope of the Chuvash, have been lost in many places. The Chuvash have addressed their prayers both to pagan and to Christian gods. Under the spreading branches of trees they have offered bloody sacrifices: slaughtered sheep and horses.*

So writes the *Produce Gazette* published by the People's Food Commissariat.

And another thing, too:

readers like to know how, once a character comes into a story—how he leaves it. And so:

and so:

That morning Nil Nilovich Tyshko drank a jug of milk, tried on several pairs of trousers, cleaned his teeth and jack boots, affixed to the door the notice:

> *Back at six o'clock Central European Time.*
> *N. Tyshko*

and got ready to go fifteen versts to have dinner at the house of his surveyor friend. It was then that Yegor Yegorovich Komynin and Yelena Yuryevna, out walking, no doubt, came to see him.

Graceful Yelena sat on the veranda steps, her hands clasped behind her head, leaning against the low railing; Yelena said:

"You know, in the old days there were different kinds of faints: Diana's faint, Medea's caprices, Omphale's vapors, faints at the right moment. And at balls ladies told secrets with patches; men stuck patches on their faces too: a patch near the right eye meant 'Tyrant' . . ."

"And allow me to ask you, mister stewdent—what are women?" said Yegor Yegorovich. "Women, mister stewdent, sir, are chimney-flyers—that's what. Witches, sir. They fly up the chimney every night."

"You're always talking nonsense," replied Nil Nilovich.

"And allow me to ask you, mister stewdent," burst out Yegor Yegorovich, becoming very animated—"what is a young leddy? A young leddy, mister stewdent, is a pump with the hole plugged up—but it's pumped all the same, sir. That's what."

Yelena burst into hysterical laughter—screamed, shouted:

"Go away, you scoundrel, away, away, you brute! Or I'll tell everything!"

Yegor Yegorovich got up and walked off, the heels of his slippers flip-flapping as he went. And when Yegor Yegorovich left, Yelena, excited and confused, dragged Nil Nilovich off to Filimonov Ravine—dinnerless. In Filimonov Ravine skulls lay about, ferns grew everywhere. Yelena laughed loudly, smiled mockingly, was indignant, snorted, talked about certain mysterious things some fools had taken it into their heads to do with her, plucked ferns absently. And when they got into the pine thickets, where the smell of resin was enough to give you a headache, suddenly, with tears in her eyes she begged Nil Nilovich, like a little girl—to save her from Yegor Yegorovich, the old fiend, the slimy wood-devil. Nilych hmm-ed dejectedly. Yelena sat down at the edge of the ravine, made Nilych sit down beside her, put her hands on his shoulders; sat quietly, defenseless as a little girl—and suddenly flecks of turbid light fled through Yelena's eyes, she began to breathe unevenly, threw back her head, and with eyes now closed, in the parching heat of the afternoon, when the smell of resin was enough to make your head spin, she sought Nil Nilych's lips with her half-open lips. Her lips were moist, salt, burning. Nilych must have closed his eyes too, because it seemed to him that light died—violet sparks showered—that he was being engulfed by something moist, salt, burning. Yelena fell back on the ground. For a moment Nilych again saw light, parching heat, pines, Yelena.

Yelena whispered:

"Kiss me here. . . ."

And Nilych's lips felt the chill of sweat between Yelena's breasts—there was the eternal bitterish female smell, which in Yelena was somehow mixed with the smell of hill mustard. The parching heat of the pines and of the afternoon must have begun to melt in that chill between her breasts —the breasts were firm, young, still unworn, with smooth nipples: this—the heat came surging back—Nilych saw in the light, the angry sun, among the pines. At this point Nilych in effect ceased to exist.

And then Yelena burst into loud sobbing as she hurriedly picked herself up from the ground.

"Don't. Don't. You're not Yegorka! Yegorka brings us bread and meat! . . . Don't follow me, go away. . . ." and Yelena left, disappeared among the pines.

Nil Nilovich was exceedingly troubled and dispirited: all day he lay about in his garden house, alternately hmming and burying his head in the pillow. No one came to see him all day, except that a peasant woman brought him a jug of milk at about six o'clock Central European Time. At dusk Yelena came by to see him—she walked in full of concern, like an old friend. Before Nilych could get up, she sat down beside him, kissed him gently on the forehead, was silent for a long time; and then again talked about mysterious things, about Yegor Yegorovich—she said that Nil Nilovich mustn't desert her that night, that he should wait for her in the sapling grove.

The sun set like a basin of red-hot brass; in the night the earth remained overhung with smoke from forest fires, darkness came yellowish, murky like windowpanes in attics —as if the nights had gone stale like bread. That year birds and frogs had fallen silent in May—only the eagle owl hooted forlornly in the ravine, and its cry smelled of dust. Nil Nilovich waited for Yelena a long time, but he waited in vain. At the edge of the sapling grove the grass had been trampled, and someone, apparently impatient and agitated, had been snapping twigs—Nilych knew at once that Yelena had stood and waited here: and for a moment the lusty smell of a young mare came from the sapling grove.

There was a crackle of branches in the grove and Sidor Merinov came out, straight at Nil Nilych. He stopped without a word.

"What do you want here?" asked Nil Nilovich.

"Just you go to bed, mister stewdent," replied Sidor sternly. "Yagorushka don't want you roaming about loose at night."

"And who may this Yegorushka be?"

"Yagor Yagorovich Kamynin. And another thing, leave Alyona Yagorovna alone too—she it was asked you not to trouble yourself about her. Time you went to bed, mister stewdent."

And Nilych—and Nilych—went away! But first he went to the mud hut to see Yegor Yegorovich; there was nobody there, the door was open, straw stuck out in matted tufts, the hut was like a mummer at Christmastide in a turned-out sheepskin coat, and all around, the earth had been trodden hard. Then Nil Nilovich went to the Commune. The Commune was dark, and only in the attic window of the empty manor house did he see a light, and from there came the sound of hymn singing. Nilych went closer—and at that moment out of the main entrance came: Yegor Yegorovich and Yelena in front, arm in arm, Anfusa, the Skopets, the women, the Merinovs behind in a cluster. Yelena was all in white, wearing a bridal veil; she walked with head bowed; Nilych stood his guard. Yelena, Yegor Yegorovich, Anfusa, the Skopets made toward Yegor Yegorovich's mud hut. Yegor Yegorovich and Yelena were left in the mud hut, the door was pulled to, light flared and went out, the Skopets and Anfusa knelt, bowed to the ground several times, and went away. It seemed to Nilych that out of the mud hut—out of the silence—came a groan; with all his strength Nilych flung at the door of the hut a stone which had been clenched in his hand since the Commune, and ran home as fast as he could run.

Nilych wanted to weep, to roar with laughter, to fight, to hide himself for fear. He came to himself in bed, already undressed; he was suddenly aware that he was exceedingly hot, and wet all over. The night seemed to him not black, but red, like red calico, filled with some species of red pyramid. He remembered how his heartbeat muffled the night—the whole bell-ringing night—and how his leg had been smarting ever since his tumble into the ravine when he was running from the mud hut. He felt that he was feverish, that his head was splitting with pain, that—in the fever—his senses were deranged, because for a long time now, mama, the Konstantinovski Land-Surveying Institute, and some bench or other had all been jumbled together—and there was no Yelena. Nilych could not tell at once whether lame Marya Yuryevna Skurlatova had really come into his room, her hair hanging loose, wearing only a shift, all limp, her breasts like udders.

In a fit of hysteria it must have been, Marya Yuryevna first flung her stiff leg up on the bed, then fell down beside Nilych; putting her arms around his neck she began to whisper hysterically:

"Don't throw me out, don't throw me out. . . . Aren't I a woman, a mother? . . . I can't take any more from them. Yegor's got no seed—they're a pack of beasts, they can't live without gods. . . . I want a baby; aren't I a woman? Everything's lost, nothing's left. . . . They eat their fill, I go hungry. . . . Don't throw me out, don't throw me out. . . ."

Nilych's head was splitting—mother, people from the Konstantinovski, the bench, danced, jostled like the red night with its teeming red triangles. Marya Yuryevna turned out to be a woman of enormous strength—she easily lifted Nil Nilych. There was no telling what had happened to his will—again and again Nil Nilych went plunging, now into some bench or other, now into Konstantinovski surveyors, now into mama, and all the while his skull was splitting in two.

. . . .

Covered by the night—
        —legs spread wide—
                —sweaty, vile, obese—
—sprawled—
                        —*Baba*-Ryazan.

Bathing in the Trubezh is strictly forbidden, for reason of the river being infected with syphilis.

Undertaker's Warehouse.

Covered by night—one with the night—sweaty, vile, raped hundreds of times, with putrid slime in the wrinkles of her ravines, with the kremlin on her belly leaning toward the Trubezh

        —and in this kremlin in the year one thousand one hundred and fifty-three lived Prince Yaro-

slav, and it was here that he apportioned to his son Rostislav—Roschislavl, the town that stands above the Oka.

Ryazan-baba

—with her houses on fivefold foundations, ochered from top to bottom, built specially for rats and bedbugs, where the merchants stifled their wives with grilles—lay Ryazan-*baba*, dying, wheezing with the wheezes of the garrison club and of automobiles in the night. Some Our Saviour or other—let's say, in the Churchyard—still stood in the churchyard, befouled by merchants and houses, like a *baba*. And that night in the house like a *baba*, in the mezzanine without a privy, before placing the chairs side by side and laying the feather bed on top, sat the man, the Jew, the Zionist—sat at the table, trying to memorize the Arabic dictionary, so that he could practice dentistry in Palestine and speak Arabic with the Arabs there. Palestine and Arabs with big teeth who had destroyed ancient Hebrew—and in the next room slept the man, the Jew, the Communist, who had locked up the telephone, since "there's definitely no dentist here, this is the military commissar's."

The very same night, in the state hostel on Astrakhanskaya—was it?—Street, the man, the Russian, the prince, lay awake. His worn-out shoes were in his suitcase, and the suitcase lay under his head; with his collar turned up, his cap pulled down tight, the prince lay, his wide-open eyes staring somewhere beyond the ceiling.

Whether it was a decree that the train dragged in with the newspapers, or a radio message that took three days getting from the station square in Ryazan to Astrakhanskaya Street, or the wires along the Astrakhan road had moaned the message—it happened in the spring of the year nineteen hundred and twenty-one. Let it be known that land—if there are less than two hundred dessiatines and if the landowners are willing to work it themselves—land is to be returned to the landed gentry, to the old owners.

The prince had done a lot of walking on his worn-out

feet, making the rounds of the Ryazan Executive Committee and Land Department: under his head, in the suitcase, alongside his worn-out shoes, lay the *document.* Prince Rostislavski had done a great deal of walking during these years. There was the day he left the estate for the last time—left it at dusk; he was wearing the same coat and cap, his collar turned up in the same way, his face like November, like wolves in November—but it was August; the prince had not gone by way of the village, where the peasant huts snickered like little old men; in Filimonov Ravine he had met small boys carrying baskets of mushrooms—the ravine was filled with the autumnal, mushroomy smell of mold, and the boys hallooed like hunters after wolves: a-lya-lya-lya-lyaa!

The prince's worn-out feet had covered a lot of ground during these years! . . . And in the suitcase—the document. And Ryazan slept as those forty men in the hostel slept in a room without windows, with nothing more than grilles, a room smothered by those forty sleepers; there's no sinning in sleep. . . . What did the prince think about that night—before tomorrow? Would his weary bones be back in their ancestral home tomorrow? The things he thought about!

There must have been no time to lose, because the prince got up while it was still dark—in towns they mutilated nights by chopping off two and a half hours—took a long time winding on wrappings and putting on shoes, bending down without wheezing. The Astrakhan road thundered with the Third International, while the Belo-omutskiye Meadows, the poetry of Ogaryov, stretched out along the Oka, a wilderness of sow thistle.

To plod on—and not to think about the versts as before; a traveler on foot can't show off like a cyclist, after all! How many roads he had tramped! And in Filimonov Ravine—toward evening—there was no sign of small boys and no smell of mushrooms; for some reason horse skulls lay about.

Lipat Merinov came out in felt boots, a scarf around

his neck, afflicted as he was with shriveling backbone. He greeted the prince amicably, shook hands—they went and sat in the Merinov house, in the big room where the beds stood, each one like Ryazan, covered with smears of gorged bedbugs. The women left the room, taking their sunflower seeds with them to the front steps. Lipat began in a feeble voice, meant to be touchingly infirm:

"Of course, of course, Yuri Georgiyevich, we heard about it. And what's more we got an order to ak'shly put General Yerliksov out and to move in there. But where are you going to sleep, where are we going to make a bed for you? In the manor house shall it be? Or maybe here? Ak'shly we could put the women out in the barn. . . . We'll make you some tea."

The prince went to the manor house. In the study, in boxes, covered with leaf makhorka—to keep the mice from eating them—lay books. The prince bent eagerly over the books, then changed his mind, and slowly straightened up. The lands of Zaraisk—"in Christ's bosom"; the prince thought—why had he come back? What for? Just as he had done back there in the hostel, he took off his shoes, put them in the suitcase, took out the flea powder from the suitcase, sprinkled the sofa with it, and lay down in his coat and cap to fall asleep immediately: the prince had got used to sleeping anywhere—best not to think why he had come. Sidor Merinov came in noiselessly and looked to see whether the table still had the inscription "table" —in order to deliver up everything to the prince according to the inventory.

> *And the apple trees—the apple trees blossom in white snows every spring. Every spring the apple trees blossom and will blossom as long as earth remains and as long as earth does not bury them at last, forever, in its white snows. On Nina's breast then, pinned to the worn cotton dress, was a spray of apple blossom, pink-white petals—youth is sweet—It was Nina too who had begged in a whisper that papa should be allowed to win at chess, and it was in Nina's presence*

that Sidor Merinov wrote "table" on every table,
"chair" on every chair in indelible pencil, wetting
the pencil with his tongue—to receive the estate
from Yerliksova, Nina, according to the inven-
tory, and to make Nina's eyes, behind her pince-
nez, look ashamed—for her papa and her brother,
who did not have enough pride.

The Town of Roschislavl

On December days, ten years or so back, street vendors
used to cry in alleyways:

"Rya-zzz-aans! Rya-zzz-aan aaa-ples!"

Words to me are like coins to a numismatist. Ryazan
apples; in Decembers, when days are short and each day
is like white smoke in alleyways, with a fire in the hearth
and long evenings with books—they used to bring Anto-
novka apples frozen to the heart, chilling you right through
to the shoulder blades; in the flesh of the apples ice
crystals glittered like fine needles; the apples seemed
rotten—smelled like very old, strong wine. In those Decembers summer is far away: and the apples in those
Decembers seemed rotten—you were afraid to touch them
—and the apples smelled of ancient wine. It's through
Ryazan that the Astrakhan road passes, it's in Ryazan that
the Holy Virgin of Kazan and Our Saviour in the Churchyard stand. That man, the Jew, the Communist, that night
in the Commune "Labor"—all night long he wandered
through the ravines, because he dreamed of a Jewish
maiden; but a week later he was back in the Commune,
and every Saturday from that time on the Merinov wives
took turns to go to him—to Ryazan, to a certain street, to
the mezzanine of a house like a *baba.* . . . Night. Palestine and Arabs whose teeth must be taken care of and
with whom one must speak Arabic, ancient Palestine—
like the ancient wine of Ryazan apples—before the feather
bed on the chairs: "There's definitely no dentist here,

this is the military commissar's. . . ." And here he is, the
second man, the Jew, the Communist—he walks into the
first man's room without knocking, and sits down on a
chair: all bounds have been passed.

"Go away, I beg of you."

"I shall do no such thing. Cramming, grandpa? Think
you'll drag your old bones to Palestine?"

"Go away, I beg of you"—in the first man's voice: a
plea for mercy, and fear. "Why must you torment a man?"

"I want to, that's why"—and in the second man's voice:
contempt and the bloodthirst of a huntsman on the
quarry's track. "The old fool's wife ran away from him—
he had to pick a young one—so he's going to Palestine
to heal his wounds? . . . Hoarding flour in your little
trunk next to your Arabs? And on the telephone today. . . ."

"Listen, why are you tormenting me? What have I done
to you? You have power, I can't do anything to you, you
can slap my face, take my bread from me: I shall say
nothing. I don't say anything about your stealing rations,
do I? I don't say anything about your borrowing a pood
of flour from me without my consent, do I? You've taken
away my telephone, you lock up the toilet so I can't use
it. . . . You moved into my apartment without any furniture, and you took everything I had, my piano. . . ."

"Well, what of it? Your wife's run off anyway, there's
no one to play the instrument."

Night.

But then, it's not only in Ryazan that there's a Holy
Virgin of Kazan and an Our Saviour in the Churchyard:
in Moscow on the Lubyanka stands the Holy Virgin of
Grebni, and on the Arbat—the Assumption in the Graveyard; churches are built to the glory of God, their bell
towers gaze up to the sky, raise their voices to the sky;
here, too, another century came, and the merchants
burned candles each weighing a pood in the churches,
and said: "Begging your pardon, God is One and Indivisible, to be sure, but economic necessity leaves us no

choice, touching on the question of putting up, as you might say, skyscrapers," and built skyscrapers shutting off the sky from the church, squeezing the churches into alleyways—incomparable churches, monuments of Mystery, of the past, and of civilization. Ryazan apples.

> *Tra-trak-trak-tra!—the automobile's footfall. The Astrakhan road is an old road. Wires trumpet the Third International to Ryazan.*

The lands of Ryazan—of Zaraisk—are in Christ's bosom. You won't scare the boys in the Executive Committees with the Third International. The parching heat is like the sound "zh," and the dust is like the sound "sh."

Famine. It is not for our highways to be told of famine, poverty, and parching heat. There in the wheat country, in places with names like Kurdyum, Nurlat, or, say, Chicken Tits, that year everything burned—to the ground. It was for our peasant, the savage—the Slav!—to steel himself, to resolve: for sure, it wouldn't be the first time he walked the land, living the life of a nomad, fleeing from place to place. To ponder a day, to ponder another day—it was for the man who had spent his life breaking his back to sit for hours on the coffer bench, with nothing to turn his hand to, cow dung before him—and to ponder and to resolve:

"We have to . . . go . . . , wife"—said "wife" to his wife for the first time, not "bitch," not "trash," without hitting her in the face.

To heap all his belongings onto the "woe"—two blankets, the feather bed, the icon; in one day to slaughter, sell, barter—the cow, the calf, the sheep: to work all day, breaking his back, as he had done always, all his life. And toward evening (they had to leave by evening without fail!) to go back into the hut for the last time, to glance, as he had done for so many years, at the icon corner, empty now, not even to cross himself, the corner being empty, to slap his knee broodingly with the whip handle.

"Well then, let's be off, wife! . . ."—and himself to walk alongside a thousand versts to his grave. . . .

Thousands of versts. It wouldn't be the first time for thousands of us to be swallowed by thousands of tracks and trails, thousands of versts.

Sha-sha! Night! Ryazan apples—the wine of roads, where the parching heat is like "zh," and dust like "sh."

. . . .

I, the writer, am writing all this. My name is Boris. Once in Moscow, in the Palace of Arts on the Povarskaya, I was playing chess with an Italian painter; and he asked me if I wasn't called Boris in honor of the Russian brigands.

"What brigands?" I asked.

"There was a time—wasn't there?—when you Russians were ruled by brigands—Yaroslavs, Olegs, Yaropolks, Borises, Igors." To the First Rome the Third Rome[23] is a story of thieves and murderers. How should they understand— Ryazan apples?

Above the Oka is the sky. At the foot of the hill are fields. But the hills themselves are scarred with gullys, covered with boulders and burial mounds: a quarry, perhaps—or was it indeed the town of Roschislavl? Who knows? Just as in the thousand years of our three-field system oats have followed buckwheat, then the field has been left fallow for a season, and the fallow field sown with winter crops, and after the winter crops, again with oats—so every hundred years the forest renews itself: for a hundred years the pine forest murmurs like the sea and mellows the air with resin; beneath it grows the sickly fir,

[23] After the fall of Constantinople in 1453 the idea that Moscow was its successor as the custodian of the true faith gained considerable currency in Russia and elsewhere. As Monk Filofey, writing in the early sixteenth century, put it, the First Rome fell because it had betrayed true Christianity, the Second Rome —Constantinople—fell for the same reason, Moscow was the Third Rome, and "a Fourth there shall not be" (Editors).

and for a hundred years fir saws cut the sky; and then comes the birch, the white birch, our own, which twines its wreaths like a girl on *semik*[24]—and after the white birch the earth can lie fallow for a hundred years. Above the Oka—sky and fallows, the hills are bald, only below the steep banks are there pines. July is over the earth, the drunken restlessness of May has passed. Terrible and strange was July that year: the fields were bare as in September when man has plundered them, and rooks flocked in the fields as if it were autumn, and the days were September crystal; but people jumbled up the weeks, mixing new dates with old:[25] July like June banked the fires of day and burned away the nights with long June twilights, when you want to embrace the world—and all the world lies before you.

Right there used to stand the town of Roschislavl: that's what I call it. I haven't read about it in books. Did they lie to me about the town of Roschislavl or didn't they?— that right there stood a town before Tarusa, Kashira, Kolomna came into being; a town stood there guarding the lands of the Oka and was the seat of the House of Rostislav. That's all I know about it; the town was surrounded by protective walls and palisades; I would build a new Kitezh, for to me history is not a lesson, but a poem.

As for me, I'm sitting in Kolomna, in Gonchary, in the parish of Nikola Beyond the Walls, in a five-windowed house, in the room where my books are, at the table facing the window, from which I can see Nikola's, where

[24] A Church holiday associated with remembrance of the dead; it had its roots in Russia's pagan past. In addition to religious observances there were games and ring-dances in the forests and on the shores of lakes and rivers; birch trees were decorated with ribbons; wreaths were cast on the waters to tell fortunes (Editors).

[25] The Soviet Union changed from the Julian calendar ("old style," "old calendar") to the universal Gregorian calendar on February 1, 1918, "old style." The changeover "advanced" time by thirteen days; thus February 1 became February 14 (Editors).

Dimitri Donskoy[26] prayed, beggarly open fences, and a
house like a chest of drawers—a coffin of a house. The
sun and the moon which sail the sky—like the sky itself,
like the haze beyond the Moskva River, which is visible
on my left—are swallowed up in smoke: forests are burning all around—in parching, choking heat. There beyond
the Moskva River, in Bobrenevo, the peasants are eating
bitter dock—a kind of weed—because they have no bread,
but they do have meadows. On my table lie, incongruously, a tape measure, a dog's skull, and dictionaries—
Russian-French, Russian-German, and Dal,[27] which I
bought from a peasant woman in the market for ten
rubles, because the paper it's printed on is no good for
rolling cigarettes. This is my Roschislavl: it is from here
that I set out to plunder—myself? Russia?—both myself and
Russia.

The summer of nineteen hundred and twenty-one, the
fifth year of the Revolution, fires, parching heat. In dry
valleys, in burial mounds, they dig up from time to time
stone *babas* covered with mosses; to us—artists—these
babas are beauty unsurpassed, but if a tiny insect were
to crawl up the breast of a stone *baba*, from the breast
to the neck, wouldn't the *baba's* breast—the insect's path
—be all gullys and potholes, the parching heat of stone,
the suffocation of mosses, weariness, sweat, desolation?
You have to stand as tall as the stone *baba* to see that she
is beauty unsurpassed—and then bow down before her as
did the ancient tribes, the Muroma, Meshchera, and Ves.
But then, neither would the *baba* of stone dug from the
earth—this beauty unsurpassed—neither would she notice
it, the crawling thing; the insect, though, would know the
path through moss and gullys. Who will stand as tall as
the year nineteen hundred and twenty-one? The year

[26] Grand Duke of Moscow, 1359–89. In 1380 he led the
Russians to a great victory against the Tartar invaders at Kuli-
kovo Field on the Don, marching from Kolomna to meet the
foe (Editors).
[27] A dictionary of the Russian language (Editors).

nineteen hundred and nineteen—stripped, naked—has been swallowed up by history.

I'm an artist—it makes no difference to me, no difference at all. I finger words—Roschislavl, Tarusa, Kashira, Kolomna, Gonchary, Nikola Beyond the Walls: to me old words are like coins to a numismatist. The numismatics of words is history. If you say a word—let's say, "Kolomna" —over and over again, it will cease to be a town with a thousand years of history, with a kremlin, monasteries, and beggars, on the Astrakhan road; the meaning of the word will be lost, its content eroded, and only the meaning of its sounds will remain: Kolomna—something round, white, smooth; Sovnarkom[28]—something sturdy, nocturnal, owlish; and Goovooz[29]—the cry of the wood-devil.

The Moscow Kremlin is hoary, overgrown with mosses. On the Spasskiye Gate the clock chimes:

"Who-fell-asleep-on-the-Spas-To-o-ower?"

Before you enter the Kremlin in the summer of nineteen hundred and twenty-one, a summer like a stone *baba* from the burial mounds—milky nights are over Moscow in July, and decrees have confused time by pushing it forward two hours —before they let you into the Kremlin on a milky night, they call the commandant's office from the Kutafya Tower. The Kremlin stands hoary; in the night's milky—moss-colored—murk soldiers stand in helmets and tunics like coats of mail in the night.

The commandant's office makes careful inquiries about name and documents, and then helmeted guards let you in—over the Troitski Bridge, through the Troitskiye Gate—into the

[28] Abbreviation for "Council of People's Commissars" (Editors).

[29] Approximate Russian pronunciation of "Guvuz"—initials standing for "Central Board of Schools of Higher Learning" (Editors).

Kremlin. Cannon mossed with murk stand like the century, Dvortsovaya Street is deserted.

If you stand on the balcony of the ancient palace from which Ivan the Terrible used to throw kittens over the Kremlin wall—all Moscow is at your feet. Ivan the Terrible's heart must have been like a roasted toad. Below, along the wall, along the battlements, paces a sentry. Zamoskvorechye[30] lies like a saucer—the one from which the merchants drink tea. There is no Arbat; the Rumyantsev Museum has replaced the horizon, scoring the sky with the eighteenth century. The brow of Lubyanski Hill is suddenly your peer. And lights, lights, lights. And the milky sky covered with mosses. And all Moscow is overhung with smoke, for all around, forests are burning. It is I, the writer, who am standing where Ivan the Terrible stood—and next to me stands a man, a writer and a Bolshevik, whose name is among the first five in the Revolution's roll of honor. The automobile, weary of idleness, has been eagerly cutting patterns through Moscow all day long, but the man is tired, and here he is, standing in an undershirt unbuttoned at the neck, shoulders sagging. Out there—Moscow, Ryazan, the lands along the Moskva, the Oka, the Volga: Russia. . . . Here—the Council of People's Commissars, power set free by October, and—again —Russia. . . . The Kremlin is hoary.

In a room where Ivan the Terrible must have prayed— a table, a sofa, a chair, a bookcase, and nothing more; and beyond the windows—the towers of the stables; it is in this room that I am to sleep. We talk. On the Spasskiye Gate the clock chimes.

"Who-fell-asleep-on-the-Spas-To-o-ower?"

A man has to stand as tall as the stone *baba*, so as not to see the gullys and open pores along the path from the breast to the neck, so as to see, as an artist would—beauty unsurpassed. Do we need to kiss her feet? Over Moscow,

[30] The area of Moscow across the Moskva River from the Kremlin, formerly the stronghold of Moscow merchants (Editors).

over Russia, over the world—Revolution, freedom unsurpassed. Who in hell, to spite God and Devil, tossed the
globe into an interplanetary Etna? What is—Mystery? If
you poke about with a surgeon's probe in the ulcer of the
Assumption in the Graveyard, which the merchants have
surrounded with ulcers of skyscrapers—what is Mystery?
Mosses on the stone breast of a *baba!* . . . To stand as
tall as the stone *baba*—surgeon's probe in hand—and yet
these *babas* were worshiped by the Merya.

But the man is tired, and there is so much human
tenderness in him.

"Time to go to bed."

"Sleep well, old friend."

The Kremlin is hoary. The cathedrals within the Kremlin walls are museums. The automobile slit the Kremlin in
the direction of the Spasskiye Gate. And as the clock
chimes—I think and think.

"Who-fell-asleep-on-the-Spas-To-o-ower? . . ."

"I! I! I! I! I!" the clock answers five times: and there
is dawn, a sheet of red flame: dusk and dawn are close.

And another morning he who is among the first five in
the Revolution's roll of honor wakened me early with the
rustling of papers—a People's Commissar; the machine is
in motion—the machine is moving into the stone *baba* of
October's freedoms. But from the balcony—daytime, working, skyscrapered Moscow, where bread is not, and bitter
dock is.

In the commandant's office—soldiers in helmets and
tunics like coats of mail. Dvortsovaya Street, Troitskiye
Gate, Troitski Bridge, Kutafya Tower, and—Moscow:

"Eee! Aaa! Ehh! . . ." "Ira,"[31] herrings, cholera . . .
busy, practical, skyscrapered: Moscow.

If you say "skyscraper" over and over again—it's an
obscene word.

Two men there must be.

> Smoke, forest fires, human fires all over Russia,
> swamp fevers, blizzards; a plague of fevers,

[31] A brand of cigarettes (Editors).

fires, blizzards—has beaten man down: Russia has broken out all over in spotted fever, and men—dwarfs—are the sores; and the Ukraine was convulsed and thrown against the Volga, the Donets, and Lithuania, as the hand of a man in high fever is convulsed and thrown against his heart, his knee against his shoulder. It is the year nineteen hundred and nineteen. Yegorkas, Nilyches, Merinovs, Yerliksovs, Rostislavskis:

words—to me—are like coins to a numismatist.

But I did go to the town of Rostislavl: there they call it Roschislav. Above the hills is the sky, below the hills—floodlands, meadows, the Oka, the forests beyond the Oka: all this is ancient like the thousand years that surround me. July —that year July was terrifying, with July's parching heat and September's emptiness, with flock upon flock of rooks in the fields—the very place where the town had stood. There is no town of Rostislavl, but there is a parish of Roschislav: in eighteen hundred and sixty-eight a new church was put up; at that time the builder outwitted the church warden—or did they join forces to swindle the peasants out of their coppers? They ate the church: in modern fashion they put up a wretched limestone box. Still, there is an inscription on the wall outside which tells that this church stands where the town of Rostislavl once was. This town of Rostislavl was built by Prince Yaroslav of Ryazan in 1153, at the same time as the town of Zaraisk, for his son Rostislav.

The priest will tell you the same thing—how the town of Rostislavl was built in 1153. And the same priest will tell you how the town perished: during the Time of Troubles Ivan Zarutski together with Marina Mnizsek and her son Ivashka—the "little bandit"[32]—advanced on the town, crossed the Oka, right over there, downstream (ever since that day the place has been called "Pristan"),[33] burned, ravaged, razed the town to the ground (and so the town has been called not Rostislavl, but Raschislav ever since). From Roschislav Ivan Zarutski wanted to march on Zaraisk, but the peasants got wind of it (and so the village is called Pronyukhovo); the Prince of Zaraisk went to meet him and gave battle—in those days they fought with pole-axes—and there's been a village Sekirina ever since. And that's all there is to say about the town, although you can read in the *Ryazan Diocesan Gazette* that the princes of Tula, Ryazan, and Suzdal used to assemble in the town of Rostislavl to march against the Mordvinians and the Meshchera. And that's all there is to say about the town of Rostislavl—and that's probably not true, either.

And another thing. In the eighties, some princess or other—the old folk still remember her, although her name has been forgotten; black-haired she was, all in black, and her eyes were like coals—drove the priest out of the parish, got it into her head to found a nunnery, gathered nuns around her, got hold of a parishless priest; she used to send her sons—who were in the Horse Guards—five thousand each a year; Meleti, the Bishop of Ryazan, used to be her drinking companion; she had papers from the Tsar. It took a visit from the vice-governor to get her out.

That's all there is to say.

That's all there is to say.

The town of Ras-chi-slav. *Gorod:* the root of the word *gorodit'*.[34] And in that year they said in the lands of

[32] Son of the second False Dimitri—the "bandit of Tushino"—and his wife, Marina Mnizsek, the Polish adventuress. Ivan Zarutski was a Cossack leader who supported the "bandit" and, later, Marina and her son (Editors).

[33] In this passage Pilnyak links the names of the villages around the vanished town and the town itself with certain words appropriate to the narration: Pristan—*pristat'* (to land); Raschislav—*raschistit'* (to clear, to raze); Pronyukhovo—*pronyukhat'* (to get wind of); Sekirina—*sekira* (poleax) (Editors).

[34] *Gorod*—town; *gorodit'*—to enclose (Editors).

Ryazan, Zaraisk—"in Christ's bosom"—that the Revolution was over.

On the fifteenth of May, fifteen hundred and ninety-three, when the Tsarevitch Dimitri was murdered in Ug-lich, the great bell of Uglich was sounded. Boris Godunov punished the bell by having one of its ears chopped off, and exiled it, minus an ear, to Siberia by way of Pelym. On the bell is an inscription: ". . . sent into exile from the town of Uglich to the town of Tobolsk in Siberia, to the Church of the All-merciful Saviour that stands in the market square, and later sounded the hours in the Sofi-skaya bell tower."

At the time of the Revolution the bell was returned to Uglich, to its old bell tower.

.   .   .   .

Was there or was there not a town of Roschislavl? I haven't read about it in books. Kolomna, Kashira, Tarusa —if you say a word over and over again its content will be eroded, and it will take on a new meaning—the meaning of its sounds.

The-town-of-Ros-chi-slavl. Words to me are like coins to a numismatist. The numismatics of words is history. Goo-vooz—the cry of the wood-devil.

Ryazan-*baba*.

Ryazan apples.

My name is Boris, I've been told that it's a brigand's name. That chauffeur—was he called Pugin?—the one who stole half of his own sheep, named his son: Motor.

About Bread

The Commune "Labor."
"And where are you going?"
"To Sapronovo."
"Get along with you, then."
"Why d'you want to know?"
"We don't let Commune folk through the village."

"Why not?"

"They don't let our herd through their pasture, and what's more, they hold out on food. So we won't let them through."

Are *chastushkas* a commentary on life, or is life a commentary on *chastushkas?* "I'm sitting on a barrel, on a barrel full of flour. And don't you think, you ——, that Russia's in your power." This conversation about the Sapronovo Commune folk took place at the edge of the village. Every Jew has something of eternity in his eyes, the mark of Judaism—the crimson thread which joins the seams of humanity. It was Jesus Christ who said: "Man shall not live by bread alone"—it takes a bit of meat, too. The man, the Jew, the Zionist—in a straw hat, a cotton suit, with a celluloid dickey, carrying a walking stick and a basket—with eyes like the third century before the birth of Christ, came to Alyoshka Kurovodov's hut in Sapronov Hills to pick up provisions.

"A-a-h! The great man himself—our Maxim Gorki!"

Those were the days fated by July, when Ryazan was down to taters, and it was a holiday. On the *zavalinka* peasants were talking:

"When we shared out dues among ourselves, they took ninety, you know, poods; and now, ak'shly, it's a hundred and twenty; tax, you know. And then like there's wool, butter, eggs. To our thinking sharing-out was nothing but a swindle. But still, they used to take most from the five richest houses, and that's a fac'. And now—I've got eight mouths to feed, and·he's only got two, but that don't make no difference—you pay according to what land you've got."

"And the peasants don't want no sharing-out by the head, neither. They want to go on living the same as they did before, that's what they say."

Alyoshka said to his mother:

"What are you standing there for with your eyes popping? You've got the samovar going—so get the hell out, go next door."

Inside the hut the walls were covered with posters—with deserters and *burzhuis*. On the floor—mats; before the icons—an icon lamp. Alyoshka—in patent-leather boots, wearing a watch and chain—smelled like Nil Nilovich Tyshko, shone like a mirror. He went out of the hut, returned, bringing with him some ham, some paper and ink; he took out a bottle from his pocket and handed over a note to be read out loud:

> *Dear Liksey Semyonych, it's so long since I seen you, meet me for a randevoo.*

"Have a drink—it'll help. It's good brew. And then write me a real beautiful letter. Here you are. Write. Tell her I'm pining away for her, but can't meet her noways. And then write to Dunka Klimova, tell her to come out walking with me. We'll see to the taters—we've got a show on tonight at the Komsomol,[35] a 'formance—we'll see to them afterward at the Commune people's, the Merinovs. The others wouldn't let us have any, they have to stretch their own taters with dock."

A crowd of young men from the village, with an accordion, came trooping in.

> *You can't get no vodka, not home brew nor shop,*
> *So drink up the varnish, boys—to the last drop! . . .*

"Nothing to eat—but life's a treat!"

The sky was swallow-streaked—as in autumn toward evening; but the heat was dropping as it does in July; all over the village cocks were crowing, and from the orchards behind the back fences came the cooings of wild doves, solitary, infrequent—again as in autumn. In a barn across the street the hand mill was champing rye; its snorting could be heard from one end of the village to the other. And dusk came down on Sapronov Hills with the greenish murk of July and the chill of September. The moon rose slowly: townspeople who had mutilated dates and hours forgot nights and Julys.

That evening in the school (O the District school stood solid and sound, O the District school, it fell to the ground!

---

[35] Abbreviation for "Young Communist League" (Editors).

A general meeting was called on the spot, they talked for a year—that's as far as they got!), that evening in the school beneath a banner with the words:

Sapronovo Cultural and Educational Circle
of the RKSM[36]

there was a show. The man, the Jew, the Zionist, with eyes like the century, Alyoshka dragged along with him—because of a misunderstanding, it must be understood; and the Jew was the only old man who passed for a young one, being clean-shaven. What with young men, girls, adolescents packed together like people in a cattle car, the wall of bodies, the buffers of female breasts, the squeaking, the squealing, the accordion, the gray-blue makhorka smoke, the smells of perspiration, pomade, powder, even iodoform, it was as jolly as Christmas holidays; and on the school desks which made up the stage, next to Marya Yuryevna Skurlatova, stood the chairman of the RKSM, wearing white elkskin breeches tucked in his boots.

"If it isn't babyface, the Soviet sweetheart, Leksey Semyonych!"

"Babyface yourself. Just you wait, I'll! . . ." and he whistled.

"Yes, sir; no, sir; anything you say, sir!"

"It's a real sharp tongue you got. . . ."

The chairman in elkskin breeches yelled with all his might:

"Comrades! The show is starting. Please be quiet and put out the lamps in the hall."

He was interrupted by lame Marya Yuryevna Skurlatova.

"Comrades. In the play there is an officer with gold epaulets. Gold-epaulet wearers have been abolished—it's just in the play. . . ."

In the darkness, suddenly quiet, there was a whisper:

[36] Initials standing for "Young Communist League of Russia" (Editors).

"Liksey Semyonych, I'm asking you, leave off pinching. Liksey Semyonych, please. . . ."

They played on the desks without a prompter; the play might have been a substitute for the discontinued express trains, and costumes—not costumes, but a Christmas fancy-dress party. And in the middle of the play—bang, clatter! . . . A lamp had fallen off a desk. There were shouts, howls, hubbub—night smells, earth smells drifted in through a broken window. The lamp was put out. The chairman of the RKSM in his elkskin breeches said:

"Comrades! . . . A lamp has fallen, now what shall it be: do we start the show right from the beginning or do we go on from where the fire started? . . ."

"Get on with it—from the beginning! . . . Ooo! Aaa!"

The man, the Jew, the Zionist with eyes like the century, having given Alyoshka the slip, left the show quietly. Auntie Ulyana, Alyoshka's mother, was lying on the stove ledge; the visitor had stretched out on the bench. The icon lamp burned in the quiet, a cricket chirped autumnally. In the village cocks were crowing.

"You asleep?"

"No."

"What's going to happen now, explain it to me, for Christ's sake."

"What do you mean?"

"I don't mean how we live—I know, hunger is hunger—not enough to go round—God sent it. . . . But what's got into people? Explain it to me, you're educated. Look how it is: Leksey knocks me in the teeth with anything handy —me, an old woman, his mother—guzzles liquor, gets girls in trouble. . . . And the girls? There's not a single one that hasn't gone wrong—all they're good for is messing around with boys in the barns. . . . But it's no use talking about the girls—they're weak in the head. The men and women have gone crazy; they get married three times over, keep running to Yagorka—and it's all out of foolishness, just plain foolishness. Trickery, spec'lation, daylight robbery. . . . They abolished the Tsar—well, he was weak in the head. But what did they abolish God for? Explain it to me, for Christ's sake, you're educated. . . ."

The old woman let her legs dangle from the stove ledge; she sat there wild-haired, frightening. To lie on the stove, to watch cockroaches, and to think—about taters. . . . And the eyes, the eyes that look at cockroaches, had existed in the third century before the birth of Christ.

"You won't say a word? I'll tell you. An-tik-christ has come. That's what. Antikchrist, the end of the world."

And late that night Alyoshka came clumping into the hut. He clattered about, gave a whistle.

"Get up. We're going."

"Where?"

"Where, he wants to know. To the Commune, that's where. . . ."

They went out, started off. They went by way of the ravine—Biryuchi Gully; a stream glinted nearby, but there was no mist; dew fell, autumnal, chill—the cotton suit soon got damp. The sky, tufted with trees, hung down like a rich vestment. Night. Autumn. Smugglers—that's what they were; if they'd been caught, they'd have been beaten up.

"Keep to the bottom. They haven't got patrols, but maybe they're on the lookout. They did beat somebody up today, a town man. No smoking, neither. . . . Dunka Klimova—she did come out walking—we had all the walking we wanted. . . . We'll soon be there."

Where and how, here among the ravines, did the Devil break his leg? The bathhouse on the Yerliksov estate stood with its back to the ravine; they were suddenly up against the bathhouse. The trees confused distances—the sky floated free from behind the trees like a vast, starred ice floe; in the heavens were worked the miracles of September, a liturgy of ice. . . . And the manor house stood in the wet dark, in emptiness, in night. . . . Taking a familiar path, Alyoshka went up to the end window, knocked, knocked again, knocked once more.

As if there were nothing out of the ordinary, a man came out—Login Merinov, secretary of the Commune "Labor," not a man, but a gnarled stump from the bottom of a pond, with felt boots on its two lower stumps.

"That you, Leksey?"

"You, Login? Bring it out."

"Who's with you?"

"A friend."

"All right, won't be a minute. I brought it all over last night. Three sacks of taters, a pood of wheat, half a pood of butter. Is your friend from Moscow?"

"No, from town. Here's the cash. It's all there, like we agreed."

"Please to meet you. You haven't got any yellow thousands?[37] People around here think the world of the yellows. . . . Whenever you need anything, mister, just come around—please to meet you. Of course they don't allow it, but they can. . . ."

Each took his load and staggered off with it—in the night, beneath the blue ice of the heavens' miracles. In the ravine, having reached safe ground, they sat down to rest, and lit up.

"Listen, listen to me, Solomon Moiseyich, I'll tell you something."

"What?"

"I've been a real friend—I showed you where, without getting anything out of it. . . . I'll tell you something. . . . Buy me—a 'locipede. . . ."

"A what?"

"A 'locipede."

"What d'you want one for?"

"Please buy me a 'locipede. I want one awful bad. You buy it for me, 'cause they'd skin me in town. Maybe someone you know—tell them I can make it in taters or butter. I do want a 'locipede awful bad."

. . . Huts in the village stood nocturnal, autumnal, dug in, clenching the earth, hugging taters, sitting on taters. The man's eyes held thousands of years. And it was he

[37] Golden-yellow thousand-ruble notes issued in 1918, bearing the Russian imperial double-headed eagle, stripped, however, of its crown, orb, and scepter (Editors).

who looked into the heavens with them, into the ice of the heavens where a fearsome, cold, numb winter was already coming into being.

An eagle owl cried out somewhere in the ravine—like a wood-devil:

"Goo-voo-ooz!"

August 1, 1921

THE TALE OF
THE UNEXTINGUISHED MOON

Chapter One

At dawn factory whistles sounded over the city. A gray murk of night, fog, and sleet trailed in alleyways, already dissolving in a dawn which seemed likely to be cheerless, frosty, and gray. At that hour in newspaper printing plants rotary presses were bringing out the final copies of the edition, and soon from the dispatch yards boys were hurrying through the streets with bundles of papers; one or two or them stood at deserted street corners shouting as if in rehearsal for the day's shouting ahead:

"Revolution in China! Army Commander Gavrilov arrives! Army Commander sick!"

It was at that hour that a train drew in at the station where trains from the south arrive. It was a special train. At the end of it was a blue lounge car—quiet, with sentries on the footboards and heavy curtains drawn behind plate-glass windows; its sides gleamed grayish where light struck them. The train had come out of the black night, from fields that had squandered the summer on luxuries and now had only winter left—fields that had been plundered in summer and abandoned to a hoary old age. Slowly and with little noise the train crept beneath the roof of the station and was switched to a siding. The platform was deserted. It was no doubt by chance that extra militia with green stripes on their uniforms stood at the gates. Three officers with rhomboids on their sleeves went through to the lounge car. There they returned salutes and stood for a while by the steps as the sentry whispered to someone inside the car; then the three went up and disappeared behind door hangings. Electric light flashed on in the car. Two army electricians began bustling about, one by the car and one under the station roof, stringing telephone wires to the car. A man wearing a threadbare spring coat and an unseasonable fur cap with earflaps approached the car. This man saluted no one, and no one saluted him. He said:

"Tell Nikolai Ivanovich that Popov is here."

The Red Army man looked slowly at Popov, examined him, noted his worn, unpolished shoes, and replied slowly:

"The Comrade Army Commander isn't up yet."

Popov gave the Red Army man a friendly smile and for some reason began to speak in a familiar manner. He said amicably:

"That doesn't matter, sonny, just you go and tell him that Popov is here."

The Red Army man went in and came back again. Then Popov climbed up into the car. Night was still trapped there—the curtains were drawn and the electric light was burning. On the table next to the lamp lay an open book, and near to it was a plate with some half-eaten gruel; behind the plate lay an unbuttoned Colt holster, its leather strap twisted like a snake. At the other end of the table stood several opened bottles. The three officers with rhomboids on their sleeves sat in leather armchairs to one side of the table along the wall, sat very respectfully at attention, holding their briefcases in silence. Popov squeezed past the table, took off his coat and cap, laid them beside him, picked up the open book, and glanced at it. An attendant, indifferent to everything in the world, came and cleared the table; the bottles he put somewhere in a corner; he brushed pomegranate rinds onto a small tray, and, having spread a tablecloth, placed on it a solitary glass in a holder, a plate of stale bread, an egg cup; he brought in two eggs on a plate, salt, several small medicine bottles; he lifted a corner of a curtain, took a look at the morning, then drew the curtain back from the windows— the cords made a forlorn hissing sound—and switched off the light; into the lounge crept a gray, frosty autumn morning. Every face was yellow in the gloom—the thin, watery light was like a yellowish discharge from an infected wound. An orderly appeared in the doorway and stood next to the attendant; the field office was already in operation; the ringing of the telephone broke the silence.

It was at this point that the Army Commander came out of the sleeping compartment into the lounge. He was a rather short, broad-shouldered man, fair, with long hair combed back. His tunic of green army cloth with four rhomboids on the sleeve was ill-fitting and wrinkled. Although his spurred boots had been polished with the utmost care, their worn-down heels bore witness to long service. This was a man whose name stood for the heroism of the Civil War, for the thousands, tens of thousands, hundreds of thousands who had stood behind him—for thousands, tens of thousands, hundreds of thousands of deaths, agonies, mutilations—for the cold, the ice-covered ground, the scorching heat of long marches—for the thunder of guns, the whistling of bullets and night winds—for bonfires in the night, for campaigns, victories and routes, and—again —for death. This was a man who had had command over armies, over thousands of men; who had had command over men, victories, death—over gunpowder, smoke, broken bones, torn flesh, over those victories which vast crowds with hundreds of red banners had acclaimed and of which the news had flown around the world—those victories after which deep holes had been dug in the sandy soil of Russia for the corpses, holes into which thousands of human bodies were flung in heaps. This was a man whose name was overgrown with legends of wars, feats of leadership, boundless valor, boldness, stubborn determination. This was a man who had the right and the will to send men to kill other men and to die.

Into the lounge came a rather short, broad-shouldered man with the good-natured, slightly weary face of a seminarian. He walked quickly, and his gait revealed both a cavalryman and a man who was very much a civilian, not at all a soldier. The three staff officers sprang to attention in his presence. The Commander came to a stop in front of them, did not offer his hand, made the sign which allowed them to stand at ease. And in this way, standing in front of them, the Commander heard their reports; each of the three stepped forward, came to attention, and reported, ". . . as commander of . . . ," ". . . in the service of the Revolution . . ." The Commander shook hands with each man in turn as he finished his report, probably without having listened to him. He then sat down in front of the solitary glass, and the attendant suddenly appeared to pour tea from a gleaming teapot. The Commander picked up an egg.

"How are things going?" he asked simply, brushing aside formalities.

One of the three began speaking, told him the news, and then asked in his turn:

"How is your health, Comrade Gavrilov?"

For a brief moment the Commander's face took on a distant expression; he said with some annoyance:

"Well, I've been in the Caucasus for treatment. I'm all right now." He paused. "I'm well now." He paused. "See to it that there are no official welcomes, no guards of honor; in general . . ." He paused. "You may go, comrades."

The three staff officers rose to go. The Commander shook hands with each of them without getting up. They left the lounge quietly. When the Commander came into the lounge Popov had not greeted him; he had picked up the book and turned away from the Commander as he leafed through it. The Commander had given Popov a sidelong glance and had not greeted him either, pretending not to have noticed the man. When the staff officers had left, the Commander asked Popov, still without a word of welcome, as if they had seen each other the evening before:

"Would you like some tea or wine, Alyoshka?"

Popov had no time to reply, because an orderly stepped forward and began to make his report to the "Comrade Army Commander": the automobile had been unloaded from the flatcar, some official letters had been delivered to the office—one of the letters was from House Number

One, it was marked "secret," had been brought by his secretary—an apartment had been made ready for him at
headquarters, a pile of telegrams and letters of welcome
had arrived. The Commander dismissed the orderly, saying that he would continue to live in the car. The attendant,
without waiting for Popov's answer, placed two glasses
on the table, one for tea and the other for wine. Popov
got out of his corner and sat down by the Commander.

"How's your health, Nikolasha?" Popov asked with real
concern, as a brother might.

"My health is as it should be; I'm back to normal, I'm
well—but, who knows, perhaps you'll have to stand in a
guard of honor by my coffin," Gavrilov replied, perhaps
joking, perhaps in earnest; if it was a joke, it was a grim
one.

These two, Popov and Gavrilov, were bound by ties of
long-standing friendship, by the underground work which
they had carried on side by side, by their work together
at a factory long ago in their young days when they had
started life as weavers in Orekhovo-Zuyevo; later they
were prisoners together at Bogorodsk, and still later they
shared the life of professional revolutionaries: exile, escape,
underground work, Taganskaya Transit Prison, exile, escape, emigration—Paris, Vienna, Chicago—and then the
thunderclouds of 1914—Brindisi, Salonika, Rumania, Kiev,
Moscow, St. Petersburg—and then the storm of 1917, the
Smolny Institute, October, the roar of cannon over the
Kremlin, and finally—one of them is Chief of Staff of the
Guards in Rostov-on-the-Don, and the other the elected
representative of the proletarian nobility, as Rykov wittily
remarked, in Tula; for one in those days—wars and command over guns, men, and death; for the other—provincial committees, executive committees, the Supreme Economic Council, conferences, meetings, and reports. For
both of them, everything—life, thoughts—devoted to the
greatest revolution, the greatest justice and truth, in the
world. But to each other they had always remained
Nikolasha and Aleksey, Alyoshka, always the close friends
of their textile-mill days, without rank or formality.

"Tell me about your health, Nikolasha," said Popov.

"Well, it's like this: I had a stomach ulcer—perhaps I still have it. You know—pains, vomiting blood, terrible heartburn—awful business." The Commander spoke quietly, leaning toward Aleksey. "They sent me to the Caucasus for treatment—the pains went, I returned to work, carried on for six months, and then, again—nausea, pains; I went back to the Caucasus. Now the pains are gone again—I even drank a bottle of wine, just to see what would happen. . . ." The Commander interrupted himself; "If you'd like some wine, Alyoshka, there's some under the seat—I brought you a small case. Open a bottle!"

Popov sat leaning his head on the palm of his hand. He replied:

"No, I don't drink in the morning. Go on."

"Well, so my health is in perfect order." The Commander paused. "Tell me, Alyoshka—why have I been brought here—do you know?"

"No."

"An order came to leave directly from the Caucasus. I didn't even stop off to see my wife." The Commander paused. "Devil knows what it can be. I can't think of anything—as far as the army goes, everything is under control; there are no conferences, nothing at all."

The Commander talked about the army and the war, and was doubtless unaware that when he talked about the army he ceased to be a weaver and became a leader of men, a Red General of the Red Army; the Commander began talking about their life in Orekhovo-Zuyevo, and was doubtless unaware that he then became a weaver—the same weaver who had at that time fallen in love with a schoolteacher from the other side of the river, who had polished his boots for her sake and walked to school barefoot to keep them from getting dusty, putting them on only when he reached a little wood near the school—the same weaver who had bought a fancy shirt with a bow tie and a hat à la devil-take-it. Yet somehow he never got any further with the teacher than talking about political pamphlets; nothing came of their friendship—the teacher turned him down. The Commander-weaver was a good, easygoing man who liked to joke and could see the funny side of things, and now he joked as he talked with his friend; only now and then would he suddenly return to the present, and then he became restless: he remembered the mysterious summons, he shifted awkwardly, and then it was a healthy weaver talking about a sick Commander: "A bigwig, a field marshal, a senator—what a laugh! And I can't even eat buckwheat porridge. . . . Yes, my friend, the Central Committee plays strange tricks on a man—you have to take it as it comes." He retreated into silence.

"Don't beat about the bush, Nikolasha; tell me, what do you suspect?" said Popov. "What was all that about a guard of honor?"

The Commander replied slowly, after a pause.

"In Rostov I met Potap"—he used the name by which a leading revolutionary, one of the "Glorious Band" of 1918, was known within the Party—"well, he told me . . . he tried to persuade me to have an operation, to have the ulcer removed or perhaps have it sewn up; there was something suspicious about the way he tried to persuade me!" The Commander fell silent. "I feel in good health, everything in me revolts against the operation; I don't want it—I'll get well without it. After all, there are no pains at all now, I've put on weight, and . . . damn it all, I'm a grown man, an old man already, a bigwig, and I have to worry about my belly. I feel ashamed." The Commander paused, picked up the open book. "I'm reading old man Tolstoy—*Childhood and Boyhood;* he wrote well; the old man had a feeling for life, for the instincts in our blood. . . . I've seen enough blood, but . . . but I'm afraid of the operation like a kid. I don't want it, they'll kill me! . . . How well the old man understood what human blood means."

An orderly entered, came to attention, made his report: they had brought a dispatch from headquarters; a car from House Number One had arrived for the Commander, he was requested to go there; some new telegrams had arrived; someone was there to pick up a package which had been sent from the south. The orderly placed a pile of newspapers on the table. The Commander dismissed the orderly. The Commander ordered his greatcoat to be got ready; he unfolded a paper. In the section in which appeared accounts of the most important events of the day the headline read: "Army Commander Gavrilov Arrives," and on the third page it was reported that "Commander Gavrilov arrives today; he has temporarily left his post in order to undergo an operation for a stomach ulcer." In the same paragraph it was reported that "Comrade Gavrilov's health gives grounds for concern," but that "the professors are confident that the outcome of the operation will be favorable."

Gavrilov—the old fighter of the Revolution, soldier, Army Commander, leader, who had sent thousands of men to die—the apex of a military machine which existed to kill, to die, to spill blood for victory—leaned back in his chair, wiped his forehead, looked intently at Popov, said:

"Listen to me, Alyoshka! There's something behind this! Yes. . . . But what can I do?" And he shouted, "Orderly, my coat!"

Chapter Two

At the intersection of two of the city's main streets, where cars, people, and drays flowed in an endless stream, a colonnaded house stood behind an iron fence. There was no signboard of any kind outside the house. Two helmeted sentries stood at the gates, which were surmounted by griffins. Past the house flowed people, the sounds of automobile horns, crowds, human time—flowed the gray day, newspaper boys, men with briefcases, women in knee-length skirts and stockings which deceived the eye, making their legs seem bare; behind the griffined gates time took its ease and seemed to be coming to a standstill. And on the outskirts of the city was another house, also in the classical style, behind an iron fence, colonnaded, flanked by outbuildings and with some mythological nonsense of hideous, grimacing faces on bas-reliefs. There were two gateways to the house; fauns made faces from the gateposts; gatehouses stood on either side, and on benches nearby sat watchmen in felt boots and aprons with brass badges on their aprons. A closed car, black with red crosses and bearing the word "Ambulance," stood near the gates.

That day the paper with the largest circulation carried an editorial "to mark the third anniversary of the return to the gold standard" which pointed out that a stable currency can exist "only when the entire economic life of the country is based on strict economic considerations, on solid economic foundations. State subsidies and the management of the national economy without regard to the budget will inevitably undermine a stable financial system." In headline type appeared: "China's Struggle Against the Imperialists." The foreign news section carried telegrams from England, France, Germany, Czechoslovakia, Latvia, America. Across the bottom of one page was spread a long article entitled "The Revolutionary Movement and the Use of Force." There were also two pages of advertisements, among which appeared in large type, "Facing Facts—Syphilis" and "A new book by S. Broide, *In the Madhouse*."

At noon a closed Rolls drew up in front of House Number One—the house which made time slow down. A sentry opened the door of the limousine and the Commander got out.

In the study at the far end of the house the heavy curtains were half drawn, and the street hurried by beyond the windows; a fire was burning in the grate; on the red felt of the desk stood three telephones, as if to affirm, in company with the crackling logs in the fireplace, the quietness of the room; the three telephones brought three of the city's arteries into the study, so that from its silence commands could be issued and so that everything going on in the city's arteries could be known. On the desk stood a writing set, bronze and massive, and in the penholder were stuck a dozen red and blue pencils. To the wall behind the desk was fixed a radio receiver with two pairs of earphones, and rows of electric buttons were lined up like a company of soldiers at attention—from one connecting with the reception room to one marked "War Alarm." Opposite the desk stood an armchair; behind the desk the unbending man sat on a wooden chair. The heavy curtains were half drawn, and on the desk an electric light burned under a green shade; the face of the unbending man was lost in the shadows.

The Commander walked across the carpet and sat down in the leather armchair.

Number One, the unbending man:

"It is not for us to talk about the grindstone of the Revolution, Gavrilov. The wheel of history, unfortunately I suppose, is turned mainly by blood and death—particularly the wheel of revolution. It is not for you and me to talk of blood and death. You remember how the two of us led half-naked Red Army men against Yekaterinov. You had a rifle and I had a rifle. Your horse was blown up under you by a shell and you went ahead on foot. Some of our men began to run and you shot one of them down with your revolver to stop the rest. Commander, you would have shot me, too, if I had lost my nerve, and I suppose you would have been right."

Number Two, the Commander:

"Well, you have got a nice little setup here—quite the minister. Is smoking allowed? I don't see any cigarette butts."

"Don't smoke—you shouldn't. Your health doesn't permit it. I don't smoke myself."

Number Two, curtly:

"Come to the point. What have you brought me here for? Don't play the diplomat with me. Let's hear it!"

"I have asked you to come here because you need to have an operation. You are a man the Revolution cannot spare. I called in the professors and they said you'll be on your feet in a month. The Revolution demands it. The professors are waiting for you—they'll examine you and find out what the matter is. I have already given the order. There's even a man from Germany."

Number Two:

"You do as you like, but I'll smoke anyway. My doctors told me there's no need for an operation and that everything will heal by itself. I feel perfectly well—there's no need at all for an operation, I don't want it."

Number One stuck his hand behind him, felt for a button on the wall, rang; a noiseless secretary entered; Number One asked, "Is there anyone waiting to see me?" The secretary replied in the affirmative. Number One made no reply, dismissed the secretary.

Number One:

"Comrade Commander, you remember how we debated whether or not to send four thousand men to certain death? You ordered them to be sent. You were right. In three weeks you'll be on your feet. You must forgive me, but I have already given the order."

The telephone rang—not the city telephone, but the internal one, which had no more than thirty or forty lines. Number One picked up the receiver, listened, asked a question, said, "A note to the French? An official one of course, as I told you yesterday. You understand—remember how we fished for trout—the French are a very slippery lot. What? Yes, yes. Get things moving. So long."

Number One:

"You must forgive me, but there is nothing further to discuss, Comrade Gavrilov."

The Commander finished his cigarette, stuck the end in among the red and blue pencils, got up from the armchair.

The Commander:

"Good-bye."

Number One:

"So long."

The Commander walked over red carpets to the entrance; the Rolls carried him into the noise of the streets. The unbending man remained in the study. No one else came in to see him. Unbending, he sat over his papers, a fat red pencil in his hand. He rang; the secretary came in; he said, "See that the cigarette butt is removed from here, from this stand!"—and again he was silent over his papers, red pencil in hand. One hour passed, and another, and still the man sat over his papers, working. Once the telephone rang; he listened and replied, "Two million rubles' worth of galoshes and textiles for Turkestan to plug up the hole in consumer goods? Yes, of course! Go to it! So long." An attendant came in noiselessly, put down a tray with a glass of tea and a piece of cold meat covered with a napkin on the small table by the window, went out. Then the unbending man rang for his secretary again, asked, "Is the confidential summary ready?" The secretary replied in the affirmative—"Bring it in." And once more the man was silent for a long time over a large sheet of paper—over columns headed: People's Commissariat for Foreign Affairs, Political and Economic Divisions of OGPU, People's Commissariat for Foreign Trade, People's Commissariat for Labor. Then into the study walked two men —the other two of the ruling "troika."

At four o'clock several cars pulled up outside House Number Two on the outskirts of the city. The house hugged the darkness, as if darkness could warm the dampness that pervaded it. At the gates of the house two militiamen took up positions next to the watchmen in aprons and felt boots. At the main entrance to the house two more militiamen took up positions. An officer with two orders of the Red Banner, supple as a willow rod, entered the front door with two Red Army men. They were met in the entrance hall by a man in a white coat. "Yes, yes, yes, of course."

The room was vast and empty. Its center was taken up by a table covered with white oilcloth, around which stood oilcloth-covered, high-backed chairs—the standard variety found in railroad stations. Along the wall stood an oilcloth-covered couch with a sheet over it, and by the couch —a wooden stool. In a corner, on a glass shelf over a washbasin, were arranged medicine bottles with various labels, a huge bottle of mercury chloride, a jar of green soap; nearby hung yellowish, unblued towels. The first cars to arrive brought professors, therapeutists, surgeons.

People came in, exchanged greetings; they were met by the man in charge—tall, bearded, bald, with a good-natured face.

Coming forward to greet him was Professor Lozovski—a man of about thirty-five, clean-shaven, wearing a frock coat and a pince-nez with a straight crosspiece, his eyes hiding in the inner corners of their sockets.

"Yes, yes, yes, of course."

The clean-shaven man handed the bearded one a wax-sealed envelope which had been torn open. The bearded man took out a sheet of paper, adjusted his spectacles, read it, again adjusted his spectacles, and with a puzzled expression passed it on to a third man.

The clean-shaven man, solemnly:

"A secret paper, as you can see—almost an order. It was sent to me this morning. You understand?"

First, second, third—snatches of conversation, whispered, hurried:

"How does the consultation come into it?"

"I came because of an urgent summons. There was a telegram addressed to the rector of the university."

"Army Commander Gavrilov, you know—the one who . . ."

"Yes, yes, yes, of course—the Revolution, the man in command of the army—the usual formula—and then, if you please . . ."

"A consultation."

The electric light made sharp-cut shadows. Someone took hold of someone else by the button of the breast pocket of his white coat; someone took someone else's arm to stroll about the room. . . .

Then: from the doorway came the clang of rifles and the stamp of heels—the Red Army men froze to immobility; in the doorway appeared the tall, slender youth, supple as a whip, with the orders of the Red Banner on his chest, came to attention facing the door; the Commander walked quickly into the reception room, pushed his hair

back with one hand, adjusted the collar of his tunic, said:
"Good day, comrades. Am I to undress?"

Then: without haste the professors sat down on the oilcloth-covered chairs, put their elbows on the table, rubbed
their hands, adjusted their spectacles and pince-nez, asked
the patient to sit down. The man who had passed the
envelope around, the one whose eyes had grown deep
into their sockets behind his straight pince-nez, said to
the bearded man:

"Pavel Ivanovich, I imagine that as *primus inter pares*
you will have no objection to taking the chair."

"Am I to undress?" asked the Commander, and put his
hand to his collar.

The chairman of the consultation, Pavel Ivanovich, gave
no sign of having heard the Commander's question, and
said slowly, taking his place at the head of the table:

"I suppose we ought to ask the patient when he first
became aware of the onset of the disease and what
pathological indications made him realize he was ill. After
that we'll examine the patient."

A sheet of paper covered with illegible professorial script
remains as evidence of this meeting of professors:

> *The report of the consultation in which took
> part Professor So-and-so, Professor So-and-so, Pro-
> fessor So-and-so (and so on—seven times).*
>
> *The patient, Citizen Nikolai Ivanovich Gav-
> rilov, appeared before us complaining of pain in
> the epigastric region, vomiting, heartburn. He fell
> ill two years ago, without realizing that there was
> anything wrong at first. Was given treatment out-
> side hospital and visited health resorts. No im-
> provement. At the request of the patient a
> consultation of the above-mentioned was called.*
>
> STATUS PRAESENS: *Patient's general condition
> satisfactory. Lungs—N. Heart—slight enlargement
> and accelerated pulse observed. Mild neurasthe-
> nia. Other organs—apart from stomach—no patho-
> logical symptoms observed. It was agreed that in
> all probability the patient is suffering from an*

ULCUS VENTICULI *and that an operation is unavoidable.*

*Those taking part in the consultation suggest
that Professor Anatoli Kozmich Lozovski should
operate. Professor Pavel Ivanovich Kokosov has
agreed to assist.*

City, date, signatures of the seven professors.

Subsequently, when the operation was over, it became
clear from private conversations that not a single professor
had in fact judged the operation to be in the least necessary, being of the opinion that the form which the disease
had taken did not indicate an operation—but nothing was
said of this during the consultation; only the taciturn German expressed the view that the operation was unnecessary, although he did not persist in face of his colleagues'
objections; and it was also told how, as he was getting
into the car to go to the House of Scientists after the
consultation, Professor Kokosov—the one whose eyes were
hardly visible behind his shaggy brows—said to Professor
Lozovski, "You know, if a brother of mine had this disease
I wouldn't operate," to which Professor Lozovski replied,
"Yes, of course, but . . . but it's a safe operation, after
all. . . ." The engine came to life and the car began to
move.

· · · ·

The unbending man in House Number One was still
sitting in his study. Drawn curtains completely covered the
windows. Again a fire was burning in the grate. The house
was steeped in silence, as if the silence had been hoarded
for a century. The man was sitting on his wooden chair.
This time thick books in German and English lay open in
front of him; he was writing with pen and ink in his
vertical script—in Russian on German linen paper. The
books lying open in front of him concerned statecraft, law,
and the use of power. Light fell from the ceiling of the
study, and now the man's face could be seen: it was a very
ordinary face, perhaps just a little hard, but there was great
concentration and no sign of weariness in it; the man sat
for a long time over his books and his writing pad. Then

he rang and a stenographer came in. He began to dictate. The foundation stones of his speech were the U.S.S.R., America, Britain, the world and the U.S.S.R., British sterling and Russian poods of wheat, American heavy industry, Chinese manpower. The man spoke loudly and confidently, and every phrase was a formula.

The moon was moving over the city.

At that hour the Commander was sitting in Popov's room in a large hotel where only Party members stayed. There were three of them; Gavrilov sat by the table and Natashka fidgeted on his lap. Gavrilov was lighting matches one after another; Natashka looked at each flame with the wonder that only a child can feel before the mysteries of this world, then she stuck out her lips and blew at the flame. It took more than one puff to put out a match, but when it did go out there was such amazement, such delight, and such awe in Natasha's blue eyes in the presence of this mystery that it was impossible to resist lighting another match, impossible not to bow one's head before the mystery that was Natasha herself. Later Gavrilov put Natashka to bed, sat down by her crib, said, "You close your eyes and I'll sing you a song"—and he began to sing, not knowing how, not knowing a single song, making a song up on the spot:

> *A goat came and said:*
> *Sleep, sleep, sleep, sleep, sleep.*

He smiled, looked slyly at Natasha and Popov, and sang the first things that came into his head—suggested by the sound of the words "sleep, sleep, sleep"; he sang:

> *A goat came and said:*
> *Sleep, sleep, sleep, sleep, sleep. . . .*
> *But don't pee, pee, pee, pee. . . .*

Natasha opened her eyes and smiled; and Gavrilov went on singing the last two lines in his unpracticed voice (he really couldn't sing) until Natasha fell asleep.

Then Gavrilov and Popov drank tea together.

Popov asked, "Shall I make you some gruel, Nikolka?"

They sat facing each other, talking slowly in low voices,

taking their time; much tea was drunk; Gavrilov had unbuttoned the collar of his tunic and was drinking from his
saucer. As they were drinking their second glass of tea,
after talking about this and that, Popov pushed away his
half-empty glass and said, after a pause:

"My Zina walked out on me, Nikolka, leaving the child
on my hands; she ran off with some engineer she used to
be in love with—devil knows who he is. I have no wish to
judge her; I don't want to dirty myself by calling her
names—but still, you have to admit she ran off like a bitch,
on the sly, without a word. And I'm ashamed of myself;
I picked her up out of the gutter—it was at the front—took
care of her, loved her, and like a fool took her to my heart
—and she turned out to be a spoiled miss. I never really
got to know the woman who lived with me for five
years. . . ." And Popov went into all the trivial details of
the separation, details which are always so painful because
of their very triviality—the triviality which obscures the
things that really matter. Then they began to talk about
their children, and Gavrilov spoke of his family life, his
three little boys, his wife, who was no longer young, but
who would always be the only woman in the world for him.

As he was leaving, the Commander said:

"Give me something to read—but make it something simple, something about good people, about real love—something like *Childhood and Boyhood.*"

Every corner of Popov's room was heaped with books,
but a simple book about simple human love, simple rela-
tionships, simple life, a book about the sun, about human
beings, and simple human joy—such a book was not to be
found at Popov's.

"There's revolutionary literature for you," Gavrilov said
jokingly. "All right then, I'll read Tolstoy again. I like that
bit about the old gloves he wore at the ball." And
Gavrilov's face darkened; he paused, said quietly, "I
didn't tell you, Alyoshka, so as not to waste time in useless talk—I saw the Chief today and I also went to the
hospital to see the professors. That bunch put on a great
show of learning. I don't want to be cut up—naturally,
I'm against it. Tomorrow I have to go under the knife.

Be sure to come to the hospital; don't forget the old man. Don't write anything to my wife or my boys. Good-bye!" And Gavrilov left the room without shaking Popov's hand.

A closed car was standing in front of the hotel. Gavrilov got in, said, "Home, to the station," and the car nosed into narrow streets. In the sidings the moon slithered over the rails; a dog ran past, yelped, and vanished where the rails stretched silently away into the darkness. A sentry stood at the footboard of the car; he froze to attention as the Commander passed. The orderly suddenly materialized in the corridor; the attendant poked his head out; electric lights went on in the car, and a real provincial silence—blue, unbroken—descended. The Commander went through to his sleeping compartment, took off his boots, put on his slippers, unbuttoned the collar of his tunic, rang—"Tea." He went into the lounge, sat down by the table lamp; the attendant brought tea, but the Commander left it untouched; the Commander sat for a long time over *Childhood and Boyhood,* reading, thinking. Presently he went into his bedroom, returned with a large writing pad, rang, said to his orderly, "Ink, please," and began to write slowly, deliberating over each sentence. He wrote one letter, read it through, thought it over, sealed it in an envelope. He wrote a second letter, thought it over, sealed it. He wrote a third letter—a very short one—wrote it hastily, sealed it unread. A numb silence filled the car. The sentry stood motionless by the footboard. Orderly and attendant were motionless in the corridor. It seemed that time itself was motionless. For a long time the letters in their white, addressed envelopes lay in front of the Commander. Presently the Commander took a large envelope, sealed all three letters in it, and on the envelope wrote, "To be opened after my death."

Chapter Three: Gavrilov's Death

The first snow fell on the day of Gavrilov's death. A white silence descended, blanching and lulling the city; blue tits which had flown in from the country with the snows were shaking snow from the twigs of trees outside the windows.

Professor Pavel Ivanovich Kokosov always woke up at seven o'clock, and it was at this hour that he awoke on the day of the operation.

The professor stuck his head out from under the blanket, cleared his throat noisily, stretched out a hairy arm to the bedside table, felt for his spectacles with a habitual motion of the hand, and saddled his nose with them, setting the lenses into the thicket of his eyebrows. On a birch outside the window a blue tit was scattering snow about. The professor put on a dressing gown, stuck his feet in his slippers, and went to the bathroom.

It was quiet in the house at the hour when the professor awoke, but when he emerged, coughing dryly, from the bathroom, his wife, Yekaterina Pavlovna, was already in the dining room stirring sugar into the professor's tea with a clink of spoon against glass; the samovar was hissing. The professor came out for his tea in dressing gown and slippers.

"Good morning, Pavel Ivanovich," said the wife.

"Good morning, Katerina Pavlovna," said the husband.

The professor kissed his wife's hand, sat down opposite her, settled his spectacles more comfortably into his eyebrows. The professor took a swallow of tea in silence, preparing to make some customary remark. But the ritual of morning tea was interrupted by the telephone. A telephone call was unusual at this hour. The professor looked sternly at the door of the study where the telephone was ringing, looked suspiciously at his wife—a plump, aging woman wrapped in a Japanese kimono—got up, and went to the telephone, every step expressing suspicion. The professor's words, spoken fretfully in what was meant to sound like an old man's voice, were swallowed up by the receiver.

"Well, well, I'm listening. Who's calling, and what's the matter?"

A voice at the other end of the line said that the call was from headquarters: they knew that the operation was scheduled for half past eight, and they would like to know if the professor needed any assistance—should they send a car for him? And suddenly the professor lost his temper; he snuffled into the receiver, began speaking irritably.

". . . Let me tell you that I'm a servant of society and not of private individuals; yes, yes, yes, let me tell you, my good man; I take a streetcar to the clinic, my good man. I do my duty according to my conscience, if you don't mind. And I see no reason not to take a streetcar today."

The professor banged down the receiver, cutting short the conversation, snorted, snuffled, returned to the table, to his wife and tea. He snorted once or twice, chewed his whiskers, and very soon calmed down. His eyes became visible again behind his spectacles; now they were wise and intent. The professor said quietly:

"Let's say Ivan the peasant from the village of Drakiny Luzhi gets sick—he'll lie on the stove ledge for three weeks, then he'll say a prayer, groan a bit, talk things over with his family, and go to the District hospital to see the doctor, Pyotr Ivanovich. Pyotr Ivanovich has known Ivan for fifteen years; during that time Ivan has brought a couple of dozen chickens to Pyotr Ivanovich as payment in kind, got to know all of Pyotr Ivanovich's children as they came along, and even pulled one of the boys' ears for raiding his pea patch. Ivan will come to see Pyotr Ivanovich, will present him with a hen. Pyotr Ivanovich will look him over, listen to what he has to say, and, if necessary, operate— quietly, calmly, competently—no worse than I would do it. And if the operation doesn't come off, Ivan will die, they'll put a cross over him, and that'll be the end of it. . . . Or even supposing some Anatoli Yuryevich Svintsitsky or other comes to see me. He'll talk about his symptoms till he's hoarse. I'll look him over thoroughly and look him over again half a dozen times, I'll find out all I can about him, and then I'll say, 'Go home, my friend, and live with your ulcer: if you're careful, you'll live another fifty years, but if you die, there's nothing to be done about it: God has called you, my friend.' If he says to me, 'Operate!' I'll do it, but if he doesn't want it—I would never think of doing it."

The professor was silent for a while.

"Today I am assisting at an operation at the hospital; we are operating on a Bolshevik—Army Commander Gavrilov."

"The one who . . . ," said Yekaterina Pavlovna, "who . . . well, according to the Bolshevik newspapers . . . a terrible name! And why aren't you operating, Pavel Ivanovich?"

"Well, there's nothing particularly terrible about him, of course," the professor replied. "As for why they've picked Lozovski: such are the times we live in—youth is all the rage, young people have to make their reputations. And still, when you come down to it, nobody really knows the patient after all these consultations, even though all our big names have examined him thoroughly—prodded him all over, X-rayed him, purged him out. But they miss the main thing—the man himself. It's not a man they're dealing with, but a formula—some General X they write about every day in the papers to put the fear of God into people. But just you make one slip in the operation and you'll end up in strange places—you won't even recognize your own father when they've finished with you."

Professor Anatoli Kozmich Lozovski's room was not at all like Kokosov's apartment. If Kokosov's apartment had preserved the atmosphere of Russia at the turn of the century, Lozovski's room had assumed its permanent shape between 1907 and 1916. There were heavy curtains, a wide sofa; naked bronze women served as candelabra on the oak writing table; the walls were covered with rugs, and over the rugs were hung second-rate paintings bought at exhibitions organized by the "World of Art."

Lozovski was asleep on the sofa, and not alone, but with a young and beautiful woman; his starched dickey had been dropped on a rug on the floor. Lozovski awoke, lightly kissed the woman's shoulder, got up energetically, and tugged sharply at the curtain cord. The heavy woolen curtain began sliding toward the corner, and the snowy day came into the room. Lozovski looked out joyfully at the street, the snow, the sky, as people look who are in love with the life pulsing through them.

At that moment the telephone rang. The telephone in the professor's room hung on the wall near the rug over the sofa. The professor picked up the receiver: "Yes, yes, I'm listening." Headquarters was on the line: should they send a car for him?

"Yes, please do! There's no need to worry about the operation, I'm sure it will be a brilliant success. About the car: that would be a very good idea, especially as I have some business to attend to before the operation. Yes, yes, please—about eight o'clock."

In the morning on the day of the operation—before it took place—Popov came to see Gavrilov. It was not yet dawn and the lights were still on; but there was no chance to talk, because a nurse came to take Gavrilov to the bathroom to administer a final enema. As he left the room Gavrilov said:

"Alyosha, read that bit in Tolstoy's *Boyhood* about what is and what isn't *comme il faut*. What a feeling the old man had for the instincts in our blood!" These were the last words that Popov heard from Gavrilov.

Just before the operation people were hurrying back and forth along the corridor connecting the operating room with Gavrilov's room, whispering, bustling about noiselessly. The evening before, a rubber tube had been inserted into Gavrilov's esophagus—a siphon to pump out gastric juice and to irrigate the stomach, the kind of rubber instrument that leaves a feeling of nausea and depresses the spirit as if it existed for the purpose of affronting human dignity. On the morning of the operation an enema was administered for the last time. Gavrilov came into the operating room wearing a hospital dressing gown and shirt and pants of coarse linen (the shirt had laces instead of buttons), with numbered hospital slippers on his bare feet (they had changed his clothes for the last time that morning—and given him sterilized things to wear); he entered the operating room pale, drawn, and tired.

In the anteroom alcohol burners hummed, water boiled in long, nickel-plated boxes; there were silent people in white gowns. The operating room was very large and painted all over—floor, walls, ceiling—with white oil paint. The room was unusually light because one entire wall was a window, and that window looked out over the river. In the center of the room stood a long white table—the operating table. Here Gavrilov was met by Kokosov and Lozovski. Both were wearing white gowns and both put on white caps, like cooks; in addition, Kokosov covered his beard with a mask, leaving only his overgrown eyes exposed. Along a wall stood a dozen people in white gowns.

Gavrilov entered the room calmly, accompanied by a nurse; he bowed silently to the professors and walked to the table; he looked out at the far bank of the river, clasped his hands behind his back. A second nurse brought in a boiling sterilizer containing instruments—a long, nickel-plated box suspended from a hook.

Lozovski asked Kokosov in a whisper:

"Shall we begin, Pavel Ivanovich?"

"Yes, yes, of course," replied Kokosov.

And the professors went to wash their hands over and over again, to pour mercury chloride solution over them, to swab them with iodine. The anesthetist checked the mask and fingered his bottle.

"Let's begin then, Comrade Gavrilov," said Lozovski. "Would you kindly lie down on the table? Take your slippers off."

Gavrilov looked at the nurse and, slightly embarrassed, straightened his shirt; she gave Gavrilov a brief glance, as if he were a thing, and smiled as one smiles at a child. Gavrilov sat down on the table, kicked off one slipper, then the other, and quickly lay down, adjusting the cushion under his head—closed his eyes. Then quickly, deftly, with practiced skill the nurse buckled the straps around his legs, binding him fast to the table. The anesthetist laid a towel on the patient's eyes, smeared vaseline all over his nose and mouth, put the mask over his face, took his hand to check the pulse, and poured chloroform onto the mask; the cloying smell drifted through the room.

The anesthetist noted down the time at which the operation began. The professors moved to the window in silence. Using forceps, the nurse began to take out and arrange on the sterilized gauze scalpels, sterilized towels, Peon's and Kocher's clamps, pincers, needles, and silk thread. The anesthetist continued to add chloroform. Silence settled upon the room. Then the patient began to jerk his head from side to side and groan.

"I can't breathe, take off the mask," Gavrilov said, and snapped his teeth.

"Please be patient a little," answered the anesthetist.

A few minutes later the patient began singing and talking:

"The ice is gone, the Volga flows to sea, my golden one, my precious one; a foolish girl am I, and love has come to me," sang the Commander, and then whispered, "Sleep, sleep, sleep." After a brief silence he said sternly, "And never give me cranberry jelly again, I'm sick of it, it isn't *comme il faut.*" He fell silent again, then shouted sternly, as he must have shouted in combat: "No retreat! Not a step! I'll shoot! Alyoshka! Brother! Full speed ahead—the land is out of sight. I remember everything. And so I know what the Revolution means, what a force it is. And I'm not afraid of death." And again he began to sing, "Beyond the Urals lives a carpenter, my golden one, my precious one. . . ."

"How do you feel? Aren't you sleepy?" the anesthetist asked Gavrilov softly.

And Gavrilov replied in his normal voice, also softly, like a conspirator:

"Not so good. I can't breathe."

"Be patient just a little longer," said the anesthetist, and poured on more chloroform.

Kokosov looked anxiously at the clock and bent his head over the patient's case history, read it through once more.

An organism can react peculiarly to certain drugs. For twenty-seven minutes they had been trying to put Gavrilov to sleep.

Kokosov called over a junior assistant and thrust his head forward for him to adjust the spectacles on the professorial nose. The anesthetist whispered anxiously to Lozovski:

"Perhaps we should give up chloroform and try ether?"

"Let's keep on with chloroform. Otherwise we'll have to postpone the operation. Awkward."

Kokosov looked around sternly and lowered his eyes, worried. The anesthetist poured on more chloroform. The professors remained silent.

Gavrilov finally went to sleep in the forty-eighth minute. Then the professors rubbed their hands with alcohol for the last time. The nurse bared Gavrilov's stomach; the skinny ribs and flat belly were exposed.

With sweeping strokes Professor Kokosov rubbed alcohol, benzine, and iodine into the area of incision—the epigastric region. A nurse brought sheets to cover Gavrilov's legs and head. Another poured half a bottle of iodine over Professor Lozovski's hands.

Lozovski picked up a scalpel and drew it over the skin. Blood spurted and the skin spread apart, sliding off layers of fat, yellow like mutton fat, with interlayers of blood vessels. Lozovski again cut into the human meat, opening the fascia—white and gleaming, interlayered with faintly lilac muscles. With a dexterity surprising in so bearish a man, Kokosov closed off blood vessels, using Peon's and Kocher's clamps.

With another knife Lozovski cut through the sac of the peritoneum. He put aside the knife and wiped away the blood with sterilized towels. Through the slit could be seen the intestines and the milky-blue sac of the stomach. Lozovski put his hand in among the intestines, turned the stomach round, and kneaded it.

On the gleaming wall of the stomach, on the spot where the ulcer should have been, was a scar—white as if molded from wax, resembling the larva of a dung beetle—a scar which showed that the ulcer had already healed and that the operation was pointless.

But at that moment, the very moment when Gavrilov's stomach was in Lozovski's hands . . .

"Pulse! Pulse!" shouted the anesthetist.

"Respiration!" Kokosov confirmed, automatically it seemed.

And then Kokosov's eyes, full of anger, of terrible anger, started out from behind his shaggy brows and spectacles, started out and swept around the room, while Lozovski's eyes, close-set, pressing against the bridge of his nose, drew even closer together, sank deeper into their sockets, merged into a single, piercing eye.

The patient had no pulse, his heart was no longer beating, his breathing had stopped, and his legs were growing cold.

It was a heart attack: the organism had been poisoned by the chloroform it had rejected. It was a certain indication that the man would never return to life, that death was inevitable and could only be postponed for an hour, ten hours, thirty hours, but no longer—by means of artificial respiration, oxygen, camphor, physiological salt solution; he would never regain consciousness; he was, in fact, dead.

There was no doubt that Gavrilov was to die beneath the knife on the operating table.

Professor Kokosov turned his face to the nurse, thrusting it forward so that she could adjust his spectacles. The professor shouted:

"Open the window! Camphor! Salt solution ready!"

An even greater silence fell upon the silent crowd of assistants. As if nothing had happened, Kokosov bent over the instruments on the table, inspected them in silence. Lozovski bent over by Kokosov.

"Pavel Ivanovich," he whispered furiously.

"Well?" answered Kokosov in a loud voice.

"Pavel Ivanovich?" Lozovski said in an even lower whisper, but now the fury had gone from his voice.

"Well?" replied Kokosov loudly, and said, "Carry on with the operation!"

The two professors straightened up, looked at each other—one with eyes fused together, the other with eyes starting out from behind shaggy brows. All at once Lozovski swayed back from Kokosov as if from a blow, as if trying to focus his gaze; his single eye became two eyes wandering about the room, then they merged again, even more completely, even more piercingly. Lozovski whispered:

"Pavel Ivanovich . . ."

And lowered his hands to the wound: he did not sew up the inner cavities, but merely basted them together. He pulled the skin together and began stitching the outer layers only. He gave an order:

"Release arms—artificial respiration!"

The enormous window of the operating room was open and the cold of the first snow came into the room. Camphor had already been injected. With the help of the anesthetist Kokosov was pulling Gavrilov's arms back and raising them, forcing him to breathe. Lozovksi was patching up the wound. He shouted:

"Salt solution!"

A woman assistant thrust two enormous needles, about the thickness of a cigarette, into the man's chest, in order to pour a thousand cubic centimeters of salt solution into the dead man's bloodstream to maintain blood pressure. The man's face was lifeless, blue; the lips had turned purple.

Then Gavrilov was untied from the table, transferred to a table on wheels, and taken back to his room. His heart was still beating and he was breathing, but consciousness did not return, and perhaps never returned, to the final moment when the heart, pumped full of camphor and salt, stopped beating, when—thirty-seven hours later —there were no more doctors and no more camphor, and he died, perhaps because up to the last minute no one was admitted to him, apart from the two professors and a nurse; but an hour before the death of Army Commander Gavrilov was officially announced, a patient who happened to be in the neighboring ward heard strange sounds, as if a man was tapping out a message, as men do in prison. In that room lay a living corpse, saturated with camphor because the proprieties of the medical profession do not permit a man to die under the surgeon's knife.

The operation had begun at eight thirty-nine, and Gavrilov was taken out of the operating room on a wheeled table at eleven minutes after eleven. In the corridor Professor Lozovski was met by the porter, who said that there had been two telephone calls for him from House Number One. The professor went to the office where the telephone was, stood a while by the window looking out at the first snow, chewed his fingers, and then approached the telephone; he penetrated to the network which had thirty or forty lines, bowed to the receiver, and said that the operation had been successful, but the patient was very weak, and they, the doctors, had judged his condition to be grave; he begged to be excused from reporting in person immediately.

Gavrilov died—that is, Professor Lozovski came out of his room with a sheet of white paper and, head bowed, announced with sadness and solemnity that the sick Army Commander, Citizen Nikolai Ivanovich Gavrilov, had passed away at seventeen minutes after one in the morning, to the great sorrow of all.

Three quarters of an hour later, toward two o'clock in the morning, several companies of Red Army men entered the hospital yard, and sentries were placed at all passageways and stairways. At that hour clouds were creeping across the sky, and hurrying after them came a plump moon, already tiring of the chase. At that hour Professor Lozovski was being taken in a closed Rolls to pay a special visit to House Number One; noiselessly the Rolls entered the gateway with the griffins, passed the sentries, and drew up at the entrance. A sentry opened the car door. Lozovski went through to the study where three telephones stood on the red felt of the desk and buttons were lined up like a company at attention on the wall behind.

It is not known what was said at that interview, but it lasted only three minutes; Lozovski came out of the study —out of the main door—out of the yard—in a great hurry, holding his hat and coat in his hands like a character out of Hoffmann; the car had gone; Lozovski walked unsteadily, like a drunken man. . . . The streets swayed beneath the moon with Lozovski in the motionless wastes of night.

Hoffmann-like, Lozovski left the study of House Number One. The unbending man remained in the study. The man stood behind the desk, leaning over it on his fists. The man's head was bowed. He remained motionless for a long time. He had been torn from his papers and formulas. And then the man began to move; his movements were angular and cut and dried as the formulas which he dictated to his stenographer every night. He began to move very quickly. He pressed a button behind him; he picked up a receiver. He said to the man on duty, "The open racer!" He spoke into the telephone to one of the ruling "troika" who must have been asleep at that hour; his voice was weak: "My dear Andrey, another one has gone— Kolya Gavrilov is dead, we have lost a comrade-in-arms. Would you mind calling Potap?"

To the chauffeur the unbending man said, "The hospital!"

Sentries stood in black passageways. The house was numb, as a place of death must be numb.

Through black corridors the unbending man made his way to Commander Gavrilov's room. He went in; there on the bed lay the body of the Army Commander; the smell of camphor was stifling.

Everyone left the room, and only the unbending man and the body of a man—Gavrilov—remained. The man sat down on the bed by the feet of the corpse. Gavrilov's arms lay along his sides on top of the blanket. The man sat for a long time by the corpse, bending over it, quiescent. Silence filled the room. The man took Gavrilov's hand, pressed it, said:

"Good-bye, comrade! Good-bye, brother!" and he left

the room, head bowed, not looking at anyone; he said:
"Why doesn't somebody open a window, it's suffocating in there!" and walked quickly down the black corridor.

Last Chapter

The evening after Army Commander Gavrilov's funeral, when brass bands had done blaring and banners were no longer lowered in mourning, after thousands of mourners had passed, and the body of the man was freezing in the earth and with the earth, Popov fell asleep in his room. He awoke at some strange hour, sitting at the table. The room was dark, and Natasha was crying softly. Popov bent over his daughter, took her in his arms, and walked around the room with her.

A white moon, weary of hurrying through the sky, filled the window. Popov went over to the window and looked out at the snow and the stillness of the night outside. Natasha slid down from his arms and stood on the window sill.

In Popov's pocket was a letter from Gavrilov, the last note which he had written the night before he entered the hospital. The note said:

"Alyosha, brother! I knew that I was going to die. Forgive me, but you are not a young man anymore. I was rocking your little girl on my knees and I was thinking. My wife is old too, and you have known her for twenty years. I have written to her. And you write to her too. Go and live together—marry if you like. Bring up the children. Good-bye, Alyosha!"

Natasha was standing on the window sill and Popov noticed that she was puffing out her cheeks and pushing her lips forward; she was looking at the moon, taking aim, blowing at it.

"What are you doing, Natasha?" her father asked.

"I want to blow out the moon," Natasha replied.

The moon, plump as a merchant's wife, swam behind clouds, wearying of the chase.

It was the hour when the machinery of the city was beginning to come to life, when factory whistles were sound-
ing. The whistles were long-drawn-out—one, two, three,
many of them—merging into a gray howl over the city. It
was quite clear that the whistles were the soul of the city
—now frosted by the moon—howling.

1926

THE FOREST DACHA

I

Grayish-brown and porous, snow still lay in the ravines; icy streams flowed from beneath it; above, the snow had already melted and little sallow spears of last year's grass pointed to the sky; the first yellow flowers had already appeared in sunny spots. Great streams of leaden gloom had been poured into the sky. A buzzard flew low over the trees, and as it passed birds were suddenly silent, and then with renewed din went on with the business of living. The swollen earth gurgled with rivulets, the warm, moist wind blew gently, carrying from somewhere far off echoing sounds of spring: perhaps it was the voices of people from the village beyond the river, or perhaps the calls of birds from their mating grounds.

The forester Ivanov came out onto the already dry porch and lit a cigarette; the cigarette smoldered in the damp and deepening twilight.

The watchman Ignat went by, carrying buckets, and said:

"Warm night, Mitrich! Feels good, don't it? . . . You wait, snipe'll be flying tomorrow and we'll be off shooting right before Easter! . . ."

Ignat went into the cattle shed. Then he came back, sat down on the steps, and rolled himself a dog-leg; the bitter smell of makhorka mingled with the sweet spring smell of rotting leaves and melting snow. Across the river church bells began to ring; the Lenten toll whined in the air for a long time, carrying far over the water.

"That must be the Seventh Gospel,"[1] said Ignat. "Soon

[1] On the Thursday of Holy Week the Passion of Christ is commemorated in the Russian Orthodox Church by twelve se-

they'll be going home with their candles. In summer the river won't come up to your belly, but today it was hard work getting across in a boat! . . . Spring! . . . I'll have to clean my double-barrel today, for sure." Ignat spat purposefully into a puddle, and took a long drag on his cigarette.

"All the signs are the cranes will settle the other side of the garden for the night—and that means that tomorrow we'll be going after woodcock," Ivanov said, and listened intently to the evening.

Ignat also listened to the sounds of sky and earth, cocking his shaggy head; he heard something he needed to hear, and confirmed:

"I'd say you're right. It's just the right time for them. . . . There's nothing I like better."

"Get the droshky hitched by dawn tomorrow; we'll go to Ratchinski Wood and look around. If we take the hill road, it'll be all right—we'll get through."

Aganka, Ignat's daughter, came dashing out onto the veranda to the right of the porch and began beating dust out of a sheepskin coat with slender brown switches. But it was still cold, and Aganka drew up one bare, red foot and then the other; she began to sing shrilly, hopping up and down on the spot:

> "A nightingale sang
> In a birch all night long—
> His love could not sleep
> For the sound of his song!"

Ignat gave her a look of tender indulgence, and said sternly:

"It's a sin, girl! It's Lent, and you're singing."

"And what of it! There's no sin nowadays!" Aganka replied, drew up her right foot, and began to beat lustily, turning her back to the porch.

Ignat shook his open hand threateningly at his daughter's back, smiled, and said to Ivanov:

---

lected readings from the Gospels, known as the "Twelve Gospels," to correspond to the twelve hours of night (Editors).

"She's a lively one! . . . Not sixteen yet, and she's playing the love game already—nothing you can do about it.
She doesn't sleep nights—always sneaking out."

Aganka turned around abruptly, tossed back her head,
and said to her father:

"What's wrong with that? I'm alive, ain't I?"

"You're alive all right, my girl! . . . But don't talk so
much."

Ivanov looked at the girl, who was like a young animal,
at her young body, her eyes that were full of spring and
bright with awareness of the "love game"; for a fleeting
moment a sadness, of which he was no doubt unaware,
showed in his tired eyes; then gaily, and louder than was
necessary, he said:

"Well, that's the way it should be, that's the way it has
to be! Love, enjoy yourself, girl!"

"Yes, let her enjoy herself. You're only young once!"
Ignat echoed.

Again the bells sounded the beginning of a Gospel.
Twilight gloom filled more and more of the sky; crows
were screaming in the trees, in the green air. Ignat bent
his head toward the earth, listening. From the distance,
from the garden, from the ravine, from the pasture, came
the calls of cranes—faint, almost inaudible in the green,
spring-alerted hum. Ignat's hairy face lengthened, reflect-
ing first serious concentration, then cunning mingled with
keen excitement.

"They're down! The cranes!" he said in a tense whisper, as if afraid of frightening them, and was suddenly
in a hurry—"Got to oil the double-barrel!"

And Ivanov too was suddenly in a hurry. Some chain
of thought—perhaps it was because he would go to watch
the cranes and would see her—brought the image of Arina
before him, so real that he felt he could almost touch her,
in her red kerchief—big-boned, strong, hot-blooded, with
her animal-soft lips.

"Get the droshky hitched at dawn, and we'll go to
Ratchinski Wood. I'll go into the woods now and take a
look."

II

Twilight wandered into Ivanov's study—the timbered walls and the stove with its cracked tiles were dimly outlined. Along one wall stood a joiner's bench and a sofa; the green baize of the desk, which time had piled untidily with all sorts of things, was plentifully spotted with candlewax—signs of long, empty nights which Ivanov had spent alone. Harness was heaped by the windows—collars, saddle-girths, a saddle, bridles; the windows were large, square, empty: on winter nights wolves came to stare at the yellow candle flames inside. But now the windows looked out onto a greenish-blue, spring-peaceful sky with an ocher streak along the horizon, against which were silhouetted the bare, knotty twigs of hawthorns and lilacs planted under the windows.

Ivanov lit a candle on the joiner's bench and, to kill time, began to fill shotgun cartridges, using a hand machine.

Lidia Konstantinovna came in: would he like to have his tea here, or would he come to the dining room?

Ivanov said he did not want any tea.

Lidia Konstantinovna had spent the years of the Revolution in the Crimea, but last summer she had come to Maryin Brod for a brief two weeks, leaving afterward for Moscow. This time she had come for Easter, and not alone: with her arrived a painter named Mintz, of whom Ivanov had never heard before. Mintz had a clean-shaven face; his gray eyes were cold behind his steel-rimmed pince-nez; his hair was long and fair. He was in the habit of removing his pince-nez and putting it back on, which made his eyes change—without the pince-nez they became helpless and malicious like the eyes of owlets by daylight; his lips were pressed together dryly and showed a weariness beyond his years; something uncertain and weak often passed fleetingly over Mintz's face; he talked and moved very noisily. They had arrived the day before, at dusk; Ivanov was not at home. Later that evening they went for a walk. They returned after one, when night was just turning gray and there was a touch of foggy chill in the air; they were met by the barking of dogs—Ignat echoed the dogs with his watchman's clapper. Ivanov had returned home at about eleven and sat by the window in his study, listening to the slow, watchful night. Owls hooted in the park all night long. Lidia Konstantinovna did not come to him, and he did not go to her.

Ivanov saw the painter for the first time in the park the next day. He was sitting on a dry turf bench and gazing intently at the river. Ivanov walked past him. In Mintz's bent figure there was something lonely and very tired.

Next to Ivanov's study was the drawing room; near the large windows with their dirty panes there remained such things as had escaped destruction: a carpet, armchairs, oil lamps—an old concert grand stood there, portraits hung on the walls.

Lidia Konstantinovna and Mintz came into the drawing room from the far end of the house. As always, Lidia Konstantinovna walked briskly, her heels clicking sharply on the floor. Ivanov remembered her way of walking—resilient, precise, the beautiful body swaying gently.

Lidia Konstantinovna raised the piano lid and began playing something gay and noisy, something alien to the mood of the worn-out drawing room, then slammed down the lid.

Aganka brought in tea on a tray.

Mintz paced the room in the twilight, his heels clicking on the parquet floor, and talked loudly, although there was sadness in his voice.

"I've just been in the park. That pond, those maple-lined walks, all those vanishing, dying, fading things—you can't help feeling sad. On the pond, where the dam is, the ice has melted already. Why can't we go back to the romantic eighteenth century, why can we only grieve for

the pipes and dressing gowns of yesterday? Why aren't
we landed nobility?"

Lidia Konstantinovna smiled ironically and replied:

"Well, yes. That's a poetic fancy. But in reality things
were much worse, very much worse. For one thing,
Maryin Brod was never a countryseat—just a forest dacha,
a forestry office, and no more . . . no more than that.
. . . I was always a stranger here. I've been here only two
days and I'm miserable already. . . ." Sadness and a
hardly perceptible note of irritation crept into Lidia Konstantinovna's voice.

"Reality and fancy? Perhaps I'm a painter because I
always perceive the latter—the hidden, the essential
beauty of things," Mintz said loudly, sadly, and added
in a low voice, "You remember—yesterday? . . . The
park? . . ."

"Yes, the park," Lidia Konstantinovna replied, wearily
and softly. "Today it's the Twelve Gospels; when I was a
little girl I loved to stand in church holding a candle; it
gave me such a good feeling inside. Ah, yes! But now I
don't love anything."

The drawing room was now completely dark. The windows set in the dark walls were greenish and tremulous.
Ivanov came out of his study wearing high boots and a
leather jacket, and carrying a gun. Without a word he
walked toward the door. Lidia Konstantinovna stopped
him.

"Sergey, are you going out again? Shooting?"

"Yes."

Ivanov paused.

Lidia Konstantinovna came close to him. Her eyes were
made up, and about her lips and on her cheeks time,
which was already carrying away her youth and beauty,
had traced fine, hardly perceptible wrinkles on the as-
tonishingly white skin. Suddenly Ivanov was keenly aware
of this.

"Do people go shooting at night in the dark? I didn't

know," said Lidia Konstantinovna, and repeated, "I didn't know. . . ."

"I'm going to the woods."

"I've come here after not seeing you for thousands and thousands of years, and we haven't talked yet. . . ."

Ivanov went out without replying. His footsteps sounded in the ballroom, then along the corridor, and died away at the far end of the big house; the back door banged. The house was old, rambling, falling to pieces.

Lidia Konstantinovna remained standing in the middle of the room, her face turned toward the door. Mintz went up to her, took her hand and raised it to his lips.

"Don't be sad, Leet," he said gently and sadly.

Lidia Konstantinovna withdrew her hand, put both hands on Mintz's shoulders, and said quietly:

"Yes, I know. I mustn't be sad! . . . Yes, I know—listen, Mintz. . . . How strange it all is! He loved me so much, and I never loved him. . . . But my youth passed here, and now I feel sad. . . . I remember everything that happened in this room—then it was all happening for the first time. And I want to bring it all back. Perhaps everything would be different then. Now I'm sorry my youth has gone, although then I used to curse it—but I would willingly forget everything that happened later. I long for warmth and security. Ah, yes, if you only knew how much he loved me! . . ."

Lidia Konstantinovna was silent for a moment, head bowed, then, tossing back her head, she gave a hollow, bitter laugh.

"Oh, what nonsense! We still have gay times ahead! It's just that I'm tired. How stuffy it is in here! . . . Mintz, open the windows! . . . Draw the blinds. . . . They live on black bread and milk here, and they're happy, but I've got a bottle of brandy in a suitcase in my room—go and get it! Light the chandeliers!"

Mintz threw open a window. From the earth rose a bracing chill and moist, sweet, spring smells. The sky was dark, and warm spring rain clouds were creeping across it.

III

The sky was impenetrable—indigo-black, dull green in the west, where low, heavy clouds could be discerned. The air was moist, warm, smelling of earth and melting snow. From the river, from the ravine, from the pasture, from the woods, from the park, came many sounds, resonant and disturbing. There was no wind at all now. Ivanov lit a cigarette; the match flared within his cupped hands, lighting up his black beard; his hands were shaking. Out of the darkness came his pointer Gek, and began to wriggle at his feet.

The church bell sounded the beginning of the last Gospel: the spring night distorted, confused the sense of distance, and it seemed that the bell was ringing close by in the dark, behind the dacha. In the yard it was dark and silent; only in the cattle shed Aganka shouted at the cows a couple of times, and there came, faintly, the sound of milk spurting into the pail.

Ivanov listened to the church bell ringing, to the quiet which enveloped the grounds, and stepped down from the porch, setting a heavily booted foot noiselessly on the ground—he was used to darkness; the dogs did not hear him, only Gek trotted by his side. In the park, cold drops fell from the trees; here the darkness was even denser. Somewhere nearby an owl stirred in the bare branches and, having made a brief sortie, gave a cry of terrible joy. The ground was soggy, heavy—it stuck to his boots—slippery, constraining movement; a sweet, persistent numbness spread through his body.

Ivanov walked through the pasture, following a clay track down into a ravine, crossed over, and made his way to a watchman's hut through the trees along the ravine's pathless edge. The hut stood in a bare spot, only the branchless trunks of three ancient pines stretched upward nearby; behind it a railroad embankment loomed grayish-brown. A dog began to bark near the hut. Gek growled, and disappeared into the darkness. Then the dogs quieted down. A man with a lantern appeared on the steps.

"Who's there?" he asked calmly. "You, Arina?"

"It's me," replied Ivanov.

"You, Sergey Mitrich? . . . Aha! . . . And Arina's still in church. She went sailing off to church! . . . Such foolishness."

The watchman was silent for a moment. "I reckon I ought to go and put the lantern out; the express should be here right about now, drat it. . . . Maybe you'd like to come in? Arinka won't be long. . . . The old woman's at home."

"No, I'm going into the woods," replied Ivanov.

"Suit yourself."

The watchman climbed up the embankment, carrying his lantern, and went toward the bridge.

Ivanov moved off into the wood, and, following the edge of the ravine, approached the steep riverbank. A train suddenly plunged from the woods on the other side of the river, its inflamed eyes reflected in the oil-black water; the train reached the bridge and rattled stridently across. . . . It was one of those moments that come only in spring when there is silence though a hundred sounds fill the air: you could hear the swollen, abundant earth breathing and drinking in moisture, twigs that had lately been weighed down by snow straightening up, new grass, not yet visible, pushing its way up through the earth. In the ravine the stream flowed mutedly, calmed by the night, but still you might have thought that some gnarled and impudent wood-devil, awakened by spring, was splashing about in the water. Beyond the ravine, beyond the woods, beyond the river, all around—birds in their mating grounds had not yet fallen silent. Below, just a few paces away, was the river; it flowed almost noiselessly, and only from far off came the blended murmur of its currents. The sky was now even darker and lower.

Ivanov leaned against a birch, stood his gun next to him, and lighted a cigarette. The flame lit up the white birch trunks, last year's dried-up grass, and a path leading down the steep bank. Arina had taken this path many times.

The bells of the village church began to ring, and where the church would be yellow candle flames appeared, then the sound of people talking drifted across. Many of these flames wandered off to right and left; a few moved down toward the river. The sounds of feet hitting the bottom of the boat and of oars were carried over the water; someone shouted:

"Wa-a-a-it! . . . Mitri-i-ch! . . ."

There was a clang of iron, probably the boat ring. Then all was still, and only the candle flames showed that the boat moved upstream, pulled out to the middle of the river, and began to move downstream. Then talk and the splashing of oars could again be heard, seemingly very near—no more than a few paces away. One of the young men made a joke; the girls laughed, then were suddenly quiet.

The boat moored near the bridge; there was much bustling about as people went ashore; the ferryman collected money, the young men were still in a clowning mood. Now it was possible to make out the crooked shapes of men and women, whose chests, knees, and chins were lit by the candles. They all followed the track that led upward, but one candle—Arina's—detached itself from the rest and began moving along the path to the watchman's hut. Ivanov was holding back Gek, who was straining toward the river.

Arina was walking up the hill slowly, firmly planting her short, broad, booted feet in the sticky mud, and breathing noisily. The candlelight molded her full breast beneath the red blouse, which could be glimpsed through the opening of her long coat, unbuttoned at the top; the light from below illuminated her inclined face, so that her lips, the gray-blue outline of her cheekbones, the arches of her black brows were clearly defined; her eyes could not be seen in the darkness; their sockets seemed enormous; the darkness retreated before the light, and the white trunks of small birches advanced.

Ivanov blocked Arina's path. She stopped close to him and sighed; Ivanov could feel her hot breath.

"You scared me," she said calmly, and held out her hand. "Evening. I've just been to hear the Twelve Gospels. You scared me!"

Ivanov drew Arina's hand to him; she pulled it away, said sternly:

"Not now; I'm in a hurry; there's no time. Don't even think of it!"

Ivanov smiled weakly and dropped his hands.

"All right then, as you like. I'll come tomorrow toward nightfall. Wait for me," he said softly.

Arina drew closer to him and replied, also softly:

"Meet me here. We can be together here—to hell with the old man. Go now, I'm in a hurry, housecleaning to do! There's a baby under my heart, I can feel it. . . . Go on, off with you!"

As Ivanov was walking home through the pasture, the first large, warm raindrops began falling from the black, invisible sky; they were few at first, splashing noisily on his leather jacket, then they began to fall more thickly, and everything merged in the resonant murmur of spring rain. Near the dacha Gek made a sudden dash toward the ravine, where cranes began to hiss in alarm; Gek started barking. Dogs on the estate answered, were echoed in turn by village dogs, then by others somewhere far away: the clear, springtime barking of dogs rang out over the earth.

In the park the glowing light of a cigarette slipped from the main walk to a side path; then by the gate Ivanov came upon Aganka.

"Sneaking out as usual? Got yourself a smoking man now?" Ivanov asked.

The girl laughed loudly, ran toward the cattle shed, splashing through the mud in the darkness, shouted, all innocence:

"I put your milk on the window sill in the study!"

Ivanov stood on the porch for a while, scraping the mud from his boots on the footscraper, stretched vigor-ously, limbering up, told himself he had better go to bed now and have a good, sound sleep, so as to be able to rise at dawn.

IV

In the drawing room, near the grand piano, above the sofa and the round table, a chandelier was burning which had not been lighted for many years—perhaps not since the last Christmas before the Revolution. Dim, yellow candlelight, dully reflected in the dusty glass pendants, fell on the piano, the tight, plush blinds over the windows, the portrait over the sofa, the sofa itself—the round table, the carpets, the poufs; but there at the other end of the room, near the doors leading to the ballroom and the corner room—where decay had entered unopposed—chairs, couches, armchairs had been removed by an unknown hand, and only old and broken furniture was piled in a corner; there light did not penetrate, there shadows gathered, grayish-brown and blurred. The blinds were tightly drawn; beyond them lay the black night, and the noise of rain.

Lidia Konstantinovna sat a long time at the piano; first she played gay trifles from operettas, then the classics, Liszt's Thirteenth Rhapsody, finishing with the naïve strains of Oppel's "Summer Night in Beryozovka"—a piece she used to play for Ivanov when they were engaged; she played it through twice. She broke off abruptly, stood up, laughed—her laughter came in short, malicious bursts; she took slow sips of brandy from a tall, narrow glass, and laughed loudly and bitterly. Her eyes were still beautiful, with the beauty of lakes when leaves begin to fall. She sat down on the sofa, leaning back, her hands clasped behind her head, which made her breasts rise high beneath her pale-blue blouse; casually, she crossed her finely stockinged legs beneath her black silk skirt, resting her feet in their patent-leather shoes on a low pouf. She kept on drinking steadily, sucking at the glass with her beautiful lips, and slandering herself, Ivanov, the Revolution, Moscow, the Crimea, Maryin Brod, Mintz.

Then she grew quiet, her eyes dimmed, she began to speak softly and sadly, a helpless smile on her lips.

Mintz drank, walked up and down the room, heels clicking noisily, and talked sarcastically, loudly, and at length. The brandy moved through his veins, arousing his tired blood; his thoughts became precise and spiteful, following one another dryly and bitterly. Whenever Mintz emptied his glass, he would take off his pince-nez for a moment: his eyes would become malicious, helpless, and drunken.

Lidia Konstantinovna shifted to the end of the sofa, covered her shoulders with a plaid shawl, tucked her legs under her.

"What a strong smell of chypre, Mintz," she said in a low voice. "All right, I'm drunk. All right, when I drink a lot, I always think there's too much perfume. It stifles me, I feel the taste of it in my mouth, my ears ring with it, I feel sick. . . . Everything smells of chypre—my perfume; can you smell it? . . . Another hour and I'll be hysterical. It always happens when I drink. I'm not happy anymore, I'm wretched, Mintz. On this very sofa I once . . . cried all night long. . . . How good it was then! I don't know what I'm saying."

Mintz paced the room with overdeliberate steps. He paused in front of Lidia Konstantinovna, took off his pince-nez, and said gloomily:

"It's different for me—when I drink I begin to understand everything only too well: that we're miserable because we don't know how the devil we go on living, and why—that it's impossible to live without faith—that your soul has been dragged through cafés, attics, and other alleyways of life—and that vileness is vileness, no matter what you say. . . . And that we've been drinking because we feel misery and emptiness, as we always do, even though we've been joking and laughing so loudly—that it's spring outside, and that there is joy and beauty there, not the kind you can see in our painted eyes and souls. And that the Revolution has passed us by, thrown us overboard, even though there's NEP[2]—which is just up our street. . . . And that . . ." Mintz did not finish, turned abruptly, and walked with exaggeratedly firm steps to the dark corner of the room where broken furniture was heaped.

"Well, of course. . . . You're right, I suppose . . . ," Lidia Konstantinovna replied. "Only I don't love Sergey, I never loved him."

"Indeed I'm right," came Mintz's stern answer from the dark corner. "People never love other people. They love themselves through others."

Ivanov came in from the ballroom carrying a gun and wearing a peaked cap and muddy boots. He went through to his study. Mintz gazed after him sternly, without a word, then followed him to the study, rested his hand on the doorjamb, said with an ironic smile:

"You've been avoiding me. Why?"

"You're imagining things," Ivanov replied.

He lighted a candle on the joiner's bench, and began to change; took off his leather jacket, hung up his gun, pulled off his boots.

"I very rarely imagine things! . . . But it doesn't matter," Mintz began coldly. "I want to tell you what a good life you have here. You have a very good life here. . . . Take me, I paint pictures, sell them, and paint more—to sell them, too. Though I don't paint at all now, and haven't for a long time. . . . I live in attics alone, because I need light, and because an attic is no place to drag a wife. . . . And for that matter, I don't even have a wife, she left me long ago! I have mistresses. . . . And I envy you because . . . because attics are very cold places. . . . You understand?" Mintz took off his pince-nez; his eyes became helpless and malicious. "In the name of all those whom life has worn out, who have exchanged the spring beauty of parks for the sensuality of sofas, who lost Russia because of those sofas—in the name of all those, I say to

2 NEP—New Economic Policy, 1921–28: a return to limited free enterprise in the U.S.S.R. (Editors).

you that you have a very good life here, and we envy you. Here it is possible to work, and even—to marry. . . . Have you ever tried writing?"

"No, never."

Mintz was silent for a while, then suddenly said in a very low, weak voice:

"Listen. We have some brandy. Won't you have a drink with us?"

"No, thank you. I'm tired. Good night."

"I need to talk! . . ."

Ivanov put out the candle, felt for the milk and bread on the window sill with the sureness of habit, began to eat quickly, standing up. Mintz stood a little while by the door, then went out, slamming it tight behind him.

Lidia Konstantinovna was sitting with head bowed, her feet resting on the carpet. Her eyes with their long lashes, like autumn lakes fringed with rushes, were clear and vacant. Her hands were clasped about her knees.

"How was Sergey?" she asked softly, without raising her eyes.

"Very unresponsive; he went to bed," Mintz replied.

He made as if to sit down next to Lidia Konstantinovna, but she got up, automatically patted her hair in place, smiled vaguely and tenderly—into space rather than at Mintz.

"To bed? Well, I suppose it is time for bed! Good night . . . ," said Lidia Konstantinovna softly. "How I hate that perfume. My head's spinning."

She moved toward the other end of the room. Mintz followed her. She stopped in the doorway. There was darkness, through which the noise of spring rain could be heard distinctly. Lidia Konstantinovna leaned against the white door, threw back her head, and began to speak without looking at Mintz; she wanted to speak seriously and simply, but sounded cold:

"I'm very tired, Mintz. I'm going to bed right away. And you go to bed too. See you in the morning. We won't see each other anymore tonight. You understand, Mintz? I don't want to."

Mintz stood, legs wide apart, hands on hips, head bowed. He smiled, sadly no doubt, and replied with unexpected gentleness:

"I see. It's all right. I understand. It's all right."

Lidia Konstantinovna stretched out her hand and spoke, as she had wanted to, with friendly simplicity:

"I know you're a cynic—embittered, lonely, tired, like . . . like an old, homeless dog. . . . But you're good and understanding. . . . You know I'll never leave you, we're two of a kind. . . . But now I shall go to him. . . . Probably for the last time."

Mintz kissed her hand in silence, turned, and went down the corridor—tall, bony, slightly stooping, his heels clicking noisily.

V

In Lidia Konstantinovna's bedroom, where there stood, as before, a mahogany double bed with a canopy, chests of drawers, cupboards, highboys, a huge wardrobe, and the smell of spurge still lingered—it was dark and cold. Outside rain came down noisily.

Lidia Konstantinovna lighted two candles by a dim mirror. On a chest of drawers were various knicknacks from her childhood, and scattered among them were things that she had brought with her the day before. The candles burned weakly, sputtering; their flames slithered dimly up the mirror.

Lidia Konstantinovna undressed, put on a loose dressing gown of green silk twill, let down her hair, and did it up in braids, which she wound about her head like a crown; all at once her head appeared very small and fragile. Without thinking, she took the stopper out of a bottle of perfume, passed her perfume-moistened hands over her neck and breasts, and immediately her head began to spin. The sheets on the bed were cold and damp; it seemed that they too smelled of chypre.

Lidia Konstantinovna sat down on the bed; she sat there

a long time in her silk dressing gown, listening to the noises of the house. Dogs kept up their howling and barking in the grounds of the dacha. Now and again crows, half-asleep, cawed from the elms in the park. The clock struck eleven, then the half hour, someone walked down the corridor, Agasha cleared away in the drawing room, Mintz paced up and down the corner room, then all was quiet.

Lidia Konstantinovna went to the window, stood looking out into the darkness for a long time. Then she left her bedroom without a sound, and went to Ivanov's study. The chill, gloom, and silence of unlived-in rooms crept up on her from all sides. The rooms were large, mute, black. In the drawing room a forgotten candle was burning dimly, a rat scampered away from the table. In the study it was again dark, and the air smelled of joiner's glue and harness.

Ivanov was asleep on the sofa, lying on his back, arms flung wide; his form could barely be made out in the darkness. Lidia Konstantinovna sat down close beside him and put her hand on his chest. Ivanov sighed, changed the position of his arms, and abruptly raised his head from the pillow.

"Who's that?" he asked.

"It's me, Sergey, it's me—Lida," answered Lidia Konstantinovna in a whisper, quickly. "You won't talk to me. I'm worn out. I came here lightheartedly, not thinking of you at all, but now all of a sudden I feel miserable. . . . Oh, how I hate this perfume. . . ."

Lidia Konstantinovna fell silent and passed a hand over her face. Ivanov sat up beside her.

"What are you saying, Lida? What is it you want?" he asked in a voice hoarse with sleep, lighting a cigarette; the flare of the match lit them as they sat together on the sofa, half-undressed. Ivanov was huge and shaggy.

"What do I want? . . . People get old, Sergey, and a lonely old age is a frightening thing. . . . I'm worn out. . . . I came here lightheartedly, and suddenly I'm miserable. I keep thinking of the past, of our life together. . . . I keep playing 'Summer Night in Beryozovka'—re-

member how I used to play it for you? Then . . . Well
. . . , people get old, and I long for a home of my
own. . . . It's the Twelve Gospels today. . . . Have we
nothing to say to each other then? . . . Did you see
Arina today?"

Ivanov was silent for a while.

"I've had my share of misery and suffering, Lida, but
that's not the point," he began. "These last four years I've
lived alone, taking leave of the past—it's gone forever.
Four years I've struggled with death, struggled to get
enough to eat. You don't know anything about that—we're
strangers. Yes, I saw Arina. I shall have a son. I don't
know whether I'm worn out, or whether it's something
else, but I'm content now; I shall bring Arina here, she will
be the mistress of the house and my wife. And I shall
live. . . . I am in harmony with some elemental force.
. . . I shall have a son. . . . Life is different now, Lida."

"But in Moscow it's the same as always—wine, theaters,
restaurants, Mintz, noise. . . . I'm worn out."

"I can't help you, Lida. I'm worn out too, but I'm at
peace now. That is something each one of us has to do
for himself."

Ivanov spoke very calmly and simply. Lidia Konstantinovna pressed her hands between her knees; she sat with
shoulders bowed, motionless, as if any movement would
have been painful. When Ivanov stopped speaking, she
got up without a word and moved toward the door, stood
for a moment in the doorway, and went out. The candle
was still burning in the drawing room. The house was
silent.

VI

Just before dawn, before the sun had risen, Ignat
rapped loudly at Ivanov's window, and shouted:

"Get up, Mitrich! I'll be hitching the horse now!"

The rain had stopped, there was a chill in the clear
morning air. Half the sky glowed pink, and a silvery mist

was rising from the ground. Ivanov went out onto the
porch and washed with icy water from a bucket. Ignat
was busy with the horse, shouting at it every now and
then.

"Ducks have just flown over, Mitrich, damn'd if they
haven't!" he shouted cheerfully.

Aganka came out of the cattle shed with a milk pail,
and chickens ran noisily after her, impatient for their
morning feed. A hen starling lighted near the birdhouse
on a tree in front of the porch, and set up a drawn-out,
monotonous "pee-ee"; two males flew down, ruffled their
feathers, whistled threateningly, and began to fight.

1917–23

THE BRIDEGROOM COMETH

Chapter One

The day before Whitsunday—on the thirteenth of May —the British ship "Francis" left Portsmouth harbor; the ship was bound for Kaapstad in Africa. En route she was due to call in at the British colony of Nigeria, there to unload and to take on cargo. And it was for the town of Rida in Nigeria that Mr. Samuel Garnet, a clerk in the British Nigerian Rubber Company, was bound on board the "Francis."

The ocean offered calm, silence, and coolness. The ship was not meant to carry passengers, and the only ones on board were people with special connections. Before lunch, at noon, the captain would make his way to the smoking room on the spar deck, and with his own hands uncork a bottle of whisky. Everything went very well. After lunch the passengers would carry deck chairs out onto the bridge and, sipping the last of their drinks and dozing intermittently, watch seagulls, dolphins, and the blue of the waves. All this time it was smooth sailing; the ocean was at peace.

Mr. Samuel Garnet had married two weeks before setting out on his expedition, and his young wife, Mrs. Samuel Garnet, was traveling with him. Mr. Garnet was blissfully happy.

He was not particularly well educated, he was far from rich, but he knew everything that a gentleman ought to know—from the Scriptures to what tie to wear with what socks, the right things to say and the witty remarks to make, how to conduct himself with people. He was going to Africa for several years; he was well versed in the procedures for corresponding with the board of the company, and knew the quality of the various kinds of rubber. Of Africa he knew little; what he did know he had learned from his Baedeker. He was young; sitting on the spar deck, observing the sea—which could be observed for endless hours—idly and at ease he went over in his mind how many pairs of socks and stockings he and his wife had brought with them, the way in which he had taken leave of the company director, the checking account he had left in London to which, at his request, his expenses were to be credited, and what his resources would be on his return to the metropolis. On his head he wore a cork helmet, from his neck hung a Kodak and a Zeiss, his legs were encased in white breeches.

His wife, Mrs. Samuel Garnet, was less adept at dealing with life, but she knew better than he in which trunks and in what order their things—linen, china, tennis rackets—had been packed; apart from books pertaining to his specialty (bookkeeping and the rubber industry), he had with him only the Baedeker: he knew that no matter where he was his favorite newspapers—the *Pall Mall Gazette*, the *Morning Post*, and the *Evening Standard*—would catch up with him; she had books, however: Shelley, Galsworthy, several books that had come out in the last few weeks, a few fashion magazines, and a fat, leather-bound notebook with the inscription, "Diary and Poems of Mrs. Samuel Garnet"; she had brought with her a great deal of writing paper and a quantity of envelopes.

She spent more time in the cabin rummaging through their things—not only because she knew that when men are sitting in the smoking room it is awkward for a woman to go there—a place where masculine conversation flows unconstrained; sometimes in the evening she would go to the quarter-deck and look over the stern at the ship's wake, back where the water swirled in ostrich plumes, and jellyfish glowed phosphorescently; there was one book about which Mr. Garnet knew nothing—a slim book of verse by an unknown poet, bearing a conventional inscription on the flyleaf; this book was kept in a case inaccessible to the eyes of men, crammed as it was with the mysteries of the feminine toilette. It should be mentioned, however, that many of the things in the case had been bought by Mr. Samuel himself and that Mrs. Samuel Garnet had done nothing in the least improper: who could condemn a woman who just two weeks earlier had been a virgin immersed in vanities and trivial follies, which she had not yet completely cast off?

The Garnets loved each other, and at ten o'clock they would go to their cabin, to emerge twenty-five minutes later, the two of them dressed in pajamas and bathrobes, to make their way through to the bathroom.

On their fifth day at sea Mr. Samuel meticulously went through the bill presented to him, checked it against his notebook—and at noon a lilac-colored strip of land became distinct on the horizon. At three o'clock the ship dropped anchor at Akassa in the Niger delta.

A radio message had been sent out before they left London. An inspection launch approached the ship. Mr. Samuel Garnet was met by a guide. In the water around the ship naked Negroes, mostly boys, darted about in their high-nosed boats.

The guide called Mr. Samuel "sir" and Mrs. Samuel "lady."

Sir Samuel Garnet was calm, businesslike, and surprised at nothing, just as if he were going ashore from a sailing boat at Brighton after a picnic. But Lady Samuel looked with amazement at the blacks, at the green water, at the strange trees on the shore—lianas, palms, and other trees that she had never seen before and the names of which she did not know.

The launch took them and their trunks aboard.

They were taken to the steamer dock in a European-style carriage to which, incongruously, an umbrella had been attached.

With a solemnity worthy of a minister of the Crown Mr. Samuel announced that he was not at all hot, but Mrs. Samuel soon said that she felt dizzy from the heat, that she was beginning to have palpitations; her husband calmed her by assuring her that they would have something cold—an ice-cream soda perhaps—at the dock. They passed by a village built of straw, silent at this hour of intense heat, where the Negroes, in spite of all the driving force of Europe, lived as they had lived from the beginning of time—naked, using hand mills and, very possibly, bows and arrows.

On board the Nigerian steamer European comfort once more prevailed: the Negroes wore white suits and spoke English. And in the ship's wake stretched exotic forests and, every now and then, plantations and Negro straw villages. Mrs. Samuel stood on deck, and wanted to see a crocodile; she was informed that although there were crocodiles in plenty here, it was nevertheless more difficult to see one than in a zoological garden.

A day later the Garnet couple reached the goal of their voyage. The company had put at Mr. Garnet's disposal a two-story, furnished cottage (there was even a small wine cellar); with the house went a two-horse carriage and four Negroes—two women and two men. The house stood on the bank of the river in a clearing near the edge of the forest, not far from the plantations. For the first few days Mr. and Mrs. Garnet carried Brownings wherever they went, fearing attacks by tigers; but it was explained to them that tigers in those parts did not attack human beings, and they hung their pistols at the heads of their beds.

At night in the forest (Mr. Garnet never said simply "forest," but invariably "tropical forests") unknown animals cried, hyenas howled: at such times Mrs. Garnet would run from her bed to her husband's. In the morning he would leave for the office and she would write up her diary.

Chapter Two

The name of this soldier-engineer—to distinguish him from millions of his brothers and sisters—is He: to distinguish him from his brothers and sisters because in both sex has been obliterated; and "He" because it will never be known whether this soldier-engineer has, or ever had, individuality, special qualities distinguishing him from his brethren.

Underground, beyond the labyrinths of subterranean passages, great chambers, larders, stalls, dormitories, and storerooms faced with his excrement and that of his brothers and sisters, where workers moved in their millions and where sentries—soldier-policemen—stood at intersections—beyond all this lay the chamber of the Mother.

Had he ever seen a medieval European castle he would have been able to compare day-to-day life in the chamber of the Mother with that of the castle; but he was incapable of thought and had never heard of medieval European castles. The cave of the Mother was vast, with vaulted ceilings and a dozen passages, some open and some secret, leading to it. There at the entrances to the chamber stood a line of fortress guards, heads lowered, mandibles facing outward. Thousands of workers labored around the Mother and hundreds of policemen urged them on. The Mother—a monster—lay in the middle of the great chamber, motionless, blind, obese, sweaty, greenish-white; her bulk was such that her back touched the ceiling. The workers—pygmies beside her—cleaned, scraped and licked her, crawled over and around her, drank her sweat. Lines of workers dragged food from the storerooms to her mouth and shoved it in. From time to time soldiers ran up to take away her excrement and to groom her. Every second the Mother was shaken by a spasm, and strain passed from her head over her belly in a wave, and every second an egg emerged; then a worker ran forward to wash the egg and carry it to the storerooms.

In this way—every second—the Mother ejects her progeny; in this way the Mother had lived for days, weeks, months, years—blind, powerless to move, hideously fat, and dripping with sweat which the workers ate.

In this way the workers drag away the eggs and the policemen-overseers prod them on—in complete darkness, through the caves, along the labyrinths built with the excrement of soldier-engineers and workers.

Close to the Mother, at her side, stood the Father, also blind and with broken-off mandibles; he too was licked all over and fed by workers, but he was able to move and to beat the soldiers and workers, driving them on.

Millions of brothers and sisters, soldiers and workers will eventually emerge from these eggs in the chambers where the eggs are stored; once they have emerged they will lose their sex and become indistinguishable from one another in order to labor, to build labyrinths, to eat, to defend themselves, to attack, to take part in campaigns, to obey, to die, to kill—never to think, only to obey: and out of these millions only hundreds will have the good fortune to be winged, to be able to fly.

Above the ramparts of the city-state, the day luminary, which He and his brethren never see, moves by day, and the night luminary, its companion, brightens the night; there the elements reign—downpours, storms, droughts, intense heat; there the world of the enemy lies.

In the center of the city is an empty square—enormous, vaulted, gothic, with four arches and innumerable columns; all around it are fungus gardens, kindergartens, food shops, workers' barracks. In the fungus gardens, where the air is stifling, flourish rare and fantastic growths —gray, spherical, odorous: spheres of various sizes—globes, giant globes, globelets, egg-shaped globes, potato-shaped globes; along the ground among the globes spread the roots which support them, slimy as the globes themselves. Among the globes and over them walk gardeners and the young. In caves beyond the gardens are buried secret stores of sweets, amber of resins and sugary juices, gums and jams. Guards stand at the entrances.

There, beyond the highways, from behind walls, towers, and embrasures, protrude the heads of armored soldiers, guards, and garrison troops—they watch the alien world, ever ready to engage in combat, to kill with their mandibles, and to die.

Far from the highways and alleyways—in the slaughterhouses—soldiers kill off slaves, old workers, old soldiers, cripples; it is there that the soldiers go to devour the dead and to carry away supplies to the storerooms. There in the prisons are slaves—rove beetles—which are caught, kept, and fed for their sweat, which has the effect of a narcotic, or of alcohol. The slaves are fatted, they cannot move; they are dragged from place to place when they are about to give birth; their corpses are carried to the slaughterhouses when they die; their sweat is kept in the storerooms, they are fed on excrement. Out there, in the world beyond the city, beyond the fortress walls, milch cows—mealy bugs—are caught: herds of them graze in corrals within the walls, they are guarded, fed, milked, grazed; they die, but new stock is constantly brought in from the outside world, from the fields, from beyond the city.

In the city, within the fortress, great building projects are under way. Excavators, masons, soldier-engineers are continuously erecting new structures; workers—millions of them—go down into the caves to eat earth, gnaw earth, and go up again to the building sites—there guards stand in rows, there the soldier-engineers are in command; there the workers deposit the earth they have brought, disgorge it, and moisten it with their excrement, while the soldier-engineers knead earth and excrement, masticating it again and raising more and more new walls, towers, vaults, and storehouses; excavators tear down old structures; then workers, hundreds at a time, drag away the stones of what were once cyclopean constructions.

The workers carry to the caves supplies from the fields and from the colonies. There in the caves gather millions of workers and soldiers to prepare for new campaigns, conquests, wars, raids.

There in the caves, alleyways, and thoroughfares the air is musty, damp, foul: they know no other. If they set out on a campaign (millions strong, ravenous) excavators go before them; the excavators dig up the earth, bore underground passages, construct galleries; along the road they build storehouses and barracks; the excavators work at night when they cannot be seen, work against time with skill, speed, determination; and only when the roads are ready, camps, food dumps, and storehouses for booty provided, do the armies—millions of workers and soldiers —begin to move; they march in well-ordered columns, while the excavators continue to push on ahead; should they encounter an obstacle, they work their way in and hollow it out from the inside until it crumbles to dust; they march unseen, in darkness, noiselessly, millions of them (and all the more terrible for that!). But sometimes their passages collapse; then columns of them march into the light, soldiers to the fore, pressed close together, millions at a time; then they hiss, seethe, threatening all before them; soldiers of the guard seize every height, set up a system of signals; the columns form into armies, commanders at the head; if an enemy interrupts their progress they do not retreat before him, they march onward to the death, and every enemy, even the white man, flees before them.

It cannot be said of this powerful state that it is an empire: the imperial power—the power of the Mother and the Father—is immobile, impotent, subordinate; as impotent and subordinate as the will and life of each citizen of the state who does not know death and goes to die for all, to die as fodder for his own sisters and slaves— for the slaves are fed on the flesh of their masters. This state never sees the light of day; the state is a machine, the state does not tolerate individuality, ownership, freedom of instinct.

He, the soldier-engineer, had taken part in many campaigns, had built many trenches, galleries, and camps for the armies, in preparation for campaigns of plunder, campaigns of war.

These were the days when for once—and only once!— the state fell into madness; the state, where folly neither was nor could be, was committing folly; these were the days when the nymphs were taking wing—the only folly, the only poetry and romance. The nymphs were endowed with sex and could love. The state knew that tomorrow

the male nymphs would take flight and that there had
been a flight of female nymphs that very morning. Last
night He and his brothers had bored through and opened
up the walls of their towers so that once—and only once!
—they would see the day luminary.

And at first soldiers went through these gates to die—
to fight, to thwart those enemies who had come to ambush
and kill the nymphs; for this day the state did not spare
the lives at its disposal, it moved into the sun, it sent out
its subjects to live and to die.

In the morning, in the sunlight, in the blue benediction
of day, silvery, winged female nymphs, endowed with sight
—with sight!—those who, if they did not die, would become
empresses of new states—began to move from the caves
toward the sun.

They passed through dark labyrinths, across dark
squares, down remote passageways toward the light, past
workers, past soldiers, and there above, on the tallest tower
of the castle, they took leave of their kin, whom they did
not at all resemble in their winged beauty; they flew toward the sun, into the blue, into the daylight, into the
open spaces, in order there, in the open, freely and by
chance, to find a lover: there in the blue spaces they were
defenseless, completely at the mercy of chance; they flew
either to live or to die, and the sun shone on them; they
flew like a silver shower; there they would find a mate.

(But later, when they did find a mate, they would
burrow into the earth together to disappear forever from
the light; they would lose their eyes, they would break off
their wings, they would lose their mandibles, forget how
to eat unaided; and the Mother, grown enormously fat
and no longer able to move, would be no more than a
propagating machine, giving birth every second for many
years. . . .)

After the nymphs had flown away and after the soldiers
—those who survived—had returned to the caves, those
who had remained behind in the old city, He among them,
closed the breaches in the walls, repaired them, to return
again to darkness, to labor, to toil: perhaps it was He who

was the last to turn back from the hill into the cave and the last to glance in the direction where the bountiful day luminary was dying and the outside world lay, the last to go back to the stillness and suffocation of darkness.

He had taken part in many campaigns and at this time He went on yet another.

He went ahead of the armies in order to open up routes for the armies—caves, galleries, storehouses, camps. His path led to some incomprehensible wooden structures, pervaded with smells not at all like those of the tropical forests; He dug tunnels under cement, deep underground, penetrating wood and tar paper; iron defeated him, but on it He raised his own lightless cement labyrinths; where He had come there was coolness, and there were no enemies; it was then that the armies began to move along the way he had opened.

He and his brother He's—soldier-engineers—started back, but He never reached his own city. He must have been old by then; in the barracks of one of the camps a dozen of his brothers approached him in order to kill and eat him; He understood this, he lowered his head and mandibles, and the nearest soldier bit off his head; he stood headless; they bit away his belly; he stood without head and without belly; he fell when they began to eat his legs; this was because his breathing apparatus and nerves were in his chest, where his legs joined his body.

Having eaten him, the soldiers marched on, back to the city: there were many He's to take his place; there were many He's.

The life of the million-brothered state was like a turbine of the utmost complexity, where millions of brothers and sisters had lost sex, individuality, sun. The million-brothered state built castles, fortresses, highways of incomparable might.

In the state nothing was left to chance and the absurd was impossible.

And yet, when the He's returned, an absurd thing was taking place in the city: the Mother had died in the imperial cave. The Mother's corpse had already been eaten by the workers. An absurd thing was happening in the state. Everyone was returning to the city: workers were coming from the fields, soldiers were arriving from campaigns: armies camped in the streets of the city—the entire city was crowded to overflowing. The corpse of the Mother had already been eaten; the Father remained below, and to him were brought nymphs—thirty-one at once. In the confusion part of the citadel had already been seized by the enemy—and there battle raged; the enemy was dragging away to captivity to serve as slaves or as food those who were now without a Mother. Armored soldiers yielded, as they died, more and more approaches to the citadel—at many points the enemy was already in control, plundering and destroying: it was there that the fighting was, and there too was death.

And yet, in the caves below, preparations were under way for a terrible campaign, a campaign of incredible boldness and audacity, one which would inevitably bring either overwhelming victory or—death. No reserves were spared in preparation for this campaign: the most precious stores were opened up, the accumulated fruit of many years' labor was consumed, all the alcohol was drunk by those who were about to march off.

The entire state was going to war against a state inhabited by its own kind, in order to carry off their Mother.

Excavators, soldier-engineers, and workers went on ahead; it was a desperate plan, a cunning plan, a colossal plan. Excavators, soldier-engineers dug underground approaches on all sides, they established bridgeheads, built fortresses and dugouts for the armies. The armies began to move out along the labyrinths. The armies were drunk. Everything was carried out with tremendous energy and in absolute silence.

And when the armies were in readiness, when all the approaches had been prepared and everything was in its place, a thousand armored troops rushed headlong to their death; the excavators broke down the last barriers and the thousand hurled themselves against the peaceful city— into its streets and storehouses, destroying and killing all in their path. Behind the thousand marched soldier-engineers and workers, blocking the roads behind them, walling off the retreat of the thousand, posting artillery. The thousand advanced gnawing, exterminating with poisons and gases, destroying, infiltrating the center and the narrow passageways; tens of thousands, hundreds of thousands defending the state threw themselves on the thousand. All the soldiers of the state marched to destroy the thousand—the thousand vanished, killed and eaten.

It was then that from the opposite direction millions of those who had sent the thousand before them burst into the city through the numerous breaches that had been blasted. They marched in columns, they captured all routes, they did not plunder—they were making for the heart of the city, where the Mother was. It was only along this route that they built new roads and bridgeheads, here to conquer or to die.

And the abode of the Mother was seized.

The soldiers guarding the Mother were killed.

Thousands of her new servants began dragging her toward the underground passages.

But it is not given to He's to think; while they were conquering another city and fighting to capture a new Mother, an enemy ravaged their city, plundered their stores, tore down bridges, led away their herds, killed their slaves, killed their brothers, killed their soldiers, killed their Father, trampled their fungus gardens; in the city built by protracted efforts and arduous toil there was an abomination of desolation. The sun shone into the ruins, which were exposed to the eyes of strangers, because chance—the absurd—had intruded into this toil, this way of life.

Chapter Three

A year of life in Nigeria, in Rida, had taught Mr. Samuel Garnet nothing. He continued to believe that there was no such place as "abroad" and that only England existed, and, as always, he ate porridge and bacon in the morning. Still, he was very interested in company business, but nobody was interested in him any more than in his conversations about how he had ordered such and such from the metropolis for Whitsunday—shoes, a suit, a saddle, film for his camera.

Mrs. Samuel Garnet's knowledge was of a different kind. She knew that she was going to have a baby soon after Whitsunday, that during the months of her pregnancy Samuel had taken up with a Negro woman, that the tree over there by the window was called a baobab. During the day she embroidered and sewed for the baby—this she did at those times when her husband was at home, or about to leave or to return (she had long since knitted him seven ties—one for each day of the week—and she would give them to him on Whitsunday); but when her husband was not at home and not expected she would sit over her diary. There in her diary she was writing a novel in which were to be found: the moon, Bourne-mouth, a moonlight sail, handclasps, near-infidelity, a se-cret ring, and a slim volume inscribed by a poet, the one with whom she, the heroine, had visited Bournemouth and with whom she had deceived her husband by holding hands. There in the diary was a reconciliation with her husband, with reality in the shape of the Negro woman from the plantations, of her husband's conversations about what kind of dress he would give her for Easter next year, and when he would allow her to bring Mother—Mrs. Garnet's mama—over from the metropolis. On the diary the words "Mrs. Samuel Garnet" had been crossed out—accidentally, of course—by an absent-minded, meditative hand, and her maiden name, Miss Elsa Deddington, had been inscribed in their place. . . .

No doubt it was pregnancy which caused tiny wrinkles to appear under Mrs. Elsa's eyes, and her eyes now moved slowly.

Mr. Garnet was a respected man in the colony, and he and his wife had been invited to stay for several days during the Whitsun holiday at the house of the company president a few dozen miles away.

Mr. Garnet returned from the trip pleased and stimulated. In the yard he spent some time joking with the Negro coachman. His wife went into the house. Soon afterward he went up to her room. She was standing at the window, looking at the baobab.

"Elsa," he began cheerfully, sat down on a chair—and fell to the floor because the chair crumbled to dust beneath him.

And it was immediately discovered that during their absence (their Negro servant, "the swine," had been too lazy to go into these rooms) the house had been attacked by termites, that terrible scourge of equatorial countries. It was dangerous to walk on the floor—it gave way and crumbled to powder; the termites had built their galleries and hundreds of passageways along the surface of cement and ironwork. Termites were everywhere.

For the first time since his childhood, when his father used to whip him, Mr. Samuel lost his composure: his desk had crumbled to dust, the bundle of pound notes—personal savings and company money which he had to account for—had crumbled to dust, and his checkbook had crumbled to dust too.

Mr. Samuel's face—tanned, solid—collapsed to a rotten, wrinkled apple.

"Elsa," he said, "it's quite possible they were gnawing away even before we left. The Negro says they're noiseless and never come out into the daylight. Didn't you see any sign of them—these corridors they make on cement—before we left?"

Mrs. Elsa made no reply: she was crying: in her hands were a pair of silver clasps—all that was left of her diary.

Last Chapter

Under the palms, in the native bazaar, Negroes were selling a great delicacy—the substance which was the excrement of termites from which the fortress of the ruined city had been built. Women traded bananas for it and took it home to cook and eat.

May 1925

THE THREE BROTHERS

I

Memory knows those honey cakes with a bitter almond in
the middle—memory hoards those honeyed days, honey
to me, who comes, after all, from the land watered by the
Irgizes.[1] There the steppe, the Trans-Volga, comes up not
against the Volga, but against the Three Brothers, which,
if I am not mistaken, are geographically part of the Yer-
geni Hills. The Volga is narrow and desolate here, although this is where its broad lower reaches begin. The
River Karaman girds Katrinstadt, and the Germans smoke
pipes to honor the Three Brothers and the steppe.

. . . .

At a quarter to seven each morning the bells of the
Kirche ring, and the entire colony sits at table drinking
coffee. At seven the bells of the *Kirche* ring, and the
entire colony is at work. With the eye of memory I look
out of the window of *Grossmutter's* house: a solitary camel
—with its snakelike neck and dragon head, its stillness,
which is the stillness of the steppe—asserts Asia, "the night
of Asia," "the wisdom of the serpent," and dragons; it is
no accident that the words "stillness" and "steppe" are
consonant. Outside the window is a deserted town square,
fifty degrees Reaumur, and the steeple of the *Kirche*,
melting in the heat; and beyond, it seems no more than
thirty paces away, stand the Three Brothers. Heinrich
Karle, my childhood friend, calls through the window:
"*Wollen wir spazieren gehen?*" I, who habitually trans-

[1] The Greater and Lesser Irgiz Rivers: tributaries of the Volga
which join it to the north of Saratov (Editors).

late everything into Russian, find this very funny: "Do we want to go for a walk?"

At a quarter to twelve the bells of the *Kirche* ring (a metallic, un-Russian sound) and the entire colony is sitting at dinner, and then, having closed shutters and undressed, as if for the night, they sleep. It is too dark to read, and I lie with my feet in the air, bite my nails, and wonder why thieves don't go about their thieving in the afternoon; how boring to remember that there never is any thieving here. The bell rings at three—that's when they drink coffee—and again at five, and at eight. At nine the entire colony is in bed again, this time for the night. The working day is disposed of—by the bell—at five. People call on friends between five and eight, before supper. Visitors are given honey cakes with a bitter almond in the middle, a small glass of wine, and invited to play a game of dominoes. *Grossmutter* has five pairs of shoes which stand on various thresholds: she wears one pair about the yard, another pair—in the cowshed, a third—in the kitchen, a fourth—in the dining room, and a fifth—in the parlor; all this for the sake of cleanliness. The floors are washed every day, and the outside of the house—every Saturday. The cowshed floor is also washed every Saturday. It is hard to say whether people were made for cleanliness, or cleanliness for people. On the landing *Grossmutter* has a wine cupboard, and I came to the conclusion that the most sensible thing to do when everyone was sleeping in the afternoon was to investigate this cupboard so that I would really fall asleep by three. My father, Andrey Ivanovich Vogau (Andreas Johannovich?) is a Russian District doctor. We are at Uncle Aleksandr's house—Aunt Leontina makes such delicious punch; how I would like to go to Katrin-Garten with Irma! But there are other things to worry about; *Grossmutter* locks the garden gate at exactly eight o'clock, when the *Kirche* bell rings; it is now ten, and my father is standing contritely by the fence; I climb over, and Father follows; in the yard he whispers to me:

"Take your boots off, Boryushka. Or else we'll make a

noise and leave footprints." Both Father and I tiptoe across the yard and along the passage in our stockinged feet so as to reach our beds without making a sound. Father lights a cigarette—and on the painted floor, shiny as a mirror, are the clear prints of our socks. Father lights a second match, sticks his cigarette in the corner of his mouth, shakes his head, and says in the language in which he uttered the first words he ever spoke: *"O mein lieber Gott";* together we sit on the floor muttering like conspirators and rubbing away the marks with our handkerchiefs. In the morning we are caught anyway—our handkerchiefs are the evidence. And now Father is sitting with my uncles, and each uncle has a pipe with a rubber mouthpiece, a scarf around his neck, and a straw hat with the widest brim imaginable pulled down over his forehead; their faces are clean-shaven, and their noses are bluish in the molten day: Father is talking to my uncles about the disorderliness and dishonesty of the Russians, about the activity and the lack of it in the District; the Germans listen, smoke, and comment gravely:

"Ho, mein lieber Gott!"

Well then. Grandmother, my dear, kind *Grossmutter* Anna, will take me across the Karaman in a cabriolet to the "wasser medau" (meaning water meadow). Dear Grandmother Anna will make me a jacket and trousers to grow into—and will take me to the shooting range where Germans compete on Sundays for the title of King of Marksmen. I arrived at Grandmother's in a boat with a torn sail, steered through the Volga's muddy waters by a purplish-faced German in an umbrellalike hat—in a boat that gleamed like a room in a Russian peasant's house at Easter, and there was a magical smell of pitch, the smell of Stenka Razin[2] to my boyish imagination. I remember the camel which for me asserted Asia—"the night of Asia" and the "serpent's wisdom" of dragons—by its sandy coat, by its stillness, which is the stillness of the steppe, and

[2] A Don Cossack, leader of the peasant uprisings of 1667–71 in the Volga and Don regions (Editors).

its bellow, encompassing the whole culture of the Turan. To this day I have a pair of woolen socks given to me by my dear, kind Grandmother Anna—red with dark-blue stripes, and as sturdy and durable as German culture itself. It was Grandmother who told me, a child, how the Germans, when they first came here to the Volga, fought the Kirghiz; once the Kirghiz caught thirty Germans in the water meadows of the Karaman and cut out their tongues; and when the Germans caught Kirghiz horse thieves they would bury them in haystacks and burn them alive; as I listened, my childish imagination pictured the green steppe nights, and always camels, many camels; Grandmother's stories gave me a very closed-in feeling. . . .

As for the rest, I suggest that the reader find out from the historians. Here are the addresses: the village of Yekaterinenstadt (or Baronsk), Samara Province, Nikolayev District, later, during the Revolution of 1917 the town of Marxstadt, capital of the Commune of Volga-German Colonists—almost a member of the Federation of Russian Republics (the town of Nikolayev was renamed Puga- chov); then—five years after the Revolution, during the Great Famine—Sterbstadt, Dietown, because some of the Germans were simply sent floating down the Volga, while others started their wagons rolling toward the Caucasus, Turkestan, even Germany. For details—see the history books, the footnotes to the volumes of the *History of the Great Russian Revolution.*

There is another childhood memory I have kept. It hap- pened in Mozhaisk, where my father practiced medicine. I used to go birdcatching with other boys on Goat Hill; we had to pass a railroad pump house and an embankment with water pipes running underneath it; and in this em- bankment was a passage, just big enough for inspectors to crawl in on all fours: the boy that I was had to crawl in too, investigating the tunnel the way boys investigate life in general: I started to work my way in, and the rotten boards gave way, the earth came down on me, and I could move neither forward nor back; I was rescued by the other boys, who pulled me out by the legs—and I remember that there, in the tunnel, I had the same closed-in feeling that I got from Grandmother's stories about the Germans whose tongues were cut out by the Kirghiz on the Karaman.

II

I spent the summer of nineteen hundred and twenty-one alone at the end of the world. Olga Alekseyevna, that kind woman, brought me boiled water to drink. The clock had stopped, and I did not rewind it. I lived in excellent harmony—with myself, the dust, and my bicycle. I took down the black curtains in the children's room and hung them in mine. To the contents of my pockets was added something I had never possessed before—a large bunch of keys. I used to get up when I awoke and go down to the river to wash and fetch water. At the market a woman I knew who had a stall used to save a large bottle of milk for me; butter and bread I brought from my wife's in Novosyolki. My sole wealth was a pood of kerosene, and I could stay up without taking the sun into account: I came to know very well the strange, greenish, tremulous dawns of June. During the wakeful night hours I wrote the tale "Ryazan Apples" and read *A History of Hunting Dogs* and *The Fishes of Russia*. Nobody came to see me. I had a bunch of keys, and it happened on occasion that the house was locked up to let the dust lie in peace, while the front-room window, peacefully open, basked peacefully in the sun. Every third day a cleaning woman came; first of all she would sit on the porch; sometimes she got the samovar going and cooked potatoes for me; then we would feast, and afterward she would sleep on my wife's bed. I usually went to Novosyolki when the cleaning woman came.

I lived in the church grounds, in a little five-windowed house; from my window I could see the ancient church, and just behind the house flowed the Moskva River. To my right lived the priest; to my left, on the other side of a vegetable patch, lived a family of petty thieves. The priest's

house was just over the fence from mine. The priest's wife
had died; he lived the life of a hermit. He walked about
his yard and his little garden dressed in a pair of white
trousers and his wife's blouse and hat. I was in my house
one morning when my nose told me that forty cesspool
cleaners must have arrived in the neighborhood. Nevertheless, I inspected the house thoroughly—and discovered
the truth (how many different truths there are!): the good
father had unsealed the pit under his back porch, and in
another part of the yard he had dug a second pit, and was
now carrying the liquid from one to the other in a bucket,
to the bottom and handle of which he had tied pieces of
rope so as not to soil his hands; dressed in his hat, blouse,
and white trousers, he did this methodically for a day and
a half. That he had to do it was a consequence of the
Revolution, as was his practice of keeping records, like a
schoolmaster, of the church attendance of his parishioners,
and of locking the church during services like the Moscow
Art Theater. The good father had a list of rites and their
cost in kind. I cannot speak of him without respect: a
hermit, he truly believed in his God, believed in Him passionately; those few—bent with age and dressed in black
—who never missed a service would lock themselves in
the church to pray together with catacombic intensity;
there in the locked church the choir's part was taken by
the congregation. To my left, on the other side of the vegetable patch, lived a peaceful family of petty thieves, in-
dustrious as ants. I observed the head of the family
dragging home water pipes for which he could have no
possible need (later they replaced stakes in the fence),
two logs, a fancy traveling case. Mother and son were
otherwise occupied: the son, a skinny boy of about ten,
spent his days, from morning to night, stealing apples, a
few at a time, which he hid inside his shirt; at night he
climbed trees for apples with a basket; his mother kept busy
drying the apples for future use. Still, my thieves lived
beggarly lives (it must not be forgotten that this was the
year of the Great Famine), and when beets, cabbages, and
cucumbers appeared in the vegetable patches, they lived

on them and nothing else. Their house was as interesting as Plyushkin's;[3] it stood in a garden on the other side of the vegetable patch, a board fence around its yard; both house and yard were piled high with all sorts of amazing junk; I was constantly tempted to buy an old harpsichord which they had. Because of the junk the house was full of dust and smelled like a metal workshop. Their prize possession was a cow, which was tended by a black crone. And this dried-up little old woman, Anfisa Markovna, the wife's sister, cast spells; she had the fame and following of—how shall I put it?—a soothsayer or a witch, the two probably being one and the same thing.

Every third day the cleaning woman came; usually all the bread had been eaten by that time, and I was by no means averse to a dish of hot soup. I had a battered old bicycle, a ladies' model, which dated back to the time when bicycles first came into existence, and which for this reason had not been requisitioned by the authorities; on this I rode to Novosyolki. There had once been a family of landowners—the Yenisherlovs; they disappeared with the Revolution, but their house remained standing in its old park planted with larch and beech, on a hill between ravines and the River Kolomenka, completely alone in the forest. During the Revolution the house was requisitioned: first by an orphanage, then by a workers' organization; later it was boarded up. And now my wife had moved into the attic for the summer with our daughter and our dog Tiny. Every time I arrived there at night (all the way corn crakes would call after me as I went by) the house, seen from the main drive, confirmed for me Turgenev's truth to life—I believed in the Turgenev girl who at any moment would come down from the veranda; by the Kolomenka frogs would be croaking. But more often I arrived during the day, to be met in the forest by my wife, stick in hand, rapt as all women are when they are soon to give birth. She is holding a stick in her hand; there is a touch of wildness about her, an air of absorbed distrac-

[3] Archetype of the hoarder—a character in Gogol's *Dead Souls* (Editors).

tion: this is because from morning till night she can think of nothing but mushrooms, and she cannot help looking for them under every bush. We are all mad about mushrooms in Novosyolki. Our attic has only one table, and not a single chair; we live on the floor, where our bedding is spread, and where our daughter Natashka's toys are, and her mirror, too. In the morning Natashka squats down by me and commands:

"Ready—aim—fire!" I leap up at the command; I eat an unleavened *lepyoshka*, smelling, as everything does here, of wild strawberries. It is of no importance to me that the house at Novosyolki has seen many things since it was built in the time of the Empress Catherine—I put on a pair of soft shoes, take a basket, and go mushrooming; I have found a spot of my own, in a ravine. At noon we count to see who has the most cepes—and all the broken window frames, roofs, and doors are festooned with strings of mushrooms. Devil knows, perhaps there is some mystic significance in these mushroom rosaries, as there is in my wife's lying-in. In the forest everything smells of wild strawberries. In the evening we are sometimes visited by another thief—Ivan Andreyevich, a peasant who, to his ruin, has taken to town ways; he is not embarrassed, for some reason, to tell us that he steals firewood from the grounds —and offers it to us; we ought to buy from him as we know him! And this is what he told us: if you take an ear of rye that should be flowering in another week, and you put this ear in a woman's hair and leave it for a quarter of an hour, it will flower before the time is out, and its golden, pollen-bearing stamens will fall out; this is because the Evil One is in women. It all seemed extraordinary to me—exactly the kind of trifle I gather, like honey, for my stories. I inquired about it, and was assured that it was true—embarrassed peasant girls also confirmed it. In the evenings mists would rise from the Kolomenka. Natashka would be sleeping. Our "winker" would be burning on the one and only table; my wife, all in white, would stand by the table braiding her hair for the night. We would talk about mushrooms. I would be lying on the floor and smoking cigarettes.

III

Once I had a day like this. In the morning (or rather afternoon) I was awakened by the postman. Within me are mingled four different bloods: German, Russian, Tartar, and Jewish—or to put it more precisely: Russo-Tartar, German, and a touch of Jewish. In the morning the postman brought me a letter from my sister, from the mother country of my Russo-Tartar ancestors. All my anguish is there, in my Russo-Tartar homeland: anguish, hatred, love, and tenderness—everything that the word "Irgiz" means to me. The Marusya who is mentioned at the beginning of the letter died of typhus and starvation in 1920 and was buried in the Donskoye Cemetery in Moscow—Marusya Lobachova, my Ledka. My sister wrote:

"I want to tell you that I love you very much and miss you often—all the more now that Marusya is dead. When I was leaving last year I saw you—you and Marusya—for the last time from the train window: you were standing in the square waving to me, and suddenly I felt that the two of you were closer to me than anyone else, and, I don't know why, whenever I begin to write to you I remember that moment—what I thought and how I cried then—and I start bawling. And I'm bawling right now.

"It really is very bad that we live apart from each other. I suppose Mama has written to you all about our life here. Father works (we go to the office together, arm in arm—very touching—carrying sacks over our shoulders and briefcases under our arms. In the department he reads out your letters and introduces me to everyone: 'My daughter, the agronomist,' which always embarrasses me), scours the District for bread, frightens everybody with talk of starvation, loses his temper when people live differently from the way he thinks they should, gets very tired. Mama cooks, gets the samovar going, mends clothes, washes dishes—forced by necessity to do the very things she dislikes most. Once in a while she and I go for a walk together, buy a few handfuls of sunflower seeds, and stroll about the hills on the outskirts of town and in Glebychev Ravine, or we go to visit relatives—usually to Aunt Dasha's. Aunt Dasha does impersonations for us: Uncle Tolya haggling as he tries to sell an old candlestick at the market, or getting the better of a peasant by giving him a broken alarm clock in exchange for two poods of squashy tomatoes; someone picking Galenka's pocket, and Aunt Katya trying to convince a crowd on Nemetskaya Street of her healing powers, assuring them that Spasokukotski[4] is founding a nursing home named after her; Aunt Zhenya selling 'delicious cold lemonade' near the hot-food stalls in the market—and making a good profit. The Krugovs live disgustingly. Uncle Tolya is a greedy old skinflint—he buys white bread and saccharin for himself on the sly and hides them from everybody, doles out a few chips of wood once a day to Aunt Dasha to light a fire under the cooking pot, forbids sitting with a lamp in the evening. Their house is filthy, overcrowded, stinking. Leonid doesn't work anywhere, doesn't do anything, lies on the sofa reading a history of French art; his wife died, and Lyuska is gradually selling off the furs and dresses her mother left. All our relatives are *burzhuis,* haggling at the market—there's no enterprise in it, or money either, just smalltime deals on 'a bit of saccharin.'"

I read the letter through and suddenly felt closed-in. I love my sister, father, and mother more than anybody. I felt closed-in, I remembered my childhood. Mozhaisk, Yekaterinenstadt. The letter was from Saratov. Still, that day, as always, I followed my morning routine: went to the river to wash, and from there, by way of the kremlin, to the market to fetch milk. An event had occurred to upset the peaceful life of my neighbors: the priest's daughter, a Communist Party member, had arrived with her three-month-old baby. It seemed strange to me that such a woman could have a child. She looked like a nun, and had an overwhelming need to go to the stake for her faith;

[4] Spasokukotski, Sergey Ivanovich (1870–1943): Russian surgeon, at the time a professor of medicine at Saratov University (Editors).

to the local Executive Committee she brought her own ideas of socialist—bureaucratic—office management; she went about always with her burning eyes lowered: the flame which consumed her was the flame of the Revolution. The baby was left on her father's hands; it cried so pitifully all the time that the priest turned for help to my neighbors on the left—to the soothsayer Anfisa Markovna; for three dawns in a row Anfisa Markovna chewed at the child's navel, cast spells to stop its crying. I don't know exactly how all this was done. In all likelihood the priest's daughter knew nothing about it at all. The priest's daughter burned only for the Revolution: there could be no compromises, and she forbade her own father to lock the church during services; she reported him to the Politburo, and the priest was obliged to agree in writing that he would not keep a register of those who came to pray and those who did not. And it was Politburo agents who one fine day hauled away all the junk accumulated by my petty thieves. In the evening Nikolai Smolenski, a nice Bolshevik, came to see me; later we were joined by Toptygin (I, who am not a Bolshevik, generally find it easier to be in the company of Bolsheviks because of their vitality and cheerfulness); we prepared a feast: Toptygin rolled up his sleeves and mixed and fried the most delicious fritters. We talked about the Revolution. And there we were: Smolenski—a Party member, Toptygin—devil knows what, a former (expelled) Bolshevik, and I—basically an anarchist who describe myself, half joking, half in earnest, as "a Bolshevik, but not a Communist": all three of us loved the Revolution as all things elemental, turbulent, shattering must be loved when there are only two things in the balance—life and death. I argued something that is perfectly clear to me: that the Great Russian Revolution had come and gone like our Russian fairy tale of Ivanushka the Fool.[5] But that's neither here nor there.

That night I had a dream. It's a quarter to seven, the bells of the *Kirche* are ringing, and the entire colony is

[5] A peasant simpleton who succeeds against overwhelming odds because right is on his side (Editors).

sitting at table drinking coffee. With the eye of memory I am looking out of *Grossmutter's* house; a solitary camel asserts Asia for me—"the night of Asia," the "serpent's wisdom" of the dragons—by its sandy coat, its stillness, which is the stillness of the steppe, and its bellow, encompassing the whole culture of the Turan. But my dreams are always milky-blue. In my dream I had to run—but you can't run in dreams, your legs are bound, and this gives you a terrible closed-in feeling. I awoke, and in half-sleep could still see—as if they were before me—the Three Brothers, *Drei Brüder,* who had taken up their positions out there on the Volga, opposite Katrinstadt. There was a disturbance outside; I opened the window: on the other side of the fence the priest was laying a curse on his daughter according to the rites of the Russian Orthodox Church, exactly as Yemelyan Pugachov[6] is anathematized in the first week of Lent.

IV

Here I end my story. The point is that if art is everything I have taken from life and poured into words, as it is for me, then every story is endless, as life itself is boundless. *Drei Brüder*—Three Brothers. It is the same as these three houses standing side by side. Ivan Andreyevich told me that rye flowers in a woman's hair. There will be another summer, and many more besides, when I shall go into the rye fields and find out for myself whether this is so. Memory knows those honey cakes with a bitter almond in the middle.

Summer 1921

[6] A Don Cossack, leader of the peasant uprisings of 1773–75 in the Volga and Ural regions (Editors).

THE TALES OF SEAS AND MOUNTAINS

1921

ALWAYS ON BUSINESS TRIPS

I

He had spent the whole day at the quarry laying charges
and blasting limestone. Below in the hollow lay the plant;
chimneys smoked, trolleys shuttled, creaking, back and
forth between the plant and the quarry. Above, wet pines
overlooked the steep bank. All day the sky had been gray
and raw; smoke from the chimneys spread over the earth
like a cloth. Charges exploded in rumblings and smoke.

He was walking home with the mine foreman, Bitzka;
the autumn darkness had already fallen, and lights burned
brightly in the generator room. The engineers' settlement
lay on the other side, on cleared forest land; small cement
houses stood in monotonous rows, and pale-blue spheres
of street lamps hummed as they burned, cutting black
shadows from the branches and trunks of pines. His leather
jacket stuck to his back, as Bitzka's jacket no doubt stuck
to his. Bitzka said:

"Soon I am home, Aleksandr Aleksandrovich, and there
is tea, the baper, the vife." Bitzka had recently married.

But in the house of Aleksandr Aleksandrovich Agrenev it
was dark, street lamps shone into the windows; the only
light in the house showed through the crack between the
tightly closed double doors of his wife's room, his beloved
wife, the only woman he would ever love—and a stranger.
He undressed, washed; rain began to fall, pattering noisily
on the roof; he picked up the newspaper. The maid came
in, said that tea was ready.

Anna stood by the window with her back to him, a book
in her hand—tall, slender, beautiful, a stranger; on the
window sill nearby stood a glass of tea; there was a misty

patch on the window. She did not turn, said, "Pour yourself some tea."

The electric light burned brightly and coldly. There was a smell of glue from new furniture. She did not say another word; her slender fingers turned the pages—she read standing, her head bent. He asked:

"Will you be out this evening, Anna?"

"What? No, I'll be home."

"Is anyone coming?"

"What? No, nobody. Will you be out?"

"I don't know—probably. Tomorrow I'm leaving on a trip, I'll be away a week."

"What? Oh yes, on a trip."

How he wanted to stay, how he wanted to talk, talk endlessly—about everything: the impossibility of living without human warmth, without love; his love for her, and the loneliness of his evenings. But he too fell silent.

"Is Asya asleep?"

"She must be by now."

On the table, on the cold, white tablecloth with its straight folds, stood a nickel teapot, a solitary glass. The clock clicked steadily.

"She won't deceive me, she won't betray me, she won't leave me, but she's a stranger, a stranger—and the mother of my child."

II

Darkness had completely enveloped the earth, street lamps cut white circles into it; rain dripped forlornly, and the factory whistle too sounded forlorn.

He walked through the park, along paths which met at right angles, in the direction of the club, changed his mind, turned off toward the school, where Nina lived. They had gone to school together in a small provincial town, and ever since—for love comes only once—he was for her the only one, for all time; she fled desperately from one end of Russia to the other, at war with herself, with the windmills of her pride, but she could not bear it, and came, broken in spirit, to live near him.

He walked down the school's dark corridors, knocked. "Come in."

She was sitting alone in the little room at a small table —plain, with a red mark on her cheek where her palm had been pressed, a gray shawl over her shoulders, a book in her hand; and he noticed with sadness that her eyes deepened and a tender light came into them; she got up, threw the book down:

"Is that you, dearest? Hello. Is it raining?"

"Hello. I've come just for a little while."

"Take off your coat—would you like some tea?" She stretched out both her arms, saying wordlessly: Thank you, thank you.

"How's everything?"

"I get tired. I'm all right. I get very tired."

In the tiny kitchen she began to heat the samovar; she set out jars of jam on the table, near the piles of exercise books; she made him sit in the only armchair—bustled about, smiled, her cheek glowed red—the mark would not go— where it had been pressed against her palm throughout the long evening—she who loved him, who had given up everything for him, and from whom nothing was wanted.

"Don't . . . fuss about. Let's talk. . . . Do sit down."

With infinite tenderness she touched his hand, came over to him.

"What is it, dearest?" She stroked his hand, burned by each touch. "What is it, dearest?"

Sometimes she would rebel, wring her hands, speak with hatred, her eyes clouding over with anger; sometimes she would fall on her knees, pleading and crying, but always she was tender, the one from whom nothing was wanted.

"What is it, dearest?"

"I'm tired. You know Anna doesn't love me. She won't leave me, she won't deceive me, but she doesn't love me. You love me—I know. . . ."

At home—walls, cold. Mine foreman Bitzka, red-cheeked, jokes all day, even when it rains. He lights the fuse and stands by. Thirty years—five tenths of a lifetime—half—ten twentieths. A blank cartridge. No tenderness. Impossible to live without human warmth.

It seemed as if the lamp suddenly went out, something warm pressed on his eyes: two palms. At first the words were soft, then wild.

"Leave, leave her, dearest. Come to me, live here. Even if you don't love me. I love you, I love you. . . ."

He was silent.

"Why don't you say something? I'll give you everything —everything is still in the future. Let me have the child. You know, she—she's dead. She doesn't need anything. Do you hear me? Let me, let me have her. . . . I'll take all the suffering on myself. . . ."

. . . .

Again the lamplight burst upon him—a small, gray human bundle fell onto the narrow, celibate bed.

So deep was the darkness outside that you couldn't see two paces ahead. Near the barracks workmen were bawling, an accordion was squealing. Someone whistled in the darkness, two fingers in mouth—and burst into roars of senseless, insolent laughter. As before, street lamps cut out white circles. He walked, lighting a path with his pocket flashlight, picking out his way automatically; Nina hurried at his side in the darkness, stepping into puddles, trying to keep up. Pines moaned in the wind, and everything was wild and terrifying. He was talking, hardly aware of it, thinking aloud:

"I don't love you, Nina. There's nothing I want from you. Anna. Anna was ordered by her father. An old family. Anna said she would never love me. She's bringing up Asya—I love my little girl; she looks at me with empty eyes, a stranger, she's a stranger too—my own daughter. I stole her mother, stole her from nothingness. I'll get home and go to bed alone. Or I'll go to Anna and she'll receive me with her lips pressed together. I don't want a daughter from you. What for? . . . And tomorrow will be the same as today."

They were already near his house in the engineers' settlement when he remembered Nina, began to worry:

"You'll catch cold, my dear, and going back is dangerous. . . ."

He stood facing her for a few seconds in silence, held out his hand.

"Well, take care of yourself."

A band of young roughs passed, someone shone a lantern on them.

"Well, if it isn't the schoolmarm. Playing around with engineers. Ho-ho-ho . . . ," they laughed, and suddenly burst into a bawdy song:

> *And so the girls all fixed a date*
> *To see the district magistrate. . . . Eh!!*

III

Before going to sleep he played a game of solitaire, ate a cold supper; there was light in Anna's room, he stood by her door a long time, knocked. "Come in." He stayed only a short time. She was sitting at a little table with a book in her hand; she laid it on top of the notebook she used as a diary. When, when would he know what was in that notebook?

"Tomorrow I'm taking the early train to Moscow on business. Here's some housekeeping money for you."

"Thank you. When do you get back?"

"In a week—that means the Friday of next week. Do you need anything?"

"No, thank you." She got up, came over to him, kissed his cheek near the lips. "Take care of yourself. Good-bye. Don't disturb Asya."

And she lowered herself into a chair by the table with her back toward him, picked up the book.

It was a wet dawn; a horse and buggy were brought up, and he drove with Bitzka along the highway to the station;

black in the rain and darkness, workmen were hurrying to reach the plant before the second whistle; as the buggy was overtaken by the director's car, the plant whistle blew. Bitzka, red-cheeked, with sparse Latvian mustaches, and wearing a bowler, looked about him with a stern expression.

"Didn't you get enough sleep, Robert Eduardovich?"

"No, that's not it. My mood is bad." He was silent for a moment. "I am forty, and my vife is eighteen. I need a serious vife who don't talk back—a good housekeeper. She all the time jokes, pulls my viskers, and laughs. It's true, I didn't get enough sleep. She give me her measurement for new shoes. . . . Vat nonsense. . . ." And he smiled with his narrow, cunning little eyes. "Vimmen . . . !"

WOLF RAVINE

I

As a child, Agrenev once heard his mother say that just that morning at nine o'clock Nina Kallistratovna Zamotkina and her daughter had gone to the apartment of the nurse Chasovnikova to slap Chasovnikova's face for breaking up the family hearth and home by her affair with Pavel Aleksandrovich Zamotkin, Nina Kallistratovna's husband. At the time the little Agrenev had a vivid picture in his mind: leading her daughter with one hand and holding a reticule in the other, Nina Kallistratovna is on her way; her gait is naturally unusual, since she is going to someone's apartment to deliver a slap in the face; she probably had to go bowlegged, or perhaps do a squat dance down the street; as for the family hearth—it was something like a Manchurian stove, the iron kind surely, since a slap was to be delivered for its sake; and it was most intriguing to imagine—Nina Kallistratovna arrives at the apartment, swings back her hand, and—lets her have it; Nina Kallistratovna's gait, the apartment, the hands—all had a hidden meaning—a most intriguing one—for a child.

This was a memory of childhood, of the little town, the provinces, where everything was out of the ordinary—like childhood itself. Here in Wolf Ravine this suddenly came to Agrenev's mind, and he felt depressed. No one would ever go to slap anyone's face on account of him. What barbarism—face-slapping; and no solution—in face-slapping. It was fall, and as he stood in the ravine waiting for Olga cranes flew low overhead, "krooh"-ing raggedly as they fell into a V formation. Then leaden clouds began to rise from the eastern horizon, the sky turned wintry, and Vega flared blue above. Olga arrived unexpectedly, late;

she was suddenly there, standing on the edge of the ravine, about to come down to Agrenev, down into the ravine.

II

Aleksandr Aleksandrovich Agrenev was a married man, and a metallurgical engineer by profession, and Olga Andreyevna Golovkiná—a girl who had finished secondary school and lived with her aunt—was a teacher. Everybody called her Olya Golóvkina, and this was wrong, because she bore an ancient Russian name, famous as far back as Peter I and Senator Golovkín. But it was then, in Peter's time, that the family suddenly fell on evil days, leaving in the town only a Golovkínskaya Street and a house on that street, which the aunt let for her living. Agrenev knew that the aunt—Agrenev did not know her name—was an old maid, had one joy in life—Olya, that in the evenings the aunt sat at the window without a lamp, waiting for Olya, and that it was for this reason that Olya walked around the block on returning home after seeing him—to cover up. The aunt was never spoken of directly, the word was mentioned only in passing, as if "aunt" were a thing. As for Olya, she was a sweet girl it's hard to say much about; she was like a willow twig, a real little provincial. The town sprawled over low hills, among fields with ancient quarries; all its energies the town poured into the plant that lay at the other end of it, and the casual conversation that took place between Agrenev and Olya in spring, soon after they met, was in the style of the town and of Olya. Agrenev happened to say:

". . . Balmont, Blok, Bryusov, Sologub . . ."[1]

Olya, that dear little willow twig, interrupted him hastily:

"I don't know much about foreign writers. . . ."

Neither Balmont nor Blok was known in the town—in the school, in the library, in the magazines—but Olya liked to

[1] Russian poets of the late nineteenth and early twentieth centuries (Editors).

recite Kozlov[2] by heart, and could speak French. The plant
lived a dark, unclean, shrill life, like a beggar-woman
wearing tatters under unaccustomedly luxurious garments.
And the plant frightened the little town with its ancient
streets—its Golovkínskayas, Zagornayas, Spasskayas; the
town lived among fields, half-smothered by the plant, but
still having some kind of life of its own.

The hollow known as Wolf Ravine lay darkly beyond the
town, in the opposite direction from the plant. To the right,
toward the river, was a wood where couples went walking. Nobody went into the ravine, because there was nothing poetic about it: it was treeless, dreary, neither deep
nor awe-inspiring. It ran along the top of a hill, dominated
the area—and lying in the small depression near the top of
the ravine one could see for a good distance all around
while remaining hidden: Aleksandr Aleksandrovich Agrenev
was a married man. But shepherd boys tending cattle in
the meadow began to notice that every evening in the
summer a man on a bicycle would turn off the main road
into the ravine, and later a girl would pass by also going
toward the ravine, hurrying like a willow twig blown by
the wind; as boys will, they shouted all kinds of dirty words
after her.

All that summer Olya kept asking Agrenev to bring her
books to read—how was it she never noticed that not once
during the whole summer did he bring her any?

III

Then there was an evening in September, after it had
been raining for several days and they had not been meeting, when everything happened that had to happen—what
comes to every girl once in a lifetime. They always met at
eight, and eight o'clock in September is not the same as
eight o'clock in June. The rainy spell was over, but a raw,
desolating autumn wind still blew, and the evening was

[2] Ivan Ivanovich Kozlov (1779–1840) or Pavel Alekseyevich
Kozlov (1841–91) (Editors).

weighed down with leaden clouds, cold, gloom. That evening the cranes were on their way south, "krooh"-ing as
they flew. The grass in the ravine had wilted and turned
yellow. The day had been sunny and Olya arrived wearing
a white dress. The shepherd boys looking after the herd
shouted dirty words. Usually Agrenev and Olya parted
here, in the ravine. That evening, truly a black one,
Agrenev was seeing Olya home, and they were both pre-
occupied with a single thought—the aunt: that she was sitting by the window without a lamp and waiting for Olya—
or had she lighted the lamp and started preparing supper?
It was essential to Olya that the aunt should be sitting by
the window without a lamp, so that she could get to her
room in the dark, because she had to change her clothes
without the aunt's knowledge. They, Agrenev and Olya,
did not even walk arm in arm, but pressed closely against
each other, their heads together, talking in whispers—
about the aunt and nothing else. Olya was unable to think
about pain, or joy, or suffering—all she could think of was
how to get in without her aunt noticing anything. And
Agrenev was bored, frightened, and depressed by the
thought of scandal. And there was a light in the aunt's
window, and that light made Olya Golovkiná tremble like
a willow twig; she said in a hoarse whisper, like a stifled
shout:

"I won't go! . . ."

But she went, a willow twig blown by the wind. They
agreed to meet the next morning in Agrenev's office at
the plant, mainly so that she could tell him about the
aunt: how she was, whether the threat of a scandal had
passed.

In the ravine, after Olya had given herself to him completely and was crying and pressing against his knees, in
the black night wild geese flying south passed directly
overhead—so low that the rustle of their wings could be
heard—honking, alarmed by the light of his cigarette, his
tenth in a row; and his heart contracted: "South, geese,
south! . . . And you have no escape, a slave, unwanted
among the unwanted." And he suddenly remembered the

slap which Nina Kallistratovna had gone to deliver on
her husband's account, the slap which no one would give
Olya Golovkiná—on his. "Olya is an accidental, unwanted
burden!" That evening as he rode his bicycle through the
town from Golovkínskaya Street and then through the plant
to the engineers' settlement, taking the shortest route because the darkness made caution unnecessary, Agrenev
thought not of Olga, but of the aunt: that she was an old
maid, that Olya was all she had, and Olya would hide her
tragedy from her; that she, the aunt, sat by the window
alone, without a lamp, evening after evening, not for Olya's
sake, of course, but because she had been dying all her
life, as the town where they knew Kozlov was dying, as
he, Agrenev, was dying, as the girl—Olya—had died. How
persistent life is! What tragedy there was in those lightless
evenings by the window!

IV

At home every morning the maid brought a tray with a
cup of coffee, already cold, into Agrenev's study. Agrenev
left for the plant when everyone was still sleeping. At the
plant there were ragged workers—men whose lives were
wretched in every possible way—Bitzka's witticisms, the
clang of the trolleys; at the plant there was—the plant, a
word that said all there was to be said. During dinner
break Agrenev came home, washed, heard his wife—white-
skinned Anna—rattling spoons on the other side of the wall.
And that was his life. It was most intriguing to imagine
—Nina Kallistratovna arrives at the apartment, swings back
her hand (Which hand? The one holding the reticule?
Or would she first transfer the reticule to the other hand?)
and slaps nurse Chasovnikova's face. Olya—dear Olya
Golovkiná, from whom like all the others nothing was
wanted!

That evening his daughter Asya came to him, made a
curtsy and said:

"Good night, papa."

Agrenev drew her to him, sat her on his knees—his beloved, his own.

"What have you been doing, Asenka?"

"When you went to the field to see Golóvkina, I played the running game with mama."

V

In the morning Olya came to his office—ostensibly on business; she was the same as always. And Olya said happily:

"Auntie didn't find out anything. She opened the door to me without a lamp and hung about in the passage, and I dashed past her as quickly as I could. Then I changed my clothes and came out to supper as if nothing had happened!"

A willow twig swept along by the wind!

In the outer office telephones rang, it was morning, abacuses clicked. They were alone in his private office, arranging their next meeting. Olya did not want to go to the ravine because the boys called dirty words. Agrenev did not tell her that they knew everything at home. As they said good-bye she pressed against him like a willow twig in the wind and whispered:

"I didn't sleep a wink last night. Have you noticed that I'm not calling you by any name—I have no name for you."

And she asked him to bring some books and to be sure not to forget them!

The town lay at such-and-such latitude and longitude. No one had ever heard of the town. As for the plant, every year something about it appeared in the industrial annuals, and occasionally—in the newspapers, when there was a strike or when workers were buried by limestone. The plant was owned by a joint-stock company; Agrenev wrote reports on the operation of his division; these reports were also printed, never to be read, and under them was the name: "A. A. Agrenev, Engineer." As for Olya Golovkiná, all the writing she did was to mark up school records and keep a diary; in the records of her section at the elementary school she entered grades opposite the name of each pupil.

THE FIRST DAY OF SPRING

This morning Mama got up in the same mood as always during these endless months; I have got into the habit of calling Aleksandr's mother "Mama." She has on a black dress and carries the white, large handkerchief she so often raises to her lips.

It is light in the dining room. The tea service stands sedately on the table, and the samovar is steaming. I am used to the sensation that the dining room gives me all the time now—as if we are about to leave for the country. This is because all the pictures have been taken down, and the mirror which hangs there for no particular reason has been covered up.

I usually get up very early, wash, and immediately pick up the papers. In the old days I hardly ever gave a thought to the papers and couldn't tell one from another, but now I can't imagine life without them. By the time tea is ready I am acquainted with everything that is going on in the world, and can tell Mama about it; Mama can't bear to read the papers.

Mama comes out of her room—it used to be Aleksandr's —tall, dressed all in black; there is something stern about her. All this is as it should be. She makes the sign of the cross over me, kisses me on the forehead and on the lips, and, as always, turns quickly away and raises the hand-kerchief to her lips. I know it comes to her mind that Yuri is dead and Aleksandr is—out there . . . and that I am the only one of the family left at her side.

We are always silent over tea, we are silent most of the time, and there is only one question that she asks:

"What do the papers say?" She always says these words in a hoarse voice. And, hardly able to control myself, the words tumbling out of my mouth, I tell her everything.

After tea I walk up and down the drawing room, looking out of the windows, until twelve; I see the plant—the same as ever—and watch for the postman.

And so, between mail, newspapers, grief—Mother's and mine—day after day passes. And always when I am waiting for letters I recall a small incident of war told to me by a wounded ensign at an evacuation post. He had a minor head wound, but I am sure he was mentally unbalanced or neurotic. He was lying on a stretcher—swarthy, black-eyed, white-bandaged. I gave him tea, but he didn't drink it; setting the mug down and holding onto my hand, he said:

"Do you know what it is—war? You dare not, you cannot know. . . . But I know. Everyone who was there knows! . . . We were going in with our bayonets—you understand?—with bayonets, that is human beings cutting, stabbing, slicing each other up. They were machine-gunning us. Well, it so happened that a private by the name of Kuzmin was beside me, and he caught two bullets at once. He fell, and not knowing where he was, not knowing anymore that I was his officer, he stretched his arms to me and screamed, 'Finish me off—bro-o-ther!' You understand? 'Finish me off, bro-o-ther!' But you can't understand—you don't dare!"

He was whispering one moment, shouting the next.

He said that I couldn't understand it. But I do understand. . . . "Finish me off, bro-o-ther!"—for me these words compress all the horrors of war, and Yuri's death, and Aleksandr's wound, and Mother's grief, everything, everything the war has brought—compress until my temples throb, and my anguish becomes physical. "Finish me off, bro-o-ther!"—how simple, how unlike everything human.

This phrase comes to my mind every day, most often in the drawing room, when I am waiting for mail. Aleksandr's letters are infrequent and matter-of-fact; he writes that he is well, that there is either no danger or that it has passed; his letters are to all of us—Mama, Asya, and me.

Today it was as always—I was waiting for mail.

The postman came—he brought several letters, and one of them was from Aleksandr. I left it to the last, waiting for Mama.

Here it is:

"My dearest Anna!

"Yesterday and today there's been no holding it back—I long for you and think of you, and only of you. When you live an untroubled, quiet life you don't notice a lot of good things. I'm talking about the flowers I am sending you. They grow right by the trench, but it's very hard to get at them, as you can get killed. Well, I've seen these flowers before, but I don't know what they're called, and I feel bad about it.

"Good-bye. I love you. Forgive the 'army' style. This letter is for you alone."

Enclosed in the letter were two violets, two small, pale-blue violets, the kind that appear as soon as the snow melts.

I gave the letter—gave it all the same—to Mama—to his mother—to read, and her lips began to tremble and tears came. She began to cry, but with her tears came laughter. And the two of us—Mama and I, one old, the other young—the two of us wept and laughed at the same time, pressing close to each other. Before this, the war was contained in the words, "Finish me off, brother." But now I have violets, two violets, from out there, from Aleksandr, which have not yet faded.

I have noticed before that awareness of spring, summer, autumn, winter seems to come to human beings all at once. I remember when I was a child on holiday in the country. It would still be summer, everything would be as usual, then one morning a wind would come up—nothing out of the ordinary—and the leaves in the vineyard, which had turned red three weeks before, would catch your eye—and all at once you felt it was autumn, all at once your mood changed, and you began to get ready to go home, back to town.

How many years has it been since I saw autumn, or winter, or spring—or felt them?

And today all at once—after summer long since gone—I felt spring.

Only today I noticed that our windows are still sealed, that I am wearing a black dress, that it is already May, that bluebells are already out in the fields. I had forgotten that I am young: today I remember it.

And I also know that I trust, love—have loved for a long time—Shurik, Aleksandr.[1] And I know that in spite of all the horror, all the absurdity, and ugliness, there are still the splendor of youth, and love, and spring, and pale-blue violets growing by the trenches.

Mama and I wept and laughed together, pressing close to each other on the sofa. Later, I went out alone to the field behind the plant—to love, to think, to dream. . . . I shall love Aleksandr as long as I live, always. . . .

[1] Shurik is one of the diminutives of the name Aleksandr (Editors).

SEAS AND MOUNTAINS

I

It's not out there in Lithuania, in the Polesye,[1] that the trenches are: on this rainy night at the Vindava-Rybinsk Station[2] in a train like a trench—the trenches are in Moscow itself. In the next compartment people are talking:

"What outfit are you with?" "Yes, yes, of course. You remember there's a ravine there, full of boulders, and a lake below; a lot of people floated off to Kingdom Come in that lake." "Allow me to introduce myself—commander of the Third Division."

"Got a light, friend? We've been on leave."

The train will move through the night toward Rzhev, Velikiye Luki, Polotsk. Those soldiers over there huddling together under a wooden seat, drinking tea, look very pleased with life. Outside, in the Vindava-Rybinsk rain, are gaslights, and the eyes of the women standing under the windows are like gaslights in the rain. There is a smell of moth balls. "Where is the commanding officer's car?" Women are not allowed in this car: there's a war going on—men only; and already the air is filled with the smell of leather, tar, and foot-wrappings—a male smell.

"Yes-yes, yes-yes. Ho-ho. He's a liar, a li-ar. No, my beauty, every man is a madman when he goes over the top!" He roars with laughter and speaks in a deep voice, very pleased with himself.

The third bell sounds. "Where is the commanding officer's car?" "Well then, good-bye!" "Ho-ho-ho-ho! He's li-ar, a li-ar, madam." "I've got a blister come up—they

1 The wooded swamplands of the western U.S.S.R. (Editors).
2 The main station of the Moscow-Vindava-Rybinsk Railroad in Moscow (Editors).

gave me new boots, and that's what did it"—this from under the seat. On the ladder used for climbing up to the top berth someone has hung new foot-wrappings—still with fresh government stamps, but already smelling strongly of sweat. The wallflower-yellow platform lights slip past into the night, women and porters glide back, a station official touches the peak of his cap, the rain begins to come down at a slant; as the train switches tracks night comes into its own.

In the rain and darkness at Rzhev soldiers climb out of windows to get tea, and stragglers with rifles clamber in; the train rattles with canteens. The rain lashes like switches in a steam bath.[3] Soldiers in the corridor are annoyed by a document check. Under the seat there is easygoing conversation—the chitchat of war.

And morning came in rosy clouds; trees are dripping, the rain has passed, the air is filled with brightness and fragrance. Velikiye Luki, Lovat; at the station—coffee, soldiers, no women. A Counterintelligence party goes through the train. Soldiers, soldiers, soldiers—rifles, rifles—canteens: men. We are no longer in Great Russia: all around are fir forests, hills, lakes; and everywhere the ground is strewn with round, smooth boulders; at train stops silent people, barefoot, but wearing sheepskin coats and hats although it is summer—Lithuanian peasants—creep out from behind the firs. Counterintelligence is a diversion, the endless, empty day is like a holiday, and there's nothing more to find out—who belongs to what outfit, how many times wounded, in what battles. Many get off at Velikiye Luki and no one gets on. All day it is quiet, and there is a feeling of holiday.

By nightfall—Polotsk; the white walls of the monastery retreat; the Dvina; the train rattles over the bridge. In this area trains move only at night, without timetable, without lights; again a fine rain is falling. The train stops and moves off again without whistles, and all around it is

[3] Reference to an old Russian custom: in steam baths bathers switch themselves with bunches of oak twigs—for cleanliness and tonic effect (Editors).

as quiet as in October; night envelops the earth. At each
station after Polotsk people get off, but nobody gets on;
the distance from the station to the trenches is thirty versts
by narrow-gauge railroad. What weariness—after Moscow,
after all the words and farewells, after the endless day!
It is just beginning to grow light, back there in the east
the sky is bottle green.

"Get up. We've arrived."

Budslav Station; a bomb from an airplane has bitten a
hole in the roof of the station building. All over the place
—on the asphalt of the platform, under the hawthorns, in
the little station garden—soldiers are lying side by side,
asleep. The bookstall has opened for the train's arrival; a
sleepy Jew stands by: Chirikov,[4] Fonvizin,[5] Verbitskaya.[6]
From somewhere in the distance the sound of mittened
hands being clapped together comes with strange clarity.
"What's that?" "That's heavy artillery pounding away."
"Where's the commanding officer? Where's the commanding officer here?" "He's asleep. . . ."

II

One week goes by in the trenches, and another one
begins. I should have written everything down from the
first day: by now one is hardly aware of such things as
the man who is hanging from the barbed wire in the
meadow out there—his head gradually coming apart from
his body. But then, I don't see much. During the day we
sleep. It is June, and there is hardly any night. This is how
I know when it is evening: I live in a dugout, and at seven
o'clock on the dot it comes under fire from the other side

[4] Chirikov, Yevgeni Nikolayevich (1864–1936): writer of the
realist school (Editors).

[5] Fonvizin, Denis Ivanovich (1745–92): playwright and
satirist (Editors).

[6] Verbitskaya, Anastasiya Alekseyevna (1861–1928): popular
writer, best known for novels in which she advocates free love
and explores sexual problems (Editors).

of the swamp; every minute a bullet comes flying—plink. Another minute, and again—plink. You can't hear the report in the noise of the shooting all around, but you can hear the bullet burrowing into the earth and the roof beams. And this goes on all night until seven o'clock in the morning on the dot. There are three of us in the dugout—the other two play chess; I've read everything there is to read, and I'm tired of lying down, walking, and sleeping. A man's life is a threadbare thing: three men can tell each other everything in three days. Yesterday a soldier came running up; one of his hands had been blown off at the wrist while he was out on reconnaissance; he shook the stump and begged senselessly:

"Finish me off, finish me off for the love of Christ! . . ."

Sometimes we come out at night to admire the fireworks. They are shooting—to kill or unnerve us: bullets are burrowing into the dugout—plink, plink, plink. We stand and admire the sight. In the distance guns yap, and suddenly the whole horizon is quivering with green light. Rockets go up one after another. Some are like the ones we used to send up on the Oka; there are some that split into two slow-moving spheres; there are huge disks made up of hundreds of points of light. But then the rockets disappear, and three fingers of light creep up from behind the forest. At first they reach out into the sky, then contract jerkily and fall with feverish haste on us, on the trenches, to the right, to the left. Their light makes our tunics seem white. In the Polesye huge wooden crosses— as big as the ones in Gogol's "Terrible Vengeance"—are placed over graves; on a hill behind us stand two crosses; one of them has tilted, and leans against the other.

Everywhere soldiers, soldiers, soldiers. Not a single old man, not a woman, not a child. This is the third week since I have seen a woman. That is what I want to talk about now, what that means—a woman.

We were having dinner once at a post outside the firing zone, and a nurse laughed on the other side of the plywood partition: I never heard more beautiful music. I can find no other words: more beautiful music. This was a nurse who was making her way through to a field hospital; her dress, her hair—what joy! She was saying something to the post commander; I do not know of any poetry as beautiful as her words. Everything in me that is fine, beautiful, chaste, everything that life has given me—comes from woman, and woman alone. There is nothing more to say.

In the evening I went to the staff-officers' cinema; I sat in a box. When the lights went down I wrote in blue pencil on the bar in front:

"I am a blonde, twenty-two years old, with blue eyes. But—who are you? I am waiting."

I had done a cruel thing.

I had written the words myself, and yet my heart contracted; I could not sit in the cinema any longer. I picked my way out through rows of benches, went to the village, wandered around the church—which did not have a single unbroken window—and gathered a small bunch of forget-me-nots in a ditch near the cemetery.

When I returned to the cinema I noticed that the box was empty, although the place was packed; I saw an officer enter the box; he took his seat in a carefree mood, prepared to enjoy himself, read what I had written—and was suddenly another man: I had injected a terrible poison into him. He left the box and went out; I followed. He started in the direction of the church. I had done a cruel thing.

I had written about the blue-eyed blonde myself—but as I walked I could see her, I longed for her to come to me—I who had written those words. Hundreds of orchestras were playing within me, but my heart was constricted as if gripped by a pair of hands. More than anything in the world I loved and longed for the blonde I had conjured up, I would have given to her all that was finest in me.

I did not go back to the cinema, but dragged myself wearily in the direction of the trenches. On the hill stood the two enormous crosses; I sat down beneath them and whispered, clenching my hands:

"Dearest, dearest, dearest. My beloved, my gentle one. I am waiting."

Far in the distance green rockets rose—the kind we used to send up over the Oka. Then the fingers of the searchlight began to fumble the darkness; my tunic was suddenly white, and a moment later a shell burst near the crosses: they had seen me and were firing at me.

Bullets were plinking—plink! plink! plink!—into the dugout. I lay down on the bunk and buried my head in the pillow. I felt very lonely, and whispered, putting into the words all the tenderness I had in me:

"Dearest, dearest, dearest. . . ."

III

Love.

Is there any truth in the romantic idea that there exists a rare kind of love, a love that comes once in a lifetime, that is stronger than seas and mountains and years, all-conquering, all-subduing, all-renewing? Love.

In the staff train—where the staff officers lived—which was standing in Budslav Station, it was known that there was such a one and only love in the life of Lieutenant Agrenev. A wife, a woman, a girl, who loves once and for all, when love is the most beautiful, the only thing in life, will stop at nothing, will get past Army- and Counter-intelligence to reach the man she loves, to see him—for nothing in the world exists but the overwhelming need of the heart.

Lieutenant Agrenev's compartment was in one of the rear cars, No. 30-05.

· · · ·

The staff train stood under cover. Lights were forbidden. In the evenings, having covered the windows with blankets, the officers gathered in the car of the commander of the XXth Corps to play *chemin de fer* and drink brandy. Someone remarked wittily that life at the front had much in common with life in a monastery; in both places the talk was only of women, and so there was no reason why monks should not be sent to the front to fast and pray.

Captain Kremnev took over the bank. The train attendant, *Pan*[7] Ponyatski, came in and called the captain outside. The others continued the game. The *Pan* told the captain that there was a woman to be had, but that it would cost a lot. The captain's knees began to tremble, he sat down weakly on the step of the car and took out a cigarette. *Pan* Ponyatski warned: no lights allowed. In the distance guns rumbled, as if a night storm was approaching. Never before had Captain Kremnev experienced keener joy than during the moments when he was sitting on the step, the physical—physiological—joy of being. *Pan* Ponyatski said again that it would cost a lot—she was waiting, and there was no time to lose.

Pan Ponyatski led him through car corridors in the dark. The cars smelled of men and leather; from behind compartment doors, where card games were probably going on, came loud laughter. In this way they walked half the length of the train. As they were crossing from one car to another a rocket flared in the distance, and in the green murk the yellow figures of the car number—30-05—glinted. *Pan* Ponyatski unlocked the door of the compartment with his key, and said:

"She's in here. Only please be as quiet as you can."

And the *Pan* turned the key behind Captain Kremnev. It was an officer's compartment; there was a smell of perfume; the sound of someone breathing came from the lower berth. Captain Kremnev threw off his jacket and sat down by the woman sleeping on the berth. His head began to spin, his mind went numb; his heart plummeted and the compartment swayed. The captain put a numb hand on the woman's knee. At this she stretched herself, awakening.

"Is that you, dearest?" she asked. "You're back?"

[7] A Polish title of courtesy (Editors).

"Yes—me," answered the captain.

And suddenly the woman shrank back in the corner, half-naked, helpless, stretching out her arms to defend herself.

"Who is it? Go away! For God's sake, go away!"

The door opened slightly; *Pan* Ponyatski's head suddenly wedged itself there, and whispered:

"Don't let her put you off, your Ex'lency, she's just. . . . Only try to be quiet." The head disappeared.

There were no more words because in the captain, as in all of us, still lurked the man who came out of the forest at train stops, barefoot and wearing a sheepskin, who "loved" a woman by knocking her senseless with a club. And so it was that the woman put up a futile resistance in the compartment; and because she resisted he wanted to throttle her, thrusting her head down into the pillows— to be even more brutal to her; then the *Pan* knocked. As he left, the captain stuffed two twenty-five-ruble notes into one of the woman's stockings.

. . . .

Love! Love that is stronger than seas and mountains and years.

The *Pan* had a master key that opened all compartments. It had not escaped the train attendants' notice that a woman had got into Lieutenant Agrenev's compartment. The lieutenant had been ordered to division headquarters for twenty-four hours. Who could tell in the dark which attendant opened the door, and which officer raped her? And anyway, would the woman dare to scream? She had no business to be where she was, and would simply be thrown out. And would she tell—tell her husband or lover —about it? What did Ponyatski know of the love that is stronger than seas and mountains? Would she tell her husband—another man—about it? Most likely she would weigh the situation, think things over, clean up—and never say a word to anyone. . . . Women. . . . Why shouldn't *Pan* Ponyatski grab himself an extra fifty rubles?

IV

Today, yesterday, the day before yesterday—fighting, retreat. Headquarters was moved out by train, but staff officers are going on foot. In the jumble of human bodies, carts, horses, guns, orderlies, bulletins, orders—nothing makes sense. Machine guns and rifles are silent. The rain lashes down. As evening fell someone said—or rather bellowed—that orders were to stop. They were stuck in a forest watchman's hut. Captain Kremnev had found some milk and cottage cheese in the cellar, and he, Agrenev and his wife, the division commander, and a few sleek, young staff officers were drinking the milk. The men had found a cow in the woods which they had slaughtered and were now roasting and eating; they had dragged in a couple of local peasant girls and were taking turns to rape them; the girls were very placid. People kept saying that it was time to get some rest, and did not notice the dawn breaking; they noticed it only when shells began to whine over the hut and a Russian battery nearby opened up. The order to counterattack was given. They trudged back in the rain—not knowing why—Agrenev, Kremnev, the three women, the men.

APPENDIX

Russian Names

Somewhere in the world there lives a man named Konstantin Konstantinovich Konstantinov. Should an English-speaking reader encounter him in print, his eyes are likely to fly past; if they stumble, the reader may pause long enough to say to himself, "Another of those Russian names!"

Actually Russian names are simple because they are consistent in their forms; furthermore, they often tell a great deal about their bearers.

Officially a Russian has only three names: his given name, his patronymic, and his family name. The last name often holds clues to the person's national or geographic origin, the social position, occupation, and even physical and other peculiarities of his ancestors. "Rostislavski" ("Ryazan Apples") is an aristocratic name; many names ending in "-ski" point to the ancestral seat of the family, in this case the ancient town of Rostislavl; the name also suggests kinship to Prince Rostislav of Ryazan, the member of one of the ruling families of twelfth-century Russia for whom the town was named. "Merinov" ("Ryazan Apples") is a peasant name, from *merin*, gelding, a term of mild abuse when applied to a man. "Popov" ("The Tale of the Unextinguished Moon"), from *pop*, priest, is a common name among clerical families and descendants of such families.

An obvious feature of most Russian last names is that they have distinct forms for men and women, the terminal "-a" being the special appurtenance of the feminine gender. The wife of "Ivanov," or his unmarried daughter or sister, is "Ivanova."

The use of Russian family names as a form of address and reference is somewhat limited. Anton Ivanovich Nekulyev ("Mother Earth") may be formally addressed and spoken of either as "Comrade Nekulyev" or as "Anton Ivanovich"—a combination of his given name and patronymic. The patronymic is a title of honor accorded to adults; it is based on the given name of the father, and its masculine and feminine endings signify "son of" or "daughter of." Thus, "Anton Ivanovich" is "Anton, son of Ivan." Similarly, "Irina Sergeyevna" is "Irina, daughter of Sergey." Among common people the patronymic alone may be used as a form of respectful address. In "The Forest Dacha" Ignat addresses the forester Sergey Dmitriyevich Ivanov simply as "Mitrich"—Ivanov's patronymic telescoped in peasant speech. For artistic reasons (to "age" a character, to reduce him socially, to express a faintly contemptuous attitude toward him) a writer may refer to a personage by the patronymic alone. To Pilnyak, Nil Nilovich Tyshko ("Ryazan Apples") is often simply "Nilych."

Russian given names in their various forms are wonderfully expressive. "Rimmochka" ("Mahogany"), for example, is diminutive of endearment of "Rimma." The use of this form implies love, fondness, or friendly intimacy between the speaker and the person addressed. A popular name usually has a whole pleiad of diminutives associated with it. "Mariya" is more often "Masha," "Manya," "Maya," "Marusya," "Maryasha"; secondary diminutives of "Mariya," or pet names based on pet names, are equally popular: "Mashenka," "Manichka," "Mayichka," and many others. Most diminutives surrounding a name are common, although unusual variants are sometimes created by intimates. In "The Forest Dacha" Lidia Konstantinovna is "Lida"—a common short form of "Lidia"—to her husband, but "Leet"—an unusual form of affectionate address—to her lover. Most pet names are sufficiently close to the full given name for the relationship to be apparent, but a few may seem totally unrelated. A case in point is the name Aleksandr: two of its most popular diminutives are

"Shura" ("Skurik" in "The First Day of Spring") and "Sasha."

If diminutives of affection convey love and friendly familiarity, pejorative diminutives express disapproval, contempt, disdain. "Mishka" and "Minka" are such forms of the name Mikhail ("Mother Earth"); "Mashka"—of "Mariya" or "Marya" ("Ryazan Apples"). Perversely, diminutives of derision are sometimes used to express special fondness for the person addressed or spoken of in this manner: "Natashka," contemptuous for "Natalya," and "Alyoshka"—for "Aleksey" ("The Tale of the Unextinguished Moon") are used as names of special endearment.

In print first names and patronymics are often seen in forms which reflect rapid, careless speech: "Yekaterina Pavlovna" is also "Katerina Pavlovna" ("The Tale of the Unextinguished Moon"); patronymics are regularly telescoped: "Nilovich," "Ivanovich," become "Nilych," "Ivanych." Class distinctions are also "heard." The "Irina" of the educated is the "Arina" of the peasants, "Yagor"—the common people's version of "Yegor." On occasion a name undergoes a thorough transformation: in "Ryazan Apples" the peasant Sidor Merinov speaks of Yelena Yuryevna as "Alyona Yagorovna." Here "Yelena" has become the peasants' "Alyona," and the base of the patronymic has shifted from "Yuri," one of the three Russian forms of the name "George," to "Yegor," the form of "George" favored by peasants, and pronounced "Yagor."

A final note on the patronymic. Children of the same father would, of course, have the same patronymic with an appropriate masculine or feminine ending. Hypothetically therefore, Lidia Konstantinovna in "The Forest Dacha" before her marriage to Ivanov could have been Lidia Konstantinovna Konstantinova and a sister of Konstantin Konstantinovich Konstantinov.